BLACK
RABBIT
SUMMER

RABBIT SUMMER

WITHDRAWN

KEVIN BROOKS

Chicken House

SCHOLASTIC INC./NEW YORK

For the very wonderful Sarah Hughes

Text copyright © 2008 by Kevin Brooks

First published in the United Kingdom in 2008 by Puffin Books, a division of
Penguin UK, 80 Strand, London WC2R 0RL.

Library of Congress Cataloging-in-Publication Data:

Brooks, Kevin.
Black Rabbit Summer / by Kevin Brooks. — 1st American ed.
p. cm.
Summary: When two of sixteen-year-old Pete's childhood classmates disappear
from a carnival the same night, he is a suspect, but his own investigation
implicates other old friends he was with that evening—and a tough,
knife-wielding enemy determined to keep him quiet.

ISBN-13: 978-0-545-05752-3 • ISBN-10: 0-545-05752-3

[1. Missing persons—Fiction. 2. Friendship—Fiction. 3. Carnivals—Fiction.
4. Drug abuse—Fiction. 5. Homosexuality—Fiction. 6. England—Fiction.
7. Mystery and detective stories.] I. Title.

PZ7.B7965Blc 2008
[Fic]—dc22

2007035322

Printed in the U.S.A.   23

First American edition, July 2008

The text type was set in ITC Slimback.
The display type was set in Gill Sans ExtraBold Display.
Book design by Kevin Callahan

ALSO BY KEVIN BROOKS

BEING

THE ROAD OF THE DEAD

CANDY

KISSING THE RAIN

LUCAS

MARTYN PIG

The summer of this story started for me on a hot Thursday night at the end of July, just as the sun was beginning to go down. I was busy doing nothing at the time — just lying on my bed, staring at the ceiling — so I didn't actually *see* the sun going down, but I'm pretty sure it was out there somewhere. Everything was out there somewhere — the sun-streaked horizon, the fading red sky, the stars, the moon, the rest of the world — I just didn't want *any*thing to do with it.

I didn't want anything to do with *any*thing back then.

All I wanted to do was lie on my bed and stare at the ceiling.

I had no idea where this lethargy of mine had come from — and I don't suppose I really cared, either — but in the three weeks or so since school had finished, I seemed to have got into the habit of not doing anything at all, and I was finding it a hard habit to break. Getting up late every morning, hanging around the house for hours, sitting out in the sun for a while . . . maybe reading a book, or maybe not. What did it matter? The way I saw it, the days and nights would pass whether I did anything or not. And they did. The mornings passed, the afternoons passed, the evenings turned into sunset nights . . . and, before I knew it, I'd be lying on my bed again, staring at the ceiling, wondering where the day had gone, and why I hadn't done anything, and why I still couldn't be bothered to do anything now.

There were plenty of things I could have been doing that night. It was still only half past nine. I could have been watching TV, or a DVD, or getting ready to go out somewhere. I could have been watching TV or a DVD and *then* getting ready to go out somewhere.

But I knew I wasn't going to.

I was happy enough doing nothing.

Happy enough?

I don't know.

I suppose I was happy enough.

So, anyway, that's what I was doing when the telephone rang and the summer of this story began — I was lying on my bed, staring at the ceiling, minding my own mindless business. The sound of the phone ringing didn't really mean anything to me. It was just a noise, the familiar dull trill of the phone in the hallway downstairs, and I knew it wasn't going to be for me. It was probably just Dad, ringing from work, or one of Mum's friends, calling for a chat . . .

It wasn't anything to get excited about.

It wasn't anything to get *anything* about.

It was just something to listen to.

I could hear Mum downstairs now—coming out of the living room, walking down the hall, quietly clearing her throat, picking up the phone . . .

"Hello?" I heard her say.

A short pause.

Then, "Oh, hello, Nicole. How are you?"

Nicole? I thought, my heart quickening slightly. *Nicole?*

"Pete!" Mum called out. "Phone!"

I didn't move for a moment. I just lay there on the bed, staring at the bedroom door, trying to work out why Nicole Leigh would be phoning me at half past nine on a Thursday night. Why would she be phoning me at *all*? She hadn't phoned me in ages.

"Pete!" Mum called out again, louder this time. "Telephone!"

I didn't really feel like talking to anyone just then, and I half-thought about asking Mum to tell Nicole that I was out, that I'd call her back later, but then I realized that in order to do that I'd have to get up and go downstairs anyway, and then Mum would want to know why I didn't want to talk to Nicole, and I'd have to think of something to tell her . . .

And I couldn't be bothered with all that.

And even if I could . . .

Well, it wasn't just anyone on the phone, was it?

It was Nicole Leigh.

I got up off the bed, stretched the stiffness from my neck, and made my way downstairs.

♥ ♠ ♦ ♣

When I got there, Mum was standing at the end of the hallway with her hand cupped over the phone.

"It's Nicole," she said in an exaggerated whisper, mouthing the words as if it was some kind of secret.

"Thanks," I told her, taking the phone from her hand. I waited until she'd gone back into the living room, then I put the phone to my ear. "Hello?"

"Good evening," a fake-posh voice said. "Is this Mr. Peter Boland?"

"Hey, Nic."

"Shit," she laughed. "How d'you know it was me?"

"I'm telepathic," I said. "I was just thinking about you when the phone rang —"

"Liar. Your mum told you it was me, didn't she?"

"Yeah."

Nic laughed again. It was a nice laugh, kind of husky and sweet, and it brought back memories of other times . . . times I thought I'd forgotten.

"I'm not interrupting anything, am I?" she said.

"What do you mean?"

"Nothing . . . it's just that you took a long time getting to the phone, that's all. And I heard your mum covering the phone and whispering."

"She always does that," I said. "It doesn't mean anything. I was just upstairs in my room . . ."

"On your own?"

I could hear the smile in her voice.

"Yeah," I said. "On my own."

"Right."

I stared at the wall, listening to the muffled silence at the other end of the line, imagining the look on Nic's face — amused, attentive, engagingly secretive.

"So, Pete," she went on. "How's it going?"

"All right, I suppose."

"What've you been doing with yourself?"

"Not much. How about you?"

"Christ," she sighed, "all I've been doing for the last three weeks is packing."

"Packing?"

"Yeah, you know . . . for when we go to Paris."

"I thought you weren't going until the end of September?"

"We're not, but Mum and Dad are away for the next few weeks and they're trying to get most of the packing done before they go. There's cardboard boxes and crap all *over* the place at the moment. It's like living in a warehouse."

"Sounds like fun."

"Yeah . . ."

I kept quiet for a while, not saying anything, waiting to find out what she *really* wanted to talk about. Nicole has never been one for small talk, and I knew she wouldn't have called me after all this time just to talk about cardboard boxes. So I just stared at the wall and waited.

Eventually she said, "Listen, Pete . . . are you still there?"

"Yeah."

"What are you doing on Saturday?"

"Saturday? I don't know . . . not much. Why?"

"You know that carnival up at the town park?"

"Yeah."

"Well, it's the last day on Saturday, and I thought we could all meet up and have a night out. Just the four of us — you, me, Eric, and Pauly. You know, for old times' sake."

"Old times?"

"Yeah, you know what I mean — the gang . . . the *four* of us. I mean, it wasn't that long ago, was it? I just thought, you know . . ."

"What?"

"I just thought we should all meet up again before it's too late."

"Too late for what?"

"Well, you're going off to college, me and Eric are going to Paris, Pauly's probably getting a job . . . this might be the last chance we get to be together again."

"Yeah, I suppose . . ."

"Come on, Pete . . . Eric and Pauly are up for it. We're going to meet in the old den in Back Lane —"

"The *den*?"

She laughed. "Yeah, I know . . . I was just thinking about it a while ago, you know, remembering how we built it and everything, and I suddenly realized it'd be a really good place to meet up for the last time. It'll be fun — just like the old den parties we used to have. Bring a few bottles, get a bit drunk . . . then afterward we can all go on to the fair together and throw up on the roller coaster." She laughed again. "You've *got* to come, Pete. It won't be the same without you."

"What about Raymond?"

Nicole hesitated. "Raymond Daggett?"

"Yeah. I mean, there weren't just the four of us in the old gang, were there? Raymond was with us most of the time."

"Well, yeah, I know. But Raymond . . . I mean, it's not really his kind of thing, is it?"

"What do you mean?"

"You know . . . going out, going to the fair, meeting up with Eric and Pauly. I just don't think he'd enjoy it, that's all."

"Why not?"

"Look, Pete," she sighed. "I'm not saying I don't *want* him to come—"

"What *are* you saying then?"

"Nothing. It's just . . ."

"What?"

"Nothing. It doesn't matter." She sighed again. "If you want Raymond to come—"

"I don't even know if *I'm* coming yet."

"Of course you are," she said, suddenly brightening up. "You're not going to say no to me, are you?"

"No."

She laughed again, but this time it sounded a little bit forced, and I got the impression that she was *making* herself go along with the joke, when in fact she wanted to be serious . . . and I didn't know how I felt about that.

There was something almost intimate about the way she was talking to me, and if I hadn't known better, I would have sworn she was flirting with me. But I *did* know better. Nicole Leigh wouldn't flirt with me. We were past all that now. We hardly even knew each other anymore. We moved in different circles. We did different things. We had different friends. All we had in common now was the shared memory of a time when we used to mess around together with Raymond and Pauly and Eric. Memories of gangs and dens, of long days down by the river, or in the woods . . . memories of breathless young kisses and awkward fumbles in the abandoned factory at the back of the lane . . .

Memories . . . that's all they were.

Kids' stuff.

"Pete?" I heard Nic say. "Did you hear me?"

"What?"

"I said, don't forget to bring a bottle."

"Sorry?"

"A bottle . . . something to drink. On Saturday."

"Oh yeah . . . right."

"We're meeting in the den at nine-thirty, OK?"

"The den in Back Lane?"

"Yeah, the one up the bank near the old factory. Opposite the gas towers."

"Right."

She hesitated for a moment. "Are you still thinking of bringing Raymond?"

"I don't see why not."

"All right. But you can't spend the whole night looking after him."

"Raymond doesn't need looking after."

"I didn't mean it like that. I just meant . . ." Her voice trailed off and I heard her lighting a cigarette. "Anyway, listen," she went on. "After the fair we're all going back to my place. Mum and Dad'll be away by then, so . . . you know . . . if you want to stay over, you're welcome." She paused for a moment, then added quietly, "No strings attached."

"Right . . ."

"OK. Well, I'll see you on Saturday, then."

"Yeah."

"Nine-thirty."

"Nine-thirty."

"All right, then. See you . . ."

"Yeah, bye."

You know what it's like when you're talking to someone, and at the time you're not quite sure what they're trying to say, but then, when they've gone, and you've had time to think about it, you realize that in actual fact you haven't got a *clue* what they were trying to say? Well, that's how I felt after I'd said good-bye to Nicole. I just stood there in the hallway, staring dumbly at the floor, thinking to myself . . .

Old times?

Den parties?

Carnivals and roller coasters?

What the hell was *that* all about?

♥ ♠ ♦ ♣

I was still standing there five minutes later when the living room door opened and Mum came out.

"All right, love?" she said.

I looked up at her. "Yeah . . . yeah, I'm fine."

She glanced at the phone, then looked back at me. "How's Nicole?"

"She's all right . . . she's moving soon. Her dad's got a new job in Paris. He's setting up some kind of theater or something. They're all moving out there in September." I didn't know why I was telling her all this. I suppose I was still a bit stunned, a bit confused. I was just opening my mouth and making noises. "Nicole asked me if I wanted to go to the fair on Saturday with Eric and Pauly."

"Sounds nice," Mum said.

I shrugged.

She said, "Don't you want to go?"

"I don't know . . ."

"It'd do you good."

I looked at her.

She smiled sadly at me. "You need to get out a bit more, Pete. Get some fresh air into your lungs. You can't spend all your time sitting around the house."

"I *don't* spend all my time sitting around the house . . . sometimes I go out and sit in the garden."

She shook her head. "I'm serious, Pete. I worry about you sometimes."

"There's nothing to worry about."

"But you never seem to *do* anything anymore. You don't go out, you're not interested in anything, you just lie around all day watching TV or sleeping." She gave me a worried look. "I mean, what about all the stuff you used to do?"

"What stuff?"

"Football . . . you used to play football every Saturday. And there was that reading group you used to go to, the one at the library. You used to really enjoy that."

I shrugged again. "I still *read* a lot . . . I'm always reading books. I just don't want to sit around talking about them."

"All right," Mum said. "What about your guitar? You haven't touched it in months . . . it's just leaning in the corner of your room gathering dust. You used to practice every night. You were getting really good at it—"

"No, I wasn't. I was rubbish."

Mum gave me another long look. "You'd tell me if there was anything wrong, wouldn't you?"

"There's nothing wrong, Mum. I'm fine—really."

"You're not worried about anything, are you?"

"No."

"Your exam results?"

"No."

"College?"

"Mum," I said firmly, "I've already told you—I'm not worried about anything, OK? I'm fine. I'm just . . . I don't know. I'm just a bit tired . . ."

"Tired? What kind of tired?"

"I don't know . . ."

She peered into my eyes, studying my pupils.

"No," I sighed, "I'm not on drugs."

She stood back and looked at me again. "I'm only trying to help, Pete."

"I don't need any help."

"You shouldn't be tired and down all the time," she said, shaking her head. "Not at your age. It's not right."

I smiled at her. "It's probably just a phase I'm going through. Hormones or something."

She tried smiling back at me, but she couldn't quite manage it. And that saddened me. I didn't like upsetting her.

"It's all right, Mum," I said quietly. "Really, everything's OK. I'm just feeling a bit funny at the moment, that's all. It's like I'm in between things, you know . . . like I'm not quite sure where I'm going. It's no big deal or anything, I just feel a bit . . ."

"Funny?" Mum suggested.

"Yeah."

She nodded. "Well, all right. But if it gets any worse—"

"I'll let you know. Honest."

She raised her eyebrows at me. "*Honest* honest?"

"Yeah," I smiled. "Cross my heart and hope to die."

I didn't get to sleep for a long time that night. As I lay in my bed, staring into the moonlit darkness, there were so many thoughts stuffing up my head that I could feel them seeping out of my skull. Sweaty thoughts, sticky and salty, oozing out of my ears, my eyes, my mouth, my skin.

Thoughts, images, memories.

The sound of Nic's voice: *If you want to stay over, you're welcome . . . no strings attached.*

The pictures in my mind: me and Nic at a party when we were thirteen, maybe fourteen, years old, locked in a bathroom together . . . too young to know what we were doing, but still trying to do it anyway . . .

You're not going to say no to me, are you?

I got out of bed then, covered in sweat, and went over to stand at the open window. The air was stuffy and thick, the night warm and still. I wasn't wearing any pajamas or anything — it was too hot for that — and although there was no breeze coming in through the window, I could feel the sweat beginning to cool on my skin.

I shivered.

Hot and cold.

It was some time in the early morning now. Two o'clock, three o'clock, something like that. The street down below was empty and quiet, but I could hear faint sounds drifting over from the main road nearby — the occasional passing car, late-night clubbers going home, a distant shout, drunken voices . . .

The sounds of the night.

I gazed down the street at Raymond Daggett's house. It was dark, the curtains closed, the lights all out. In the pale glow of a streetlight, I could see the alleyway that leads around to the back of his house, and I could see all the crap that littered his front yard — bike frames, boxes, skids, garbage bags. I stared at Raymond's bedroom window, wondering if he was in there or not.

Raymond didn't always spend the night in his room. Sometimes he'd wait until his parents were asleep, then he'd creep downstairs, go outside, and spend the night in the garden with his rabbit. He kept the rabbit in a hutch by a shed at the bottom of the backyard. If the night was cold, he'd take his rabbit into the shed with him and they'd snuggle up together in some old burlap sack or something. But on a warm night, like tonight, he'd let the rabbit out of its hutch and they'd both just sit there, quietly content, beneath the summer stars.

I wondered if they were out there now.

Raymond and his Black Rabbit.

It all started for Raymond when he was eleven years old and his parents gave him a rabbit for his birthday. It was a scrawny little thing, black all over, with slightly glazed eyes, a matted tail, and big patches of mangy fur down its back. I think Raymond's dad bought it off someone in a pub or something. Or maybe he just found it . . . I don't know. Anyway, wherever his dad got it from, Raymond was pretty surprised to get a rabbit for his birthday. Firstly, because he hadn't asked for one, and this was the first time in his life he'd ever gotten anything from his parents without asking for it. Secondly, because his parents usually forgot his birthday. And thirdly, as Raymond admitted to me later, he didn't even *like* rabbits at the time.

But he didn't let his parents know that. They wouldn't have been pleased. And Raymond had learned a long time ago that it wasn't a good idea to displease his parents. So he'd thanked them very much, and he'd smiled awkwardly, and he'd held the rabbit in his arms and stroked it.

"What are you going to call him?" his mother had asked.

"Raymond," said Raymond. "I'll call him Raymond."

But he was lying. He wasn't going to call the rabbit Raymond. He wasn't going to call it anything. Why should he? It was a rabbit. Rabbits don't have names. They don't *need* names. They're just dumb little animals.

It was probably about a year or so later that Raymond first told me his rabbit had started talking to him. I thought at first he was just messing around, making up one of his odd little stories — Raymond was always making up odd little stories — but after a while I began to realize he was serious. We were down at the river at the time — just the two of us, hanging around on the bank, looking for voles, skipping stones across the river . . . the usual kind of stuff — and as Raymond started telling me about his rabbit, I could tell by the look in his eyes that he believed every word he was saying.

"I know it sounds really stupid," he told me, "and I know he's not *really* talking to me, but it's like I can hear things in my head."

"What kind of things?" I asked him.

"I don't know . . . words, I suppose. But they're not really words. They're like . . . I don't know . . . like whispers floating in the wind."

"Yeah, but how do you know they're coming from the rabbit?" I said. "I mean, it could just be some kind of weird stuff going on in your head."

"He tells me things."

I stared at him. "What kind of things?"

Raymond shrugged and lobbed a pebble into the river. "Just things . . . he says *hello* sometimes. *Thank you.* Stuff like that."

"Is that it? Just hello and thank you?"

Raymond gazed thoughtfully across the river, his eyes kind of glazed and distant. When he spoke, his voice sounded strange. "A fine sky this evening . . ."

"What?" I said.

"That's what Black Rabbit said last night. He told me it was a fine sky this evening."

"A fine sky this evening?"

"Yeah . . . and green is fresh like water. He said that, too. *Green is fresh like water.* And the other day he said *This good wooden house* and *Straw smell blue sky.* He says all kinds of things."

Raymond went quiet then, and I couldn't think of anything else to say, so we just sat there for a while, not doing anything, just staring in silence at the murky brown waters of the river.

After a minute or two, Raymond turned and looked at me. "I know it doesn't make any sense, Pete, and I know it's kind of weird . . . but I really like it. It's like when I get home from school every day and I go down to the hutch at the bottom of the backyard and I feed Black Rabbit and give him fresh water and let him out for a run and clean his hutch . . . it's like I've got this friend who tells me stuff that's OK. He says stuff that doesn't hurt me. It makes me feel good."

Two years later, when Black Rabbit died of a fungal infection of the mouth, Raymond cried like he'd never cried before. He cried for three days solid. He was still crying when I helped him bury Black Rabbit's body in an empty cornflakes box in his backyard.

"He told me not to cry," Raymond sobbed, filling in the hole, "but I just can't help it."

"Who did?" I asked him, thinking he meant his dad. "Who told you not to cry?"

"Black Rabbit . . ." Raymond sniffed hard and wiped the snot from his nose. "I know what to do . . . I mean, I know he's not gone."

"What do you mean?"

"He told me to bring him home."

I didn't know what Raymond was talking about at the time, but when I went over to see him the next day and found out that he'd been down to the pet shop and bought himself another black rabbit . . . well, I still didn't understand what he was talking about, but I kind of realized what he meant. Because, as far as Raymond was concerned, the rabbit he'd gotten from the pet shop wasn't just another black rabbit, it was the *same* Black Rabbit. Same eyes, same ears, same jet-black fur . . . same whispered voice.

Raymond had done as he was told — he'd brought Black Rabbit home.

I shivered again. The sweat had dried on my skin now, and I was beginning to feel cool enough to get back into bed. I stayed at the window for a while longer, though, thinking about Raymond, wondering if he was out there . . . sitting in the darkness, listening to the whispers in his head.

A fine sky this evening.

This good wooden house.

Straw smell blue sky.

I thought about what Nicole had said — about Raymond not wanting to go to the carnival on Saturday — and I knew she was probably right. I was pretty sure that he'd want to go if it was just me and him, but I didn't know how he'd feel about meeting up with the others. I didn't know how I felt about it myself, either. Nicole and Eric? Pauly Gilpin? It just seemed so . . . I don't know. Like stepping back into the past: back to grade school, sitting together at the back of the class; back to middle school, watching out for each other in the playground, hanging around after school, spending our weekends and school vacations together . . .

We were friends then.

We had connections: Nicole and Eric were twins, Nic and me pretended we loved each other, Pauly looked up to Eric, Eric looked after Nic . . .

Connections.

But that was then, and things were different then. *We* were different. We were kids. And we weren't kids anymore. We'd moved on to junior high school, we'd turned thirteen, fourteen, fifteen, sixteen . . . and things had gradually changed. You know how it is — the world gets bigger, things drift apart, your childhood friends become *people you used to know.* I mean, you still *know* them, you still see them at school every day, you still say hello to them . . . but they're not what they were anymore.

The world gets bigger.

Not everything changes, though.

Raymond and me had never changed. Our world had never gotten any bigger. We'd always been friends. We'd been friends before the others, we'd been friends with the others *and* apart from the others, and, in lots of ways, we'd been friends in spite of the others.

We *were* friends.

Then *and* now.

And so the idea of us all getting together again on Saturday . . . well, it just felt really strange. A bit scary, I suppose. A bit pointless, even. But at the same time it was sort of exciting, too. Exciting in a strangely scary-and-pointless kind of way.

I'd turned away from the window now and was gazing over at a black porcelain rabbit that I keep on top of my chest of drawers. It was a sixteenth birthday present from Raymond. A black porcelain rabbit, almost life-size, sitting on all fours. It's a beautiful thing—glossy and smooth, with shining black eyes, a necklace of flowers, and a face that seems to be frowning. It's as if the rabbit is thinking about something that happened a long time ago, something saddening, something that will always prey on its mind.

I don't usually get all emotional about stuff, but I was really quite touched when Raymond had given me the rabbit. Everyone else had given me the kind of presents you expect on your sixteenth birthday—Mum and Dad had given me money, a girl I'd gone out with a couple of times had given me a night to remember, and I'd gotten a few cards and jokey little things from friends at school — but this, Raymond's rabbit . . . well, this was a *proper* present. A serious present, given with thought and feeling.

"You don't have to keep it if you don't want to," Raymond had mumbled awkwardly as he'd watched me unwrap it. "I mean, I know it's a bit . . . well, you know . . . I mean, if you don't like it . . ."

"Thanks, Raymond," I'd told him, holding the porcelain rabbit in my hands. "It's wonderful. I love it. Thank you."

He'd lowered his eyes and smiled then, and the way that'd made me feel was better than all the best Christmas and birthday presents rolled into one.

I looked at the rabbit now — its porcelain body shimmering in the moonlight, its black eyes shining and sad.

"What do you think, Raymond?" I said quietly. "Do you want to go to the carnival, take a trip down memory lane? Or should we both just stay where we are, hiding away in our own small worlds?"

I don't know what I was expecting, but the porcelain rabbit didn't say anything back to me. It just sat there, black-eyed and sad, gazing at nothing. And after a while I began to feel pretty stupid — standing by the window in the middle of the night, naked and alone, talking to a porcelain rabbit . . .

Mum was right — I definitely needed to get out a bit more.

I shook my head and got back into bed.

TWO

The houses in our street, Hythe Street, are all pretty much the same — flat-fronted terraced houses with small front yards and walled back gardens. The gardens on my side of the street back onto a scrubby little hill that leads down to the river, while the back gardens of the houses on Raymond's side of the street look out over a shared alleyway and a dilapidated church to the main road that runs parallel to Hythe Street. This main road, St. Leonard's Road, runs south from the town center all the way down to the docks at the bottom of the hill, about half a mile or so from Hythe Street.

The alleyway that leads around to the back of Raymond's place isn't the nicest place in the world. It's quite cramped, for a start, kind of narrow and poky, and it has high brick walls on either side that shut out the light, so even in the middle of summer it's always pretty gloomy and damp. The crumbly old walls are topped with barbed wire and broken glass, and for some strange reason the bricks have always been stained with layers of grimy black soot. The alleyway is also the place where everyone leaves their trash, so it's always cluttered with crap — bulging black garbage bags, overflowing trash cans, empty bottles, beer cans, dog shit . . . all kinds of muck. So, like I said, it's not the nicest place in the world, but I always used the alleyway whenever I went around to see Raymond, and he always used it whenever he came around to see me.

It was our route to each other.

It must have been around midday on Friday when I left my house and headed down the street toward Raymond's place. The sun was burning high in the sky, filling the air with a bright white haze, and as I crossed the road and entered the alleyway I could feel the stickiness of melted asphalt clinging to the soles of my sneakers. It was that kind of day — the kind of day when the heat is so thick that *everything* seems to slow down and melt, including your brain. And I was already suffering from a brain-melting lack of sleep anyway. But despite all that, I was actually feeling surprisingly fresh. I'd changed out of the dirty clothes I'd been wearing for the last three days, I'd taken a shower, I'd even managed to get some of the knots out of my hair. God knows why I'd bothered. I mean, I was only going to see Raymond, and he'd never cared what I looked like. I don't think he'd ever cared what *any*one looked like.

But I *was* feeling kind of OK, and even as I followed the alleyway down to Raymond's back gate, and the sunlight gave way to the cold shadows of the blackened brick walls, I still felt better than I had for a long time.

The gate was closed when I got there. It's a big old wooden gate, too tall to see over, so I couldn't see if Raymond was in his garden or not, and I couldn't hear anything, either. But I knew he was in there. I always knew. I'd stood at his gate so many times over the years that I could somehow *feel* if Raymond was in his garden or not. I've never understood how it worked, this feeling, but it always did. And it was always right. In fact, I trusted the feeling so much that if ever I felt he wasn't there, I didn't even have to open the gate. I could just turn around and go home without so much as a flicker of doubt.

He was there today, though.

I knew it.

The gate led me through to the bottom of the garden, and when I looked over to my right I saw Raymond sitting on a rickety old wooden chair by the shed. He didn't seem to have noticed me, though. He was just sitting there, gazing out over the garden, his eyes fixed on nothing and his head perfectly still. The only movement I could see in him was a very faint fluttering of his lips, as if he was whispering secrets to himself under his breath. Apart from that, though, he was as still as a statue.

The rabbit hutch beside him was empty, its wire-mesh door wide-open. I glanced around the garden — a scrubby mess of sun-browned lawn and overgrown borders — and I spotted Black Rabbit squatting in the shade of a lilac bush. He wasn't doing much — just sitting there, looking around, lazily twitching his nose.

"Hello, Pete."

At the sound of Raymond's voice, I looked over and saw him smiling at me.

"Hey, Raymond," I said. "How's it going?"

He nodded his head, still smiling. "Yeah, everything's OK . . . you know . . . nice and hot." He looked up, then almost immediately looked back at me again. "Blue skies," he said.

"Yeah . . ."

As I started walking over toward him, I couldn't help smiling to myself. Raymond had always made me smile. His face made me smile, his smile made me smile, everything about him made me smile. It was strange, really, because most people thought Raymond was a really weird-looking kid . . . and, in a way, I suppose he was. His head was too big for his body, his eyes were a bit loopy, and there was something about the way he dressed that always made him look childishly small. He didn't actually *dress* childishly, and he didn't look anything like a child, either. It's just that his clothing always seemed to somehow diminish him. I used to think it was because his parents bought most of his clothes from charity shops, and they usually bought them a size too big so he'd have plenty of time to "grow into them." But over the years I'd seen Raymond dressed in all kinds of clothes — brand-new shirts, the perfect size . . . shapeless coats, baggy shorts, even skin-tight jeans (forced on him once by his mother) — and eventually I came to realize that it didn't matter what he was wearing — old clothes, new clothes, too big or too small — *everything* made him look small.

But I *liked* the way he looked — his weirdness, his difference, his oddity. It suited him. It helped to make him what he was.

It also helped to make his life really hard sometimes.

But right now—as he got up from his chair, went into the shed, and came back out carrying another rickety chair for me—right now, he was fine. I watched him, still smiling, as he set the chair down next to his, swept the dust off it, and gestured awkwardly for me to sit down.

I sat.

Raymond sat.

We grinned at each other.

"So," I said, "you're doing all right, then?"

He nodded, smiled, then glanced over at Black Rabbit. The rabbit was still just sitting there, not doing anything.

I said, "He's getting big."

"Yeah . . ."

I gazed at the big black rabbit. It was actually Black Rabbit the Third. Black Rabbit the Second had died from an infected rat bite last year. Raymond had been sad for a while, but he hadn't cried this time. He'd just buried him in the garden, right next to the original Black Rabbit, and then he'd gone out and bought another one. Although, to Raymond, it wasn't another one, because by now he was convinced—or at least part of him was—that Black Rabbit lived forever.

I looked at Raymond now. He was watching his rabbit, just sitting there watching it, perfectly content. And part of me envied him for that. I knew it was wrong of me, because I knew that Raymond's peace of mind wasn't quite normal—whatever that means—and I knew that he had stuff going wrong in his head, but every now and then I couldn't help thinking how nice it must be to find such contentment in the simplest of things.

A lawn mower had started droning away in the distance now, and I could smell the drift of freshly cut grass in the air. *Green is fresh like water,* I found myself thinking. *A fine sky this evening . . .*

I wiped a bead of sweat from my brow.

"Nicole rang me last night," I said to Raymond.

He looked at me. "Nicole?"

"Yeah . . . she was asking if we wanted to go to the fair tomorrow night. You know, the carnival up at the town park?"

Raymond didn't say anything, he just gave me a puzzled look.

"Yeah, I know," I told him. "I was a bit surprised to hear from her myself. What it is, though, she's got this idea about us all meeting up again, you know, the old gang . . . like a going-away party kind of thing."

"Who's going away?"

"Nicole and Eric . . . they're moving to Paris in September."

"Yeah, I know."

"And Pauly's not going on to college—"

"Pauly?"

"Yeah."

"Pauly's going to the fair?"

Raymond's eyes were starting to look troubled now.

"It's all right," I told him. "We don't have to go if you don't want to. I mean, I'm not really sure I want to go myself."

"She likes you," Raymond said.

"What?"

"Nicole — she likes you."

"Yeah, well," I said. "She likes you, too. She always has."

"Not like that."

"Like what?"

"Like she likes you," he said, smiling at me.

I frowned at him. *"What?"*

He didn't say anything for a moment, just carried on smiling at me, but then his eyes blinked stiffly, his face suddenly dropped, and his smile disappeared. "Is Pauly going to be with Wes Campbell?" he asked.

It was a good question, a question I'd been asking myself ever since Nicole had phoned me — if Pauly Gilpin was going to be there, did that mean that Wes Campbell and his boys were going to be there, too?

Wes Campbell was two years older than the rest of us, and when we were kids, he used to scare the shit out of us. Him and his boys — a bunch of tough kids from Greenwell Rise, a rough part of town on the other side of the river — they were the ones we were always running away from. I remember once, when me and Raymond were riding our bikes back from town . . . I suppose we must have been about ten or eleven at the time, or maybe a little bit older. Anyway, we were riding along this little lane by the river, a shortcut back from town, and suddenly I heard this whizzing sound, like something had just cut through the air, then a quick dull pop, and then something *ping*ed off the frame of Raymond's bike. Raymond heard it, too, and we both pulled up and looked around, and that's when we saw one of Campbell's boys. He was standing in a little copse beside the lane, pointing an air rifle at us. As he grinned and pulled the trigger again, we hit the pedals and got going, and then Campbell and some other kids suddenly appeared from farther down the lane, and some of them had air rifles, too, and they were shouting and laughing and chasing the shit out of us, scaring us both to death . . .

Christ, I'd never been so frightened in my life. And Raymond . . . well, Raymond was so terrified that he pissed himself. I've never forgotten it. I was pedaling along like a madman behind him, my legs pumping, my lungs bursting, and when I first heard the splashing sound I didn't realize what it was. I was so intent on getting away from the kids behind us that I barely even noticed it. It wasn't until Raymond's bike started to slow down in front of me, and I looked up to see what he was doing . . . and I saw him standing up awkwardly on his pedals, kind of squirming around and fiddling with his fly . . . and even then, it took me a moment to realize that his pants were soaked and a stream of yellow liquid was spraying out into the air behind him.

There were other bad times with Campbell, too. And it wasn't just me and Raymond who suffered, either. Campbell had it in for all of us—Eric, Nicole, Pauly . . . anyone who was smaller than him, basically. Smaller or different. Weaker or younger . . . whatever. I'm sure you know how it is. I mean, we all have our Wes Campbells when we're eleven years old, don't we?

That kind of stuff was mostly in the past now. None of us had had any trouble from Campbell recently, but we'd all been scared shitless of him at the time. Which was why it was so strange that in the last couple of years or so, Pauly had started hanging around with Campbell and the others. I'd seen him in town with them, mobbing it up in the High Street, and I'd heard rumors that he went out drinking with them, too.

So, yeah, I knew what Raymond meant about Pauly and Campbell, and to a certain extent I shared his concerns. But at the same time, I kind of understood that things change — people grow up, their fears move on, their childhood nightmares don't haunt them so much anymore. It wasn't like that for me or Raymond, and understanding it didn't make it any easier to accept. But, as far as I was concerned, if Pauly wanted to spend his time cozying up to our childhood nightmare . . . well, that was up to him. There wasn't much I could do about it, anyway.

I looked at Raymond. "It'll just be the five of us at first," I told him. "Me and you, Nicole, Eric, and Pauly. Nicole wants us all to meet up in the old den in Back Lane, you know — the one up the bank by the factory. Just the five of us . . . no one else allowed. Like a den party."

Raymond smiled warily. "A den party?"

"Yeah, just like the old days — bring a bottle, have a few drinks . . ."

"No one else allowed?"

"No one else."

Raymond was starting to relax a bit now. The troubled look was fading from his eyes, and he was beginning to seem cautiously interested. He'd always liked being in the dens — I think he felt safe and comfortable in them. To the rest of us, they were just places to go, places to be, places to do things we weren't supposed to do. But to Raymond I think they were some kind of sanctuary, a refuge from the big bad world. He even used to go to the dens on his own sometimes, which I always thought was a pretty cool thing to do — just sitting there on your own, hidden away in a secret place, no one knowing where you are . . .

I wish I'd had the courage to do that.

"So," I said to Raymond, "what do you think? Do you want to go?"

He shrugged. "I don't know . . ."

"We could just go to the den, if you want . . . just for an hour or so. We don't have to go on to the fair afterward."

"What about Pauly?"

"He'll be all right . . . don't worry about it. I mean, you know what he's like — he'll just be the same old Pauly with us."

"Same old Pauly," Raymond muttered.

"Yeah, I know . . ."

"He used to come around here."

"I know."

"He made me think he was OK."

Raymond was beginning to look saddened again now.

"It's all right," I told him. "It doesn't matter if you don't want to go. I mean, it's no big deal or anything."

He looked at me. "You want to go, don't you?"

I shrugged. "I really don't mind."

He smiled. "I can tell."

"Tell what?"

"You want to see Nic."

"No, I don't —"

"I can tell."

"Well, you're wrong . . ."

He shrugged, still smiling at me.

I shook my head. "Why would I want to see Nic?"

"Because . . ."

"Because what?"

"I don't know . . . just because."

I shook my head again. "You don't know what you're talking about, Raymond."

He grinned at me. "I know."

"I mean, I wouldn't *mind* seeing her . . . just to say good-bye and everything . . . but I'm not bothered if I don't." I looked at him. "There's nothing between us anymore, if that's what you're thinking."

"Right," he said.

I glared at him, trying to look annoyed, but it was impossible. The way he was just sitting there, staring wide-eyed at me, grinning his head off . . . I couldn't help smiling at him.

"I don't even know why I'm listening to you," I said.

"Pardon?"

I grinned at him. "You think you're funny?"

He laughed. "I *know* I'm funny."

♥ ♠ ♦ ♣

We carried on sitting there for a while, just soaking up the sun and talking about stuff — exam results, college . . . nothing important — and then around two o'clock we both heard the sound of the front door slamming, and Raymond said he'd better go inside.

"It's my dad," he said, suddenly very serious. "He'll probably want something to eat."

Raymond didn't like talking about his parents, so I didn't ask him where his dad had been, or why he couldn't get something to eat for himself, I just nodded and started to get up.

"What about tomorrow then?" I asked him. "Do you want to give it a go?"

"Yeah, I suppose . . ."

"You sure?"

He nodded vaguely, but he wasn't really paying attention to me anymore — he was concentrating intently on the back door of his house, looking out for his dad.

"I'll come around here about nine," I told him. "Is that OK?"

He didn't answer.

"Raymond?" I said.

He glanced at me. "What?"

"Tomorrow night — I'll come around at nine o'clock."

"OK . . ."

His head snapped back to the house again as he heard his dad's voice calling out — *Raymond!*

"I'd better go," he said quickly, scuttling off toward the house. "I'll see you tomorrow."

"Yeah, see you, Raymond," I called after him. "And don't worry about anything . . ."

But he was already halfway across the garden now, and I knew he wasn't listening to me anymore. I watched him as he opened the back door and hurried into the house, and I wondered, as I'd wondered so many times before, what kind of life he had in there.

It was hard to imagine.

His parents had never been up to much. They were cold people, ugly-minded, uncaring . . . the kind of parents who make you appreciate your own.

I stared at the house for a moment, trying to picture what happened behind those brick walls, but all I could see was a formless haze of dull gray mist. Cold ugly voices, resentment, hidden feelings.

I sensed something then — a soundless movement — and when I looked down at my feet I saw Black Rabbit flopping past me and hopping back into his hutch.

He didn't look at me.

He didn't twitch his nose at me.

His voice didn't whisper inside my head . . .

Be careful.

Don't go.

. . . and even if it did, I didn't hear it.

I didn't know it then, but as I left Raymond's garden that day and started walking back home, I'd just made the biggest mistake of my life.

THREE

The next day, Saturday, was one of those days when you wake up in the morning, too hot to sleep, and you feel so sweaty and breathless that all you want to do is throw off the duvet and lie there naked, hoping in vain for a breath of cooling air to drift in through the open window . . .

But it never comes.

There's no cool air out there, just a blazing white sun and a burned-blue sky and a heat so heavy you can see it.

After I'd finally managed to peel myself off the bed and shuffle wearily into the bathroom, I took a cold shower, dressed in a T-shirt and shorts, and went downstairs. A fan was blowing in the kitchen, and all the windows were open, but the house was still uncomfortably hot. I went outside and found Mum sitting on a kitchen chair, sipping tea and smoking a cigarette. She was wearing shorts and a T-shirt, too, and although she looked really good in them — kind of baggy and scruffily cool — she also looked pretty tired and worn out.

"I thought you'd given up smoking," I said to her, nodding at the cigarette in her hand.

She smiled at me. "I have."

"Doesn't look like it."

"It's just the one . . . I needed it."

"Yeah, well," I said, "you'd better not let Dad catch you."

"He's still asleep."

"What time did he get in?"

She shrugged. "I don't know . . . a few hours ago. Around eight, I suppose."

"When's he got to go back?"

"This afternoon."

She took a long drag on her cigarette and gazed down the garden. Her smile had gone now, and she had a worried-about-Dad look in her eyes. She was always worried about Dad, especially when he was working nights.

My dad's a police officer — a detective sergeant in the Criminal Investigations Department — and it's hard for Mum sometimes. It's hard for both of us, really. Even when Dad isn't working late or doing nights, neither of us gets to see him that much. There's always something keeping him busy — overtime, paperwork, courses, training. I don't really mind not seeing him too much. I mean, I don't *like* it, but I'm used to it. I've grown up with it, just as I've grown up with and gotten used to all the other crap that goes with being the son of a police officer — the suspicions, the wariness, the stupid jokes. It's not that I don't *like* Dad being a policeman, because I do. As far as I'm concerned, it's a pretty cool thing to do. It's just that sometimes I wish he had a more normal job. An ordinary job. Nine to five,

Monday to Friday. No weekend overtime, no worried Mum, no tired-out Dad.

I looked at Mum now, and I knew she didn't really care too much about the long hours and the overtime and the fact that Dad was tired all the time. The only thing she was really worried about—the only thing she'd ever been worried about—was that every time Dad left for work, there was always a chance he wouldn't come home.

She put out her cigarette and smiled at me. "Everything all right?"

I smiled back. "Yeah."

"Good. How's Raymond? You went to see him yesterday, didn't you?"

"Yeah, he's all right. You know . . . same old Raymond. He's coming to the fair with us tonight."

Mum raised her eyebrows.

"What?" I said.

She shook her head. "Nothing . . . what time are you going?"

"About nine." I flapped my T-shirt, trying to cool myself down. "A few of us might go back to Nicole's place afterward. She and Eric are having a little going-away party. They said I can stay over if I want."

Mum grinned. *"They* said?"

"Yeah," I said, blushing slightly. "Pauly's probably going to be there, and Eric . . ."

"And Nicole."

I shook my head. "She's just an old friend, Mum."

"I know," Mum laughed. "I'm only joking."

"Is it all right if I stay over?"

She nodded. "I don't see why not. Make sure you take your phone with you, though. And be careful, OK?"

"Yeah."

She wiped some sweat from her forehead and squinted up at the sky. The air was shimmering now, hazing in the heat, and in the distance I could see things that weren't there — silver seas, floating reflections, mirrors on the horizon. The heat was distorting the world.

"You'd better take a jacket tonight," Mum said.

I looked at her. "What?"

"I think we're in for a storm."

I spent the rest of the day doing nothing — just hanging around, waiting for the night to come around. I didn't like admitting it to myself, but I was really looking forward to going out for a change. I was still a bit wary of seeing Nicole and the rest of them, and throughout the day I kept hearing the echoes of a faint whispered voice somewhere in the back of my mind — *be careful, don't go . . . be careful, don't go* — but I was determined to ignore it. I hadn't been out anywhere for ages. I hadn't felt excited for a long time. I wasn't going to let some stupid whispering voice spoil my day.

I couldn't hear it anyway.

It wasn't there.

Dad woke up around midday, and I managed to see him for about ten minutes or so before he went back to work. He was in a hurry — sitting in the kitchen, bolting down some bacon and eggs — so we didn't have much time to talk.

"Are you all right?" he asked me.

"Yeah."

"Doing anything tonight?"

"Me and Raymond are going to the fair."

He nodded, chewing vigorously. "Well, be careful up there."

I smiled to myself, wondering how many more people were going to tell me to be careful.

"I mean it, Pete," Dad said. "There's been a bit of trouble up at the fair the last few nights, so make sure you keep your eyes open, OK?"

"What kind of trouble?"

"Just the usual stuff — fights, drugs, people getting robbed. It's going to be really hot and crowded up there tonight, so it's probably going to be even worse."

"I'll be careful, Dad," I promised.

"Yeah," he smiled, "I know you will." He took a big gulp of tea, wiped his mouth, then got up from the table and rubbed his unshaven chin. "Right," he said, "well, I'd better get going, I suppose."

Later on, around six o'clock, when Mum nipped out to the corner shop on St. Leonard's Road, I went into the little room at the back of the kitchen where Dad keeps his wine and I picked out the cheapest-looking bottle I could find. Dad likes his wine, and there were quite a few bottles in there, so I didn't think he was likely to miss one.

Then I went back upstairs, hid the bottle away, and started getting ready.

I put some music on — *Nevermind*, Nirvana.

I showered again.

Deodorized.

Picked out some clothes — combat shorts, baggy T-shirt, sneakers, no socks.

Got dressed to more music — *Elephant*, The White Stripes.

Studied myself in the mirror. Changed my shirt, changed it back again . . . changed my shorts, changed them back again . . .

And then I just hung around some more — lying on the bed, trying not to get too sweaty . . . trying not to ask myself why I was making so much effort, why I cared what I looked like, why I was feeling so tingly and weird . . .

Why anything?

Why not?

Be careful . . .

Shut up.

At five to nine, I went downstairs and popped my head around the living room door to say good-bye to Mum. She was sitting on the sofa, watching TV.

"I'm going now," I told her.

"OK," she smiled. "Have you got a jacket, in case it rains?"

I showed her the backpack in my hand, taking care not to knock it against anything. I could feel the weight of the bottle of wine inside.

Mum nodded. "Got your phone?"

"All charged up."

"OK," she said. "Well, have a good time then."

"Yeah."

She smiled. "And don't do anything I wouldn't do."

She always says that whenever I go out — *don't do anything I wouldn't do.* I've never understood what it means.

Raymond was waiting for me at the bottom of his garden when I arrived. Black Rabbit was in his hutch, and Raymond was just standing there, gazing out over the garden. He was wearing cheap denim jeans and a zip-up black hoody.

"Aren't you too hot in that?" I said to him.

He looked at me. "It's going to rain later on."

I held up the backpack in my hand. "Can I leave this in your shed?"

He nodded.

I went over to the shed, took out the bottle of wine, wrapped it in a plastic bag, and threw the backpack inside.

Raymond patted his pocket and smiled at me. "I've got some, too."

"What?"

He glanced furtively at his house, then turned his back on it and leaned toward me. "Rum," he whispered.

"Rum?"

He grinned. "One of those little bottles, you know . . . pocket-size. Mum drinks it with milk."

I stared at him. "Rum and *milk*?"

He nodded. "She likes it with a box of chocolates."

It sounded pretty weird to me, but then Raymond's mum had always been pretty weird. Once, when Raymond had opened his packed lunch at school, the entire Tupperware box was filled with raisins. Nothing else, just a box full of raisins.

"Come on," I said to Raymond. "Let's go."

We left by the alleyway and headed up the street.

It was really nice being out and about—the sun was still burning down, music was drifting out from open windows . . . there was a real kind of Saturday-night feel to the air. Things were happening. People were going out, or getting ready to go out. The night was coming alive.

"All right?" I asked Raymond.

He smiled at me. "Yeah."

At the top of our street there's a gated lane that leads down to the river, and as we approached it, a scruffy-looking guy with dirty blond dreadlocks came up the lane and climbed over the gate into the street. He was tall, in his twenties. He had pierced eyebrows, a ring in his lip, and he was wearing worn-out white coveralls with the pant legs rolled up. I'd never seen him before, but as we turned left toward St. Leonard's Road, and the dreadlocked guy went past us, heading down Hythe Street, he nodded his head at Raymond. Raymond smiled and nodded back at him.

"Who's that?" I asked Raymond when the guy was out of earshot.

"I don't know," he said. "I've seen him down by the river a couple of times. He's got a trailer down there."

"A trailer?"

"Yeah."

"Since when?"

"A few weeks."

"What is he — a traveler or something?"

Raymond shrugged. "I don't know."

We crossed St. Leonard's Road and headed straight on along the little pathway that runs between the old factory parking lot and a row of car repair places. At least, they used to be car repair places. They're all closed down now — either boarded up or just abandoned. Beyond them, over to our right, I could see the tops of the old factory buildings looming up darkly against the bright evening sky.

The factory's been empty and derelict for as long as I can remember. It's a huge place, a sprawling expanse of dull gray buildings, workshops, offices, tanks and vats, chimneys and towers. It's even got its own little reservoir — a small concrete lake surrounded by big black pipes and filled to the brim with stagnant green water. God knows what it was used for. I think the factory used to make engines for trains or airplanes or something . . . but I could be wrong.

Anyway, as we headed along the pathway toward Back Lane, I realized that we were both gazing around at the old factory with the same distant look on our faces.

"You know it's been sold, don't you?" I said to Raymond.

"Yeah . . . they're knocking it down to build houses. It's all fenced off everywhere now."

I nodded. I could see the brand-new high metal fencing they'd put in to replace the crappy old wire-mesh stuff that used to be there. The wire-mesh fencing had been easy to get through. Even if you didn't know where all the gaps were — which we did — all you had to do was find a loose bit, lift it up, and crawl underneath. We used to spend hours messing around in the old factory.

"Do you remember that time your dad caught you in there with Nic?" Raymond said.

"He didn't catch us *in* there," I corrected him. "We were just coming out."

"Yeah," Raymond grinned, "but your dad still went mad, didn't he?"

He'd actually gone madder than mad, he'd gone totally ballistic. I'd never seen him so angry. Me and Nic were only about thirteen at the time, and the first thing Dad had yelled at me was — WHAT THE *HELL* WERE YOU TWO *DOING* IN THERE? Which was kind of embarrassing. And even when I'd finally convinced him that we hadn't been doing anything *illegal*, he still didn't let up. He just went on and on for hours about how dangerous it was, how stupid, how thoughtless, how irresponsible . . .

I found out later that a twelve-year-old boy had been found dead in an abandoned warehouse a few days before. The poor kid had just wandered into the warehouse on his own and fallen through some loose floorboards or something. When his parents reported him missing, Dad had been part of the investigation team, and when the kid's body was eventually found, it was Dad who'd had to inform the parents.

"You all right?" Raymond asked me.

"Yeah, I was just thinking . . ."

"About what?"

"Nothing . . . it doesn't matter."

We'd reached the end of the pathway now, and ahead of us lay the narrow dirt track that we called Back Lane. It isn't really called Back Lane — I don't think it's called anything officially. It's just a dirt track — the kind of nameless path that doesn't appear on maps — and most people don't even know it's there. The local kids all know about it because it's a shortcut up to the town park, but the only adults you'll ever see in Back Lane are dog walkers and dossers and the occasional weirdo or two.

The air suddenly cooled as we entered the lane, the bright sun blocked out by the steep wooded bank that rose up on our right toward the factory fence. The ground beneath the hillside trees was covered with a dense thicket of brambles and weeds.

"I hope the den's still there," I said.

Raymond looked at me. "Why shouldn't it be?"

"I don't know . . . someone might have trashed it or something."

"It'll be there."

"How do you know?"

Raymond shrugged. "I don't . . . I'm just saying, that's all. I'm just saying it'll *probably* be there."

I looked at him. His face seemed pale.

"Are you still OK with this?" I said.

"Yeah . . . I think so."

"It's not too late to change your mind, you know."

He didn't say anything for a while, we just carried on walking in silence. And that was fine with me. I hadn't been in Back Lane for a long time, and I was happy enough just looking around, remembering how everything was. It was strange how it all seemed so familiar. The lane itself, still rutted with bike tracks. The bank on our right, dark with trees. And on our left, another steep bank, this one leading down to a wasteground area of concrete and weeds that stretched away across to the docks. At the far end of the wasteground, the huge rusted cylinders of two derelict gas towers glinted dully in the sun.

"The star's going out tonight," Raymond said quietly.

I stared at him. "What?"

He looked at me, his eyes pale and glassy. "Black Rabbit," he whispered. "That's what he said this afternoon — *the star's going out tonight.*"

"The stars are going out tonight? What stars?"

"No," Raymond said. "The star *is* going out . . . not stars. *The* star."

"What star?"

Raymond blinked, and all at once his eyes seemed to clear. He seemed lost for a moment or two, but then he blinked again, looked at me, and his face broke into a grin.

"What?" he asked me. "What are you looking at?"

I frowned. "Are you all right?"

"Yeah . . . why?"

"Nothing . . . I was just checking . . . Raymond?"

As I was speaking to him, his eyes had changed again, only this time they weren't pale or glassy, they were just staring straight ahead, glazed with fear.

"Raymond?" I said again.

"You said he wouldn't be here . . ."

"Who?"

"You *said* . . ."

For a moment I thought he was talking about Black Rabbit again, but when I turned my head and followed his gaze, I suddenly realized what he meant. About fifty feet ahead of us, four or five kids were hanging around by the junction of a little pathway that branches off Back Lane and heads down to the wasteground. At first, I only recognized one of them — Pauly Gilpin. But when I shielded my eyes against the sun and took another look, I realized that the kid standing beside Pauly was Wes Campbell.

"It's all right, Raymond," I said. "There's nothing to worry about."

"You said he wouldn't be here."

"Yeah, I know . . . but he's not going to do anything." I smiled at Raymond, trying to reassure him. "Come on," I said, "just keep walking. It'll be all right."

It wasn't a particularly confident smile, and I'm pretty sure that Raymond wasn't fooled by it, but we both kept walking anyway. Neither of us *wanted* to, but the only other option was to turn around and start running away, and somehow that felt even scarier than *not* running away.

"They've seen us," Raymond said.

"I know."

I could see now that there were five of them: Pauly, Campbell, and three hard-looking kids from Greenwell Rise. Pauly was his usual hyperactive self — jigging around, waving his arms, grinning like a madman — but I could tell by the nervous look on his face that he wasn't quite sure of the situation. It was as if he wasn't quite sure who he was supposed to be looking at. Me and Raymond? Or Campbell and the others? His eyes were flicking around like pinballs. Campbell and the other three didn't have any doubts, though. They were all just standing there, hard as hell, their eyes fixed coldly on Raymond and me.

My heart was beating hard as we approached them, and I wondered if I looked as scared as I felt. Or worse — if I felt as scared as Raymond looked. He looked terrible — his face drained of color, his eyes unblinking, his skin all tense and twitchy. *Nothing's changed*, I thought to myself. *He's still that petrified little kid who pissed himself on his bike . . .*

We were almost at the junction now. The three Greenwell kids were just slouching around in the background, all of them dressed in their TK Maxx gangsta gear — skanky white track pants, XXL basketball shirts, chains, rings, bright white Nikes. Campbell was standing beside Pauly, and he looked just as intimidating as ever. The angular face, chiseled and lean. The dark narrow eyes, the slightly crooked mouth, the high forehead topped with razor-cut black hair. He hadn't changed one bit. In his short-sleeved

Rockport shirt and his spotless white jeans, he looked like a psychopathic catalogue model.

As we slowed to a halt in front of them all, I kept my eyes on Pauly. He had a scrunched-up plastic bag in his hand, shaped like a bottle, so I guessed he was on his way to the den. But what was he doing here with Campbell?

"All right?" he said chirpily, grinning from me to Raymond. "How's it going?"

I nodded at him and spoke calmly. "Hi, Pauly."

He smiled at Raymond. "Y'all right, Rabbit?"

Raymond stiffened slightly at the name, but he didn't say anything. He'd gotten used to the names a long time ago — Rabbit, Bunny Boy, Mental Ray — but he'd never forgiven Pauly for starting it all. And neither had I. Raymond had always been known as a slightly weird kid, but a few years ago, when he'd confided in Pauly about Black Rabbit, and Pauly had gone around telling everyone else . . . well, from that moment on, Raymond had never been known as anything *but* weird.

"Yeah, good one, Pauly," I muttered.

He grinned hesitantly at me. "Say what?"

"Have you seen Eric and Nic yet?" I asked him.

"I'm just on my way," he said, his eyes flicking furtively at Campbell.

"Where you going?" Campbell said to him.

Pauly grinned at him. "What?"

Campbell just stared at him for a moment, then he looked over at me. "Where you going, Boland?" he said.

I shook my head. "Nowhere, really . . ."

"Nowhere?"

"The fair."

Campbell said nothing, just carried on staring at me. He had the kind of eyes that drill right through you and make you go cold inside. I watched, guiltily relieved, as he turned his attention to Raymond.

"Yeah?" he said to him. "What are *you* looking at?"

Raymond just stood there, unable to speak.

Campbell stared at him. "What's the matter with you? You got something wrong with your head or something?"

Pauly snickered.

Campbell turned his stare on him. "What?"

"Nothing," Pauly said, grinning nervously. "I was just—"

"The fucker's sick, Gilpin. It's not *funny.*"

Pauly hesitated for a moment, his eyes flicking around, trying to work out if Campbell was joking or not. When he realized that no one else was smiling, he looked back at Campbell and grinned again. "What?" he said innocently, shrugging his shoulders. "I didn't *mean* anything. I was just, you know . . . I mean, Raymond's all right. I was only . . ."

His voice trailed off as Campbell turned away from him and looked at me. "What do *you* think, Boland?" he said, tilting his chin at Raymond. "You think he's all right?"

"What's it to you?" I heard myself say.

Campbell smiled then, which surprised me. It was a genuine smile, no menace intended, and just for a second I saw a completely different Wes Campbell—harmless, friendly . . . charismatic, even.

"You like him, do you?" he said to me.

"What?"

"Bunny Boy there . . . you like him?"

I didn't know what to say. Like him? Did I *like* him? I mean, what kind of question was that?

Campbell looked at Pauly. "He likes him."

Pauly grinned awkwardly. His mouth twitched as he looked for something to say, but nothing came out. He glanced over at me, then quickly turned back to Campbell again. Campbell's smile had disappeared now. He was staring dead-eyed at Pauly.

"Friends," he said quietly.

Pauly frowned. "What?"

"You know what a friend is, Gilpin?"

Pauly didn't know whether to laugh or not. He glanced anxiously around again, looking for clues as to what he should do, but the Greenwell kids were just as blank-faced as before, and there was no way he was getting any help from Raymond or me. He blinked quickly a couple of times, nervously licked his lips, then turned back to Campbell.

"I don't get it," he said. "Is this some kind of joke or something?"

"No joke," Campbell said coldly. "Just a simple question — do you know what a friend is?"

"Yeah," Pauly snorted, pretending to be offended, "of course I know what a *friend* is. Why shouldn't I?"

For a moment or two, Campbell just carried on staring at him, then all at once his eyes lost their coldness, his face broke into that smile again, and he stepped up and gave Pauly a friendly pat on the arm.

"See?" he said casually. "That wasn't so hard, was it?"

Pauly grinned, not quite so nervous now, but still a little unsure.

Campbell gave him another reassuring pat on the arm. "We'll see you later then, OK?"

"Yeah . . . where're you going to be?"

But Campbell didn't answer him. He'd already turned around and was heading off down the pathway toward the wasteground, the three Greenwell kids following along behind him. He wasn't smiling anymore. His friendly face had shut down as soon as he'd turned away from Pauly. I'd seen it disappear — *click* — like a light going off. And now, as I watched him go, it was hard to believe he'd ever smiled in his life.

I turned to Raymond.

He was watching Campbell, too.

"Are you all right?" I asked him.

He nodded.

"Are you sure?"

"Yeah . . ." He looked at me, his brow furrowed. "He's weirder than me, isn't he?"

"Who — Campbell?"

"Yeah."

I laughed. "Yeah, I think he probably is."

The den in Back Lane is hidden away at the top of the bank, about three-quarters of the way along the lane. You can't see it from ground level, and unless you know exactly how to get there, it's almost impossible to find. And even when you *do* know how to get there, it's still pretty tricky.

"It's up there," Raymond said, pointing up the bank.

"Where?"

"There . . . you cut through those brambles over there —"

"Where?"

"There, by that tree stump."

I couldn't even *see* any tree stump. It was getting on nine-thirty now and the sun was starting to go down. It wasn't really dark yet, and the air was still hot and sticky, but the light in the lane was beginning to fade to a dim and shadowy blur.

"He's right," Pauly said, muscling in between Raymond and me. "It's there, look." He pointed up at the bank. "You go around the back of that stump, then along that little ridge and up through the brambles —"

"Shut up, Pauly," I said.

He gave me his hurt-little-boy look. "I'm only trying to help."

"Yeah, right," I said. "Pauly Gilpin — Mr. Fucking Helpful."

"What's that supposed to mean?"

"It means you're bad," Raymond said.

We both looked at him.

"Bad?" Pauly grinned. "You mean *baad* like Michael Jackson?"

Raymond couldn't help smiling then, and that was all the encouragement Pauly needed. He put down his plastic bag and started dancing around, singing loudly in a stupid American accent: *"Because I'm baad, I'm baad . . . shit!"*

Raymond laughed as Pauly moonwalked into the bank and fell over, and I found myself smiling, too. I didn't *want* to, but it *was* pretty funny.

That was the thing about Pauly — no matter what you thought of him, no matter how much you *wanted* to hate him, he could always redeem himself by making you laugh. But I knew it was all part of his act. Make them laugh, make them smile, make them forget about everything else . . .

I looked at him now, rolling around on his back, wiggling his arms and legs in the air, whooping and shrieking like Michael Jackson in pain.

"Come on, Raymond," I said, stepping up onto the bank. "Let's go."

FOUR

We used to have dens all over the place — down by the river, along the lane into town, in the little woods at the back of the old factory parking lot. Most of them were pretty ramshackle things — a few wooden boards jammed into the ground, a couple of old skids stuck between a gap in some trees. Sometimes we'd fix it all together with bits of old rope or something, maybe throw some plastic sheeting over the top . . . but they weren't really made to last. We'd just pick up whatever we could find, stick it all together, and that was that.

But the den in Back Lane was different. I can't remember *why* we decided to put so much effort into it — I expect we were probably just bored and didn't have anything else to do — but I know that it took days to build. It was really hard work — finding exactly the right spot, scouring the old factory for building materials (old doors, corrugated metal, rusty nails), lugging it all back to the top of the bank, fixing it all together, plugging the gaps between the walls, covering the outside with branches and brambles . . . we even gave it a little door and a skylight in the roof. And when it was all finished, it was amazing. Hidden away at the top of the bank, but not too close to the factory fence, it was virtually invisible. Even when you were standing right in front of it, it was hard to tell it was there. And once you got inside, it was almost like being in a proper little room. It wasn't huge or anything, but it was just about high enough to walk around in without having to stoop too much, and there was easily enough room for the five us to slouch around on the floor, which is mostly what we did. The floor wasn't really a *floor*, but we'd cleared the ground, and we'd stamped it down, and after we'd slouched around on it for a couple of weeks, it was almost as hard as concrete.

We spent most of that summer in the Back Lane den. Hot summer days, rainy days, shadowy evenings, and candlelit nights. We just about lived in there. God knows what we did all day — all I can remember is sitting around talking, making stupid plans, messing around . . .

Messing around.

Yeah, there was that. There was all *kinds* of messing around.

And the den parties, of course. We had lots of den parties that summer. Steamy nights, stolen cigarettes and bottles of booze, getting drunk, getting sick, getting overexcited . . .

Me and Nicole.

Breathless in the candlelight . . .

Kids' stuff.

"What?" said Raymond.

We'd reached the top of the bank now, and I'd kind of forgotten Raymond was there. I also hadn't realized that I'd been thinking out loud.

"Sorry?" I said to him, pausing for breath.

"I thought you said something."

"When?"

"Just now."

I shook my head. "I didn't say anything."

Raymond looked at me for a moment, smiling secretly to himself, then he turned his head and gazed across at a suddenly familiar-looking patch of ground over to our left.

"There it is," he said.

In the graying light, I could see the overgrown brambles spreading out over the roof of the den, and beneath the brambles, I could just make out the faded blue paint on the boards of the roof. The skylight — a cracked old windowpane, fixed with bent nails over a hole in the roof — was still intact.

"It looks all right, doesn't it?" I said to Raymond.

He smiled at me. "I told you it'd still be here."

"Yeah, you did."

I glanced over my shoulder and looked down the bank at Pauly. He was scrambling up behind us, breathing hard and cursing at the brambles.

I looked back at Raymond. "Do you want to wait for him?"

"No."

We walked over to the den and stopped in front of the door.

"After you," I said to Raymond.

"No, after *you*," he smiled, waving me forward.

I paused for a moment, breathing in the hot thundery air, then I stooped down and opened the door.

"Hey, Pete."

"Who's that?"

Nicole laughed. "Who do you think?"

"Christ," I said, edging my way inside, "I can hardly *see* in here."

"Let me in," Raymond said from behind me.

"Hold on."

I took a step forward.

"Shit!" Eric cried out. "That's my foot!"

"Sorry."

As I stepped to one side, I cracked my head on the roof — "Shit!" — and then Raymond stumbled into me, almost knocking me over, and I stepped on Eric's foot again.

"Christ, Boland! What are you *doing*?"

"It was Raymond —"

"I didn't *do* anything," Raymond said.

Then Pauly bulldozed his way through the door behind us — "Watch out! I'm coming in!" — and *he* tripped over something — "Fuck!" — crashing into Raymond, and Raymond crashed into me, and I toppled over and almost landed in Nicole's lap.

"Watch it!" she cried.

"Sorry."

"What's going on?" said Pauly. "Why's it so *dark* in here?"

"It's the night," Eric said drily. "The lack of sunlight."

Raymond laughed.

Pauly shoved him.

Raymond bumped into me again.

"Keep still, for Christ's sake!" I yelled, nearly losing my balance again.

"Why don't you all just shut up and sit down?" Nicole suggested.

It was a good idea.

Once we'd all settled down and made ourselves comfortable, everything started to calm down a bit. It was pretty cramped in there, and it took us a while to sort ourselves out (so that we weren't sitting too close to each other, or kicking each other's feet), but we got there eventually. I'm not sure if I did it on purpose, but I ended up sitting next to Nicole. She was on my right, sitting against the far wall. Raymond was on my left. And Eric and Pauly were sitting opposite me.

The air inside the den was hot and sticky, and it smelled kind of earthy and raw — a heady mixture of brambles, sweat, warm breaths, and skin.

"Anyone remember to bring a candle?" Eric said.

We all looked at each other, shaking our heads, then Raymond reached into his pocket and pulled out two white candles. As Eric clapped his hands — "Well done, Ray" —

Raymond lit one of the candles and placed it on the ground.

"It's vanilla," he said to no one in particular.

As the candle flickered, lighting up the gloom, I gazed around the den. The walls were leaning in a bit, and there were a few stray bramble stems creeping in through gaps in the roof, but apart from that, it seemed in pretty good order.

"It's a lot smaller than I remembered," I said, gazing up at the roof.

"Maybe it shrank in the rain," said Nicole.

I looked at her.

She smiled. "Of course, it *could* just be that we're all a bit bigger now."

"A *bit* bigger?" Pauly said, leering at Nic.

"Piss off, Pauly," she told him.

He grinned.

Pauly was always saying stuff like that — crass, jokey, sexy kind of stuff — and I knew it wasn't worth bothering about. It was just him being stupid. Mr. Funny Guy. But it *did* bother me. Not because I thought it was wrong or insensitive or sexist or anything, but simply because I was thinking pretty much the same thing myself. Nicole *did* seem to have grown quite a lot . . . and I couldn't quite understand it. I mean, it was only just over three weeks since I'd last seen her, and although we didn't hang around together anymore, I still saw her at school pretty much every day. But somehow she just looked so different now — older, fuller, sexier. I knew it was probably just her makeup and everything — darkened eyes, reddened lips — and the way she was dressed — low-rise jeans, a flimsy little cropped white vest — and the way she'd slicked back her short blonde hair, so she looked kind of icy and hot at the same time . . .

"Are you all right, Pete?" she said to me.

"What?"

"You're staring."

"Am I?"

"Yeah."

"Sorry."

She smiled. "That's all right."

"Who wants a drink?" Pauly piped up.

I looked over to see him brandishing a bottle of tequila.

"It's the special stuff," he said, unscrewing the cap and taking a slug. "Whooh-*hoo!*" he howled, rolling his eyes. "Very special in*deedy!*"

"What's so special about it?" Eric asked.

"Here," Pauly said, passing him the bottle. "Suck it and see."

As Eric took a drink, we all started bringing out the bottles we'd brought. It was a pretty varied selection — a bottle of wine, a few cans of Coke, a half-bottle of Bacardi, Pauly's tequila, Raymond's bottle of rum.

"What the hell's *that?*" Pauly said, sneering at the grimy little bottle when Raymond brought it out.

"It's rum," Raymond told him.

"It's half-empty."

Raymond shrugged, looking embarrassed.

I glared at Pauly.

"What?" he said to me.

Nicole nudged me and passed me the tequila bottle. I carried on staring at Pauly for a moment, telling him silently to lay off Raymond, then I raised the tequila bottle to my lips and took a drink. I'd never drunk tequila before, and at first it tasted pretty good — kind of smoky and sweet and warm. But then, as it seeped down into my throat, I felt the heat of the alcohol burning up inside me, and I started coughing and spluttering.

"Christ!" I gasped.

"Juicy, eh?" Pauly grinned.

"Juicy?"

"Yeah," he laughed, lighting a cigarette. *"Jooooseeee!"*

The den party had started.

As the bottles got passed around, and Pauly started rolling a joint, Nicole began telling us all about Paris — the new house, her dad's new job, the theater, the schools, how excited she was . . .

"What about you?" I asked Eric as Nic paused for a moment to take the joint off him. "Are you looking forward to going?"

He shrugged. "I'm not sure if I *am* going yet. I might stay here for a while."

"Why?"

"No reason," he said, glancing at Nic. "I just haven't made up my mind if I want to go or not."

"What are you going to do if you stay here?" I asked him.

"I haven't really thought about it. I might go to college, I might go to college in Paris —"

"Coll*age*," Pauly said.

"What?"

"It's French for college — coll*age*."

Eric shook his head. "I might do some work in Dad's theater."

"What kind of work?"

He shrugged. "Lighting, stage design . . . I don't know. I'll just see how it goes, I suppose."

"What about you, Nic?" I said. "What are you going to do?"

"You could sell onions," Pauly suggested.

Nic looked at him. "Yeah, that's a good idea."

He grinned.

Nic passed me the joint. I was already feeling pretty woozy from the drink, so I didn't smoke much of it — just a couple of quick puffs — then I passed it across to Pauly.

"What about Raymond?" he said.

"He doesn't smoke."

"Why not?" Pauly offered the joint to Raymond. "Come on, Rabbit, enjoy yourself."

Raymond looked at me.

"Do you want it?" I asked him.

He shook his head.

"He doesn't want it," I told Pauly.

I could see Pauly thinking about having a laugh with Raymond, trying to persuade him to smoke the joint, and I could see him glancing at me, wondering what I'd do if he *did* start trying to persuade him . . . and in the end he just shrugged — who cares? — and gave up.

Eric smiled at Raymond. "How you doing over there, Ray?"

"All right, thanks."

"Enjoying your rum?"

"Not really."

"You want some Coke?"

"Yeah."

Eric passed him a can of Coke. "You looking forward to college?"

"Who, me?" Raymond said.

"Yeah."

"I suppose . . ." He popped the Coke, took a long drink, then burped, and took another long drink.

"Better?" said Eric.

Raymond nodded. "It's hot."

Eric smiled again, then looked at me. "Are you definitely going then, Pete?"

"To college?"

"Yeah."

"I think so . . . I mean, as long as I get the grades I need."

"What are you going to take?" Nicole asked me.

"English, media studies, and law."

"Law?"

"Yeah."

"Why?"

I shrugged. "I don't know . . . I couldn't think of anything else."

"I'm doing art," Raymond said.

Nic looked at him. "You're *crap* at art."

He smiled. "I know."

It was true — Raymond *was* crap at art. He couldn't draw to save his life. He was an absolute genius at everything else — physics, math, English, chemistry — but for some weird reason he only wanted to study art.

Nic nudged me again and offered me the bottle of wine. "You want some of this?"

I looked at her, and just for a moment her face seemed to dissolve into a series of patterns and shapes . . . triangles, rectangles, bright red lines . . . and her skin seemed to be rippling with energy. I closed my eyes for a second and shook my head.

"Pete?" I heard her say.

When I opened my eyes again, her face was back to normal.

"Shit," I said, turning to Pauly. "What the hell's in that joint?"

"Uh?"

"The joint . . . what is it?"

He grinned dozily at me, swaying slightly. "The joint?"

"Yeah."

"It's the juice," he said.

"What?"

"The juju juice," he slurred, widening his eyes and taking another swig of tequila.

"He's out of it already," Nic said to me.

"Yeah . . ." I looked at her. "Are *you* feeling all right?"

"I'm feeling fine," she said, putting her hand on my leg and smiling at me. "How are *you* feeling?"

My head kind of whirled for a moment, and I could feel tiny pinpricks where her hand was touching my leg. "I'm feeling pretty good, actually," I said. "Kind of . . . what's the word?"

"Warm?"

"No."

"Hot?"

"Velvety," I said.

"*Velvety?*"

I smiled at her. "Yeah."

"What does *velvety* feel like?"

"I don't know . . . like velvet."

We started laughing then, giggling away like overexcited kids. Nicole was laughing so much that she lost control and doubled over, clutching her belly, and as her head rolled briefly against my thigh, I felt the weirdest sensation tingling up and down my leg. It was like . . . God knows. Like gossamer threads brushing against my skin.

"What's she doing down there, Boland?" Pauly called out. "I mean, come *on* . . . get a room, for Christ's sake!"

Nicole sat up quickly and glared at him. "Why do you always have to be such a twat, Pauly?"

He grinned at her. "Someone's gotta do it."

"Yeah, and you're the expert."

Pauly winked at Eric. "Your sister thinks I'm a twat."

Eric said nothing, just sat there puffing languidly on a cigarette.

Pauly blinked drunkenly at him. "You with anyone tonight?"

"What?"

"Are you *with* anyone?"

"Like who?"

"I don't know . . . anyone . . ."

Eric just stared at him.

Pauly blinked again. He had a strange expression on his face — kind of trancey, a bit spaced-out — and he didn't seem to notice that Eric was getting annoyed with him. As Eric shook his head and turned away, Pauly carried on looking at him, grinning like a kid with a secret.

After a moment, he said, "You know Stella's going to be there tonight, don't you?"

Eric froze.

Pauly grinned.

Eric turned slowly and looked at him. "What did you say?"

"Yeah," Pauly grinned. "Stella Ross . . . she's going to be at the fair—"

"Who told you that?" Eric said quietly.

Pauly shrugged. "I don't know . . . someone . . . can't remember. I just heard it somewhere . . ."

He was looking really out of it now — blinking all the time, his head wobbling from side to side, his eyes glazed. I watched him as he looked down at the ground, staring at nothing, and just for a moment he seemed incredibly sad. But then he closed his eyes and took a deep breath, and when he looked up again, the sadness had gone, and his grin was as manic as ever.

"Stella Ross, eh?" He leered at Eric. "I don't suppose *you've* bothered downloading her pictures?"

Stella Ross was something of a local celebrity. Her father, Justin Ross, used to be the drummer in a band called Secret Saucer. They were one of those hippie groups that were really big in the early 70s — long hair, long songs, drum solos, dry ice . . . that kind of thing. By the time they split up — sometime in the 80s, I think — they'd sold about a trillion records and they were all living in big country mansions with recording studios in their basements and Ferraris parked in their driveways. That's what Dad told me, anyway. He also told me that Justin Ross used to be a "hell-raiser" — taking drugs, smashing up hotel rooms — but about fifteen years ago he'd "seen the light" (these are all Dad's words, by the way, not mine), and he'd sold all his Ferraris and his country mansion, married a beautiful young model, and they'd set up home on a working farm in a little village about ten miles from St. Leonard's.

His wife, Sophie Hart, was also pretty rich, so together they were worth a huge heap of money. But Stella never saw any of it. She was their only daughter, and because they'd both seen the ugly side of celebrity (Sophie was an ex-hell-raiser, too), they were determined to bring up Stella as "normally" as possible. Which is why — despite their millions — Stella ended up at the same school as us.

I didn't actually know her that well, but she was really good friends with Eric and Nic, and she shared their passion for acting. They performed in all the school plays and stuff, and they were always singing and dancing, dressing up, dreaming of the days when they'd all be big stars. Most of us thought that if any of them were going to make it, it'd be Nicole. Eric was always a bit too intense about everything, especially himself. Stella had the looks, but not much talent, and although her parents knew all the right people, they refused to do anything to help her, which *really* pissed Stella off. Nicole, though . . . well, Nicole didn't need any help. She had everything—talent, looks, energy, confidence. So it was a big surprise when Stella turned up at school one day and announced that she'd landed a part in a TV commercial. She was around fourteen at the time, and it turned out later that she'd got this part by getting all cozy with the sixteen-year-old son of one of her parents' friends who just happened to be a well-known film director. The TV commercial was for a big supermarket chain. It was one of those serial ads, the sort of thing that runs for a few months, then a new one comes out, but with the same characters, and then another one . . . like installments in a stupid little story. This one featured an endearingly quirky family—father, mother, daughter, son. Stella played the daughter. Her character started off as a cute, but sassy, teenager—all sweetness and charm and innocence—but as the commercials developed, so did Stella's cute little teenager, and within a year or so she was beginning to get the kind of tabloid attention that didn't really fit in with the supermarket's wholesome family image, so they dropped her from the ads. Stella had already left school by then—I think she was being tutored at home—and the only time any of us saw her, including

Eric and Nic, was when she was in the papers and on TV, which was pretty much all the time. She was doing all sorts of stuff by then — photo shoots for *Loaded* and *FHM*, talk shows, appearances in music videos — but mostly she was just famous for being Stella Ross. The Wild Child, the Fifteen-Year-Old Hell-raiser, the Girl of Every Boy's (and Every Man's) Dreams.

About six months ago, after a wild night out at some swanky club in London on her sixteenth birthday, Stella ended up in a hotel room with a guy called Tiff. Tiff was a singer with a boy band called Thrill who'd recently come third in a second-rate talent show on cable TV. Apart from Stella and Tiff, no one really knows exactly what happened that night, but within a few days their relationship had broken up and a series of intimate photographs of Stella had appeared in a Sunday newspaper. They were pretty grainy pictures, shot on a mobile phone, and they didn't really show very much — the newspaper edited out all the naughtiest bits — but suddenly the whole world was talking about them. The newspaper that published the pictures was one of those papers that's always ranting and raving about pedophiles, and now here they were, happily showing pictures of a near-naked girl who'd only just turned sixteen. So, of course, all the other newspapers went mad, calling them hypocrites, purveyors of filth, while at the same time showing edited versions of the photos themselves, just to let us see what they were talking about. And then another series of pictures appeared, this time on the Internet, and these weren't edited at all, and so the story just kept going and going . . . and all the time, Stella got more and more famous . . .

And Eric and Nicole despised every second of it. They were jealous, for a start, especially Nicole. She'd always hated the whole famous-for-being-famous kind of thing, and what made it even worse for Nic was that Stella had been her friend. They'd dreamed of stardom together, they'd grown up imagining what it would be like, but now that Stella had actually made it, she didn't want anything to do with Nicole. She didn't call her. She didn't text. She didn't e-mail. She didn't return any of Nic's messages. She acted as if she'd never even known her.

With Eric, though, it was slightly different. Just before she'd left school, around the time she was beginning to get famous, Stella had gone out with Eric a few times. They were both only fourteen then, so it wasn't really a relationship or anything, they just used to meet up in town, maybe go to the movies . . . that kind of thing. Then one night, at an end-of-semester dance at school, we were all just hanging around at the back of the assembly hall, waiting for some crappy local band to come on, when all at once a side door opened and Stella came bursting in, crying her eyes out. The side door led out to the school grounds, so we all just assumed she'd been out there with Eric, doing whatever they did, and they'd had an argument or something. But then, a few minutes later, Eric came in through the side door, too, and he looked incredibly calm. In fact, he looked almost serene. Without saying a word to anyone, he walked across the hall, got up onto the stage, and went over to the microphone.

Everyone was watching him now, wondering what the hell he was doing . . . everyone, that is, except Stella. When Eric had come in, she'd given him the most hateful look I'd ever seen, and then as soon as she'd seen him getting up on the stage, she'd just turned around and stormed out. And when Eric started talking into the microphone, I understood why.

"I don't know if this is the right time or the right place," he'd announced, his voice booming out through the speakers, "and I'm not trying to make a big deal out of it or anything, but I just wanted to let everyone know that I'm gay."

And that, in a very big nutshell, was what Pauly was talking about in the den that night. Eric and Stella, their history, the photographs of her on the Internet, the fact that Eric was gay . . . all that and more, and everything it meant, it was all there in that one stupid sentence: *Stella Ross, eh? I don't suppose you've bothered downloading her pictures?*

If Eric was offended by Pauly's remark, he didn't show it. He just stared at him for a moment, his eyes quietly thoughtful, then he shook his head and turned away.

Pauly looked over at me. "Have you seen them, Pete?"

"Seen what?"

"Stella's pictures . . . the ones on the Internet."

"No," I lied.

He grinned. "I bet you have."

"Christ," Nicole muttered, passing me the joint again.

Pauly looked at her. "What?"

"You . . ."

"What *about* me?"

"You're *obsessed* with her."

"I'm not obsessed—"

"Yes, you are. You've always been obsessed with her. Even before she started flashing her tits around—"

"She doesn't—"

"Shit," said Nic, "you were having wet dreams about Stella Ross when you were twelve years old."

Pauly wasn't grinning anymore. "I don't know what you're talking about," he said sulkily.

Nicole glared at him. "Yeah, you do."

Everything went quiet then. Pauly went back to staring at the ground, Nicole lit a cigarette, I stubbed out the dead joint, and Raymond just sat there, gazing at nothing. Eric seemed worried about something. The cigarette in his hand had burned down to a stub, but he didn't seem aware of it—he was just sitting there, staring into space, chewing intently on a thumbnail.

As I studied him in the flickering candlelight, the angles of his face seemed to shift, and just for a moment he looked *exactly* like Nicole. I'd experienced the same thing with Eric before. Although they were twins, Eric and Nic weren't exactly alike, and most of the time Eric's face bore little resemblance to his sister's. Physically, they were both very similar—same nose, same mouth, same eyes—but somehow the same features didn't add up to the same thing. On Nic, they were beautiful. But on Eric, for some reason, they just didn't quite fit together, and this gave his face a strange kind of almost-beauty — neither ugly nor beautiful, but at the same time both ugly *and* beautiful. Sometimes, like now, when Eric's face momentarily become Nic's, it was like watching a blurred picture slowly coming into focus — becoming what it was meant to be. This time, though, as Eric's face morphed into Nic's, it also took on the weird patterns and shapes I'd seen on Nic's face earlier . . . triangles, rectangles, cones, and pyramids . . . and when he moved his hand, dropping his dead cigarette to the ground, I saw trails in the air, slow-motion afterimages of the movement . . .

I closed my eyes.

"I'm going," I heard someone say.

The voice sounded odd — slow and deep, thick and distorted.

"You coming, Nic?"

When I opened my eyes again, Eric had gotten to his feet and was looking over at Nic. His face was pure Eric again.

"Nic?" he said.

"I'll catch up with you at the fair," she told him. "I just want a word with Pete."

I looked at her.

Ignoring me, she turned to Pauly. "In private."

"What?" he said.

"I need to talk to Pete about something."

"So?" Pauly shrugged. "I'm not stopping you."

Eric nudged him with his foot. "Come on, don't be such a wanker."

Pauly looked up at him and grinned. "You gonna buy me some cotton candy?"

Eric smiled. "I'll kick the shit out of you if you don't move your arse."

"Fair enough," Pauly said.

As Eric helped him to his feet, Nic glanced over at Raymond. "Do you mind?" she said, smiling at him.

He stared at her for a moment, blinked his eyes, then looked at me.

I didn't know what to do. It didn't feel right, asking him to leave. I knew he wouldn't feel comfortable on his own with Pauly and Eric, so he probably wouldn't want to go on to the fair with them, and I didn't like the idea of him going home on his own. It was dark now. It was ten o'clock, Saturday night, and that's not a good time for *anyone* to be on their own in Back Lane, let alone Raymond. But, at the same time, I didn't want to embarrass him by letting the others think he needed looking after.

I don't know how much of that is true. I suppose some of it is, maybe most of it. I mean, I really *was* worried about Raymond, and I really *did* feel responsible for him . . . but I know, deep down, that my overriding desire was to be on my own with Nicole.

I looked at her now, wanting to ask — how long will we be? — but I just couldn't say it.

She smiled at me. "Don't worry."

I didn't know what she meant.

I turned back to Raymond. He was still looking at me, still just waiting. It might have made things a bit easier for me if there'd been some anger in his eyes, or even a bit of disappointment or something, but there was nothing. Nothing but trust.

"If you want to wait—" I started to say.

"It's all right," he said simply. "I'll see you at the fair."

I stared at him, surprised. "Are you sure?"

He nodded and started to get up.

I just watched him, unable to speak.

"Don't worry," he said, smiling at me.

"Right . . ." I muttered.

I sat there in silence, watching them go: Eric first, stooping quickly through the door; then Pauly, leering over his shoulder at us; and then Raymond. I thought he'd look back at me as he left, maybe say a few words, or wave good-bye. But he didn't. He just ducked down through the doorway and disappeared into the night.

I listened to him following Eric and Pauly down the bank, their fading footsteps stumbling through the darkness, then I turned my attention to Nic. She'd shuffled away from the wall and was sitting in front of me now—her legs crossed, her face glowing palely in the candlelight, her eyes fixed steadily on mine.

"So," she said quietly, "here we are again."

"Yeah . . ."

"Just the two of us."

I wiped sweat from my forehead.

She took off her shoes and smiled at me. "Hot, isn't it?"

FIVE

verything was kind of OK for a while. Me and Nic just sat there talking about stuff — Paris, Stella, school, college — and it didn't feel too awkward or anything. We were both a bit drunk, I suppose, and a bit whacked out from the dope, and Nic kept taking quick little sips from the bottle of tequila that Pauly had left behind, so I'm not sure if either of us really knew what we were talking about. But it didn't seem to matter. In fact, the way Nicole was jabbering away — spewing out words like a machine gun — I hardly had to say anything at all. So I didn't. I just sat there, watching her as she talked — staring at her mouth, her moving lips . . . the candlelit colors shimmering on her skin. The more I stared, the more vivid the colors became, and as they grew brighter and brighter, the darkness of the den seemed to close in all around us. It was a nice feeling, like sitting in a bubble of light, and there was something about it that made me feel I was inside something alive. It was as if the den had some kind of primitive consciousness, and now that the others had gone, it was adjusting its size to make us feel cozier.

"Are you all right?" Nicole said suddenly.

I blinked. "What?"

"Your eyes . . . they look really spacey."

"Spacey?"

"Yeah," she smiled. "Like big black saucers."

"Must be the drink," I said.

Nic laughed. "You never could handle it, could you?"

"What do you mean?"

She smiled. "You always used to get like this at a den party."

"Like what?"

"All dreamy and stupid . . . like you're living in a different world."

"Dreamy *and* stupid?" I said.

She laughed again. "Stupid in a nice way."

"So you're saying I'm stupidly nice, is that it?"

"Yeah," she said, looking into my eyes, "but mostly just nice."

Everything seemed to change then. The atmosphere, the heat, the silence . . . it was all suddenly different. Heavier, stiller, more intense. I could taste the dark sweetness of Nic's perfume in the air. I could feel the sweat oozing from my skin.

"What happened to us, Pete?" Nicole said quietly.

"What do you mean?"

"You know . . . me and you, everything we did, everything we had . . . I mean, how come we ended up so far apart?"

"I don't know," I shrugged. "Things change, I suppose . . ."

"They never changed for me."

She was leaning in close to me now, staring so intently into my eyes that I had to look away for a moment. I didn't really believe what she was saying, and I knew she didn't believe it, either — she knew as well as I did that we *had* both changed — but as she moved a little closer to me, and I felt her hand on my thigh . . . well, I couldn't have cared less about the truth just then.

"Do you remember that time in the bathroom?" she said softly.

I looked up at her. "The party at your cousin's place?"

"Yeah." She smiled. "We came pretty close then, didn't we?"

I nodded, my mouth suddenly dry.

She said, "Do you think we would have done it if her parents hadn't come back?"

"Maybe . . ."

She moved her hand on my thigh. "It doesn't seem right . . ."

"What?"

"That we never got around to it."

I was feeling incredibly strange now — my heart was thudding, my skin was tingling all over, my whole body was buzzing with a warm liquid energy.

Nic said, "And now we'll probably never see each other again."

We looked at each other, knowing each other.

Nothing needed saying.

Nic's eyes never left mine as she sat back and started to ease off her vest. I watched, mesmerized, as she crossed her arms, slowly pulled the vest over her head, and dropped it to the ground. I tried to stay cool, forcing myself to concentrate on her eyes . . . but it wasn't easy. Her eyes were burning into me now, watching my reaction as she raised her arms and ran her fingers through her hair, subtly flexing her body.

"You can look if you want," she said.

I looked.

She moved her hands slowly down her belly, rested them for a moment on the waist of her jeans, and then she started popping open the buttons. I couldn't breathe. I couldn't do anything. All I could do was sit there and watch, all dreamy and stupid, as she leaned back a little, slid out of her jeans, then got down on all fours and started crawling toward me. She looked like some kind of miracle beast — her naked flesh in the candlelight, her dark eyes on fire — and for a second or two I felt strangely frightened. But the fear was nothing compared to everything else I was feeling. I was physically hurting now. Aching inside. My heart was pumping so hard that I thought it was going to burst out of my skin.

As Nic crawled up to me, I started moving my legs to give her some room.

"It's all right," she said. "Just stay there."

She got to her knees, straddled my lap, and leaned in close to me, resting her hands on my shoulders.

"I'm not hurting you, am I?" she asked.

I shook my head.

"Good." She smiled. "I wouldn't want to hurt you."

"No . . ." I muttered.

She stared into my eyes for a moment, her head cocked slightly to one side, then she gently ran her finger down my face.

"What are you thinking about?" she said.

I wanted to say—what do you *think* I'm thinking about?—but I didn't. I just looked at her.

She smiled again. "You know what you said about Stella earlier on?"

"Stella . . . ?"

"Yeah, you know . . . when you told Pauly that you hadn't seen those pictures of her on the Internet." Nic raised her eyebrows at me. "Is that right? You really haven't seen them?"

I didn't know what to say. I didn't want to think about Stella . . . I didn't want to think about *anything*. I put my hands on Nic's hips.

"I'm not interested in Stella," I said, trying to change the subject.

Nic took hold of my hands, keeping them still. "No," she said, "neither am I. I'm just curious, that's all."

I felt the first flutter of something I didn't want to feel then.

Nic said, "You don't *mind* me asking, do you?"

"No," I sighed, "of course not. I just don't see—"

"I only want to know if you've seen them or not."

Her voice was a little bit slurred now, and there was something unsettling in her eyes—a strange kind of uncontrolled steadiness.

She carried on smiling at me. "Can you imagine how Stella must feel? I mean, she must *know* what everyone's doing when they look at those pictures . . . how do you think that makes her feel?"

I shook my head. "I'm not sure I really want to talk about it—"

"I mean, God . . . if that was me . . ." She looked away for a moment, her eyes gazing at nothing, then suddenly she turned back to me. "Would you look at naked pictures of *me* on the Internet?"

"Listen, Nic—"

"No, come on, Pete," she said, pouting her lips and running her fingers through her hair. "What d'you think?" She struck a pose—hands behind her head, thrusting herself forward—and although I knew she was only joking, mocking the artificiality of pornographic pictures, I kind of got the impression that she was only half-joking, too. But while a part of me was still in thrall to the miracle of her half-naked body, she didn't really look very sexy anymore. She just looked drunk.

"You don't have to do this, Nic," I said quietly.

"Do what?"

"You know . . ."

She glanced down at herself, then looked up, smiling seductively. "What's the matter? Don't you like it?"

"No, it's not that . . . I just think—"

"What? You just think what?"

Everything felt wrong now. Nic felt wrong, I felt wrong, the whole situation felt wrong.

"I'm sorry," I said to her. "I don't think we should do this."

Her face froze. "You what?"

"I just can't . . ."

She smiled awkwardly, glancing downward. "Is it . . . you know . . . is something wrong?"

"No . . . no, nothing's wrong. I just don't think this is the right time."

She frowned. "What are you talking about?"

"This," I said. "Me and you, it just doesn't feel right . . ."

She grinned, shifting herself in my lap. "It feels all right to me."

I moved away from her.

She stopped grinning and her eyes went cold. "What the hell's the matter with you? I mean, Jesus *Christ* . . ."

"Come on, Nic," I said, reaching out to calm her down. "There's no need to get angry . . ."

She slapped my hand away.

"Sorry," I said, "I was only trying to—"

"Fuck you, Pete," she hissed.

There wasn't much I could say to that, so I just sat there, letting her glare at me. Her face had completely changed now. It was dead-looking, vicious, hard as nails. Her once-glowing skin was dull and white, and her eyes were black with rage.

"You're enjoying this, aren't you?" she said nastily.

"Of course I'm not—"

"Humiliating me."

"I didn't mean to—"

"Making me feel like a whore."

I shook my head. "Listen, Nic. I'm sorry, OK? I'm *really* sorry. I know how you must feel—"

"You don't know how I *feel*."

She pushed herself away from me then, shoving me hard in the chest, and all I could do was sit there and watch as she picked up her clothes and started to get dressed. She was stumbling all over the place now, hopping on one leg, trying to pull on her jeans, almost falling over . . .

"Do you *mind*?" she said, glaring over her shoulder at me.

I lowered my eyes.

"Christ," I heard her mutter.

I stared at the ground, dazed and confused, not knowing what to think or what to do. My head was spinning, my skull was tightening . . . I was nowhere. And I didn't understand why. I just stared at the ground, not knowing anything, utterly incapable.

I didn't raise my eyes again until I heard Nicole cursing and kicking an empty bottle out of her way as she moved toward the door. As I looked up, she paused for a moment, dug something out of her jeans' pocket, and threw it over to me. It landed in the dirt at my feet — a packet of condoms.

"Enjoy yourself," she said coldly.

I looked up at her.

She turned away and stooped down to the door.

"Are you going to be all right?" I asked her.

"What do you care?"

"I can walk with you along the lane, if you want . . ."

She laughed, a dismissive snort, and then she was gone. I listened to her angry footsteps stomping down the bank, and I heard her stumble once or twice, and then after a while her footsteps faded away and there was nothing to hear but the stillness of the night and the sigh of my own stupid heart.

SIX

didn't want to go to the fair after that — I didn't *want* to do anything — but I didn't feel like going home, either, and I knew if I stayed where I was, sitting alone in that soured silence, trying to think myself into a time and a place where nothing had happened and everything was still all right . . . well, I knew that was hopeless. Something *had* happened. Everything *wasn't* all right. And if I carried on trying to think myself out of it, I'd probably just end up crying instead.

Crying for what, I didn't know.

For being an idiot?

For getting things wrong?

For trying to make things right?

I had no idea.

All I knew was that I couldn't just sit there feeling sorry for myself — I had to *do* something. And the only thing I could think of — the only thing that had any point to it — was going to the fair to find Raymond.

I took a final swig of tequila, shuddered and coughed, then got to my feet and got going.

♥ ♠ ♦ ♣

It wasn't as dark along the lane as I'd imagined. The night sky was starless and black, and the moon was nowhere in sight, but there was just enough light drifting up from across the wasteground to let me see where I was going. It was a strange kind of light — a hazy mixture of distant streetlights, headlights passing on the dockland roads, and a muted glow from Greenwell Rise on the other side of the river — and as I walked along the narrow path, everything around me seemed to shiver with an unnaturally dull luminescence. The gas towers shone black. My sneakers were bright white. The wall of a factory building at the top of the bank shimmered with a gray-green flatness, like the deadened shine of a blank TV screen.

I wondered if it was real, or if it was just me. Me and the drink. Me and the dope. Me and the stifling black heat. I didn't really feel drunk or stoned anymore, but I was definitely still feeling weird. Kind of buzzy, liquidy, all warm and tingly inside. My senses were heightened, and I was acutely aware of everything in and around me: the ground under my feet, the darkness, the light, the distant sound of the fairground, the sweat on my skin . . . I could even feel the blood in my veins. It was throbbing in time to a faint metallic roar that was rushing around in my head — *whi-shoosh, whi-shoosh, whi-shoosh* — like the sound of an old washing machine in an empty basement.

I felt sick.

Numbly nauseous.

I was aching in places I didn't know existed.

But, for some inexplicable reason, none of this seemed to bother me very much. In fact, in a weird kind of way, it somehow felt quite pleasant. And as I walked on through the dreamy gray darkness, I actually started to feel a bit better. I still didn't feel great or anything, and my head was still twisted up with all kinds of stuff, but I was beginning to accept that whatever had happened with Nicole, and whoever's fault it had been, it wasn't the end of the world.

It was just one of those things.

I mean, no one had *died*, had they?

No one had been hurt.

It was just one of those mixed-up, shitty little things . . .

That's what I kept telling myself anyway — *it was just one of those things . . . there's no point worrying about it, trying to understand it . . . it was nothing, just something that happened* — and by the time I'd reached the end of the lane, I'd pretty much convinced myself that I was right. There *wasn't* any point in thinking about it anymore. All that mattered now was getting to the fair, finding Raymond, and getting us both safely home.

Of course, if he'd had a mobile phone, I could have just called him instead. But he didn't. His parents had never let him have one. And it'd been so long since I'd called Eric or Pauly that even if I'd had their numbers, they'd more than likely have changed them by now.

Not that I really wanted to speak to either of them, anyway.

And, besides, I was almost at the town park now.

The sounds of the fairground were getting louder and louder — a swirling cacophony of music and machinery, screams and laughter, the booming crackle of amplified voices — and as I came out of the lane and headed down a little street, I could feel the excitement rippling through the air.

The town park is usually locked up at night — not that that stops anyone from getting in — but tonight the gates were wide-open, and the usual dark emptiness of the nighttime park was ablaze with the lights of the fair. The fairground itself only took up a small part of the park — a ragged circle of rides and trailers at the far end of a pathway on the right-hand side — but the flashing lights and the whirling noise spread out all the way across the playing fields, and as I headed up the pathway toward the fair, everything seemed weirdly mixed up and out of place. The lights in the darkness, the noise in the emptiness, the sounds of excitement surrounded by dullness . . .

The night was still hot, and the air was getting thicker and heavier. It smelled thundery and electric. I could smell other things, too — the meaty stink of overcooked burgers, the sweet scent of perfume and cotton candy, the heat of exhaust fumes and burning lights. It was all too much for me, and for a moment I thought I was going to throw up. But after I'd paused for a minute and taken a few deep breaths, the nausea quickly passed, and in its place I was suddenly filled with a burst of skin-tingling energy.

As I moved on along the path, I felt like I was walking on air.

♥ ♠ ♦ ♣

Although I was already used to the lights and the noise of the fair, the sudden explosion of sound and movement as I entered the fairground literally took my breath away. It was staggering. The blaring music, the crashing drums, the strobing lights, the flashing lasers . . . people screaming, sirens wailing, everything spinning . . . whirling wheels, stars and spaceships, thousands of faces, a million booming voices swirling around in the air — *HERE WE GO!! HERE WE GO!! EVERYONE'S A WINNER!! . . . IT'S C-C-C-C-CRAZEEE!!!*

I could feel the sound of it all thumping in my heart.

B-BOOM BOOM BOOM . . .

The lights burning my eyes.

C'MON C'MON!! ANY PRIZE YOU LIKE!!

The crash of the rides rolling and ripping all around me — TERMINATOR! METEOR! TWISTER! FUN HOUSE! — throwing out madness into the night.

It was hard to feel sane as I moved along the walkways between the stalls and the kiosks and the giant spinning rides. There were so many people — pushing and shoving, laughing and shouting — and so many different sounds blaring out from loudspeakers on poles . . . everything was all mixed up together — rock 'n' roll music, twanging guitars, Wham!, Madonna, Duran Duran . . .

Jesus *Christ.*

It was like listening to the favorite songs of a dozen middle-aged lunatics all at the same time — *WAKE ME UP BEFORE . . . HER NAME IS . . . YOU GO-GO . . .*

*HER NAME IS RIO AND . . . WE WILL WE WILL . . . I WANNA
TAKE YOU THERE . . . WHO LET THE . . . JUST LIKE
A CHILD . . . DOGS OUT . . . ROCK YOU . . .*

I couldn't see where I was going through the bustle of
the crowds, but it didn't really matter, because I didn't know
where I was going anyway. I was just walking—just going
with the flow, hoping to find Raymond. I was also hoping
to find some toilets. My bladder was beginning to ache, my
belly felt worryingly shitty, and I was starting to feel sick
again, too. I paused by a stall for a moment and let out a
quiet burp. It tasted sour.

"Try your luck, mate?" I heard someone say.

I looked around at the stall and saw a ponytailed man
offering me three cheap-looking darts. He nodded at a
dartboard at the back of the stall.

"Forty-five or more," he said, "any prize you like."

I gazed around at the prizes—stuffed animals, Scooby-
Doos, Garfields, and Tweety Pies. A row of teddy bears were
fixed to the wall, hanging by their necks, like furry little
dead men hanging on the gallows.

"Pound a throw," the ponytailed man said. "Any prize
you like."

But I wasn't listening to him anymore. I'd heard
something from somewhere over to my right, a subtle change
in the sound of the crowd, and as I stepped away from the
stall and leaned to one side to see what was happening,
something inside me already knew what I was going to see.
So I wasn't too surprised when I spotted Raymond's face
up ahead, and just for a second I felt a warm glow of relief

spreading right through me . . . but it didn't last very long. When I saw who Raymond was with, and what he was doing, everything inside me suddenly went cold.

He was with Stella Ross.

I couldn't believe it.

Raymond and Stella . . . ?

What the hell was he doing with her? And, more to the point, what the hell was she doing with him? She was Stella Ross, for Christ's sake. She didn't hang around with people like Raymond. Even when she was at school, before she got famous, she wouldn't be seen *dead* with people like Raymond. But there she was now, strolling along through the fairground with him . . . her arm around his shoulder, hugging him, talking to him, smiling her bright white smile at him.

As I moved closer, pushing my way through the crowd, I realized that they weren't alone. Stella had her *people* with her — a couple of big security guys, a bunch of well-dressed hangers-on, a guy with a film camera on his shoulder, another one with a big furry microphone on a pole. They were all trailing along behind her, and the guy with the camera was filming her, and everyone around them — all the *ordinary* people — were getting out of their way, then lining up as they passed to get a better look at Stella Ross in the flesh. And there was a lot of flesh to look at. She was all dressed up in some kind of trailer-trash chic — tight denim shorts, thigh-high boots, a cut-off cowboy shirt with most of the buttons undone.

She was kissing Raymond now, holding him close and planting her bright red lips on his cheek . . . but she wasn't looking at him. Her eyes were grinning at the camera. And as she kissed him again, smearing lipstick all over his face, I could see all the people around her smirking at each other, having a good laugh, watching the beauty playing with the beast.

I didn't know why, but that's what she was doing. She was playing with him, toying with him. Pretending that he was her *boyfriend* or something. It was just a big joke to her — the beautiful celebrity flirting with the weird-looking loser — and it made me feel sick. It was like watching someone teasing a dog. And, just like a dog, Raymond didn't seem to care. He was just playing along with it — smiling at Stella, wide-eyed and excited, grinning while everyone laughed at him . . .

I didn't get it.

Raymond wasn't stupid.

He must have *known* what was going on.

But he didn't seem bothered at all.

At least, he didn't *look* as if he was bothered about anything. It was hard to tell with Raymond. But I was pretty sure that he wasn't doing anything he didn't want to do. And that was the only thing that made me hesitate for a moment as I moved through the crowds toward Stella. *He's happy enough*, a voice in my head said. *Why not just leave him alone?* But it didn't strike me as much of an argument, and it didn't do anything to slow me down.

I'd nearly reached Stella and Raymond now. The crowds had thinned out in front of them, and as I closed in on the slow-moving entourage, I could see that the camera was pointing at me, and the two big security guys were moving out in front of Stella to cut me off.

"Raymond!" I called out. "Hey, Raymond!"

He looked around suddenly, his eyes wide-open, and when he saw it was me, he grinned like a madman and raised his thumb. As Stella glanced over to see who he was looking at, the two security guys stepped in front of me and blocked my way.

"It's all right," I started to say, "I'm a friend —"

"Get back," one of them said.

"I just want to —"

"Get *back*."

When I didn't move, the one who'd spoken to me put his hand on my shoulder and started to force me back. It was like being pushed by a bulldozer. After he'd shoved me back a couple of paces, though, I heard Stella's voice calling out to him.

"It's all right, Tony!" she yelled. "He's a friend. You can let him through."

Big Tony took his hand away and stepped to one side.

"Hey, Pete!" Stella called out. "It *is* Pete, isn't it? Pete Boland?"

I walked up to where she was standing with Raymond. She still had her arm draped around his shoulder, and they were both just standing there, smiling at me. The guy with the camera was still pointing it at me.

"Sorry about that, Pete," Stella said, nodding at the security guy. "I didn't know it was you." She flicked back her perfect blonde hair and smiled at me again. "How are you, anyway? You look *great* . . . God, I haven't see you for —"

"Raymond?" I said, looking into his eyes. "Are you OK?"

He nodded.

"Come on," I told him. "Let's get out of here."

"Hold on," Stella said to me, "what do you think you're doing?"

I just looked at her.

She glanced at Raymond, gave him a squeeze, then looked back at me. "Ray's with me tonight," she said with a smile. "I'm showing him how to have fun. You're welcome to join us, if you want."

"No, thanks." I looked at Raymond again. He was beginning to look uncomfortable now. I could see the growing fear in his eyes, the anxiety, the confusion. It was almost as if he'd only just realized where he was and what he was doing. "Come on, Raymond," I said quietly. "I'll buy you a hot dog."

He flicked a quick glance at Stella, then started to move away from her. She tightened her grip on his shoulder and pulled him back.

"What's the matter?" she said, pouting at him. "Don't you *like* me anymore?"

He grinned awkwardly at her.

She smiled at me.

I glanced at the guys with the camera and the microphone, and just for a moment an unknown and unsettling image flashed through my head — something white, something sad, something vaguely familiar—but it was gone before I had time to think about it. I shook it from my head, walked up to Stella, and stopped right in front of her. I looked at her for a second or two, then I leaned forward and spoke quietly in her ear, so no one else could hear what I was saying. "Stop fucking about with him," I whispered, "OK?"

Her smile didn't waver. "Or else what?"

I didn't have an answer to that, so I just stared at her. Although she was still smiling at me, there was no trace of humor in her face. No joy in her eyes. All I could see was a cold, mocking emptiness. It was the look of a girl who truly believed she was the only worthwhile thing in the world.

"You're going to wish you hadn't done this," she said casually.

"Am I?"

She smiled. "You've got no idea . . ."

Everything went strangely quiet then. Just for a moment, the maddening sounds of the fairground seemed muffled and distant, as if they were underwater, and the babbling chatter of the crowds all around us faded into a barely audible hum. The lights faded, too. The brightness dulled, smothered by the blackness of the night, and all I could see with any real clarity was Stella's dark eyes staring deep into mine. Then, all at once, something cracked—a sharp electric sound, like the amplified lash of a whip—and everything came back to life again. The music, the lights, the crowds, the rides . . .

Stella laughed and took her arm from Raymond's shoulder. "I was only looking after him for you," she said to me. "You can have him back now." She glanced at Raymond. "All right?"

He nodded at her.

"Go on, then," she told him. "Go and get yourself a hot dog."

Raymond looked at me.

I suddenly felt really tired. I was too hot, too sweaty. My body was aching all over and my head was buzzing with too much of everything. I wanted to say something to Raymond, something helpful and reassuring, but I couldn't seem to find my voice. So I just stepped over, took him by the arm, and quietly led him away.

We didn't say anything to each other for a while, we just walked along through the bustling crowds, heading vaguely toward the far end of the fairground. I didn't know why, but I thought it might be quieter there, a bit less manic, and I was hoping to find some toilets, too. I was getting pretty desperate now.

It was slow-going through the swarms of people, and as we approached the far end of the fair, instead of getting quieter, everything seemed to get louder and busier. More people, more noise, more madness. I didn't understand it at first, but after a while I realized that it was just one of those places — the kind of fairground place that attracts all the gangs and the kids looking for trouble. There were loads of them — most of them hanging around a big bumper-car place, some of them drinking from cans of beer, others just slouching around, looking hard. The bumper-car place was huge, a massive wooden arena of crashing cars and bright blue sparks, screams and thuds, booming rap music. As we passed it by, making sure we didn't bump into anyone, the crash of the cars and the raging rant of the rap music faded into the rattle and whirl of an adjoining tilt-a-whirl ride. Lights flashed — *EVOLUTION!!!* — and Madonna's baby-girl voice boomed out — *Just like a child . . .*

"Nicole," Raymond shouted in my ear.

"What?" I shouted back.

He stopped and pointed over at the ride. The seats were whizzing round, spinning and whirling, moving up and down, and it was hard to make out anything in the blur of lights and screaming faces . . . but then I saw her. She was in a seat with two other girls. I recognized one of them — a school friend of Nic's — but I didn't know who the other one was. They all looked fairly wrecked — wild-eyed and crazy — and as they whirled round and round, I could see that one of the carny guys had already moved in on them. He looked pretty much the same as every other carny guy I'd ever seen — cool and lean, rough and easy, not a care in the world. He was standing behind Nicole's seat, his arms draped casually over the back as he leaned in and turned on the charm. With the lights strobing on and off, and the ride spinning round and round, it was like watching something played out in a slow-motion flick book: the carny guy leaning in, Nicole ignoring him, the other two flirting . . . flick, flick . . . Nicole looking over at me, our eyes meeting for a second . . . flick, flick . . . Nicole leaning back, smiling up at the carny guy . . . flick, flick . . . her hand on the back

of his neck as he leans down and whispers in her ear . . .
flick, flick . . . flick, flick . . .

Flick, flick.

Heaven help me . . .

Madonna was still singing as I walked away and left
Nic to it.

"Are you all right?" Raymond asked me.

"Yeah . . . I'm fine. Do you know where the toilets are?"

He looked around for a while, then shook his head.
"There's some trees over there."

We were sitting on a bench in the relative peace and quiet
of some children's rides near the far end of the fairground.
It was too late for little kids, and the rides — bouncy castles
and miniature merry-go-rounds — were too tame for anyone
else, so everything was dark and deserted.

I looked at Raymond.

"What?" he said.

"You know what."

He grinned.

I sighed. "You know what she was doing, don't you?"

"Nicole?"

"No, Stella."

He shrugged and looked away.

"Come on, Raymond," I said. "You know what I mean . . .
why did you let her do it?"

"Do what?"

"She was laughing at you . . . they all were. They were
taking the piss . . ."

"I know."

"So why did you let them do it?"

"I don't know . . ."

"Didn't it bother you?"

He didn't answer me, he just shrugged again, and I didn't know what else to say. It was just so hard with Raymond. His usual state of mind was "not quite right," so whenever he seemed quite normal, like now, it usually meant that he wasn't quite right. And that was always pretty hard to work out. So I did what I usually do when I don't know what to do — I didn't do anything. I just sat there, looking around, trying not to think about Nicole and the carny guy.

After a while, Raymond said, "Stella means star."

I looked at him. "What?"

"The star's going out tonight," he said. "Stella's going out . . ." He turned and looked at me. "She kissed me."

"Yeah, I know. Come here . . ." I took a tissue from my pocket and wiped a smear of lipstick off his face.

"I feel weird, Pete," he said quietly.

I smiled at him. "You *are* weird."

"No," he muttered, "I mean *really* weird. I feel like . . . I don't know. It's like I feel like I'm someone else."

"Someone else?"

"I keep seeing things . . ."

"What kind of things?"

"Things that aren't there. Strange shapes and colors . . . I don't know." He squinted into the distance. "It's kind of like the air's moving . . ."

"You didn't smoke any of Pauly's dope, did you?"

"No."

"Does your skin keep tingling?"

"Sort of . . ."

"Does your belly hurt?"

"Yeah . . ."

"Do you feel sick?"

"A bit."

"Me, too. Let's go and find the toilets."

I saw Nicole again as we walked back around the other side of the fair. She was sitting with the carny guy on a wooden crate at the back of the ride. He had his feet up on a generator, and she had her hand on his thigh, and they were both drinking something out of paper cups.

"What's she doing with him?" Raymond asked me.

"Enjoying herself," I said.

We still hadn't found the toilets when Raymond suddenly stopped beside a drab-looking canvas tent. The flap of the tent was open, and a sign above it said:

MADAME BAPTISTE
FORTUNE-TELLER

"Come on, Raymond," I said. "I'm going to burst if we don't . . . Raymond?"

But he was already entering the tent.

"Shit," I muttered.

I could see the toilets now. They were just up ahead, about fifty feet away—two or three rows of dull blue Portaloos. I looked longingly at them for a moment, desperately wanting to go, and I knew it'd probably be OK if I did. I mean, I'd only be a minute or two . . . Raymond would probably still be here when I came back. But *probably* wasn't enough. I'd rather put up with a bursting bladder than have to go looking for Raymond again. So I took a deep breath, gritted my teeth, and followed him into the tent.

SEVEN

T he only fortune-tellers I'd ever seen before were the kind you get in crappy old films and TV programs, so I suppose that's what I was expecting to see: a wrinkly old gypsy woman with long black hair and long black fingernails, hunched over a crystal ball . . . rings on her fingers, silver bangles on her wrists, a shawl draped around her shoulders. But the woman sitting at a table with Raymond wasn't like that at all. She wasn't hunched over a crystal ball, she didn't have long black hair, and she wasn't old and wrinkly, either. I guessed she was about forty, maybe a bit younger. Or maybe a bit older. It was hard to tell. She had dark eyes, very pale skin, and her dark brown hair was braided tightly and coiled into a bun on top of her head. Despite the heat, she was wearing an old-fashioned brown woolen dress, buttoned up tightly to her neck. And that was pretty much it — no rings on her fingers, no silver bangles, no gypsy shawl draped around her shoulders. She didn't look very mysterious at all. But as I stood there in the doorway of the tent, and she sat there gazing calmly at me, I found it hard to take my eyes off her.

"Come in, please," she said, beckoning me over.

The air in the tent was surprisingly cool and quiet, and as I moved away from the entrance and headed over to the table, the sounds of the fairground outside seemed to soften and die in the silence. On the table, which was covered with a plain black cloth, there was a lighted candle and a pack of cards. Raymond was sitting with his back to me, and as I stopped behind him and put my hand on his shoulder, he glanced over his shoulder and smiled at me.

"Take a seat," the woman said to me, nodding toward an empty chair beside Raymond.

"I'm all right, thanks," I told her, backing away slightly. "I'll just stand here, if that's OK."

She smiled serenely. "You're in a hurry, perhaps?"

I shrugged.

She looked at me. "You're not a believer."

"Sorry?"

She didn't say anything for a moment or two, she just kept looking at me. It felt a bit unnerving, as if she was studying me, reading me, searching me for secrets. Of course, I knew she didn't have any mystical powers or anything, and I knew all this fortune-telling stuff was just a scam . . . I mean, if she could *really* see into the future, she wouldn't be sitting in a tent in the middle of a town park on a Saturday night, would she? If she could *really* see into the future, she'd be rich and famous, a billionaire . . . she'd be the most powerful woman in the world.

So, no, I wasn't a believer.

The only thing I believed in just then was the eye-watering ache in my bladder.

"You can go if you wish," the woman said to me.

I looked at her, not sure what she meant.

She smiled at me. "We'll still be here when you come back."

"I'm fine, thanks," I muttered.

She gazed at me for a moment longer, still smiling calmly, then — with a slight nod of her head — she turned her attention to Raymond.

"So," she said quietly, looking into his eyes, "let's see what we know." She picked up the pack of cards. "Are you quite comfortable?"

Raymond nodded.

She smiled. "Not too hot?"

He shook his head.

She said, "You've had a long night . . . both of you. Things to remember."

Raymond said nothing.

I watched the woman's hands as she placed the pack of cards on the table and spread them out in a line, facedown. There were no pictures or patterns on the backs of the cards — they were a plain dark red — and when the woman flipped the cards over, I was surprised to see that they were perfectly ordinary playing cards — Hearts, Clubs, Diamonds, Spades . . . the usual fifty-two cards. Nothing fancy, nothing special.

"You like animals," the woman said to Raymond.

"Yes . . . yes, I do."

She gathered up the cards and placed the deck on the table again. "Animals," she said quietly. "You feel close to them."

"Yes."

"They make you feel good."

I couldn't see Raymond's face, but I knew he was smiling.

The woman placed her right hand on the tablecloth — palm down, fingers spread out. She studied it for a moment, removed her hand from the table, and then — with the index finger of her left hand — she started sketching the outline of something around the space where her hand had been. Her finger didn't leave a mark on the dull black cloth, so I have no idea *how* I knew what she was drawing . . . but there was no doubt in my mind that it was a rabbit.

She looked at Raymond. "He's not black enough, is he?"

Raymond stared at the invisible picture. "Not quite . . ."

"I need a paler hand."

I knew what she meant. The paleness of her skin had made the black of the cloth seem even blacker, but it still wasn't as black as Black Rabbit.

"He's softer, too," Raymond said.

"Of course."

The woman smiled again. She slowly wiped her hand over the cloth, erasing the invisible picture, then she picked up the pack of cards again. I watched her closely as she started to shuffle them, trying to follow the movement of her hands, but all I could see was a blur of moving cards. Her hands didn't seem to move at all. She finished the shuffle, tapped the pack into shape, and placed it on the table in front of Raymond.

"Cut the cards, please," she told him.

"Anywhere?"

"It's your fate, Raymond."

He reached out for the cards. His hand hovered hesitantly for a moment, then he carefully cut the pack. The woman told him to put his cards on the table. He put them down, and she slid the two piles into the middle of the table.

"Pick one, please," she said.

Raymond reached out a finger, hesitated again, then touched the pile on his left. The woman removed the other pile, putting them out of sight under the table, and picked up the remaining cards. She closed her eyes, took a couple of deep breaths, and started to deal the cards. She turned them over incredibly slowly, placing each one very carefully, side by side, face up on the table. By the time she'd got to the third card, I was already starting to think to myself — *God, this is going to take ages* — but then she suddenly stopped. Her eyes opened, she put the rest of the pile to one side, and she gazed down intently at the three cards on the table.

Something happened to her then. I didn't know what it was, and it only lasted a moment, but in that moment she looked as if she'd seen something terrible. Her eyes went cold, her body stiffened, and a faint startled breath seemed to catch in her throat. I thought at first that she was having a heart attack or something, but then I realized it was the cards. There was something about them that shocked her, something that only she could see. I had no idea what it was. All I could see were three perfectly ordinary playing cards: the Nine of Spades, the Ten of Spades, the Ace of Spades. Whatever the woman had seen in them, though, and whatever it had meant to her, she was very quick to cover it up. Before I'd had a chance to think about it, she'd already composed herself and was very nearly back to normal. If it wasn't for the slight quiver in her voice as she started explaining the cards to Raymond, I might have thought I was imagining things again.

"Your past, Raymond," she said softly, indicating the card on her left, the Nine of Spades. "You've not always had the happiest of times, have you?" She looked at him. "It's been hard . . . looking for things, things that weren't always there." She paused for a moment, glancing down at the cards again, and I could see the sadness weighing her down. "There was a time, I think, when you had what you needed. When you were young . . . I think you had some closeness then. You had some security. But there have been too many troubles since. Too many misunderstandings . . . misplaced desires." She looked up again, her eyes seeming to reach out across the table. "Nothing is to *blame*, Raymond," she whispered powerfully. "These things . . . your world . . . the way you see things, the way the world sees you . . . these things are *your* things, your *life* . . . you know that, don't you?"

"Yes," Raymond breathed.

"You know the moments of light."

He nodded.

She looked down at the cards again. "Your cards," she muttered, moving her hand over all three of them, "three Spades . . . their darkness tells me of hard times. Confusion. Anxiety. Perhaps even . . ." She hesitated a moment, placing her finger on the middle card, the Ten of Spades. "Your moments of light . . . you must hold on to them. Even now . . ." She tapped the card. "This is now . . . the present. A time of great change. The things around you are moving—your friends, your places, your . . ." She frowned slightly. "Your concerns." She looked up at Raymond. "You have great kindness."

He shook his head. "No . . ."

"Selflessness, then. You care for others without thinking of yourself."

Raymond said nothing.

The woman smiled. "Your moments of light put the darkness to shame."

Raymond was never very good with compliments, and as I looked down at him, sensing his awkwardness, I couldn't help smiling at the flush of embarrassment reddening the back of his neck. I had no idea what was going on, but whatever it was, it somehow gave me an immense sense of pride.

It was a nice moment—a moment that seemed to float in the air—and as I stood there in the cooling silence of the tent, I didn't want it to end. I wanted it to *be* the end—no more words, no more noise, no more nothing. If I could have waved a wand and magicked us both out of there while that moment was still all there was . . .

But there was no magic.

There never is.

The moment always ends.

I looked down as Raymond nervously rubbed the back of his neck. I saw his hand, his bitten-down fingernails, the dusty shine of his unruly black hair . . . and I saw him lean forward and point to the last card on the table, the Ace of Spades, his eyes fixed anxiously on the woman.

"Is this my future?" he asked her.

I could see a strange conflict in her eyes as she looked back at him, and when she spoke, her voice was surprisingly hesitant. "It's difficult sometimes . . ." she told him. "I have to read each card in relation to the other cards . . . and sometimes this can make things unclear . . ."

"It's a bad card," Raymond said. "The Ace of Spades."

"Not necessarily—"

"The death card."

The woman shook her head. "It's not that simple, Raymond. Yes, it can be a very destructive card, but it can also mean the end of the bad times and the beginning of something new." She looked at him. "Life is not life without death."

Raymond stared at her. "Is someone going to die?"

She didn't answer him for a moment, and I felt like screaming at her—*don't hesitate, for God's sake, just say no!*—but she seemed curiously reluctant to commit herself. I realize now that it was a difficult question to answer. *Is someone going to die?* Well, of course, *someone* was going to die. Someone, somewhere, is always going to die. But that wasn't what Raymond had meant, and the woman was perfectly aware of that.

"Our futures are infinite," she said eventually. "Every second of every day, we choose which way to go. And every time we make that choice, another aspect of ourselves—

another self—makes a different choice. So everything is always possible, and everything always happens. But because we are only one among an infinity of ourselves, the odds of *anything* happening to us, at any particular time or place, are almost nonexistent."

"But things happen," said Raymond.

"Yes, things happen."

"Bad things?"

She nodded. "Sometimes . . ."

"Tonight?"

She gazed silently at Raymond for a second or two, her eyes gleaming darkly, then she slowly leaned back in her chair and smiled. "Tonight," she said, "you should go home. It's late. You've had a long day." She glanced up at me. "And I think your friend here is anxious to be somewhere else."

Despite everything, I found myself smiling at her.

She smiled back at me, then stood up and gazed down at Raymond. He didn't move for a moment, he just sat there, perfectly still, staring intently at the cards on the table.

"Raymond?" the woman said.

He looked up at her.

"Go home," she said gently.

He seemed a little unsteady as he got to his feet, and when he turned around to face me, his skin was very pale.

"Are you all right?" I asked him.

"Yeah," he said, smiling. "Yeah, I'm all right." He looked around the tent for a moment, frowning slightly, as if he wasn't quite sure where he was, then he turned back to the woman and bowed his head at her.

"Thank you," he said.

She bowed back. "Thank *you*."

They carried on looking at each other for a while, and I thought one of them was going to say something else, but after a few seconds Raymond just turned around and started heading for the doorway. As I turned to follow him, I heard the woman calling out quietly.

"Wait, please," she said.

I thought she was talking to Raymond, but when I glanced over my shoulder I saw her scuttling up to me, her eyes fixed on mine. I looked around and saw Raymond disappearing out of the tent.

I quickly turned back to the woman. "I'd better go —"

She put her hand on my arm and looked me in the eye. "Look after him," she whispered urgently. "I know you don't believe in these things, but please . . . take care." She squeezed my arm, then gave me a little shove. "Go . . . be with your friend. Take him home."

Raymond was waiting for me outside the tent. He was just standing there, seemingly oblivious to everything around him — the crowds, the noise, the lights, the madness — and as I went up to him, I could see that familiar lost and lonely look on his face. The quietness, the stillness, the faint secret fluttering of his lips.

"Hey," I said to him.

He looked at me.

I smiled. "The toilets are just over there."

"Toilets . . ." he muttered, gazing slowly in the direction of the Portaloos.

"I don't know about you," I said. "But I *really* need to go."

He didn't say anything, he just carried on staring into the distance.

I took his arm. "Come on, let's go."

"You don't really believe in any of that stuff, do you?" I asked him as we walked over to the toilets.

"I don't think it matters . . ."

"What doesn't?"

"Anything."

"Yeah," I said, "but the future . . . all that weird stuff about infinity and choices . . . I mean, she's supposed to be a fortune-teller, but it seems to me like she was trying to say that it's impossible to know what's going to happen."

"It doesn't matter," Raymond said again.

I didn't know what else to say. I mean, what *can* you say when someone keeps telling you that nothing matters?

"It's all *right*," Raymond said suddenly. "I know there's nothing to worry about. They're only cards. Cards don't mean anything." He looked at me, his eyes worryingly bright. "What I can't understand is where we are."

I shook my head. "I don't know what you mean."

"Where are we in time?" he said. "You know . . . where do we exist? *When* do we exist? In the past, the present, the future? I mean, we don't live in the past, do we? And we don't live in the future. So that only leaves the present."

He was grinning a bit too madly for my liking now. "But when's the present?" he said. "When *is* now? How long does it last? A second, half a second . . . a millionth of a second? You can't just be alive in a millionth of a second, can you? It doesn't make sense."

None of it made any sense to me.

Raymond suddenly flinched and clutched at his stomach.

"What's the matter?" I said.

"I think I'm going to be sick."

I quickly ushered him over to a vacant Portaloo. "It's all right," I said, opening the door for him. "You'll be all right . . ."

He groaned and heaved.

"Go on," I told him, guiding him inside. "I'll wait for you . . ." I glanced at the adjacent cubicle and saw that it was vacant. "If I'm not here, I'll be in there, OK?"

He stumbled inside and pulled the door shut.

I heard him retching and throwing up, and the sound of it made *my* belly start heaving. Swallowing hard, I hurried over to the Portaloo next door, yanked it open, and got to the toilet just in time.

EIGHT

only stayed in the Portaloo for as long as it took to do what I had to do, but unfortunately I had to do quite a lot, and you can't exactly rush things when you're in a situation like that, can you? I mean, I'm not going to go into any details or anything, but if you've ever been stuck in a shoebox-size cubicle, desperately trying to empty yourself from too many orifices all at the same time . . . well, I'm sure you'll understand.

I did my best, though — I *tried* to hurry — and I'm pretty sure I wasn't in there for *all* that long. Three or four minutes, maybe . . .

Five at the very most.

And, besides, I'd told Raymond to wait for me, hadn't I? *If I'm not here*, I'd told him, *I'll be in there.*

I'd *told* him that.

But I suppose I should have known better.

I should have known he wouldn't be there when I came out.

I wasn't worried at first, I just assumed he was still in the toilet, and even when I saw someone else going into the Portaloo next to mine, which I *knew* was the one that Raymond had been in, I still didn't want to admit to myself that anything was wrong. I'd got the Portaloos mixed up, that was all . . . I'd made a mistake. Raymond must have been in another one . . .

But I knew I was only kidding myself.

Why else would I be looking around, trying to see where he was . . . why else would my heart be beating so hard?

He'd gone. He wasn't there.

"Shit," I muttered.

I stayed where I was for a while, just looking all around, but it was so hard to see anything through all the crowds, and everything was still spinning and whirling and flashing and crashing, and the lunatic music was still blaring out . . . it was useless.

Raymond could be anywhere.

I looked over at the fortune-teller's tent, wondering if maybe he'd gone back there, but all I could see was the fortune-teller herself, standing quietly in the doorway of the tent, watching all the people pass by. She hadn't seen him, I was sure of that. No matter what I thought of her — and I still didn't know what that was — I knew she wouldn't be standing there so calmly if she'd seen Raymond walking around on his own. I could still hear the urgency in her voice — *Look after him . . . be with your friend . . . take him home* — and there was no doubt in my mind that she'd meant it.

No doubt at all . . .

I started walking toward her.

♥ ♠ ♦ ♣

I really don't think that I *did* have any doubts, I was simply heading back to the fortune-teller's tent because I didn't know where else to go. She was *there*, that was all, a familiar face in the crowd, and even if she didn't know anything — and I was fairly sure that she didn't — at least I could talk to her. And there was something inside me just then that really *needed* to talk to someone.

I was still looking around as I walked, still keeping my eyes open for Raymond, and as I passed a little burger stand, about twenty feet away from the tent, I thought for a moment I'd found him. A bunch of kids in front of me were making a lot of noise and shoving each other around, and as one of them dived to one side and barged another one into a passing group of girls — causing a gap to appear in the crowds — I caught a quick glimpse of a sad-looking face up ahead . . . a face that I knew. I realized almost immediately that it *wasn't* Raymond, and even as I started moving to one side to get a better look, I already knew who I was going to see.

It was Pauly.

He was sitting on a bench over to my left, just a few feet away. The bench was set back in a little gap between the burger stand and a row of litter-filled oil drums, and Pauly was just sitting there, all on his own, staring straight ahead.

I don't know what made me do it, but instead of just going up to him, I found myself edging around the back of the burger stand and watching him from the shadows. Physically, he didn't look anything *like* Raymond, and despite my guilt-fueled desperation to see Raymond's face, it was hard to believe that I'd mistaken Pauly for him, even if it had been only for a moment. But as I stood there watching Pauly now, I began to see things in him that I hadn't really seen before — a lostness, a loneliness, a darkness — and I realized that maybe he wasn't that different from Raymond after all.

He hadn't moved since I'd been watching him — he was still just sitting there, slightly hunched over, and he was still just staring straight ahead, peering intently through the passing crowds at something on the other side of the walkway. I leaned to one side and followed his gaze, trying to see what he was looking at. It was hard to focus on anything at first — the streams of people kept getting in the way — but after I'd been staring for a while, my eyes got used to looking through the spaces in the crowds, and I began to see things quite clearly.

Between the far end of the Portaloos on the right, and three parked fairground trucks on the left, there was a ragged square of shadowed ground. Another truck blocked the back of the square, and behind it I could just make out the railings of the park and the dimly lit street beyond. Generators were chugging away at the back of the trucks, their thick black cables snaking out in all directions, and the trampled ground was littered with empty beer cans and burger boxes. The square was relatively dark — the high-sided trucks shading it from the lights of the nearest rides — but there was still enough residual light to make out the faces of the figures hanging around in the shadows. Most of them were just faces, the kinds of faces you'd expect to see in a nowhere place—hard and empty, hooded, drunk. They weren't doing much, just the usual slouching around, watching and waiting, hoping for something to happen. Just off to one side, though, standing with their backs to one of the trucks, there were two figures I *didn't* expect to see.

Eric Leigh and Wes Campbell.

That's who Pauly was watching—Eric Leigh and Wes Campbell.

I looked back at Pauly for a moment, wondering what the hell was going on, then I turned my attention back to Eric and Campbell. Although they looked quite comfortable with each other—standing side by side, talking quietly, their shoulders occasionally touching, their heads occasionally nodding—they both seemed kind of anxious about something. Their eyes kept flicking around, especially Eric's, and it was pretty obvious he'd rather be somewhere else. As I carried on watching them, I realized that their attention was fixed on something, or someone, in the darkness at the back of the Portaloos, and I thought for a moment that it might be Raymond. Maybe he was hurt or something . . . maybe he'd come out of the Portaloos and something had happened to him, he'd got beaten up or something, and now he was lying in the darkness at the back of the Portaloos . . . ?

But I quickly dismissed that idea. Even though Eric had never really cared too much about Raymond, I was still pretty sure that he wouldn't just stand there doing nothing if he knew that Raymond was hurt.

No, I told myself, *even Eric wouldn't do that.*

I still carried on looking, though, scanning the area around the Portaloos, just in case something *had* happened, but there was no sign of anything untoward, no evidence of anyone getting beaten up . . . and definitely no Raymond. I saw some of the people I'd seen with Stella earlier on—a few of her hangers-on, the guy with the camera, one of her security men—and I watched them for a while, but they didn't seem to be doing anything. They were just hanging around, trying to look cool—which wasn't that easy in front of a row of Portaloos. I couldn't see Stella anywhere, so I guessed she wasn't with them anymore . . . and even if she had been, I was pretty sure that Raymond wouldn't have hooked up with her again.

Or maybe he would . . . ?

Christ, I didn't know *what* to think.

I shook my head—sick of myself for not knowing what I was doing—then I went over and sat down beside Pauly.

It took him a second to realize who I was, and as soon as he did, his face suddenly changed. The sadness disappeared, the loneliness left him, and he was back to his old grinning self.

"Hey, Pete . . . you all right?"

His eyes seemed blurred for a moment, and I wondered briefly if they were trying to catch up with the rest of his face, trying to fit in with the mask . . .

"What's the matter?" he said, rubbing his eyes and frowning at me. "What are you looking at?"

"Nothing . . ." I looked away from him, shaking my head again, forcing myself to concentrate. "Listen, Pauly," I said. "Have you seen Raymond?"

"Yeah," he grinned, "he's a funny-looking kid with a big head—"

"Have you *seen* him?" I repeated.

"Why? Have you lost him?"

I stared hard at Pauly, trying to show him that I knew what he was beneath his mask, that he didn't *have* to keep being Pauly all the time. I don't know if it made any difference, but at least he stopped grinning.

"The last time I saw Raymond," he sighed, "he was with Stella Ross." He smiled faintly. "She was parading him around like he was her pet monkey or something."

"You haven't seen him since?"

"No."

"You sure?"

"Yeah, I'm *sure* . . ."

He took a bottle of Vodka Reef from his pocket. It was already opened, but the cap had been jammed back on again. As he flicked off the cap and took a quick drink, I saw him glance over at Eric and Campbell. He tried to make out that he was just looking around, not looking at anything in particular, but he didn't do a very good job of it.

"Are they still there?" I asked him.

"Who?"

"Eric and Campbell."

He looked at me, and for a fraction of a second I could see the confusion in his eyes as he tried to decide how to react. He knew that I'd seen them now, but he didn't know if I'd seen him watching them or not. "Yeah . . ." he said hesitantly, nodding his head and trying to grin. "Yeah . . . I thought it was them." He glanced casually at the square again, pretending to be mildly interested. "Yeah . . . yeah, they're still there." He offered me the Vodka Reef. "You want some?"

The night was still warm and sticky, and after all the throwing up and everything else I'd just done, I was feeling pretty thirsty and dry. My throat felt horrible, too — sour and stale with the taste of puke.

"Have you got any water?" I asked Pauly.

He laughed.

I nodded at the bottle in his hand. "What's in it?"

He glanced at the label. "I don't know . . . vodka, orange, something else. You want it or not?"

I took the bottle from his hand and drank deeply. It was slightly fizzy, slightly orangey, but mostly just vodka-ey. It didn't make me feel any better.

"What are they doing over there?" I asked Pauly.

"Who?"

"Eric and Campbell."

He shrugged. "I don't know."

"Are they friends or something?"

He shrugged again.

I looked at him. "I thought you were *in* with Campbell?"

"So?"

"So how come you don't know what he's doing with Eric?"

"Why should I?"

"They're both friends of yours, aren't they? I mean, you know Eric, you know Campbell—"

"I know lots of people. Just because I know them doesn't mean I know what they're doing all the time." He grinned at me. "Do you know what everyone *you* know is doing all the time?"

"That's different—"

"Do you know what Nic's doing right now? And what about Raymond? Shit, you don't even know where your Bunny Boy *is*, do you?" He laughed. "I thought you were really *concerned* about him, anyway."

I glared at Pauly, wanting to smash the bottle into his face, wanting to wipe that idiotic grin off his face . . . but I knew he was right. I'd forgotten what I was supposed to be doing. I shook my head in self-disgust. What the hell was the *matter* with me? Why couldn't I do anything right? Why couldn't I do *anything*?

Even as I was trying to think about it, and I saw Pauly suddenly get up from the bench and start hurrying across the walkway, I still couldn't seem to do anything. All I could do was sit there and watch him as he threaded his way through the crowds, heading for the spot where Eric and Campbell had been . . .

But they weren't there anymore.

And when I looked back to see where Pauly was, I couldn't see him anywhere, either. He'd gone, disappeared, melted away into the crowds . . .

Just like everyone else.

♥ ♠ ♦ ♣

I felt so bad then, so dumb and dazed and overloaded . . . everything I felt was too much. I was too heavy to stand up. Too tired to do anything. The bottle of Vodka Reef in my hand was too cold and too glassy, and it looked too orangey not to drink. I knew I shouldn't drink it, that it wouldn't do me any good, but I didn't seem to have any choice. The bottle just lifted itself to my mouth, tipped itself up, and the next thing I knew it was empty.

I carefully put it down.

Burped sweetly.

And closed my eyes.

NINE

Do you know what it's like when your head keeps roaring and whirling and spinning, around and around and around, and you feel so sick that you think your body's going to turn itself inside out, and it hurts so much that you wish you'd never been born?

Do you know what that's like?

It's like the end of the world, only worse.

The end of the world that never ends.

It's shitness, sickness, guilt, regret . . . an inner pain that kills you forever, a pain that's always been there, and will always be there, whether you're dead or alive or anything in between.

That's what it's like.

And that's pretty much what it was like for me for the rest of that night.

I didn't know if it was just the drink that was screwing me up — the tequila, the vodka, whatever else I'd had — or if it was something else. The weirdness of the night, the heat, the noise, the lights . . . or maybe it was just me. Maybe I was losing it, cracking up, going mad. I really didn't know.

But whatever it was, it didn't really matter, because there wasn't anything I could do about it anyway. All I could do was keep going.

So that's what I did.

After I'd finally managed to heave myself up off the bench and get moving, I just kept going — walking, stumbling, searching all over the fairground, trying to find Raymond. I didn't have much sense of the time, and although I kept looking at the clock on my mobile, I also kept forgetting what it said, so I don't really know how much time I spent wandering around the fair. It felt like a couple of hours or so, but I'm really only guessing.

It was all too vague.

I was trying to be rational in the way that I searched, trying to follow some kind of plan, but the layout of the fairground didn't seem to have any plan. Everything was just all over the place. There was nothing to guide me, no sense of direction, and no matter how hard I tried to follow a route, I just couldn't do it. All I could do was keep going, keep wandering, keep looking, and keep hoping.

I looked everywhere.

Every walkway, every ride, every stall. The gaps between the rides. Around the backs of the rides. The bumper cars, the tilt-a-whirl, behind the Portaloos. The burger stands, the twisters, the roller coaster . . .

Nothing.

The fortune-teller's tent was all closed up. The deserted spot near the children's rides was still deserted . . .

Nothing.

No Raymond.

No sign of him anywhere.

I didn't come across Pauly, either. No Pauly, no Eric, no Campbell, no Stella. The only familiar face I saw was a very quick — and very dazed — glimpse of Nicole.

I was heading down a walkway at the far edge of the fair, in between the roller coaster and the place where all the fairground vehicles were parked, when I saw Nicole and the carny guy coming toward me. He had his arm around her shoulder, and they both looked pretty unsteady, staggering and weaving all over the place as they walked. The carny guy seemed happy enough in his drunkenness, all loopy smiles and rolling eyes, but it was hard to tell how Nic was feeling. Even if I hadn't been so out of it myself, I still don't think I would have known what to make of her. She was smiling, but her eyes were dead. She was holding on tight to the carny guy, but at the same time she looked as if she couldn't bear touching him. And as they both approached me, she looked right into my eyes, but she didn't seem to recognize me.

"Hey, Nic," I said, stepping in front of her. "Have you seen Raymond anywhere? I've been looking all over the place . . . Nic? Nicole?"

She didn't answer me. I don't think she even heard me. And before I had a chance to say anything else, the two of them had veered off the walkway and were stumbling off into the darkness toward the fairground vehicles.

I didn't carry on looking for much longer after that. It was getting pretty late by then. The crowds were beginning to thin out, some of the rides were closing, and I'd just about had enough. I must have walked around that fairground at least a dozen times, and I couldn't see any point in walking around it anymore. I'd already looked everywhere. There wasn't anywhere else to look. What more could I do?

And, besides, I was starting to feel sick again. And my head was throbbing. And my feet hurt. And I was still feeling so weird . . . hearing weird noises, imagining weird sensations inside my body, seeing weird things. I just didn't know what was real anymore.

And I still don't know, even now.

All I know — or *think* I know — is that I was sitting on a pile of wooden boards near the exit, trying to decide what to do next, and the last few fairground stragglers were wandering past me, heading back home, and I was beginning to think that maybe I should join them. Just forget about everything. Forget about Raymond, call it a night, and go home.

Get some sleep.

Get up in the morning.

Get back to normality.

I was trying to imagine it: Sunday morning, the church bells ringing, the sun shining brightly as I made my way down the street toward Raymond's. Along the alleyway, turn left, down to Raymond's back gate, feeling for his presence . . .

And that's when I felt it.

His presence.

Right here, right now. And when I raised my head and looked across the fairground, I saw him.

He was on a merry-go-round — an old-fashioned, brightly colored merry-go-round. It was about fifty feet away from me, just to the right of the fairground entrance, and I couldn't understand why I hadn't seen it before. I'd been everywhere, I'd searched every inch of the fairground, I'd seen everything there was to see — every ride, every stall . . . absolutely everything. So why hadn't I seen this merry-go-round? I mean, how could I have missed it? It was right there, right in front of me — a beautifully painted carousel, like something from a dream. A rainbow circle of wooden horses — white horses, silver horses, bright red horses, spotted horses — with golden saddles and sparkling blue eyes and luscious flowing manes . . .

And Raymond.

He was right there, too. Sitting astride a jet-black horse, holding on tightly to the scrolled silver pole, smiling at me as the merry-go-round slowly revolved . . .

I knew it couldn't be real.

A fairground organ was playing, pipes and drums swirling in the air, and I could hear the sound of children's laughter — excited voices, faint cries of delight . . . but there weren't any children around. There was hardly anyone around at all. The only other person I could see was a slightly odd-looking man with a mustache, standing in the shadows, watching the merry-go-round. He looked like an overconcerned father, keeping an eye out for his child . . . but there weren't any children on the merry-go-round. There was no one on the merry-go-round.

Only Raymond.

I watched him as he came around again. He was still smiling at me, still gripping the curlicued pole, but this time his jet-black horse was a rabbit. A horse-size rabbit. It was a beautiful thing — glossy and smooth, with shining black eyes, a necklace of flowers, a painted face that seemed to be frowning . . .

I smiled to myself.

The carousel kept turning, taking Raymond away, and as I waited for him to come around again, I wondered what would happen if I went over and joined him. There was plenty of room for me, plenty of horses or rabbits to ride . . . we could sit there together, like two lost cowboys riding in circles, both of us going nowhere, and I could ask Raymond how he was feeling and where he'd been and what he'd been doing . . .

But after a while I realized it was too late. He wasn't there anymore. The merry-go-round was still turning, but the horse-size rabbit was just a horse again, and its golden saddle was empty.

Raymond had gone.

And so had the man with the mustache.

I wasn't really aware of much after that. I suppose I must have known what I was doing, and where I was going, and I remember thinking to myself at the time how wonderfully clear everything was . . . and it *was*. Everything in and around me was clearer than it had ever been before: my thoughts, my senses, my feelings, the world. But it was the kind of clarity that only works in isolation — like the concentrated beam of a spotlight, lighting up one thing at a time — and every time the spotlight moved on, focusing brightly on something else, I'd forget what had been left behind in the darkness.

It was like existing in a series of perfectly lucid moments, none of which were connected. It was just one thing, then another thing. One thought, another thought. One step, another step . . .

One step at a time.

That's all I was doing as I left the fairground and headed back across the park — taking one step at a time. One step, another step . . . along the pathway, away from the lights, into the darkness . . . one step, another step . . . one step, another step . . . all the way down to the park gates. They were still open, and I wondered briefly — and pointlessly — if they'd stay open all night, or if someone was supposed to shut them . . . and if so, who? A fairground worker? Someone from the town council? A policeman?

I paused outside the gates and looked around, trying to decide which way to go. The little street that led up to Back Lane was on my right, and the street on my left would lead me around to Park Road, then along the other side of the old factory, and eventually back to the north end of St. Leonard's Road.

I checked the time on my mobile.

I don't know why I bothered — whatever time it was, it didn't matter. And by the time I'd put the phone back in my pocket, I'd already forgotten what time it was, anyway.

As I looked over to my right again, I thought I saw someone turning off the little street into Back Lane. It was only a very brief glimpse, and the street was pretty dark, and I was finding it really hard to focus on anything more than a few feet away . . . but just for a moment I was convinced that it was the odd-looking man with the mustache. I didn't actually see his face, so I couldn't tell if he had a mustache or not, but there was just something about him — a feeling, a sense . . . his slightly hunched posture, the way that he moved . . .

He *moved* like an odd-looking man with a mustache.

I didn't know why the sight of him bothered me, and I knew I was probably just seeing things, anyway. In fact, a few moments after he'd gone, I was already pretty sure that he'd never been there in the first place. But even so, I could still feel my heart beating hard as I turned left and started heading away from Back Lane, and I didn't stop looking over my shoulder every ten seconds or so until I'd reached the street-lit security of Park Road.

Eric and Nic's place is about two-thirds of the way along Park Road, about a hundred feet or so past the main entrance to the old factory. It's a big old detached house, set back from the street, with a small front garden, a graveled driveway, and posters all over the windows. Mr. and Mrs. Leigh are the kind of people who like to put posters in their windows: local theater productions, protest meetings, Green Party politics . . . that kind of thing.

I didn't know if I'd been meaning to go to Eric and Nic's place or not, and even as I opened the front gate and started walking up the path, I still didn't know what I was doing there. I was so tired and wrecked by now that my brain seemed to have shrunk. It was still there, still thinking, but it felt so small . . . so far away. It was as if my skull had thickened, so most of my head was solid bone, and all that was left of my thinking mind was a tiny little cavity deep down inside.

What are you doing here? it said.

What?

What are you doing here?

I don't know.

There's not going to be any farewell party . . .

I know.

Nicole won't be here, she'll be off somewhere with her carny guy.

I don't want to see Nicole.

So what are you doing here?

I don't know.

Are you looking for Eric?

No.

Pauly?

God, no . . .

Raymond?

Yeah, that's it. Raymond. I'm looking for Raymond. That's what I'm doing here—I'm looking for Raymond.

And why would Raymond be here?

I don't know.

Did you tell him you were coming around here after the fair?

I can't remember . . .

Christ, it's hot . . .

I was at the front door now, swaying slightly, trying to remember if I'd told Raymond anything about coming around here after the fair . . . but it was too hard to think anymore. My head was too thick.

I leaned back and gazed up at the house. The lights were all out, the curtains drawn. Everything felt still and empty. I knew there was no one home, but I reached up and rang the bell, anyway.

It sounded the same as it had always sounded — a distant *ding dong* — and just for a moment I remembered all the times I'd stood here before, ringing this bell, calling on Nic, calling on Eric, awkwardly saying hello when one of their parents answered the door. Mr. Leigh, with his craggy face and his shoulder-length hair and his slightly unsettling blue eyes. And Mrs. Leigh, always embarrassing me with her low-cut dresses and her black-haired beauty and her dark and sexy French accent . . .

But there was no one home now.

No one was in.

The house was empty . . .

What are you doing here?

I couldn't remember . . . it was something about . . . I was trying to remember something, but I couldn't remember what it was. Something about Raymond . . . something about . . .

What was it?

I was too tired to remember.

I sat down on the front step.

The air was hot.

The night sky rumbled faintly in the distance.

I was so tired . . .

I put my head in my hands and closed my eyes.

woke up to the sound of the world exploding, and for a nightmarish moment I thought I'd died and gone to hell. My head was throbbing, my eyes were burning, the air all around me was booming and rumbling . . . and then something flashed in the distance, and another huge crash of thunder ripped through the sky, and as the rain started falling, pouring down like a tropical storm, everything suddenly came back to me.

Eric and Nic's place . . .

I was at Eric and Nic's place. I was sitting on the front step, getting soaked to the skin, and it seemed to be daylight. I was cold, confused, my backside ached . . .

I must have been sitting here for hours.

I must have fallen asleep . . .

Lightning flashed again, thunder boomed, and suddenly the rain was really lashing down. I stretched the stiffness from my legs and painfully got to my feet. My clothes were already soaked through, so there wasn't much point in getting out of the rain, but I edged back into the doorway, anyway. I was shivering, feeling sick. My hand shook as I reached into my pocket, took out my mobile, and checked the time.

It was 6:02 a.m.

I put the phone back in my pocket, took one last look at the still-empty house, then I turned around and started walking.

There was no one around as I headed back home along Park Road. The thunderstorm was fading into the distance now, but the rain was still pouring down, and no one in their right mind was going to be out and about at this time in the morning. The streets had that tired-out Sunday morning feel to them — the morning after the Saturday night before — and I don't mind admitting that I took some kind of pitiful pleasure from the gloom and the emptiness all around me. I *wanted* everything to be miserable. I'd been through a night of madness. I'd lost Raymond. Messed it all up with Nicole. I was cold, I was wet, my head was still throbbing . . .

I *wanted* to feel sorry for myself.

So I did.

I walked through that cold summer rain, sulking and shivering and hurting, and I let myself wallow in whatever misery I could find. I knew it was stupid and selfish and childish, but I didn't really care anymore. I wanted to wallow. I wanted to be selfish and childish. I wanted to be the guy in the movie who's down on his luck and all alone in the rain, and if I could have had some miserable music playing in the background, and a million people watching me on TV, I probably would have wanted that, too.

But you can't have everything, can you?

So I just carried on moping in my unseen silence — along Park Road, down St. Leonard's Road, left into Hythe Street, up to the lane that leads down to the river . . .

The gate to the lane was open, its padlocked chain smashed off. There were fresh tire tracks leading down to the river, and I could smell the stink of burning rubber in the air. It wasn't anything to worry about, just another stolen car. Almost every weekend there's at least one or two left burning by the river. They usually smolder there for a few days or so before the police eventually tow them away, and then a man from the town council comes along and fixes a new padlock and chain to the gate, but it never makes any difference. The kids who steal the cars *like* driving them down to the river, they *like* racing them around for a while before setting fire to them, and that's all there is to it.

I walked on.

It was still raining, but not so heavily now. The thunderstorm had left the sky with a washed-out daylight darkness, and as I moved down the street toward my house I could see a faint glow of light in the kitchen window. Dad's car was parked in front of the house, so I guessed he'd just got back from work and was making himself a cup of tea before he went to bed.

I wondered how wrecked I looked. Dad could always tell . . . he just had to look at my eyes and he'd know what I'd been up to. Mind you, he was usually pretty good about that kind of thing. I mean, he never really made a big deal about anything, but he wasn't a pushover, either. If he ever thought I'd gone too far, he wouldn't just leave it. He'd want to talk to me, man to man, tell me a few home truths . . .

And I couldn't face that right now.

I didn't want to be a man.

I didn't want to know any home truths.

So I crossed the street — like *that* made me invisible — and carried on down to Raymond's place.

His house was dark, as miserable and dingy as ever, and as I followed the alleyway around to his back gate, I could feel a cold shiver creeping inside me. Something felt wrong. There was something missing, an emptiness . . . a lack of something. I paused for a moment and looked around. Wet trash bags were slumped all over the place, their sodden guts strewn across the path — wads of stained tissue paper, chicken bones, bits of grayed meat — and as I breathed in deeply, trying to steady myself, my stomach lurched at the fetid smell of rotten waste. I closed my eyes for a second, concentrating on keeping the sickness down, and in that momentary darkness I suddenly knew what the emptiness was. It was Raymond . . . his presence. It wasn't there. There was nothing there. No feeling of Raymond at all. I couldn't feel his presence *or* his absence . . .

All I could feel was a sudden sickening fear.

I didn't want to open my eyes then.

I didn't want to see anything . . .

But I knew that I had to.

I opened my eyes and looked down.

I saw the ground at my feet, the cracked concrete path . . . that small gray world of stones and grit, asphalt repairs, insects and dust. I saw a trail of shallow brown puddles and rainy scuff marks leading up to Raymond's gate. And at the foot of the gate, where the ground was dry, I saw blood.

There wasn't very much of it, just a few scattered spots . . .

But blood is blood.

Its redness screams like nothing else.

And it was there . . .

Screaming its violence at me.

Christ, it was *blood*.

It made me feel cold and small, like a child in an unknown place, and as I slowly looked up at the gate, something inside me switched off. I didn't know what I was doing anymore. I was just doing it. And when I saw what was hanging on the gate, impaled on a rusty nail, I simply didn't believe it at first. I *couldn't* believe it. It had to be something else — a discarded glove or something . . . an old black T-shirt, scrunched up into a ball . . . or maybe the remains of a child's soft toy.

But it wasn't a toy.

Soft toys don't bleed.

They don't have flies buzzing around their eyes.

No . . .

I closed my eyes, hoping it would go away . . . but when I opened them again, Black Rabbit's severed head was still there, still skewered to the gate, still dripping red in the rain.

ELEVEN

Everything drained out of me as I stood there looking at that gruesome vision on the gate. I just couldn't take it in. It was too out of place, too wrong. Too sick to understand. It was Raymond's rabbit, his immortal Black Rabbit, but it wasn't a rabbit anymore. It wasn't even a rabbit's head. It was just a thing, a small black brutalized thing. Teeth, fur, bone, blood . . . rain and flies . . . a dead skull hanging on a rusty nail.

Oh God . . .

I looked down at the ground, breathing steadily, trying not to be sick. I was drenched in sweat now. My legs were shaking. And I could feel a hollow sickness rising in my belly.

Oh God . . .

I doubled over, clutching my stomach, and threw up.

My body felt a bit better after I'd been sick, but my mind was still numbed with shock. And I suppose that's why I didn't just turn around and go straight home. It would have been the sensible thing to do. Go home, get Dad, let him deal with the rest of it . . . whatever that might be.

But I wasn't sensible.

I was *in*sensible.

I was just doing whatever I was doing, without even thinking about it.

There really wasn't anything in my mind as I stepped up to the gate, averting my eyes, and nudged it open with my elbow. My head was empty. The garden was empty, too. I paused in the gateway for a minute . . . two minutes . . . standing perfectly still, listening hard, staring through the gloom at the rain-soaked lawn, the muddy borders, the dripping bushes. There was no one there. Nothing that shouldn't have been there. I took a deep breath, stepped through the gateway, and looked over at the garden shed. The door was open, and a few bits and pieces were scattered outside the doorway—an old shovel, some blue plastic sacks, a roll of wire-netting. My backpack was there, too. But I didn't wonder about that for long. Instead, my eyes were drawn to the rabbit hutch beside the shed . . . or, at least, what was left of it. It was smashed to pieces. Someone had ripped it apart and stomped it into the ground.

Just to one side of the ruined hutch lay the headless remains of Black Rabbit. His pitiful body was lying in a puddle—his neck gaping open, ripped and red . . . his sodden black fur darkened with blood.

One of his back legs had been hacked off.

I completely lost it then. Everything boiled up inside me—the shock of it all, the sickness, the fear—and I just started running. Down the garden, away from the horror, down to the back of Raymond's house.

"Raymond!" I called out, hammering on the back door. *"Raymond!"*

I probably sounded like a madman or something, but I didn't care. I just kept thumping on the door, screaming at the top of my voice . . .

"Raymond! Are you there? It's me, Pete . . . Raymond? *Raymond! RAYMOND!!"*

. . . until, eventually, I heard the clatter of an upstairs window opening, and a guttural voice called down from above.

"What the *fuck's* going on?"

I stepped back from the door and looked up to see Raymond's dad leaning out the window, glaring angrily at me. I'd obviously just woken him up — he was bare-chested, his eyes all bloodshot and sleepy — and he looked like he wanted to kill me.

"It's me, Mr. Daggett," I called up to him, "Pete Boland."

He squinted at me. "Whuh . . . ?"

"I need to see Raymond," I told him. "It's really important —"

"Raymond . . . ?"

"Yeah — is he there?"

"Christ's sake, boy . . . d'you know what *time* it is?"

"Yeah, I know, I'm sorry —"

"Go on," he groaned, waving his hand at me. "Piss off."

"No, you don't understand —"

"I'm not telling you again."

"He's missing."

Mr. Daggett hesitated for a moment, rubbing his eyes. "Who's missing?"

"Raymond . . ."

"What d'you mean — *missing*?"

"I don't know where he is," I said. "I mean, he's probably not actually *missing* . . . but we were at the fair together, and we got split up . . . and I think something might have happened . . ." I was getting all flustered now, trying to work out how to explain everything. "His rabbit," I spluttered, pointing up the garden, "someone's killed Raymond's rabbit . . ."

I heard Mrs. Daggett's voice then, a faint and irritated whine. "What is it, Bob? Who're you talking to?"

"It's nothing," Mr. Daggett told her. "Go back to sleep."

"I can't sleep with all that noise, can I?" she snapped. "What's going *on*, for God's sake?"

"It's just some kid," Mr. Daggett sighed, "wants to know where Raymond is."

"What kid?"

"The one from up the road, you know . . . the copper's kid."

"What's he want?"

"I just *told* you . . . he's looking for Raymond."

"He's not here."

Mr. Daggett looked over his shoulder at her. "You sure?"

"Yeah, he's not been in all night . . . probably out in the garden again. Come on, Bob, shut the window. I'm trying to get some sleep here."

Mr. Daggett turned back and looked down at me. "He's not here."

"He's *not* in the garden," I told him. "Someone's been up there, someone's smashed up the rabbit hutch and . . . no, *hold on.*" Mr. Daggett was starting to close the window. "*Wait* a minute," I yelled at him. "What are you *doing*? You can't just . . . hey, *listen to me!*"

The window slammed shut.

"Mr. *Daggett!*" I shouted.

The curtains closed.

"Shit."

I stood there for a few moments, staring angrily up at the window, wanting to scream and shout and *make* Mr. Daggett listen to me . . . but I knew it was a waste of time. He didn't give a shit—about Raymond, about Black Rabbit, about anything—and that was that. There was no point getting angry about it, was there?

I turned around and started running again—back up the garden, past the carnage, through the gate, down the alley . . .

The rain was getting heavier again now, but I barely even noticed it. I was running on fear and anger. Up the street, through the front gate, around the back of the house, slamming open the kitchen door and breathlessly barging in . . .

"Pete?" said Dad. "What is it? What's the matter?"

He was sitting at the kitchen table, a big mug of tea in his hand. He was shocked to see me, and I could see the sudden alarm in his eyes, but there wasn't any panic in his voice. Just a calm and controlled concern.

"It's Raymond . . ." I gasped, trying to get my breath back, "I think something's happened to him . . . and his rabbit's—"

"All right," said Dad, getting to his feet. "All right, just calm down a minute, take your time . . ." He came over and put his arm around my shoulder and guided me over to the table. "Sit down," he said quietly, "take some deep breaths."

I sat down, breathing slowly, trying to calm myself.

"Are you all right?" Dad said. "I mean, you're not hurt, are you?"

I shook my head.

He sat down next to me. "Do you want some water?"

"No . . . no, I'm OK, thanks."

"Sure?"

"Yeah . . . I'm fine."

Dad put his hand on my arm. "OK, tell me what happened."

I didn't tell him everything, obviously. There wasn't enough time, for one thing, and I honestly thought that most of what happened wasn't really relevant, anyway. But there was also a lot of stuff that I just *couldn't* tell him about—the drinking and the smoking, all the weird stuff that happened, the thing with Nicole in the den . . .

I mean, he was my dad.

You can't tell your dad everything, can you?

But I told him as much as I could: how Raymond had gone missing at the fair, how I'd looked for him everywhere, how I'd gone to his house and found his mutilated rabbit . . .

"What time was this?" Dad asked me.

"Just now, about ten minutes ago . . ." I looked at the clock on the kitchen wall. It was nearly quarter to seven now. "It must have been around six-thirty."

Dad nodded. "So, you saw this rabbit's head on the gate . . . what did you do then?"

I told him about the smashed-up rabbit hutch and the remains of Black Rabbit, and how I'd woken up Mr. Daggett and tried to talk to him.

"And what did he have to say?" Dad asked.

"Not much . . ." I shook my head. "He didn't want to know, Dad. I tried to tell him about Raymond, but he just didn't care . . ."

"Did he check to see if Raymond was in his room?"

"No . . . but I heard Mrs. Daggett telling him that Raymond hadn't been home all night."

"Were they expecting him home?"

"I don't know . . ."

Dad looked at me. "I thought you were staying the night at Eric and Nicole's?"

"Well, yeah . . . but I don't know if Raymond was supposed to be coming with me or not. I mean, Nicole didn't actually invite him . . . and it didn't happen, anyway."

"What didn't happen?"

"The thing at Eric and Nicole's . . ."

Dad frowned. "It didn't happen?"

"No."

"Why not?"

"I don't know . . . I kind of lost touch with Eric and Nic at the fair, and then I spent hours looking for Raymond —"

"So where have you been all night?"

I rubbed my eyes. "I went to Eric and Nic's place, but there was no one there . . ."

"And?"

"I waited for them."

"All night?"

"I fell asleep on the step."

"You fell asleep?"

"Yeah, I was tired . . ."

Dad looked into my eyes. "How much did you have to drink?"

I shook my head. "I was just *tired*, Dad. It was late, I'd been walking around the fair all night . . ." I looked at him. "What do you think we should do about Raymond? I'm really worried about him."

Dad sighed. "I'm not sure there's all that much we can do at the moment."

I stared at him in disbelief. "How can you *say* that? We've *got* to do something . . . he's missing, his rabbit's been killed —"

"We don't *know* that he's missing, Pete," Dad said calmly. "He could be anywhere . . ."

"Like where?"

Dad shrugged. "With some friends —"

"He hasn't *got* any friends."

"He could be at home, for all we know."

"But he's *not* . . . his mum said he hasn't been home all night."

"I know, but we don't *know* that, do we?"

"He's *missing*, Dad. You've got to *do* something . . ."

"Just calm down a minute," Dad said, putting his hand on my shoulder. "I didn't say I'm *not* going to do anything, but I can't just report him missing because you don't know where he is—"

"Why not?"

"Listen," Dad said, "let me go and speak to his parents and see what they have to say. All right? If Raymond's not there, I'll get them to report him missing, and then we can start looking for him."

"Yeah, but what if they don't *want* to report him missing? You know what they're like, Dad . . . they don't give a shit about him. They never have. And what about his rabbit? I mean, can't you just get forensics or someone to go around there and take a look at it?"

Dad shook his head. "Come on, Pete . . . you know I can't do that."

"Why not?"

"It's a rabbit . . ."

"Yeah, I know, but someone cut its head off and hung it on the gate."

Dad started to get up. "I'll sort it out, OK? I'll go over there now. Just let me tell your mum where I'm going first . . ."

As he shuffled wearily across the kitchen toward the door, I stared at the table, trying to work out how I felt. Of course, I was glad that Dad was doing something about Raymond, and I kind of understood why he couldn't do anything more . . . I mean, I *knew* it made sense to check things out first, and I *knew* the dead rabbit was only a dead rabbit . . . and maybe I *was* just worrying too much, jumping to stupid conclusions . . . maybe I was making a big fuss about nothing.

But what if I wasn't?

What if . . . ?

Dad was in the doorway now, and as I looked over at him and started to say something, his mobile rang. He took it out of his pocket, flipped it open, and put it to his ear.

"Boland," he said.

I watched him as he listened, and I could tell by the look on his face that it was police stuff, something important.

"Yeah," he said, "yeah, I know who she is . . . when was this?"

He glanced at me then, and there was something in his eyes that I didn't understand — some kind of secrecy, or maybe suspicion.

"Can you give me half an hour, sir?" he said into the phone. "I was just about to do something . . . no, no, I understand . . . yes, of course . . . OK, I'll be there in ten minutes."

He closed the phone and sighed heavily.

"What is it?" I asked him.

He looked at me. "I have to go . . . they want me back at the station."

"But what about Raymond?" I said. "You can't just leave it—"

"I'm sorry, Pete," he said. "That was the detective chief inspector. I've got to go back in."

"Why?"

He looked slightly awkward for a moment, almost embarrassed. "Look, I'll call in on the Daggetts before I leave, and I'll try to get someone to check out the rabbit—"

"Why do you have to go, Dad?"

He sighed again. "A girl's gone missing . . . her parents called in about an hour ago." He looked at me. "It's Stella Ross."

I was too confused to say anything for a while. I just sat there, staring at nothing, trying to get things clear in my head. Stella Ross was missing . . . Raymond was missing . . .

Stella . . .

Raymond . . .

The beauty and the beast.

Disembodied voices echoed through my head:

The star's going out tonight . . .

Stella's going out . . .

You're going to wish you hadn't done this . . .

"Pete?" said Dad. "Are you all right?"

I looked at him. "Stella's missing?"

He nodded. "She was at the fair, apparently . . . but she didn't come home, and her phone's switched off. No one knows where she is—"

"No one knows where Raymond is, either."

"I know, Pete, but this is different . . ."

"Why? What's *different* about it?"

Dad just looked at me, not sure what to say.

I shook my head. "It's because she's famous, isn't it? She's a *celebrity* . . . her parents are celebrities—"

"They've reported her missing, Pete. We have to look into it."

"Yeah, right," I said coldly. "It's nothing to do with who she is, is it?"

"It's not a question of who—"

"No? So how come your DCI just called you? He's never called you about a missing person before, has he? I mean, he wouldn't bother calling you if Raymond was reported missing, would he?"

"Raymond's not news," Dad said quietly.

"So *what*?" I spat. "That shouldn't make any difference."

"I know it *shouldn't* . . . but it does."

Dad looked at me then, trying to make me understand. And I *did* understand. I knew exactly what he meant, and I knew it wasn't his fault, and I knew there was nothing he could do about it.

But that still didn't make it right.

"Look," Dad said, "I have to go now, OK?"

I looked at him. "Are you still going to talk to Raymond's parents?"

He nodded. "I'll give you a ring as soon as I've spoken to them, and I'll see what I can do about the rabbit. And don't worry too much, OK? I'm sure everything's going to be fine."

"Yeah . . ."

"Tell Mum I'll call her later on."

"OK."

He smiled at me, picked up his car keys, and turned to leave. I watched him go, still not knowing how I felt about anything. There was too much to feel, too much I didn't understand—Raymond, Stella, Raymond and Stella, Raymond and me, Stella and me . . .

"Did you see her?" Dad said.

He'd stopped in the doorway and was looking back at me.

"See who?" I asked him.

"Stella Ross. Did you see her at the fair?"

"Uh, yeah . . ." I said hesitantly. "Yeah, I saw her. I talked to her, actually."

His eyes narrowed. "You *talked* to her?"

"Yeah . . ."

Dad stared at me then, a long and thoughtful look, and for a moment or two he wasn't my dad anymore—he was just a policeman. And I'd never felt more guilty in my life.

"I want you to stay at home today," he said sternly. "Do you understand?"

"Why?"

"Just do it, all right?"

"Yeah, OK."

He nodded. "I'll speak to you later."

After Dad had gone, I just hung around in the kitchen for a while, waiting for the phone to ring. Outside, the rain had stopped falling, and the heavy black clouds were beginning to clear from the sky. It looked like it was going to be another hot day.

I felt like shit.

My head was all thick and fuzzy, my mouth was bone dry, and I kept burping up a horrible taste of sour gas. Everything inside me felt numb and distant.

I went to the toilet.

Washed my face.

Tried to scrub some of the fur off my teeth.

Then I went back into the kitchen again.

Sat down at the table.

Got up, went over to the fridge.

Drank half a carton of orange juice.

Almost threw up.

Sat down at the table again.

Waited for the phone to ring.

It was half past eight when Dad finally called. Mum was still upstairs in bed, and I snatched up the phone as soon as it rang so it wouldn't wake her up.

"Hello?"

"Pete . . . it's Dad. Listen, I'm running late, so I can't talk for long. I just wanted to let you know that I saw Mr. Daggett, and I made him check Raymond's room —"

"Was he there?"

"No, but they don't seem to think it's anything to worry about. They said that Raymond often goes off on his own —"

"No, he *doesn't*."

"Well, that's what they told me. They said it's not unusual for him to stay out all night."

"No, he just stays out in the garden sometimes, that's all. He doesn't *go* anywhere."

"I'm sorry, Pete, but there's not much more I can do just now. Give it another hour or two, OK? If he's not back by then, I'll send someone around."

"What about the rabbit? Did you see it?"

"Yeah . . ."

"What do you think?"

"I don't know . . . I mean, I know it's pretty bad, but there's a lot of sick people around, Pete. This kind of stuff happens — dead dogs, tortured cats, mutilated horses, all sorts. I'd be surprised if it's got anything to do with Raymond, but I'll see if I can get someone on to it. It might not be for a while, though."

"Yeah, but what about — ?"

"Sorry, Pete, I've really got to go now. Don't forget what I told you about staying at home, all right?"

"Yeah."

"We'll talk later."

The line went dead.

I hung up the phone, sat down at the table, and looked out the window. It was a big world out there. A world where everything was possible, and anything could happen.

I wondered if it already had.

TWELVE

I was still sitting at the kitchen table when I heard the familiar sound of Mum coming down the stairs in her slippers. I glanced up at the clock and was surprised to see that it was nearly ten o'clock. I'd been sitting there for over an hour—thinking about things, trying to fit things together, trying to make sense of it all. But it hadn't done me any good. I was just as confused as ever. In fact, if anything, I was even more confused now than I had been before. All I could see in my head were pieces of things, fragments of the night, memories of stuff that had happened—and that's all it was to me: stuff that had happened.

"Morning, Pete," Mum said brightly as she came into the kitchen. "Did you have a good time at the fair?"

I looked up and smiled wearily at her.

"God," she said, "you look *terrible*. What's the matter? Are you sick or something?" She glanced quickly around the kitchen. "And where's Dad? Isn't he back yet? I thought I heard him talking to you earlier on."

I didn't really want to start explaining everything again, but I knew I'd never get away with not telling her anything, so I settled on something in between. I told her about Stella, that Dad had been called back to work because Stella's parents had reported her missing, and I told her that I'd asked Dad to check up on Raymond because we'd got split up at the fair and I hadn't been able to find him. But I didn't let on how worried I was, and I didn't tell her about the rabbit, either.

She still had a lot of questions, of course — why was Stella Ross at the fair? did you see her? is Raymond all right now? — but I managed to fob her off with a few mumbled replies, and then I told her that I was really tired, and I wasn't feeling very well, and perhaps it'd be best if I went to bed for a while.

I'm pretty sure she knew what I was doing — I could tell by the way she looked me in the eye and slowly nodded her head — but she didn't say anything. She just gave me another knowing look, nodded again, and started to make some tea.

"Do you want me to bring you a cup?" she asked.

"No, I'm all right, thanks. I just want to get some sleep."

"Right . . . well, off you go, then."

I looked at her for a moment, feeling kind of guilty again, then I went up to my bedroom, got out my mobile, and punched in Eric and Nic's home number.

"Yeah?"

"Eric?"

"Yeah, who's that?"

"It's Pete."

"Oh, right . . . hi, Pete. How's it going?"

His voice sounded strange, a bit breathless and nervous, as if he'd just been caught doing something he shouldn't have been doing.

"Are you all right?" I asked him.

"Yeah . . . yeah, I'm fine . . ."

He didn't sound fine.

I said, "Raymond's not there, is he?"

"Raymond? No . . . why should he be here?"

"No reason . . . I'm just trying to find him, that's all. He didn't go home last night. You haven't seen him, have you?"

"No, not since the fair. He was with me and Pauly when we got there, and then he just kind of wandered off . . . I didn't see him again all night."

"You didn't see him with Stella?"

"Stella?"

"Yeah . . ."

"Stella Ross?"

"Yeah, Raymond was—"

"I didn't see Stella," Eric said defensively. "What makes you think I saw her? And what's *she* got to do with anything, anyway?"

"Nothing, I was just saying—"

"Did *you* see her?"

"Only briefly—"

"When?"

"I don't know . . . about ten-thirty or something, maybe eleven." I paused for a moment then, suddenly realizing that I probably shouldn't be talking about Stella.

I mean, if she *was* missing, if something *had* happened to her . . .

"Pete?" Eric said. "Are you still—?"

"Is Nicole there?" I asked him.

"Nicole?"

"Yeah."

"Uh, no . . . no, she's not here."

"Do you know where she is?"

"Me? No . . . I haven't seen her since I left the den last night. Isn't she with you?"

"No."

"Oh, right . . . I thought maybe you two had got together or something."

"No," I told him, "we didn't get together. I just wanted to ask her if she'd seen Raymond, that's all."

"Right . . . well, like I said, she's not back yet. I think she must have stayed out somewhere else last night. I mean, I got back about three o'clock or something, and she wasn't here then—"

"Sorry?"

"What?"

"You got back to your house about three?"

"Yeah, something like that. I was pretty out of it, to tell you the truth." He laughed, trying to sound like one of the lads, but it wasn't very convincing. In fact, nothing about him was very convincing. I didn't know why he was lying to me, but I knew that he was. He *had* to be. I was *there* at three o'clock in the morning. I was sitting on the front step of his house, for God's sake.

"Anyway, Pete," he said quickly, "I'd better go. When Nic comes back I'll get her to call you, OK?"

"Yeah . . . OK . . ."

I was still trying to understand why he was lying, and why he sounded so strange—one minute nervous, the next minute harsh and defensive. It was almost as if he was two different people.

"I'll see you later, Pete—"

"Hold on, Eric," I said, "before you go . . . have you got Pauly's number?"

"What?"

"Pauly's phone number."

"Why d'you want his number?"

He'd gone back to being the harsh Eric again.

I said, "I just want to ring him and ask him about Raymond."

"Pauly won't know anything."

"How do *you* know?"

"Well . . . he would have said, wouldn't he? I mean, if he'd seen Raymond . . ." Eric's voice trailed off, and I got the feeling that he was struggling to find the right words. "I haven't got it, anyway," he said bluntly. "I mean, why would *I* have Pauly's number?"

"What about Nic?" I said. "She must have called Pauly to tell him about Saturday night—"

"Look, I've got to go, OK?"

"Yeah, but—"

"I've got to *go*."

"All right . . . but if you see Raymond—"

"I'll let you know."

He hung up.

I stared at the phone in my hand for a moment, trying to picture Eric's face — trying to work out why he'd lied to me, why he'd sounded so strange — but I couldn't see anything. No face, no clues, no answers. Mind you, I've always found it quite hard to picture Eric, so it probably didn't mean all that much. I mean, I'm not saying that Eric's *forgettable* or anything, because he's not. In fact, to most people, Eric's completely *un*forgettable. Proud, principled, confident, mature . . . you know, one of those people who *believe* in themselves. He's always been like that, even when he was a kid. He always seemed slightly older than the rest of us, slightly bigger . . . a bit more grown-up. The kind of kid who *doesn't* think farting is the funniest thing in the world. The kind of kid who *isn't* confused all the time. The kind of kid who can grow a mustache at fourteen years old.

That's what Eric was like.

And I've always found it quite hard to picture people like that.

I've always found it quite hard to like them, too, and as I closed the phone and went over to the bedroom window, I found myself wondering if there'd ever been anything about Eric that I *had* actually liked. I was pretty sure there had to be something . . . I mean, there has to be *something* to a friendship, doesn't there? But the only thing I could think of just then — the only thing about Eric that had ever appealed to me — was Nicole.

♥ ♠ ♦ ♣

I stood at the window for a while then, trying not to think about anything, just gazing out at the street, the houses, the parked cars, the sky. It was all so familiar that it didn't look like anything. Raymond's house looked the same as it always did, too — dark and dull in the morning sunlight, the curtains closed, the front yard littered with rubbish . . .

I knew I had to go back there.

I didn't *want* to.

All I wanted to do was lie down on my bed and go to sleep. Just lie down and close my eyes, forget about thinking, forget about Raymond and Stella and Eric and Nicole . . . just go to sleep and forget about everything.

Something made me look over at my black porcelain rabbit then, and just for a moment I thought I could hear a fairground organ playing, and somewhere in the distance, the sound of children's laughter . . .

Every second of every day, we choose which way to go . . .

A whispered voice.

Bring me home.

I blinked my eyes, and suddenly everything was quiet again. No voices, no music, no children's laughter. There was just me, standing at my bedroom window, knowing what I had to do.

As I started to change into some clean clothes, I remembered what Dad had said to me — *I want you to stay at home today.*

Do you understand? — and I tried to convince myself that I hadn't actually told him that I *would* stay at home. I knew that I had, of course, but if you really want to make yourself believe something, it's not all that hard.

You just have to believe it.

By the time I'd gotten changed and gone downstairs, I was pretty sure that Dad hadn't even said anything about staying at home in the first place.

"Mum!" I called out from the hallway. "I'm just going out for a while, OK?"

"Where are you going?" she called back from the kitchen.

"Just out," I told her. "I won't be long."

"Hold on, Pete—" she started to say.

But I was already closing the door.

I called around to Raymond's again first, only this time I went to the front door. I kind of guessed that his mum and dad wouldn't be very pleased to see me, so I wasn't too surprised when Mrs. Daggett opened the door and immediately started glaring at me. It wasn't a very attractive sight. Her hair was all lank and greasy, her eyes were pale and slightly glazed, and she was carelessly dressed in a shabby old bathrobe.

"What do you want now?" she said, lighting a cigarette.

"Is he back yet?"

She put her hand on her hip and stared at me. "Christ . . . how many more times d'you have to be told? We've already had your old man around here, poking his snout in—"

"I just want to know if Raymond's back, that's all."

"No, he's not back."

"Aren't you worried?"

"Not particularly." She took a drag on her cigarette. "What's it got to do with you, anyway?"

"Have you seen what someone's done to his rabbit?"

She grinned. "He probably did that himself."

I stared at her, shaking my head. "What if something's happened to him? Have you thought about that? I mean, what if someone's got Raymond—?"

"No one's *got* Raymond, for Christ's sake," she snapped. "He's probably just wandering around on his own somewhere, talking to the fucking sky or something . . ." She took another puff on her cigarette, and as she hungrily sucked in the smoke and quickly breathed it out again, I got the feeling that maybe she wasn't as unconcerned as she wanted me to think.

I watched her as she leaned out of the doorway and flicked some ash from her cigarette. The sunlight dulled her eyes. She blinked, sniffed. Leaned back in again.

She looked at me, jerking her chin. "What?"

"Nothing . . ."

She shook her head. "Why would anyone want to do anything to Raymond, anyway?"

"I don't know . . . why would anyone want to cut off a rabbit's head? It doesn't matter *why*, does it?"

She sniffed again. "Yeah, well . . . Raymond's not stupid. He can look after himself . . ." She looked at me, her eyes frighteningly intense. "There's nothing *wrong* with him, you know."

"I know."

"He'll be all right."

There didn't seem to be anything else to say after that. We both just stood there for a second or two, waiting out the silence, then Mrs. Daggett slowly moved back into the dimness of the hallway, her paleness fading into the gloom, and without another word she quietly closed the front door.

I went down to the river then. It had always been one of Raymond's favorite places, and I knew he still spent a lot of time down there — just walking around, or sitting on the bank — and if, for whatever reason, he was simply hiding away somewhere, he couldn't have picked a much better place. There were all kinds of sanctuaries down there — bits of woodland, old bridges, hidden pathways and tracks . . .

It was a good place to go to hide away from the world.

There was still a faint stink of burning rubber in the air, and as I turned the corner at the end of the path and headed down toward the river, I could see the wreck of the burned-out car smoldering away on a patch of wasteground over to my right. It looked like a Ford Focus, but it was hard to tell. There wasn't much left of it. The tires had burned off, the windows were smashed, and the chassis was just a scorched gray shell.

I didn't pay much attention to it.

It was just another burned-out car.

Across from the wasteground, parked between the riverside path and a steep wooded bank, was a small white trailer. I guessed it belonged to the dreadlocked guy I'd seen climbing over the gate on Saturday night. *I've seen him a couple of times by the river,* I remembered Raymond telling me. *He's got a trailer down there.*

And I wondered . . .

How well do you know him, Raymond?

Well enough to pay him a visit?

Well enough to trust him?

It wasn't a particularly clean trailer, but it wasn't disgusting or anything. It was just a bit grubby — mud-spattered, rained-on, dirty white. The towing hitch at the front was propped up on bricks, and there was a cylinder of propane gas standing in the muddy ground beside the door.

I slowed down as I walked past the trailer, trying to see inside, but the windows were blanked out with sheets of cardboard taped inside. I wondered why . . . why block out your windows? And I wondered why I was so scared of knocking on the door.

Just do it, I told myself. *What's the matter with you? Just knock on the door, for Christ's sake.*

I knocked on the trailer door.

Nothing happened.

I knocked again. "Hello? Is anyone there? Hello?"

No one answered me.

I tried the door handle, but it was locked.

"Raymond?" I called out, knocking again. "Raymond . . . are you in there?"

Nothing.

I gazed up at the bank behind the trailer. It was higher than the bank in Back Lane, but not so thickly wooded. Industrial waste from a warehouse at the top of the bank was scattered among the trees — rusted bits of old machinery, polystyrene blocks, broken skids, tangles of plastic packing material . . .

We'd built a den up there once, I remembered, a ramshackle old thing made from sheets of corrugated iron, and as I scanned the top of the hill, looking for any signs that it was still there, I wondered briefly why we'd always seemed to build our dens at the tops of steep wooded banks. I suppose we'd thought they were safe up there. Safe and secret, out of the way. The kind of place where no one can see you, but you can see them . . .

The kind of place that Raymond liked.

I couldn't see the old den anywhere. No ruined remains, no rusted sheets of corrugated iron. I cupped my hands to my mouth and called out up the bank. *"RAYMOND! RAAY-MOND!"*

There was no answer.

I called out again, louder this time, but there was still no reply. I thought about climbing up the bank to take a closer look, but there didn't seem much point. There were too many places to hide up there, too many nooks and crannies . . . it'd take me all day to check them all.

So, with a final useless glance at the trailer, I headed off along the path.

♥ ♠ ♦ ♣

The path that runs alongside the river is actually made up of lots of different paths, but they all head in the same general direction — along the river, through some little woods, under a tunnel, over a bridge, then around the back of some vegetable plots and out on to a road called Magdalen Hill. If you go down Magdalen Hill, it's a shortcut to the town center, but if you turn left and head up the hill, it leads you over a crossroads into Park Road.

And that's the way I went after I'd wandered around the river for an hour or so. I'd gone through the woods, calling out Raymond's name again. I'd checked all the hiding places I knew about around the tunnel and the bridge. I'd even searched along the riverbank wherever it was possible. But I hadn't come across any sign of Raymond.

So now I was going back to the fairground.

I didn't know if it'd do any good or not, and I didn't know what I was going to do when I got there, but it seemed like a reasonable thing to do — follow your tracks, go back to the beginning, see if there's anything there.

Everything was still pretty quiet along Park Road, but the sun was out now, and it wasn't raining anymore, so the streets weren't quite so empty and miserable as they had been before. There were a few people around — an old man washing his car, a couple of young kids kicking a ball around, a hungover-looking guy shuffling down to the shops — but none of them said anything to me.

Although I didn't stop when I passed Eric and Nic's house, I could see that there were a few windows open now, and the house didn't feel empty anymore. I wondered again why Eric had lied to me about getting home at three o'clock, and I tried to think if there was any way at all that it could be true. I would have been asleep at the time, so if he'd been really out of his head — so whacked out that he could hardly see — maybe he'd simply stumbled into the house without even noticing me? Or maybe he'd got the time completely wrong? Maybe it *wasn't* three o'clock . . . maybe it was a lot earlier, or a lot later . . . ?

Maybe . . . ?

There were lots of other maybes, none of which I really believed, but I kept on thinking about them, anyway, and by the time I'd reached the end of the road I was so wrapped up in my thoughts that even when I saw a familiar-looking figure shambling around the corner ahead of me, it still took me a moment or two to realize who it was. She was walking slowly — her head bowed down, her hands stuffed wearily into her pockets — and she didn't look too happy. Her hair was uncombed, her makeup smeared . . . she looked as if she'd been crying. Her eyes were fixed miserably to the ground, so she didn't see me coming until we'd almost bumped into each other.

"Nicole?" I said.

She looked up suddenly, slightly shocked, and stopped in front of me.

"Hey, Pete . . ." she said, blinking her eyes and running her hand through her hair. "What are you doing here?"

She seemed pretty dazed and blurry. A bit embarrassed, too.

"Are you all right?" I asked her.

"Yeah, yeah," she said, forcing herself to smile. "I'm OK . . ."

"Are you sure?"

"Yeah . . . why?"

"You look like shit."

"Thanks a lot." She blinked her eyes again. "You don't look so great yourself."

"Yeah, well . . . it was a long night."

"Yeah?"

"I lost Raymond."

"You what?"

"He went off on his own last night, at the fair . . . I spent ages looking for him, but I couldn't find him anywhere. And he never went home, either."

"Shit," said Nic. "Do you think he's all right?"

I looked at her, suddenly realizing that she was the first person I'd spoken to who'd expressed any genuine concern for Raymond. I wasn't really surprised, because although Nic hadn't been too keen on him coming to the fair in the first place, I knew she'd always had a soft spot for him. There'd been other times in the past when she hadn't always *wanted* him to be there, times when she just wanted to be with me, but even then she'd always been OK with him. She liked him. Not just for what he meant to me, or what I meant to him — although I'm sure that was part of it — but basically I think she just liked him for what he was. She cared for him.

And then I recalled the fortune-teller's words: *You have great kindness*, she'd told Raymond. *You care for others without thinking of yourself.*

"Did you see him at all last night?" I asked Nic.

She ran her hand through her hair again and sighed. "Christ, Pete . . . I don't know. I can't seem to remember *any*thing about last night." She blew out her cheeks and shook her head. "I don't know . . . it's really strange. I mean, I can sort of remember some of it, you know, like blurred flashes of things, but most of it's just a blank."

"What about Raymond? Do you remember seeing him?"

"Well, yeah . . . when he was in the den . . ." She glanced awkwardly at me for a moment. "But after that . . . I'm not sure. I think I saw him *somewhere* at the fair . . . but I can't remember when or where."

"Was he on his own?"

She closed her eyes and put her hand to her head, trying to remember. "I don't know . . . I think I might have seen him twice. Or maybe that was someone else . . ." She sighed heavily and opened her eyes again. "I'm sorry, Pete . . . I really can't remember."

"That's OK," I told her. "If you do remember anything though—"

"Yeah, I'll give you a ring."

I nodded. "I'll be out for a while, so call me on my mobile. Have you got my number?"

"I've got your old one somewhere, but I don't suppose that's any good."

She was right — the number she had was at least three or four mobiles out of date.

"Have you got a pen?" I asked her.

She pulled a tube of lipstick out of her pocket, passed it over, and offered me her arm. I paused for a moment, watching as a police car moved slowly past us, then I took hold of her hand, twisted the lipstick, and started writing my mobile number on her arm.

"Listen, Pete," she said quietly, "about last night . . ."

A drop of sweat dripped from my head onto her arm.

"I know this is a stupid question," she went on, "but we didn't actually *do* anything, did we?"

"No," I said, pretending to concentrate on the lipstick in my hand. "No, we didn't do anything. Don't you remember what happened?"

"Well, kind of . . . I mean, I remember some of it, and I know we *started* doing something, you know . . ." She put her hand to her head. "God, I just remember feeling so *weird* . . . like my body was exploding. It was like I was totally out of control or something."

I let go of her hand and gave her back the lipstick.

Nic looked at me. "I'm sorry, Pete . . . I mean, if I messed things up . . ."

"It's all right," I told her. "No one messed anything up. It was just a really weird night . . ."

She nodded sadly. "Yeah . . ."

I gazed back at her for a moment, wondering what to say, and then we both looked up as a helicopter passed low over our heads. The chopping sound of the blades filled the sky for a moment, and I shielded my eyes against the sun and watched the dark shape of the helicopter as it banked to the left and started circling over the town park.

"What's going on?" Nic asked me. "Is that a police helicopter?"

"Yeah . . ."

"Do you think it's something to do with Raymond?"

"I don't know . . . probably not." I looked at her. "Listen, I'd better go . . ."

"Are you going back to the fairground?"

"Yeah."

"Do you want me to come with you?"

"No . . . it's all right, thanks. I'm just going to have a quick look around . . ."

"Are you sure?"

"Yeah . . ." I smiled at her. "You look as if you could do with getting home, anyway."

She looked at me. "OK . . . well, I'll call you if I think of anything . . ."

"Yeah, thanks."

We stood there for a moment, neither of us quite sure how to end things, then Nic touched my arm, said, "See you later," and started walking off. I watched her for a second or two, wondering briefly what kind of night she'd had with the carny guy, and whether or not she really couldn't remember anything about what had happened in the den . . .

Then I shook it all from my head and got going.

♥ ♠ ♦ ♣

In the summer light of a Sunday afternoon, the fairground seemed to have died. Without its lights, without all its music and its noise, it just seemed to lie there, jaded and dull. All its energy had gone. All its madness, its movement, its life . . . all that remained was a formless scattering of machinery, scaffolding, canvas, and vehicles.

The carnival was moving on.

Some of the rides had already been dismantled and packed away, leaving large patches of dead yellow grass where they'd stood, while others were still in the process of being taken down. The sound of hard work drifted in the air as I wandered around — buzzing drills, thumping hammers, the dull clink of scaffolding coming down. The fairground people were too busy packing up to take much notice of me, and if any of them wondered what I was doing there, they didn't seem to show it. I got a few glances, a few curious looks, but that was about it.

The whole place seemed a lot smaller than I remembered, and it didn't take long to walk around and take everything in. There wasn't much left to see. The Portaloos were all gone, and most of the surrounding litter had been swept up and cleared away. The fortune-teller's tent wasn't there anymore. There was no tilt-a-whirl, no bumper cars, no children's rides. And in the place where the old-fashioned merry-go-round had been, or the place where I *thought* it had been, there was absolutely nothing. No patch of yellowed grass. No litterless imprint in the ground. No sign that it had ever been there at all.

I should have felt puzzled, I suppose. Or, at least, a little bit curious. But as I stood there by the fairground entrance, gazing over at the empty space where I thought I'd seen Raymond riding a horse-size black rabbit, everything seemed so ordinary and drab that it was hard to feel anything at all. Even the sight of the police helicopter, standing alone in the middle of the grass, and the patrol car parked down by the gates . . . even that didn't seem to mean anything. The two uniformed police officers from the patrol car were just strolling around the fairground, occasionally stopping to talk to some of the fairground workers, but they didn't seem to be in any great hurry. And the two figures inside the helicopter were just sitting there, not doing anything at all.

I looked over at the area where all the fairground vehicles and trailers were parked, and I wondered if I should try to find the fortune-teller. Rationally, I knew it was pointless, a complete waste of time. No matter how much she'd *seemed* to know about Raymond, I knew it was all just an illusion. Words, mind games, trickery . . . whatever you want to call it. It's simply not possible to know about things that haven't happened yet.

"Excuse me."

The voice came from behind me, and when I looked around I saw one of the uniformed police officers coming toward me.

"Do you work here?" he said.

"Sorry?"

"Are you with the fair?"

"No . . ."

He stopped in front of me, wiping sweat from his brow. "Do you mind telling me what you're doing here?"

"I'm not doing anything," I said, "I was just . . . I don't know. I was just looking around . . ."

"Just looking around?"

"Yeah . . ."

He looked at me. "What's your name, son?"

"Pete Boland."

"Boland?"

"Yeah."

"Where do you live, Pete?"

"Hythe Street."

"Number?"

"Ten."

He nodded. "Were you here last night?"

"At the fair, do you mean?"

"Yes, at the fair."

"Yeah . . . yeah, I was, actually."

"What time did you get here?"

"About ten-thirty, I think."

"And what time did you leave?"

I shrugged. "Around midnight."

He nodded again. "So, you just came up here this morning for another look around the fair . . . is that it?"

"Yeah . . . well, no . . . I mean, I didn't really *mean* to come up here. I was going to see some friends on Park Road, but they weren't in, so I just came up here to hang around for a bit, you know . . . to pass the time."

"Right. So you'll be going back to your friends' place now?"

"Yeah."

"On Park Road."

"That's right."

He smiled at me. "Off you go, then."

As I turned around and started walking away, I could feel him watching me, and I wondered why I hadn't told him about Raymond, and why I hadn't asked him what was going on . . .

God, why was I so *pathetic*?

I didn't look back to see if the police officer was still watching me until I'd reached the park gates. Even then, I was feeling so stupidly paranoid that I didn't risk looking back until I'd actually turned left at the gates and taken a few steps toward Park Road, just in case he *was* still watching me. But he wasn't. I couldn't see him anywhere. I looked again, just to make sure, then I quickly turned around and headed back the other way, toward Back Lane.

Apart from a bunch of skateboard kids hanging around the gas towers, the lane was quiet and deserted. There were no dog walkers around, no dossers, no weirdos, no odd-looking men with mustaches. No sign of Raymond, either. In fact, there was no sign of anything. I was keeping my eyes open as I walked, looking all around—down at the ground, up at the bank, into the trees—but I didn't really know what I was looking for. I was just looking, I suppose. Just looking . . .

Actually, come to think of it, I wasn't really looking at all. I mean, my eyes *were* open, and they *were* moving around, and if I *had* seen something . . . well, that would have been fine—or *not* fine, depending on what I'd seen—but all I was really doing was trying to keep my mind occupied so I wouldn't have to think about what I might find when I got to the den.

I knew that everything might be all right, that I might get to the den and find Raymond sitting there, alive and well . . . and I also knew that I might not find anything at all. But there was another possibility, and that was the one that was bothering me, the one that I didn't want to think about. But the closer I got to the den, the harder it was *not* to think about it, and as I started clambering up the bank, threading my way through the bushes and brambles, I couldn't help imagining the worst.

It was the rabbit, I suppose . . . the image of Black Rabbit's severed head on the gate, its blank eyes staring at nothing. I just couldn't get that picture out of my mind. And I couldn't stop it from playing tricks with me, either, making me see things I didn't want to see.

A rabbit's head with Raymond's eyes . . .

Raymond's head with rabbit's teeth . . .

Black fur, black clothes . . .

Whispered voices . . .

Blood and flies . . .

There it is.

I'd reached the top of the bank now, and as I stood in front of the den, breathing hard, everything looked the same. The overgrown brambles, the wooden boards, the faded blue paint on the roof. Everything was just the same.

It looks all right, doesn't it?

I told you it'd still be here.

Yeah, you did.

I glanced over my shoulder and looked down the bank. There was nobody there. I turned back to the den and stepped up to the door.

After you.

No, after you.

I paused for a moment, listening to the echo of Raymond's voice, then I stooped down and opened the door.

There was nothing in there. No nightmares, no bodies, no blood . . . just a scattering of empty bottles, a stale smell of cigarette smoke and sweat, and a sweetly dark memory I wanted to forget.

THIRTEEN

Mum was watching TV in the living room when I got home. She was perched on the edge of the sofa with a cigarette in one hand and the remote control in the other, and she was so engrossed in whatever she was watching that I didn't think she'd seen me come in.

"Hey, Mum," I said. "Has Dad rung—?"

"Hold on," she said, turning up the volume on the TV. "I think this is about Stella."

"What?"

"Sky News," she said, nodding at the TV. "They're talking about Stella."

I turned to the TV and stared at the picture. *BREAKING NEWS* it said at the bottom of the screen, *TEENAGE CELEBRITY FEARED MISSING*. The newsreader—a smartly dressed woman with a very small head and very big hair—was holding a piece of paper in her hand and peering at a laptop.

". . . these reports are still unconfirmed," she was saying, "but we understand that Essex police were alerted by Mr. and Mrs. Ross earlier this morning, and officers are currently carrying out an investigation in the area of

St. Leonard's where Miss Ross was last seen." The newsreader put down the piece of paper and looked gravely into the camera. "Stella Ross," she said in summary, "apparently reported missing this morning." She glanced at her laptop again, pressed a button, then turned back to the camera. "Our reporter, John Desmond, is in St. Leonard's now, and we'll be going over to him shortly for a further update. In the meantime, I think we can go back to Sheila McCall in Baghdad . . ."

Mum hit the mute button and looked at me. "Well," she said, "it looks like Dad's going to be busy."

"Yeah . . ."

"This is going to be a big one."

"If it's true."

"What do you mean?"

I sat down. "I don't know, Mum, it just seems a bit . . . I don't know. I mean, I saw Stella last night at the fair. She was with loads of people. There was even a guy with a camera there."

"So?"

I shook my head. "It just seems a bit strange, that's all."

"What's so strange about it? She's a young girl, her parents don't know where she is —"

"Yeah, but she's Stella Ross, Mum. She's a star, she travels all over the place, all over the world . . . her parents probably don't know where she is *most* of the time. And now, just because she didn't come home from some stupid little fair, they call the police straightaway?" I looked at Mum. "Doesn't that seem a bit odd to you?"

She shrugged. "Maybe they know something we don't."

"Yeah, maybe . . ."

I glanced at the TV. A woman with a microphone was standing in a rubble-filled street, talking and waving her hands around. Behind her, dead bodies in black bags were being loaded into the back of a truck.

"Did you find Raymond?" Mum asked me.

"No," I said, looking at her. "He's still not home."

"Have you talked to his mum and dad?"

I nodded. "They don't care."

"I'm sure they do —"

"They don't," I said bitterly. "Nobody cares . . . not about Raymond. I mean, he's not a *celebrity*, is he? He's not good-looking, he doesn't have famous parents, he doesn't have millions of sad old men ogling him on the Internet . . . why *should* anyone care about him? He's just a dumb-looking weird kid."

"Come on, Pete," Mum said softly, "it's not like that."

"Yeah, it is. He's just as *missing* as Stella, isn't he? He's just as vulnerable as her . . . in fact, he's *more* vulnerable. But they're not talking about him on the news, are they?" I looked at the TV again. They were showing a photograph of Stella now. It was a publicity shot — all golden hair and shining eyes, lots of cleavage, a superstar smile. "See?" I said to Mum, waving at the screen. "I bet they wouldn't show a photo of Raymond like that on the news."

She gave me a slightly puzzled look, and I knew what she meant — yes, it *was* a stupid thing to say, and, no, it *didn't* make sense — but I think she knew what I was trying to say. I stared at the TV as she turned up the volume.

". . . is the daughter of Justin Ross and Sophie Hart," the newsreader was saying. "She first came to fame as a feisty teenager in a popular and award-winning series of TV commercials, and has since gone on to star in pop videos, soap operas, fashion magazines . . ."

As the newsreader jabbered on about Stella's famous parents, her sheltered upbringing, and her more recent tabloid notoriety, a series of pictures and TV clips flashed across the screen showing Stella in all her glory: dancing in videos, posing for magazine covers, acting badly in soaps. The more intimate photos from the Internet weren't shown, of course, and they weren't actually mentioned, either. But there were enough hidden hints and unseen winks to put us all in the picture.

It was kind of sickening, really. The TV people had nothing to report. There was no information. No facts. No *news*. They were just talking, gossiping, speculating, filling in time. It was like watching some kind of grim entertainment show.

"Look," said Mum, pointing at the screen. "Isn't that Nicole?"

The newsreader was talking over a film clip now, explaining that it was an exclusive piece of video footage, allegedly filmed at a carnival in St. Leonard's on Saturday night. The film clip didn't last very long, no more than twenty seconds or so, but they kept playing it over and over again, and as I leaned forward and stared breathlessly at the screen, I realized that Mum was right. Nicole *was* there. You could just make her out at the beginning of the clip—out of focus, in the background, entering the fairground. She was on her own, looking pretty pissed off . . . as if she'd just been insulted by some stupid guy in a den. As the camera zoomed in on Stella's laughing face, Nicole disappeared from the picture for a moment, but then Stella turned and looked over her shoulder, as if something had just caught her attention, and as the camera panned out again, I could see that she was looking at Nic. Nic was walking up to her now, a false-looking smile fixed to her face—as if she was just saying hello to her old friend Stella—but her old friend Stella wasn't even bothering to pretend to smile back at her. She was looking at Nic as if she'd never seen her before. Like—who the hell are you? Nic looked puzzled for a moment, then her puzzlement turned to an angry frown as Stella turned away, blowing her off, and just for a second or two I saw a flash of rage in Nic's eyes—a glare of naked hate—and then the camera zoomed back to Stella's laughing face again.

It was all really quick, the camera work a little bit shaky, and everything was slightly out of focus, but there was no doubt it had happened. Stella had blown off Nic at the fair, and Nic hadn't liked it one bit.

I didn't know if that meant anything or not.

All I knew was that Sky News had the film, and if they had that piece of film, they probably had the rest. Which meant they probably had film showing Stella with Raymond . . .

The star's going out tonight . . .

. . . and Stella with me . . .

You're going to wish you hadn't done this . . .

Stella and Raymond.

Raymond and Stella . . .

"Pete?" Mum said, breaking into my thoughts. "Did you hear what I said?"

I looked at her. She was still perched on the edge of the sofa, and she still had the remote in her hand. The TV was muted again now. The room was quiet, the news had moved on to Afghanistan, and Mum was staring at me with a worried look on her face.

"What's on your mind?" she asked me.

"Nothing . . ."

"Come on, Pete," she sighed. "What aren't you telling me?"

"About what?"

"What do you think?" she said. "Stella Ross, the fair . . . whatever happened last night." Her eyes narrowed. "You know something about it, don't you?"

I gave her an innocent look. "What makes you think that?"

"I'm your mother, Pete. I know when you're hiding something—"

"I'm not *hiding* anything—"

"No?"

She was giving me one of those looks now, the kind of look that makes you lower your eyes and stare at the floor, hoping you don't look as guilty as you feel.

"What is it, Pete?" she said softly. "Come on, you can tell me."

"I don't know anything, Mum," I muttered, still staring at the floor. "Honest . . . I'd tell you if I did. I'm just really worried about Raymond, that's all. I don't know what to do about him, you know . . . I don't know what to think."

Mum nodded slowly. "What about the others who were there last night? Nicole, Eric, Pauly . . . maybe they know where he is."

I shook my head. "They haven't seen him."

"Do you think he might know something about Stella?"

"What?" I said, looking up.

"Raymond," she said cautiously. "I mean, if he's missing, and Stella's missing . . ."

I'd been trying not to think about that. Ever since Dad had got the phone call from his DCI, I'd been trying to ignore the possibility that Raymond's disappearance might have something to do with Stella's. I didn't want to believe it — and I *didn't* believe it. What was there to believe? All that stuff at the fortune-teller's about people dying and bad things happening . . . ? That didn't *mean* anything. And Raymond's words, or Black Rabbit's words — *the star's going out tonight* — they didn't mean anything, either. Rabbits don't talk, for a start. And wherever Raymond had got the words from — from himself, from his weirdness, from whatever voices he had in his head — he couldn't have known they had anything to do with Stella, because he didn't even know that she was going to be at the fair.

At least, I didn't *think* he knew . . .

But they *had* been together at the fair.

And Mum was right, they *were* both missing now.

Stella and Raymond.

Raymond and Stella . . .

As I looked at Mum again, I suddenly felt incredibly sad. "Raymond wouldn't do anything bad," I said quietly, shaking my head. "He wouldn't hurt anyone . . . he couldn't . . ."

"All right, Pete," Mum said. "It's all right —"

"No, it's not," I whispered, my voice quivering now. "It's *not* all right. Nothing's all right."

I tried to get some sleep after that, but all I could do was lie on my bed and stare at the mute TV, waiting for something to happen. Sky News kept showing the video clip of Stella and Nic at the fair, and I kept watching it, wondering if it meant anything . . . and wondering when they were going to show the rest of it.

Stella with Raymond . . .

The star's going out tonight . . .

. . . and Stella with me . . .

You're going to wish you hadn't done this . . .

The haunting words kept burning away in my head.

I was still lying on my bed, still staring at the mute TV, when I heard the phone ringing downstairs. I heard Mum coming out of the living room, walking down the hall, picking up the phone . . . and I heard her talking quietly for a few minutes. I couldn't hear what she was saying, but I could tell from the tone of her voice that she was talking to Dad. And it wasn't hard to guess what they were talking about.

I waited, listening . . . and just for a moment my mind flashed back to Thursday night when the phone had rung and the summer of this story had begun. I'd been lying on my bed then, too. Busy doing nothing, just staring at the ceiling, minding my own mindless business . . .

"Pete!" Mum called out now. "Dad's on the phone!"

I didn't move for a moment. I just lay there on the bed, staring blindly at the bedroom door . . . lost in a world of nothing.

"Pete!" Mum called out again, louder this time. "Come on, hurry up. Dad wants to talk to you . . . it's important."

I shook the nothingness from my head, got up off the bed, and made my way downstairs.

"Hi, Dad," I said, taking the phone from Mum's hand. "Have you found —?"

"I told you not to go out."

"I didn't —"

"Don't *lie* to me, Pete. I know where you've been."

"I only —"

"Look," he said angrily, "when I tell you to stay at home, you stay at home. Do you understand?"

"Yeah, but —"

"Do you *understand*?"

"Yes, Dad. Sorry."

"All right, listen," he said quickly, "I have to go in a minute . . . things are getting complicated. I don't know if they're going to let me . . ."

"What?" I said. "Let you what?"

"Nothing, it doesn't matter. Look, I want you to stay at home with your mum for the rest of the day. Don't go anywhere, and don't talk to anyone. Have you got that?"

"Yeah—"

"And I mean *any*one, Pete. Do you understand? I don't care who it is—the media, your friends, the police—"

"The police?"

"I'll explain later. Just don't say a word about anything until you've talked to me first. I'll be home in a while—"

"But why—?"

"Just *do* it, Pete."

"Yeah, OK . . ."

"Right, I've got to go—"

"Have you heard anything about Raymond yet?"

"No, but we're looking for him. His mother called in about an hour ago. We're going to need a written statement from you about last night—"

"A statement?"

"Later . . . I'll explain everything when I get home. Just sit tight for now, and I'll see you as soon as I can."

Mum tried talking to me for a while after that, asking me what Dad had said, and what I'd said to him, but I wasn't in the mood for answering questions, so I just mumbled and muttered and kept shrugging my shoulders, and eventually she gave up and let me go back to my room.

Dad had sounded really strange on the phone, and I didn't understand why. I knew why he was angry with me, and I knew he was under a lot of pressure, but the rest of it—his reluctance to tell me anything, his insistence that I didn't talk to anyone else, even the police—I just didn't understand it. It was almost as if he was trying to protect me from something . . .

Or maybe he was protecting *himself*?

I lay on my bed, stared at the TV, and thought about it.

I was still trying to think about it an hour or so later when my mobile rang. I answered it quickly, hoping that Mum wouldn't hear anything, and I kept my voice low.

"Hello?"

"Pete?"

"Hey, Nicole. How are you—?"

"Have you heard about Stella?" she said quickly.

"Yeah . . ."

"I've just seen it on the news. Christ, Pete . . . what the hell's going on? Why do they keep showing that bit of film from the fair? Have you seen it?"

"Yeah."

"Shit . . . it makes me look like *I've* got something to do with it."

"No, it doesn't—"

"Of *course* it does. Stella's gone missing, and there's me staring at her like I want to *kill* her or something . . . I mean, shit, how can they *do* that? That's *me* on the film . . . they can't just keep showing it without *asking* me or anything, can they?"

"I don't know, Nic . . ."

"Shit," she said again, and I heard her lighting a cigarette. "What do you think's happened to her, Pete?"

"I don't know—"

"Do you think Raymond's got anything to do with it?"

"No."

She hesitated for a moment, puffing on her cigarette, and when she spoke again her voice seemed a little bit calmer. "The police are going to want to talk to us, aren't they?" she said.

"I expect so—"

"What have you told your dad?"

"About what?"

"Last night."

"I told him what happened."

"Everything?"

"No, not everything . . . but he knows most of it."

"Did you tell him about the den?"

"No, I just told him that we went to the fair."

"What about *after* the fair?"

It was my turn to hesitate now, but as I wondered how much I ought to tell Nic, and how much she already knew, I realized that I'd already told her too much, anyway, and that simply by talking to her I was doing exactly what Dad had told me not to do. *Don't go anywhere*, he'd told me, *and don't talk to anyone.* But this wasn't just *anyone* I was talking to, was it? This was Nicole. And it felt OK. And I *needed* to feel OK.

"I went back to your place after the fair," I told her.

"Yeah?" she said cautiously.

"After I'd looked everywhere for Raymond, I stopped off at your place on the way home. I thought he might have gone back there."

"What time was this?"

"I don't know . . . pretty late. There was no one in."

"Yeah," Nic said, "I don't think Eric got back until about three or something—"

"I was there at three o'clock."

She sniffed. "Well, maybe he got back at half past—"

"No, he didn't."

"How do you know?"

"I fell asleep on your step. I was there all night. Eric didn't get back until at least six in the morning."

I listened to the silence on the line, wondering what Nic was going to say. Did she know that Eric had lied to me, or was she simply repeating what she'd been told?

"Does your dad know?" she said quietly.

"Know what?"

"That you were at our place all night. I mean, did you tell him that Eric wasn't there?"

"Yeah . . . yeah, I think so. Dad was home when I got back, and he asked me where I'd been all night."

Nic sighed. "Look, Pete . . . Eric was just embarrassed, that's all. He only lied to you because he was embarrassed."

"Embarrassed about what?"

"You have to promise not to tell anyone."

"I can't do that, Nic. If the police start asking me questions, I'm not going to—"

"All right," she said. "I didn't mean that. I just meant, you know . . . don't tell anyone else. Don't go spreading it around."

"Spreading *what* around?"

She sighed again. "Eric . . . well, he got a bit drunk last night, and he ended up spending the night with someone."

"So?"

She cleared her throat. "Well, it was someone . . . someone he shouldn't have spent the night with . . . an older guy. I mean, he wasn't *that* old or anything, you know, he wasn't like some dirty old man, he was only about twenty-five or something . . . and he was perfectly OK, you know . . . it's just that Eric would never have slept with him if he hadn't been drunk, if you know what I mean."

Yeah, I thought to myself, remembering the carny guy. *Yeah, I know exactly what you mean.*

"He made a mistake," Nic said. "That's all it was, Pete. A mistake. He slept with a guy for the wrong reasons. He knows it was wrong, and he wishes he hadn't done it, and now he feels really bad about it." She paused for a moment. "Do you know what I'm saying?"

"Yeah," I said, "I think so."

"So, you know . . . that's . . ."

The signal started breaking up then.

"Nic?" I said. "Are you still there?"

". . . if anyone . . . hello?"

"Can you hear me?"

"Hello? Pete?"

The line went dead.

I tried ringing her back, but her phone was busy — I guessed she was trying to ring me. So I cut the connection and waited for her to call, but nothing happened. I gave it a couple of minutes, then rang her again, and this time I couldn't get a signal.

So I gave up and just lay there, thinking about what she'd said, and I wondered again why Eric was lying. I mean, this thing about sleeping with some older guy, and being really embarrassed about it — it just didn't make sense. Even if it *was* true, and Eric *had* been embarrassed — which, knowing Eric, I very much doubted — that still didn't explain why he'd lied to me. He could have just told me he'd spent the night with someone. He needn't have told me who it was, and he must have known I wouldn't have asked, so there wouldn't have been anything to be embarrassed about.

So why lie?

And why was he with Wes Campbell last night at the fair?

And Stella, I thought about Stella . . .

And Pauly.

But most of all, I thought about Raymond.

Raymond . . .

His face, his smile . . . his loopy eyes.

His parents — too many troubles, too many misunderstandings.

His moments of light — *the star's going out tonight.*
His future: the death card.
Is someone going to die?
Life is not life without death.

My mind started drifting then, and after a while I suppose I must have fallen sleep, because the next thing I knew I was opening my eyes to a darkened room, and the air was hushed with the sounds of the night. I was sweating, shivering. Hot and cold. I was awake. But not quite awake. I wasn't asleep, and I knew I wasn't dreaming, but I felt as if I was. My head was floating, my mind disconnected. My senses didn't seem to belong to me anymore. The darkness had a strange silver light to it, and in the dark light I could see the shapes of things shifting. The TV was still on, shimmering with 3-D colors. My CD player was smiling at me. My skin was velvet, the air was white. The ceiling above me was a million miles away, another universe. It had mountains, rivers, valleys, roads.

Children were laughing up there.

A fairground organ was playing.

And the porcelain rabbit on my chest of drawers was a horse . . . a horse with a frown . . . a necklace of flowers . . . and a mustache.

The flowers were dripping blood.

The horse was a rabbit, twitching its porcelain nose . . .

Whispering to me.

Black Rabbit was whispering to me.

Take me home . . . bring me home . . .

"Raymond?" I heard myself mutter.

Bring me home.

"Where are you?"

Nowhere.

"Where *are* you, Raymond?"

Everywhere . . .

"What happened to you?"

Nothing. It doesn't matter.

"Raymond? What's happening?"

He was changing now, looming over me like a great black giant . . .

Pete . . . ?

. . . with a giant head and a giant mouth and a giant hand, reaching out for me.

"Peter?"

The giant voice was deep and slow and without a point of origin. It was distended, everywhere, nowhere. It was terrifying. I cowered away, whimpering like a baby, covering my eyes with my senseless hands . . .

"What's the matter, Pete? What are you doing?"

The voice was suddenly soft.

And familiar.

And when I opened my eyes and blinked away the sweat, everything was back to normal again. My room was just my room. There were no smiling CD players, no talking rabbits or horses with mustaches. There were no black giants with giant heads and giant hands. There was just my dad, standing beside my bed, reaching out gently toward me.

FOURTEEN

I don't think Dad really believed me when I told him there was nothing to worry about, that I'd just been having a nightmare, but I don't think he wanted to believe anything else, either. I mean, he might have *thought* I was crazy, or delirious, or whacked out of my head on drugs or something, but he didn't want to believe it. So he just stood there for a while, quietly watching me as I sat up on the bed and wiped the sweat from my face, and then, after a minute or so's thoughtful silence, he sighed to himself — putting his doubts to one side — and sat down carefully on the edge of the bed.

"Are you sure you're all right?" he said.

"Yeah . . ."

"You don't *look* all right."

I smiled at him. "It was just a nightmare, Dad. Really . . . I'm fine."

I wasn't, of course. I was nowhere *near* fine. I felt heavy and numbed, as if someone had injected lead into my veins. My limbs were tingling, my eyes were too big, and my head . . .

God, my head felt *so* weird.

"How come you're dressed?" Dad said.

"What?"

"It's not even eight o'clock yet."

I looked around, rubbing my eyes, suddenly confused as to what time it was. I'd assumed it was around midnight or something, but now Dad was saying it was eight o'clock, which didn't make sense, because it wouldn't have been dark if it was only eight o'clock in the evening . . . but then, as I looked over at the window and saw the sunlight streaming in, I realized that it *wasn't* dark anymore . . . of *course* it wasn't dark. It was eight o'clock in the *morning*.

It was Monday morning.

I'd been asleep for God knows how long.

I couldn't *believe* it.

I looked at Dad, trying to hide my surprise. "I was tired," I told him. "I must have fallen asleep watching TV."

He glanced over at the television. It was still tuned to Sky News. They were talking about stocks and shares.

I said to Dad, "Have you just got back from work?"

He nodded. "About half an hour ago."

"I thought you were coming home yesterday? You said on the phone you'd be back in a while—"

"Yeah, I know, but things started happening . . . I couldn't get away." He looked at me. "We need to talk, Pete. And we don't have much time."

"What do you mean?"

He paused for a moment, looking into my eyes. Then he took a deep breath and said, "One of my colleagues is coming around here in about half an hour to talk to you about Raymond and Stella. I don't know if he's actually going to take a written statement just yet, but he's going to want to know everything that happened on Saturday night. And I mean *everything*—do you understand?"

"I've already told you what happened."

"You haven't told me everything, though, have you?"

I shrugged.

He said, "Look, this is really important, Pete. I know it might be a bit difficult for you, but the police have to know what happened—"

"Why can't I just tell *you*?" I said. "Why do they have to send someone else around to talk to me? You could take a statement from me, couldn't you?"

Dad shook his head. "It's not that simple, I'm afraid."

"Why not?"

"Because you're involved." He took another deep breath, and as he slowly let it out, I could sense the exhaustion seeping out of him. "You were with Raymond," he said wearily, "and Raymond's still missing. And you were both at the fair when Stella Ross disappeared." He looked at me. "You're involved, Pete. And I'm your father. And that means that I *can't* be involved."

"Why not?"

"Conflict of interest," he said simply. "If anything ever came to court, and one of the witnesses turned out to be the son of one of the investigating officers . . . well, the case wouldn't even *get* to court." He sighed. "So, as of seven o'clock this morning, I'm officially off the case. I shouldn't even be talking to you about it, really."

"But you are."

He smiled at me. "I'm doing my best."

I looked at him. "Is there any news about Raymond?"

He shook his head. "Not yet."

"What about Stella?"

He looked at his watch. "Look, we've only got about twenty minutes before . . ."

He stopped talking and listened as a car pulled up outside. I heard a car door open and shut — *clunk, clunk* — then footsteps moving toward the house. Dad got up and went over to the window.

"Shit," he said, glancing at his watch. "He's early."

The doorbell rang.

Dad turned from the window and looked at me. "You know John Kesey, don't you?"

I nodded. John Kesey was a detective sergeant who'd worked with Dad for years. They were friends outside work, too. Good friends.

"All right, listen," Dad said quickly. "I want you to tell John the truth, OK? Whatever he asks you, no matter how awkward you feel about it, just tell him the truth. Do you understand?"

"Yeah, but —"

"I'll be there when he talks to you, but don't think you have to hide anything from me." He came over and put his hand on my shoulder. "Look, I know about the bottle of wine you took, OK? And I know you got a bit drunk . . . and I expect you did some other things that you don't want me to know about, too. But it doesn't matter. All right? Just tell the truth, and don't hide *anything*. OK?"

"Yeah . . ."

The doorbell rang again.

"Right," Dad said, heading for the door, "let's go."

When we went downstairs, Mum had already let John Kesey in, and they were both waiting for us in the living room. Kesey looked pretty much the same as he'd always looked — kind of pale and sickly, as if he spent all his time in darkened pubs. He was about the same age as Dad, but he looked more worn-out and stressed. He had tired eyes, nicotine-stained fingers, and his breath smelled of stale beer and mints.

He nodded at Dad as we came into the room.

"John," Dad said, nodding back. "You're early."

"Yeah, sorry, Jeff, we couldn't wait. You know how it is . . . I can wait in the car for a few minutes if you want —"

"No," Dad told him, "you're all right."

"Sure?"

"Yeah."

Kesey looked at me. "All right, Pete?"

I nodded.

He smiled at me.

Dad said to him, "Do you want some coffee or something?"

"Yeah, that'd be great, thanks."

Dad looked at Mum. "Do you mind, love?"

Mum glanced at me, smiled, then looked back at Dad. I thought for a moment she was going to say something to him, but she didn't. She just looked at him for a few seconds, letting him see what she was thinking — whatever that was — then she turned around and headed out to the kitchen.

Dad said to Kesey, "Are you taking a statement?"

"Not just now," Kesey told him. "The DCI just wants to put everything together first. We still don't really know what we're looking at." He looked at me again. "We just want to ask you a few questions, if that's OK."

I shrugged.

Dad said to him, "Any problems with me sitting in?"

Kesey shook his head. "As long as you don't —"

"Yeah, I know. I'll keep my mouth shut."

Kesey looked slightly embarrassed. "Look, I'm sorry, Jeff. I know this is really awkward for you —"

"It's fine," Dad said gruffly. "No problem. Let's just get on with it, shall we?"

By the time we'd all sat ourselves down — me on the sofa, Kesey in the armchair beside me, and Dad in another armchair by the window — Mum had come back in with two cups of coffee. She gave one to Dad, the other one to Kesey, then turned around and walked out without saying anything.

"All right, Pete," Kesey said, taking a sip of his coffee, "all we're going to do here is go over what happened on Saturday night, OK?" He put down the coffee cup and opened his notebook. "This isn't an official interview, and you're not under arrest or anything, we're just making some preliminary inquiries and we need to know a few details. Is that all right?"

"Yeah."

"Good . . . OK, well, I'm sure you know that Raymond Daggett has been reported missing by his parents, and according to your dad, you might have been the last person to see him. Is that right?"

"Yeah."

"And this was at the fairground on Saturday night?"

"Yeah . . . well, it was Sunday morning, actually."

"OK, Sunday morning. So you and Raymond went to the fair together?"

"Sort of . . ."

"What do you mean — *sort of*?"

I *tried* to do what Dad had told me, I *tried* to tell Kesey the truth, and at first I didn't have any problems. I told him straightaway that I'd taken a bottle of Dad's wine, and that Raymond had taken some drink from his parents, too. Then I told him how we'd met up with the others in the den, and I explained where it was, and who the others were, and I admitted that we'd all been drinking (I didn't mention the dope), and that I'd stayed behind in the den with Nicole when the others had gone on to the fair . . .

"Hold on a minute," Kesey said at that point. "You stayed behind in the den with Nicole?"

"Yeah . . ."

"What did Raymond do?"

"He went on to the fair with Pauly and Eric."

"Right . . . but you stayed behind with Nicole?"

"Yeah."

"For how long?"

"I don't know . . . about twenty minutes maybe, something like that."

I saw Kesey glance quickly at Dad, then he turned back to me. "Why did the two of you stay behind?"

"Nic wanted to talk to me," I told him. "In private."

Kesey didn't say anything, he just looked at me.

"We used to be pretty close," I explained, trying not to blush. "I mean, we used to hang around together quite a lot when we were kids, and she just wanted to talk about it, you know . . . talk about the old times."

"Right," said Kesey. "So that's it? You just talked about the old times?"

I felt something holding me back then, some kind of . . . I don't know. Some kind of instinctive warning, maybe. It's hard to describe, but it was as if there was something inside me — an insistent whisper in the back of my mind — telling me to be careful, don't say too much . . . you don't have to tell him *everything*. I didn't really understand it, but I'd already made the mistake of *not* listening to things I didn't understand, and I wasn't going to make the same mistake again.

"Pete?" Kesey said. "Are you all right?"

"Yeah . . . sorry. I was just . . ."

"Just what?"

"Nothing." I smiled vaguely at him. "Sorry, I've forgotten what I was saying."

"You were telling me about Nicole," he said patiently. "Remember? You were in the den with her, talking about the 'old days.'"

"Right, yeah . . ."

"And that's all you did? The two of you just talked?"

"Yeah."

"Nothing else?"

"Like what?"

He smiled knowingly at me. "Come on, Pete, you know what I'm talking about — you and Nicole, alone in the den . . . you've both had a few drinks . . ."

"We just talked about stuff," I said casually, holding his gaze. "That's all. Nothing happened."

"All right," he said, his smile quickly fading. "So how come Nicole ended up going to the fair on her own?"

I hesitated. "What do you mean?"

"I'm not stupid, Pete," he said wearily. "I've seen the film clip they keep showing on the news, the one with Stella at the fair. That's Nicole in the background, isn't it? The girl that Stella snubs . . . that's Nicole Leigh."

"Yeah."

"And she's just arrived at the fair."

"Yeah."

"On her own."

"So?"

"So where were you? I mean, if the two of you were in the den together, having a nice friendly chat together, why didn't you go to the fair together?"

I couldn't think of anything to say for a moment. I just stared at him, trying not to look too stupid.

He said, "Do you see what I'm saying?"

"Yeah," I mumbled, lowering my eyes.

"What happened, Pete?"

I took a deep breath and looked up at him. "It was nothing . . . I mean, we just had a bit of an argument, that's all."

"You and Nicole?"

"Yeah."

"You had an argument in the den?"

"Yeah."

"What was it about?"

"Nothing, really . . ."

"It must have been about something."

I shook my head. "It was just one of those things, you know . . . we'd both had too much to drink, I said the wrong thing, Nicole got a bit angry with me . . ."

Kesey raised his eyebrows. "What did you say to make her angry?"

"I can't remember."

"You can't remember?"

I shrugged again. "Like I said, it was just one of those things . . ."

He stared at me for a moment, letting me see that he wasn't too happy with my answer, and then he just nodded. "All right," he sighed, "so the two of you had an argument. What happened then?"

"Nic left the den and went on to the fair on her own."

"Was she still angry with you?"

"I suppose so."

"What did you do after she'd left?"

"Not much . . . I stayed in the den for a while, maybe five minutes or so, and then I went on to the fair."

Kesey looked at me. "Do Stella and Nicole know each other?"

The sudden change of subject caught me off guard. "Sorry?"

"Stella and Nicole," he repeated slowly. "Do they know each other?"

"Well, yeah . . . I mean, they used to be friends when Stella was still at school, but they kind of drifted apart when Stella got famous—"

"So they're not friends anymore?"

"Not really."

"Is that why Stella ignored Nicole at the fair?"

"I don't know. Probably . . ." I looked at him, suddenly realizing what he was getting at. "They don't *hate* each other or anything," I told him. "I mean, if you're trying to suggest that Nic—"

"I'm not trying to suggest anything," he said calmly. "Do you know where the film clip came from?"

"What?"

"The video of Stella at the fair . . . do you know who made it?"

"It was just some guy with a camera," I said. "He was with Stella. There was a guy with a microphone, too."

"They were with Stella?"

"Yeah, she had loads of people with her."

"What did the cameraman and the guy with the microphone look like?"

I couldn't really remember what they looked like, but I did my best to describe them. As I sat there mumbling away—*one of them was tallish, the other one was a bit shorter*—and Kesey sat there diligently writing it all down, I began to realize that if the police didn't know who'd made the film, then they probably hadn't seen any more of it. Which meant they probably didn't know that Raymond had been with Stella at the fair, or that I'd taken him away from her. And *that* probably meant . . .

"So you saw her then?" Kesey said suddenly.

"Who?"

"Stella Ross. You saw her at the fair?"

I looked at him.

He said, "I mean, if you saw these two guys with the film equipment, and you're telling me that they were with Stella . . ."

"Yeah," I said. "Yeah, I saw her."

"Did you talk to her?"

"Only briefly . . ." I shrugged. "We just said hello, you know . . . I used to know her at school."

Kesey smiled. "She didn't ignore *you* then?"

"No."

"What time was it when you saw her?"

"Quite early . . . around ten-thirty, eleven. I'd only just got there."

"What was she doing?"

"Not much . . . just walking around, you know . . . soaking up all the attention."

"And you just said hello to her?"

"Yeah."

"Anything else?"

I shook my head. "I was trying to find Raymond. I felt bad about letting him go on to the fair without me."

"Why?"

"He's a bit . . . he sometimes gets a bit anxious about things."

"Anxious?"

"Yeah."

Kesey wrote something in his notebook, then looked back at me. "So you went looking for Raymond?"

"Yeah."

"And?"

I carried on with the story then, only this time I was even more careful with the truth. I told Kesey how I'd found Raymond at the fair, but I didn't go into any details. I told him how we'd gone to the fortune-teller, but I didn't tell him what she'd said. And I told him how I'd lost track of Raymond at the Portaloos, and how I'd spent the next couple of hours looking for him, but I didn't say anything about anything else.

"So what time did you actually leave the fair?" Kesey asked me.

"I don't know . . . it was pretty late. Gone midnight."

"And you went straight home?"

"No, I stopped off at Eric and Nic's place."

"Where's that?"

"Park Road. I thought Raymond might be there."

"But he wasn't?"

"No."

"Did you talk to Eric or Nicole?"

I shook my head. "They weren't in."

"So what did you do then?"

"I waited . . ."

"For how long?"

"I don't know . . . I fell asleep."

Kesey grinned at me. "You fell asleep?"

"I didn't *mean* to . . . I just kind of sat down on the front step, and I suppose I was a bit drunk, you know . . ."

"What time did you wake up?"

"About six o'clock . . . it was raining. I walked back to Hythe Street and went around to Raymond's to see if he was home . . . but he wasn't. And someone had killed his rabbit—"

"And that's when you came back here and saw your dad?"

"Yeah . . . I tried talking to Mr. and Mrs. Daggett about Raymond first, but they didn't seem too bothered. So I ran back home and told Dad."

"Right." Kesey looked at me. "Why did you go back to the fairground on Sunday morning?"

"Sorry?"

"You know what I'm talking about, Pete. Why did you go back there?"

"To find Raymond. I was worried about him."

"That's not what you told the police officer who asked you what you were doing there."

"What?"

"Come on, Pete," Kesey said, grinning at me again. "The uniformed cop at the fair on Sunday morning. He spoke to you, remember? He asked you what you were doing there, and you told him that you were just looking around. You didn't mention anything about Raymond."

"Yeah, I know—"

"And when he asked you what time you'd left the fairground on Saturday, you didn't say anything about stopping off at Eric and Nic's place on the way back, did you?"

"Well, no—"

"Why not?"

"I don't know . . . I just . . . I wasn't trying to hide anything—"

"Like what?"

"Nothing . . . I mean, there's nothing *to* hide. I just meant, you know . . . I just wasn't thinking straight." I looked at Dad, then back at Kesey. "I'm sorry, OK?"

"Yeah, all right," he said quietly. "As long as you're telling us everything now."

"I *am*—"

"Because we'll find out if you're not. You know that, don't you?" He tapped his notebook. "This is all going to be checked. So if there's anything else you think you might have *forgotten*, now's the time to tell me. Do you understand what I'm saying?"

"I've told you everything."

"I hope so," he said. "Because the more we know, the better chance we have of finding Raymond."

"Yeah, well," I said sullenly, "if you'd started looking for him as quickly as you started looking for Stella—"

"All right, Pete," Dad said, cutting me off. "Let's not get into all that."

Kesey glanced over at Dad, and I saw a look in his eyes . . . a look that meant something, something between him and Dad, but I couldn't work out what it was.

"Is that it?" Dad asked him. "Have you finished?"

Kesey nodded. "Yeah, I think that'll do for now." He closed his notebook and put it away. "We might need to talk to you again, Pete," he told me. "Obviously, if Raymond and Stella turn up, and hopefully they will, that'll be the end of it. But if we don't find them soon, you'll need to make a written statement, and we'll probably have to ask you a few more questions. OK?"

I nodded.

He looked at me, his eyes full of unanswered questions, and I'm pretty sure he was going to say something else, but Dad didn't give him a chance.

"Yeah, well, thanks a lot, John," he said, getting up and crossing the room. "And thanks for letting me stay. I appreciate it."

Kesey smiled at him. "No trouble, Jeff. Thanks for being so good about it."

"Are you going back to the station now?"

"Not yet . . . I've got a few more people to see."

"Right."

"What about you?" Kesey said.

Dad shrugged. "Back on at six tonight. Paperwork, reports, you know . . . anything to keep me out of the way."

"Why don't you just take some leave?"

"I need the money. There's no overtime when you're on leave."

"Right . . ."

They carried on chatting as Dad ushered Kesey out of the room, and it sounded friendly enough, but I could tell they were both feeling a bit awkward, and I guessed it had to be pretty hard for them: Dad having to stand back and let Kesey get on with it; Kesey having to get tough with his close friend's son . . .

It was an awkward situation.

And I got the feeling that it wasn't going to get any better.

Dad didn't say much to me after Kesey had left. I knew that he wanted to talk to me, but I think he thought that I'd had enough for now. And he was tired, too, almost dead on his feet.

"I'm going to get a couple of hours' sleep," he told me. "If that's all right with you."

"Yeah, fine."

"And I think you ought to try and get some sleep, too," he said. "You look shattered."

"OK."

"I'll wake you up around midday, and then we'll talk."

"Right."

He looked at me, trying to concentrate, trying to work out what he wanted to say . . . but he couldn't get hold of it. Whatever it was, he just couldn't do it. He put his hand on my shoulder and gave it a slight squeeze.

"See you in a couple of hours," he said.

I nodded. "See you, Dad."

I watched him as he shuffled wearily out of the room, and I listened as he climbed the stairs. I heard him open the bedroom door, then quietly close it, and I could just make out the faint mutter of voices as he started talking to Mum. I couldn't hear what they were saying, but I guessed they were talking about me.

I went upstairs to my bedroom, making sure that Mum and Dad heard me, then I quietly tiptoed back down again, crept out the back door, got my bike out of the garden shed, and quietly wheeled it around the back of the house and out onto the street.

FIFTEEN

reenwell Rise is a maze of flat roads and granite-gray houses that all look the same. It's a place where seven-year-old kids throw rocks at passing cars, and twelve-year-old kids rule the streets. It's a place where dogs are weapons, not pets, and cats are there to be killed. It's a place where everyone knows everyone else, and everyone knows if you don't live there. And if you don't live there, or if you don't know anyone who lives there, you'd better not hang around there too long.

The hard streets were almost deserted as I pedaled up into the heart of the maze, but that didn't mean there was no one around. It just meant that I couldn't see them. I could feel them watching me, though, as I rode on through the sullen gray heat — past scraps of playing fields, dog-shit paths, lock-up garages, burned-out cars, roads that didn't go anywhere . . .

The sun was beating down.

My sweat was cold.

The nowhere eyes were everywhere.

Pauly Gilpin's house was a pebble-dashed gray thing at the end of a street full of pebble-dashed gray things. It had dirty windows, a shit-colored door, and a scabby front yard of cracked concrete and weeds. I got off my bike, wheeled it up to the front door, and leaned it against the wall.

I rang the bell and waited.

It felt really strange, being at Pauly's place. It felt as if it ought to be familiar, but it wasn't. And as I stood there waiting, staring at the paint-peeled door, I found myself thinking about the past again, about the times when Pauly and the rest of us used to hang around together, and it suddenly occurred to me that we'd hardly ever gone around to Pauly's place back then. In fact, as far as I could remember, I'd only ever been there twice before. And even then, I hadn't been invited inside.

But that was a lifetime ago . . .

When Pauly finally opened the door, he had the same unmasked look about him that I'd seen when he was alone at the fair — the lostness, the loneliness, the darkness. He was barefoot and bare-chested, dressed only in jeans, and I guessed he'd only just woken up. His hair was uncombed, his eyes were heavy, and it took him a few seconds to recognize me.

"Pete?" he said, blinking and rubbing his eyes. "Hey . . . what're you doing here?"

"I need to talk to you," I told him.

"Yeah?" He was looking over my shoulder now, his eyes instinctively scanning the streets. "You should have called first," he said, still not looking at me. "I was just about to go out—"

"Have the police spoken to you yet?" I asked him.

His eyes suddenly focused on me. "What?"

"The police—have they been in touch with you yet?"

"About what?"

"What do you think?"

"Oh, right . . . Stella. Yeah, I saw it on the news." He shook his head. "I couldn't believe it . . ."

There was no sense of real disbelief in his words, they were just words—the kind of things you say when you're expected to say something. The look of puzzlement on his face didn't seem too genuine, either.

"Why'd the cops want to speak to me?" he said. "I don't know anything about Stella—"

"Raymond's missing, too."

"Raymond?" he said. "What's Raymond got to do with it? He wasn't even . . ."

"He wasn't even what?"

Pauly hesitated, a quick nervous grin. "What?"

"Raymond wasn't even *what*?" I repeated.

"No, nothing . . . I mean, he wasn't on the news . . . Raymond wasn't. You know, there wasn't anything about Raymond on the news."

I stared at him. He was avoiding my eyes again now, pretending to look down the street at something. He scratched the back of his neck, rubbed his bare belly, picked at a scabbed cut under his eye . . .

"Are you going to ask me in?" I said to him.

"What?" He grinned.

"Ask me in."

"I was just going out —"

"Don't you want to know what the police were asking me?"

"They've talked to you?"

I nodded. "This morning."

"What did you tell them?"

"Let me in," I said, "and I'll tell you."

There was no summer in Pauly's house. Despite the heat outside, everything inside was cold and clammy and dim. It felt like a house that had never seen any light.

As I followed Pauly up the narrow stairs to his bedroom, I wondered where his parents were. Sleeping? At work? Downstairs? I hadn't seen or heard anyone else, and the house felt really empty, but I got the feeling that it always felt like that, so there was no way of knowing if his parents were at home or not. Not that it really mattered. But as I was thinking about it, I realized that I didn't actually know anything about his parents. I couldn't remember ever seeing them, and I couldn't remember Pauly ever mentioning them. They might not even be a *them*, for all I knew. They could be divorced, separated, dead . . .

"Mind the newspaper," Pauly said as we reached the landing. "The fucking cat's been sick again."

I stepped over a sheet of stained newspaper and followed Pauly into his bedroom.

It wasn't very nice in there. I mean, I'm not saying *my* bedroom's the tidiest place in the world, but Pauly's room wasn't just untidy, it was a filthy stinking mess. There was crap all over the place—empty KFC boxes, piles of dirty clothes, overflowing ashtrays, flies buzzing around unwashed plates. The bed was unmade, the sheets all grubby and stained, and the whole place smelled really bad, kind of sour and sweaty and stale. Everything about the room made me feel dirty—the dirty floor, the dirty cheap furniture, the dirty pictures tacked carelessly to the walls. The curtains were closed, so there wasn't much light, but there was enough to see that some of the pictures pinned to the walls were computer printouts of Stella. They were sad and seedy little things—letter-size sheets, badly printed in black-and-white, grainy shots from the Internet.

"What?" said Pauly as he saw me looking at them. "They're only pictures. Don't tell me *you* haven't seen them."

"I haven't got them all over my wall."

"What are you trying to say?"

"They're pictures of *Stella*, Pauly," I said. "Stella's missing—"

"So what? You think *I* had something to do with it?"

"I didn't say that—"

"You think I'd have her picture on my wall if I'd had anything to do with it?"

I looked at him. "I'd take them down if I were you," I said. "Before the police get here."

"Why'd they want to see me anyway?" he said. "What've you told them?"

"Nothing. They asked me about Saturday night, that's all. I had to tell them about the den."

"What about it?"

"They wanted to know who was there."

"Why?"

"Raymond's missing, for Christ's sake. That's *why*."

"Oh, yeah . . . I thought you meant . . ."

"What?"

"Nothing." He went over to his bed, picked up a shirt from a pile of dirty clothes, and put it on. "So what's happened to him then?" he said casually, moving over to a cluttered computer desk. "Raymond, I mean. Where is he?"

"If I knew that," I sighed, "he wouldn't be missing, would he?"

"Yeah, right . . ."

Pauly was standing at his computer desk now. He had his back to me, so I couldn't see what he was doing, but I could tell from the vagueness of his voice that his mind wasn't on Raymond. He was concentrating on something else — picking something up, putting it in his pocket, picking up something else, opening a drawer, putting something in it, closing the drawer . . .

"I told the police you were at the den," I said, "but I didn't say anything about later on."

He turned and looked at me. "Later on?"

"When I saw you by the Portaloos. Remember? You were sitting on a bench, and I was looking for Raymond, and you were watching Eric and Campbell."

"I wasn't *watching* them —"

"Yeah, you were. I was standing behind you for about five minutes. I was watching you."

His face darkened. "You *what*?"

"You were watching them, Pauly. I know you were."

He was staring at me now, his eyes cold and hard, and just for a moment there was something about him that scared me. It wasn't a physical fear. I mean, I didn't actually think he was going to *do* anything to me. But I could see the possibility of some kind of violence in his eyes. It was really weird, as if he was someone else, someone I'd never known.

And I wondered then if I'd *ever* known him.

The moment didn't last very long, though, and as he shrugged his shoulders and lit a cigarette, his eyes lost their coldness and the Pauly I *did* know came back.

"Yeah, well . . ." he said, blowing out smoke. "What if I *was* watching them? There's no law against watching people, is there?"

"Why were you watching them?"

He stared at me, thinking things over, then he moved over to his bed and sat down. "All right," he sighed, resting his cigarette in an ashtray, "I *was* watching them, OK? But I don't see what that's got to *do* with anything. I was just watching them, you know . . ."

"Why?"

He closed his eyes and put his hands to his face, and for a second or two I actually thought he was going to start crying. But he didn't. He just rubbed his eyes and slowly dragged his hands down his face, as if he was preparing himself for something really difficult. He took a breath, opened his eyes, picked up his cigarette, and looked at me. "Look," he said. "I just wanted to know what they were doing, OK? That's all. I saw them together, and I didn't know . . . you know . . . I didn't know *why* they were together. Eric and Wes. It wasn't right, you know?"

"Why not?"

The scab under his eye had come off and the cut was bleeding. He wiped it with his hand, then wiped his bloody hand on the bed. "You know what Eric's like," he said nastily. "He doesn't belong with people like Wes."

"What do you mean?"

"You know what I mean." He tilted his chin at the window, indicating the streets outside. "This is our world — mine and Wes's. Eric's got nothing to do with it. If he came down here, he wouldn't last five minutes."

"What — because he's gay?"

"No, because he's Eric."

It might not sound as if it made much sense, but at the time I thought I knew what Pauly was trying to say. Wes Campbell was one thing, and Eric was another. Whatever they both meant to Pauly, they weren't meant to have any connection. They were different parts of his life. Different circles, different lives. They didn't *belong* together.

"Where did they go?" I asked him.

"What?"

"Eric and Wes. At the fair, when you left me on the bench — you followed them, didn't you?"

Pauly didn't say anything for a moment. He fingered the cut on his face again, wiping off a little more blood, then he stubbed out his cigarette, got to his feet, and started heading for the door. "I need a piss," he said. "Won't be a minute."

He closed the bedroom door as he left.

The bathroom was right next door to his bedroom, so I could hear him going in and shutting the door. I waited until I heard him peeing, then I crossed over to his computer desk and quietly opened the drawer. Lying on top of a jumble of CDs and DVDs was the stuff Pauly had picked up from the desk and hidden away: a plastic prescription bottle full of small blue pills, a lump of cannabis in plastic wrap, and some sparkling white powder in a little ziplock bag.

As I was standing there looking down at all this stuff — wondering what the pills and the powder were, and why Pauly had bothered hiding them away from me — I heard the faint mutter of his voice from the bathroom. It sounded like he was talking to someone. I listened hard, trying to work out what he was saying, but all I could hear was the *sound* of his voice — a low, cautious whispering . . . too muffled to make any sense.

After a minute or so, the whispering stopped and I heard the toilet flush. I closed the desk drawer and went back over to the other side of the room.

"Sorry about that," Pauly said as he came back in.

I watched him as he went over and sat down on his bed. He didn't look at me, and he didn't say anything, either, he just sat there — staring at the floor, chewing his lip, jiggling his heel up and down.

"Who were you talking to?" I asked him.

"Uh?"

"I heard you talking —"

"When?"

"Just now, in the bathroom. I heard you talking to someone."

"Not me," he said, shaking his head. "It was probably the people next door . . . you can hear everything through these walls." He looked up and grinned at me. "You wouldn't *believe* what I hear sometimes . . . I mean, just the other night —"

"I don't really want to know, thanks."

He shrugged. "Suit yourself."

I looked at him. "You still haven't told me about Eric and Wes."

"What about them?"

"I asked you where they went."

He frowned. "When?"

"At the fair," I said patiently. "When you followed them. Where did they go, Pauly?"

He shook his head. "I don't know."

"You *followed* them —"

"Yeah, I know . . . but I couldn't find them." He looked at me. "Honest, Pete . . . I don't *know* where they went. I thought I saw them going through that little side gate — you know, the one that leads out into Port Lane — but when I got there, there was no one around. I mean, I *looked* for them, I went up and down the road for a bit, but I couldn't see them anywhere."

"So what did you do?" I asked him.

"Not much," he shrugged. "I hung around the gate for a while, just in case they came back . . . and then I went home."

"So you didn't see them at all?"

"No."

"And you've got no idea where they went?"

"I just *told* you—"

"Have you seen either of them since?"

"No."

"Have you spoken to them on the phone?"

"What's this—?"

"Have you?"

"No."

"Why not?"

"Why should I?"

"I'm just asking."

"Why?" he said, staring at me. "I mean, what does it matter? What's all this got to do with anything anyway?"

I looked at him then, wondering what he was . . . and who he was . . . and what I was doing here in this dirty little room. What *was* I doing? Why *was* I asking him all these questions? Was it simply because I wanted to know why Eric had lied about Saturday night? I mean, what *did* it matter? What *did* it have to do with anything?

"I don't know . . ." I heard myself whisper.

My voice seemed a long way away.

"Yeah, well," said Pauly. "I've got to be somewhere else . . ."

His voice . . . his words . . .

"Pete?"

"Uh?"

"What's the matter?"

"What?"

"Listen," he said, glancing quickly at a clock on the wall. "I've really got to go, OK? So, you know . . . if you don't mind —"

"You're bleeding," I told him.

"What?"

"That cut under your eye . . . it's bleeding again."

Pauly didn't say anything after that. He just wiped the blood from his face and walked out of the bedroom. I followed him silently down the stairs. He didn't say anything when he opened the front door and showed me out, and when I stopped on his step, staring stupidly at the empty space where my bike had been, he just gave me one of his grins.

"Shit," I said.

Pauly was still grinning as he went back inside and shut the front door.

Riding my bike was another one of those things that I'd pretty much given up in the last few months. Just like football and playing the guitar, it simply didn't interest me anymore. So I wasn't really that bothered about my bike being stolen. And, if I'd been anywhere else, I wouldn't have been bothered about having to walk home, either. But I wasn't anywhere else — I was in Greenwell Rise. And even as I left Pauly's house and started walking up the street, I could already see a bunch of hard-looking kids hanging around the corner up ahead, and I knew they were watching me, waiting for me, waiting to have some fun . . .

and I also knew that they had my bike. I could see one of them sitting on it, a shaven-headed kid of about fourteen. As I looked at him, he grinned at me, stretched out his leg, and stamped his foot into the spokes.

It's hard to look casual when you're scared, but I did my best — casually crossing the road, casually pretending that I hadn't seen anything, that I was just some kid . . . just going somewhere else. I casually turned left and headed down a side street.

I didn't actually start running then — you don't start running until you really have to — but I was walking pretty quickly. The side street led me down to a little pathway, through to another street, and then I turned left again, down to the end of the street, then down another pathway and across a little playing field, and from there I could see the road that runs alongside the docks.

I stopped for a moment and looked over my shoulder. The Greenwell kids were following me. They weren't running or shouting or anything, they were just idly following along behind me. There were about half a dozen of them — white track pants, basketball shirts, gold chains glinting in the sun.

As I hurried on down to the dockland road, I kept glancing over my shoulder to see what they were doing. At one point, I saw three of them peel away from the others and head off away from them, almost doubling back. I didn't understand it at first, and I wondered for a moment if I was just being paranoid. Maybe they weren't following me after all? Maybe they just happened to be going in the same direction as me, and now three of them just happened to be going somewhere else? But then I saw *where* they were going, and I suddenly realized what they were doing. The three who'd split away from the others weren't just going somewhere else, they were heading down to the far end of the dockland road, blocking my way back to St. Leonard's Road.

My only option now was to cross over the dock road, find my way into the wasteground, and head up into Back Lane.

The wire fence that screens the wasteground from the road used to be a rusty old thing full of holes, so it used to be really easy to get through, but it wasn't anymore. It was a new fence, a lot higher than the old fence, and as I crossed the dock road and stopped in front of it, there wasn't a hole to be seen.

I looked back across the road and saw the three Greenwell kids heading straight for me. They were about a hundred feet away now. And when I looked to my right, I could see the other three moving toward me from the far end of the road.

"Shit," I said.

I hadn't really been all that scared until now. I'd been a bit worried, and I'd had that horrible fluttery feeling in my belly, but I hadn't really thought I was in any real danger or anything. I mean, I'd been scared, but I hadn't been *running* scared. Now, though . . . well, now I was beginning to feel more and more trapped.

So now it *was* time to start running.

I headed off to my left, away from the kids coming down the dock road, and as I ran I kept my eyes on the fence, looking for a way into the wasteground. I could hear rapid footsteps behind me, so I knew the Greenwell kids had started running, too, but I didn't waste any time looking around at them. I just kept going.

I was trying to think as I pounded along the pavement, trying to work out where to go and what to do if I couldn't get into the wasteground — *where does this road take me to? where can I go from there? how can I find a way back home without getting the shit beaten out of me?* — and I was just beginning to realize that I didn't have a clue where I was going or what I was going to do, when suddenly I saw a gap in the fence. It was right at the end of the wasteground, just next to the parking lot of a grotty little docklands pub — a section of fence where the wire mesh had been ripped away from its supporting post and folded back, leaving just enough room to squeeze through into the wasteground.

I lunged through it, gashing my arm as I went, and then I quickly looked around to see where the Greenwell kids were. They'd all joined up again now, the six of them running in a ragged group along the road, no more than fifty feet behind me.

I got going again, running hard across the wasteground toward the gas towers.

I was feeling more hopeful now. I knew where I was again, and I knew where I was going, and I knew that if I could just get past the gas towers, then up the steep hill and into Back Lane, I'd probably be OK. I knew every inch of Back Lane, and once I was there, I'd have all kinds of options. I could head for home, or back toward the town park, or up the bank and into the old factory. If necessary, I could even just find somewhere to hide. So I was running without too much fear now, just running fast, but not too fast, trying to keep steady, trying to avoid all the rocks and garbage and holes in the ground . . .

The wasteground is a weird kind of place. I don't know what it used to be, or even if it used to be anything, but it's always had a really strange feel to it. It's hard to explain, but it's almost as if it's a separate little world, with its own unique atmosphere and terrain. The ground is mostly bare. An uneven expanse of crumbly old concrete, covered with a thin layer of sand and soil, it's dotted here and there with strange little bushes and stunted trees that never seem to get any bigger. There are piles of rocks and rubble all over the place, huge heaps of tangled metal, and several deep ponds full of oily gray water. The whole place looks gray. Even the bits of it that aren't gray — the bushes and the trees, the thick green moss surrounding the ponds — it all *looks* gray. But then, beyond all the grayness, on the high concrete walls that span the far side of the wasteground, where the skateboard kids spray-paint their comic-book scenes of cities and streets, there's a wonderful explosion of vibrant color. Metallic reds, sunburst yellows, purples and greens and electric blues . . .

It's incredible.

And then there's the atmosphere, the wasteground air, with its faint but insistent smell of gas. It's always been there, this vaguely unsettling odor, even though the gas towers have been empty for years, and it always seems to smell the same. It's never weaker, never stronger. It's always just *there* — an ever-present scent in the air. But the strangest thing of all is that as soon as you leave the wasteground, as soon as you step through the fence, or climb the bank into Back Lane, the smell of gas is suddenly gone.

So, yeah, like I said, it's a weird kind of place, the kind of place that makes you think . . . but I don't suppose I should have been thinking about it just then. Because if I hadn't been thinking about it just then, if I hadn't been gazing around as I ran, thinking about the weirdness of the wasteground, I might have seen the two kids standing in the shadows of the gas towers earlier, and I might have had more time to think . . .

But I didn't.

They were standing just to the right of the nearest gas tower, and I didn't see them until they'd stepped out in front of me, blocking my way, and I'd almost run into them. I stopped just in time, turned quickly to the left, and ran off around the other side of the tower. They didn't make much of an effort to get hold of me, and they didn't come rushing after me, either . . . and I suppose I should have realized then what was happening. But I was too busy being scared to think straight. It wasn't until I'd reached the other side of the tower, and I looked up to see where I was going, and I saw Wes Campbell standing in the middle of the path, looking at me with a mocking smile on his face . . .

That's when I realized what was happening.

SIXTEEN

"Hey, Boland," Campbell said to me. "You all right? You look a bit hot and bothered."

He'd chosen a good spot to wait for me. With the gas tower to my right and a thick spread of brambles to my left, he was blocking the only way forward. And I didn't have to look over my shoulder to know that the Greenwell kids were behind me. I could hear them — muttering and laughing, getting their breath back, lighting cigarettes.

I was trapped.

All I could do was stand there and watch as Campbell started moving toward me. Grinning softly, his eyes fixed coolly on mine, he didn't stop walking until he was almost on top of me.

As I stepped back a little, he raised his eyebrows and smiled at me.

"What's the matter?" he pouted. "Don't you like me?"

Someone behind me snickered.

I said to Campbell, "Pauly rang you, didn't he?"

Campbell shrugged. "Pauly's always ringing me."

"He told you I was at his house—"

I stopped talking as Campbell leaned in close to me and placed his finger on my lips. It was a curiously gentle gesture, almost intimate. But it was also incredibly menacing.

"Shhh," Campbell whispered, leaning in even closer. "You talk too much . . . you know that, don't you?"

I found myself nodding at him.

He stared at me for a moment, his eyes only inches from mine, then he slowly took his finger from my lips, smiled at me again, and took a step back. "I just want a little chat with you, OK? Just me and you . . . is that all right?"

I didn't know what to say to that, so I didn't say anything.

Campbell carried on staring at me for a while, then eventually he raised his eyes and looked over my shoulder, turning his attention to the Greenwell kids behind me. "All right," he told them, nodding his head, "you can go now. Wait for me back at the corner."

"How long you gonna be?" one of them said.

Campbell gave him a look. "Just wait for me."

I heard a few mutterings, the scuffle of moving feet, then the sound of shuffling footsteps as they all turned around and headed back across the wasteground. As Campbell watched them go, I wondered what they'd do if I turned around and called out to them — *Hey, hold on, don't go . . . don't leave me alone with him . . .*

But it was too late now.

They were gone.

And I *was* alone with him.

And he was looking at me as if he could do whatever he wanted.

And I didn't like it one bit.

"You're not going to do anything stupid, are you?" he said.

"No."

"That's good." He smiled. "Because I don't want to hurt you, I just want to talk to you. All you've got to do is keep your mouth shut and listen, and everything'll be all right. OK?"

"Yeah."

"That's not too difficult, is it?"

"No."

"Good." He jerked his head toward a stack of old bricks next to the gas tower. "Sit down over there."

I went over and sat down.

When Campbell came over and sat down next to me, I didn't know if he was sitting too close on purpose, or if it was just something he did without thinking—an instinctive tough-guy thing, invading your space to intimidate you. Whatever the reason, I found myself shuffling away from him, but almost immediately he put his arm around my neck and pulled me back toward him.

"Where are you going?" he said, tightening his arm.

"Nowhere," I muttered, almost choking. "I was just, you know . . . I was just getting comfortable . . ."

He loosened his grip and draped his arm around my shoulder. "Is that better?"

I couldn't say anything.

He grinned at me. "Are you *comfortable* now?"

I'd never felt less comfortable in all my life, but I nodded at him, anyway.

"Good," he said. "Now, listen . . . are you listening?"

"Yeah."

"Right . . . this is what you're going to do, OK? You're going to stop poking your nose into things that don't concern you. You're going to forget whatever you saw at the fair. And you're not going to ask any more questions about anything. Do you understand?"

"No . . ."

He sighed. "I thought you were supposed to be smart?"

"I don't know what you mean —"

"It's not *difficult*, for Christ's sake. You didn't see anything, you don't know anything, you don't *want* to know anything. Which bit of that don't you understand?"

"I was only asking Pauly about Raymond —"

"Who?"

"Raymond . . . Raymond Daggett."

"Who the fuck's Raymond Daggett?"

"He was with me the other night, you know . . . Saturday night, in Back Lane —"

"The spazzy kid?"

"Raymond's not —"

"Fuck *Raymond*," Campbell said angrily, gripping my neck again. "I don't give a shit about *Raymond* . . . this has got fuck all to do with *Raymond*. This is just me telling you to keep your fucking nose out, all right?"

"Or else what?" I heard myself say.

There was a split second's silence then, just enough time for me to wonder if I could have said anything *more* stupid, then Campbell's arm suddenly tightened around my neck and he leaned to one side and violently yanked my head down. As my body doubled over, my legs flew up into the air, and I ended up kind of half-sitting and half-lying on the stack of bricks, with one arm jammed under my chest, the other one scrabbling around, trying to find something to hold on to, and my head shoved down between Campbell's legs.

It was ridiculous.

I was scared to death.

But it was still ridiculous.

I could hardly breathe, my head was exploding with pain, but even as Campbell tightened his grip, squeezing my throat so hard that I thought my neck was going to snap . . . even then, I was still faintly aware that my head was shoved down between his legs, and that didn't feel right at *all*. I actually felt kind of embarrassed about it. God knows why. I mean, it wasn't as if I'd chosen to be in this situation, and there were far more *useful* things I could have been feeling than a vague sense of irrational embarrassment.

Or maybe there weren't?

Maybe that's what happens when you think you're going to die — you concentrate on the trivial things to take your mind off the horror. You think of embarrassment rather than pain. You concentrate on the spotless white jeans of your killer, rather than the fact that he's strangling you. You smell his scent, a darkly sweet perfume, and you wonder where you've smelled it before . . .

You think of the darkness, closing in around you . . .

The darkness.

The stars . . .

Going out.

Dark silence.

White plains.

The blackness . . .

It was everywhere now.

Hey!

It was a nice feeling . . . like sitting in a bubble of light . . .

Boland?

. . . in some kind of primitive consciousness . . .

Hey, Boland!

Someone was shaking me now, shaking the life back into me, and I could hear a distant voice in the sky.

"You listening to me, Boland?"

"Yuhh . . ."

A whisper.

"Look at me."

I opened my eyes. I was lying on the ground at Campbell's feet — lying on my back, looking up at him. My throat hurt. My neck hurt. The sun was too bright.

"Look at me."

I sat up slowly and looked at him. His face was blurred, cold and waxy.

"Next time I won't let go," he said. "Do you understand?"

I nodded, wincing at the pain in my neck.

Campbell squatted down in front of me and stared into my eyes. "No more questions, all right? You don't know anything. You didn't see anything. And this never happened." He reached out his hand and gently lifted my chin. "Do you hear me?"

"Yeah."

"Good."

He let go of my chin, patted my cheek, then got up and walked away.

SEVENTEEN

My neck started stiffening up quite badly as I walked back home along the lane, and every time I breathed in, I could hear a weird kind of scraping sound in my throat. My head was aching, too, and I had lights in my eyes — little flashing lights, like tiny white stars. But apart from that — and considering what Campbell had just done to me — I didn't actually feel too bad.

Not physically, anyway.

Mentally, I was falling apart.

I was scared, for one thing — and when I say scared, I mean *really* scared. Shaking-inside scared. *It's all right*, I kept telling myself. *It's nothing to worry about. It's just a delayed reaction, some kind of emotional aftershock . . . it's perfectly natural to feel like this.* But it didn't feel perfectly natural — it felt like I'd never feel normal again.

And I couldn't think, either. I just couldn't seem to get anything straight in my mind. The thoughts were there — thoughts, memories, facts, feelings — but I couldn't do anything with them. They wouldn't keep still. They just kept buzzing around in my head, like a room full of flies, and every time I tried to grab hold of one, all I'd get was a handful of nothing.

I couldn't reason.

I couldn't *connect* anything.

I had flies in my head.

And lights in my eyes.

You don't know anything. You didn't see anything . . .

Next time I won't let go.

The air was too hot to breathe.

When I reached the end of Back Lane and started crossing over to Hythe Street, I thought for a moment that the flashing lights in my eyes had suddenly gone into overdrive, and I wondered briefly if I was going to pass out again, but then I realized that the lights I was seeing now weren't white, they were blue, and they weren't the kind of lights that only I could see . . .

They were the flashing blue lights of police cars.

There were two of them, parked at the corner by the gate to the river, and as I crossed over St. Leonard's Road and started up Hythe Street, I could see more blue lights flashing farther down the street. A uniformed cop was stringing crime scene tape across the road, trying to keep back a growing crowd of onlookers, and there were other officers milling around the cars, talking on radios. I was vaguely aware of sirens wailing in the distance, and the faint *chop-chop* of a circling helicopter, but all I could really hear was the sound of my heart pounding in my chest as I pushed my way through the crowd and ducked under the crime tape.

They've found Raymond, I was thinking. *Oh God, they've found Raymond* . . .

"Hey!" the officer shouted, hurrying toward me. "Hey, *you!*"

I ignored him and kept walking. The gate to the river was open, marked off with crime tape, and two crime scene investigators in paper suits and overshoes were walking carefully along the edge of the path. As I neared the gate, the cop caught up with me, grabbing me by the arm and pulling me back.

"Come on," he said gruffly. "Out."

I tried pushing him away, but he was a pretty big guy, and as soon as I started struggling he just twisted my arm up around my back and began shoving me toward one of the police cars.

"Hold on," I said, "just a minute —"

"Shut up."

"No, you don't understand —"

"Mike!" he yelled at one of his uniformed colleagues. "Get this kid out of here, will you?"

I saw Dad then. He was coming up the street from the direction of our house, his eyes taking everything in, and when he saw me being shoved around by this big police officer, he immediately started running.

"Hey!" he shouted, waving his hand. "Hey, Diskin!"

The cop who was holding me looked in Dad's direction.

"What are you *doing*?" Dad called out to him. "Let him *go*!"

"Jeff?" Officer Diskin said as Dad came running up to him. "What are you—?"

"Let him go," Dad said breathlessly.

"But he was—"

"He's my son."

"Your son?"

As Dad nodded, Diskin loosened his grip on my arm.

Dad looked at me. "Are you all right?"

"Yeah . . ."

"What the hell are you doing?"

"Nothing . . . I was just—"

"He was heading down there," Diskin told Dad, indicating the gate. "I had to stop him. I didn't know—"

"What's going on, anyway?" Dad asked him, looking around. "Have they found something?"

Diskin hesitated. "I'm not sure . . . we were told, you know . . ."

"What? You were told not to tell me?"

The officer shrugged. "You'd better talk to the lead detective."

Dad looked at Diskin for a moment, then he just nodded. "Where is he?"

"I think he's still down at the river."

"Is Kesey with him?"

"I think so, yeah."

Dad nodded. "All right . . . thanks, Diskin."

Diskin smiled awkwardly. "Yeah . . . look, I'm sorry about this, Jeff. But you know how it is . . ."

"Yeah," Dad said. "I know how it is." He turned to me. "Come on, Pete, let's get you home."

But we didn't go home just then. As Officer Diskin went back to controlling the onlookers — who'd now been joined by a crowd of press reporters and TV crews — Dad led me off to a relatively quiet spot just behind one of the police cars. We were still inside the taped-off area — which I could see now was blocking off the street in both directions — and I could tell from the looks that Dad was getting from his colleagues that they all knew he wasn't supposed to be here, but none of them actually said anything.

"What's happening, Dad?" I said, rubbing my neck. "What have they found? Is it Raymond?"

"I don't know . . . I've only just woken up. I don't know any more than you do." He looked at me. "Are you all right? Did Diskin hurt you?"

"No," I told him. "I've just got a bit of a stiff neck."

Dad looked at me. "I thought you were supposed to be in your room?"

"I couldn't sleep . . . I went for a walk."

"Where?"

I shrugged. "Nowhere . . . I was just walking . . ."

He shook his head. "You're really starting to annoy me, Pete. I mean, look at all this . . ." He waved his hand around. "This is serious stuff — police, press, TV people . . . and you're part of it, Pete. You're *part* of it, for Christ's sake. You can't just keep wandering off on your own all the time—"

"Jeff?"

We both looked up at the sound of Dad's name, and I saw two men coming toward us from the direction of the gate. One of them was John Kesey, and I guessed the other one—an older man with a reddened face—was the lead detective, George Barry. Both of them were wearing suits, and they were both sweating hard in the afternoon sun. As they came up and stopped in front of us, Kesey gave Dad a friendly nod, but Barry just glared at him.

"What the hell are you doing here, Jeff?" he said sternly. "I thought we'd agreed—"

"I live here, sir," Dad told him calmly. "My house is just down the street. I didn't know this had anything to do with the investigation. I just saw all the commotion and came out to see what was happening."

"I see," said Barry.

"What *is* happening?" Dad asked Kesey.

"You don't need to know," Barry said before Kesey could answer.

As Kesey shrugged, half-smiling at Dad, I saw Barry glance at me.

"What's he doing here?" he asked Dad.

"Nothing," Dad sighed. "He was just trying to get back home."

"Well, get him out of here, for Christ's sake." Barry shook his head. "Come *on*, Jeff, you know we can't afford to mess this up. Go on home . . . now. Both of you."

"Yes, sir," said Dad.

He nodded at Kesey, and I saw a quick look pass between them, then he put his hand on my shoulder and led me away. As we ducked under the crime tape and started edging our way through the crowd, I could see cameras flashing from across the street. I could see people watching us, too. Neighbors, strangers, TV reporters. But I didn't really take any notice of them. I was too busy staring at the police car parked outside Raymond's house.

As soon as we got back home, Dad made a quick call on his mobile, then he told me to go and wait in the living room.

"Why?" I asked him. "What's going on?"

"Just do it, will you?" he said. "I'll be back in a minute."

As I went into the living room, I heard him go into the kitchen and start talking to Mum, and then I heard his mobile ring. I listened for a while, but I couldn't make out what he was saying, so I crossed over to the window and tried to see what was going on at Raymond's instead. I couldn't see all of his house from here, and most of the curtains were closed anyway, but I could see that the police car was still there.

I didn't know what that meant. Were the police just talking to his parents? Were they questioning them? Or were they giving them the bad news about what they'd just found at the river?

I didn't want to believe that.

I couldn't.

Christ, I couldn't even *think* about it.

I took a deep breath and rubbed the moisture from my eyes.

God . . .

I breathed in again, trying to steady myself . . . and suddenly something came to me. A smell . . . something in the air . . . something that reminded me of something. I sniffed again. Flowers. There was a vase of flowers on the windowsill. I leaned down and breathed in their scent. No, that wasn't it . . . it wasn't the *smell* of the flowers that reminded me of something, it was just the *memory* of smelling . . . smelling something else.

Smelling darkness.

That was it.

That darkly sweet scent that I'd smelled on Wes Campbell . . .

That was it.

I'd just remembered where I'd smelled it before.

The living room door opened then, and I turned to see Dad and John Kesey coming in. I quickly wiped my eyes again and moved away from the window.

"It's all right, Pete," Dad said, noticing the look in my eyes. "It's not Raymond. John's just filled me in on what they've found at the river, and at the moment it doesn't look as if it's got anything to do with Raymond."

I breathed out a sigh of relief.

It's not Raymond.

But the relief didn't last very long.

"What do you mean?" I asked Dad.

"Sorry?"

"You said that *at the moment* it doesn't look as if what they've found has got anything to do with

Raymond." I looked at him. "What have they found?"

Dad hesitated, glancing at Kesey.

"You might as well tell him," Kesey said. "It'll be all over the news soon, anyway."

Dad thought about it for a moment, then nodded. "All right," he said wearily. "But you have to realize that this is all unofficial, Pete. John shouldn't be here, and neither of us should be telling you anything. So, if anyone asks . . ."

"Yeah, I know. This never happened."

"Right."

We all sat down then — me and John Kesey on the sofa, and Dad in the armchair.

"A couple of hours ago," Dad said to me, "the police got a call from an old man about something he'd found by the river. He was walking his dog, apparently, and the dog went after a rabbit, and when it came out of the bushes it had a bloodstained shirt in its mouth."

"Shit," I breathed.

"Anyway," Dad went on, "this old chap called the police, and they sent some officers around to take a look . . . and they found some other things."

"What kind of things?"

Dad looked at Kesey.

"Clothing," Kesey said. "A pair of denim shorts, some underwear, a pair of black boots —"

"That's what *Stella* was wearing."

"Yeah, we know," Kesey told me. "Her parents have already identified the clothing as hers."

"What about Stella?" I said. "I mean, is she —?"

244

"There's no sign of her, so far," Kesey said. "We've got dozens of people down there now. They're scouring the whole area inch by inch. If she's down there, we'll find her."

I looked at Dad for a moment, then turned back to Kesey, and for the first time I wondered what he was doing here. If he wasn't *supposed* to be here, and he wasn't *supposed* to be telling us stuff that we weren't meant to know . . . then why *was* he here?

"Listen, Pete," he said somberly, shifting in his seat to face me. "I know this is all a bit confusing for you at the moment, but if there's anything you haven't told us yet, and I mean anything at *all* . . . well, now's the time to get it off your chest. Before things get too serious."

"What do you mean?"

"No one knows I'm here, OK? No one knows I'm talking to you. So anything you tell me now is strictly off the record. Do you understand what I'm saying?"

"Not really, no."

He sighed. "All I'm trying to say is — if you *know* something, anything, that can help me find out what happened, I can use it now without making it official. As long as we get the right result, no one's going to care where I got the information from." He looked at me. "I can keep you out of it, Pete. But you have to help me, and you have to do it now. We're not investigating a murder yet, but things aren't looking too good. And once it all starts kicking off . . . well, there won't be much I can do for you then."

"Why do you want to keep me out of it?"

"Why?" he said, frowning at me. "Why do you *think*? I've known your dad for years, that's *why*. We're friends, we look after each other. That's what friends *do*." He stared at me, narrowing his eyes. "And you're not *guilty* of anything, are you, Pete? I think you probably *know* something, but the only thing you're guilty of is keeping it quiet."

"Why would I do that?"

"You tell me." He looked at me. "Are you scared of something?"

"What?"

"Is someone threatening you?"

"No one's *threatening* me."

"So why won't you talk to us?"

"I *am* talking to you—"

"Are you trying to protect someone?"

"No."

"What about Raymond?"

"What about him?"

"Look, I know he's your friend, and I know you want to look after him—"

"That's what friends *do*, isn't it?"

Kesey smiled. "The best thing you can do for Raymond right now is tell us everything you know. If he's got anything to do with Stella—"

"He hasn't."

"Are you sure?"

"Raymond wouldn't hurt anyone."

"People do strange things, Pete. Especially if they're—"

"If they're *what*?" I said angrily. "There's nothing wrong with Raymond—"

"I didn't say there was—"

"He's not fucking ab*normal*—"

"Pete!" Dad snapped.

I ignored him, glaring at Kesey. "That's what this is all about, isn't it? All this *concern* for me, everybody wanting to *help* me . . . it's all *bollocks*. You're just trying to get to Raymond through me."

"That's not true—"

"Yeah, it is. You've already made up your mind about him, haven't you? He's a bit of a *weirdo*, he's gone missing at the same time as Stella, so he *must* have done something to her. That's it, isn't it? Simple as that."

"Nothing's simple—"

"Fucking right," I said.

Dad jumped out of his seat and came marching over to me then, and I knew that I'd gone too far, and that he was going to start yelling at me . . . but when I looked up at him, I was surprised to see that he didn't look angry at all. He just looked really worried, and a little bit scared. And then I realized that I was crying. And I started feeling pretty frightened myself, because I'd never cried like this before. I wasn't shaking or trembling or anything, I was just sitting there, perfectly still, and the tears were literally *pouring* down my face . . .

And I couldn't work out if the tears felt hot or cold.

Like blood or sweat.

And I didn't understand why it mattered.

But it did.

And that scared the hell out of me.

Dad decided not to go into work that night. I told him that I was OK, that he didn't have to stay at home for my sake, but he said that he wasn't just doing it for me, that he had a few things to talk over with Mum, anyway . . . which might have been true, or it might not. But it wasn't worth arguing about.

Anyway, he called the station and told them he wasn't coming in, and he spent most of the rest of that night in the living room with Mum. I sat with them for a while, drinking tea and half-heartedly nibbling at a sandwich, then I made my excuses and went upstairs to my room.

I turned on the TV, lay down on my bed, and watched Sky News.

The only fresh information they had about Stella was that she'd been due to fly out to Barbados with her parents on the Sunday morning to celebrate their twentieth wedding anniversary, which was why her parents had reported her missing so quickly. They'd been booked on a nine o'clock flight, and they'd been planning to leave home at six in the morning. So when Stella still hadn't returned by five, her parents had tried calling her mobile, only to find that it was dead — no answer, no dial tone, no voice mail, no nothing. They'd started ringing around then, calling everyone they could think of who might have known where Stella was, and after a while it became apparent that she hadn't been seen since the early hours of the morning. And that's when they'd called the police.

Apart from that, and the fact that several items of clothing had been found by a river in St. Leonard's, and that the police were still searching the area, the rest of the news was just a rehash of the same old stuff. There was no confirmation that the clothing was Stella's, and no mention of any blood, so I guessed the police were keeping as much information to themselves as possible. Not that the news reporters didn't keep *speculating*, of course. There was speculation about this, speculation about that . . . expert opinions, unconfirmed reports, discussions, views, theories, ideas, and lots and lots of film footage showing Stella's home, the fairground, the town park, the scene at the end of Hythe Street . . .

There was no mention of Raymond.

Nothing about a missing teenage boy.

And I wondered if that was another thing the police were trying to keep quiet. Or maybe, as Dad had admitted, Raymond just wasn't *news*. But I guessed it wouldn't be long before he was.

It was around nine o'clock when my mobile rang. I was still lying on my bed, staring at the TV, still trying to get my head around everything . . .

I flipped open the phone and put it to my ear. "Hello?"

"Pete?"

"Yeah."

"It's Eric. Can you talk?"

"Sorry?"

"Is it safe to talk? I mean, your dad's not there, is he?"

"No, I'm on my own."

"Great. Listen, I just wanted to talk to you about Saturday night, you know . . . all this stuff about Stella? Shit . . . have you seen what they're saying on the news? They think they've found some of her clothes at the river—"

"Yeah, I know."

"Shit," he said again. "I just can't believe it. I mean, I know this kind of stuff happens, but when it's someone you know, and it happens really close to you . . . I mean, the *river*, for God's sake. You can almost *see* the river from your place—"

"I know."

"Yeah, yeah . . . of course you do." I heard him light a cigarette. "Do you think they've found anything else?"

"Like what?"

"I don't know . . . I just thought you might have heard something. You know, from your dad . . ."

I didn't say anything.

Eric cleared his throat. "I mean, is your dad, you know . . . ? Has he been talking to you about it?"

"Why do you want to know?"

"Come *on*, Pete," he said, slightly irritated. "Look, I'm *sorry* I lied to you about Saturday night, OK? But it didn't mean anything. I was just—"

"Yeah, I know," I told him. "Nic's already explained everything. It's all right, Eric. You don't have to apologize."

"Yeah, well . . . it's just a bit embarrassing, that's all. You know how it is when you get a bit drunk . . ."

"Yeah."

"Anyway, the thing is . . . well, it's just that it could make things a bit awkward for me now. I mean, the police are probably going to want to talk to us about Stella, aren't they?"

I kept quiet, waiting for him to go on.

"Do you think they *will* want to talk to us?" he said.

"Probably."

"Yeah, they'll have to, won't they? We all knew her, and we were all there . . . and they've got that film of her blowing off Nic—"

"And you used to go out with her."

"What?"

"You used to go out with Stella."

"Yeah, but—"

"They'll probably want to talk to *all* her old boyfriends."

"Yeah, I suppose . . ." He anxiously cleared his throat again. "That's what I mean, though, Pete. If the police find out that I lied to you about where I was on Saturday night . . . well, it could make things a bit difficult for me. So, you know, I need to know . . ."

"You want to know who I've talked to. Is that it?"

"Yeah."

"You think I might have told the police that you lied to me?"

"I don't know, do I? Look, I'm not saying you would have done it on *purpose* or anything . . . I mean, I don't even know if you've talked to the police yet, anyway."

"I have."

"Really?"

"Yeah."

"What did you tell them?"

I had to think about that. I really had to sift through all the things I'd told Dad and John Kesey about Saturday night . . . and all the things I *hadn't* told them, too. It was hard to remember, and for some reason it made me feel kind of detached from myself. It was like thinking about lots of different Pete Bolands. There was the Pete Boland who'd talked to Dad in the kitchen after seeing Black Rabbit's severed head on the gate. There was the Pete Boland who'd talked *officially* to John Kesey, and the Pete Boland who'd talked to him unofficially. And there was the Pete Boland who was trying to remember it all now.

"Pete?" said Eric. "Are you still there?"

"Yeah, hold on, I'm just thinking . . ."

"What's there to *think* about?" he said sharply.

"Do you want me to tell you or not?" I snapped back at him.

"Yeah," he said, "yeah . . . sorry. I'm just a bit —"

"I told them the truth, Eric. That's all. I told them that I went around to your place after the fair, that no one was in, and that I fell asleep on the step."

"So they know I didn't go home?"

"Yeah."

"But not that I lied to you about it?"

"No."

"Thanks, Pete," he sighed. "God . . . that's a relief."

There was so much I wanted to say to him then — *you can keep your thanks, Eric . . . I know you're still lying . . . I notice you haven't mentioned Raymond at all . . . and, by the way, have you heard from Wes Campbell recently?* — but I could hear that soundless voice again, that unknown whisper in the back of my mind, and it was telling me to keep my thoughts to myself.

And, besides, I'd just heard Dad's footsteps coming up the stairs.

So I just said, "I've got to go now, Eric," and before he could reply, I quickly ended the call.

EIGHTEEN

"How are you feeling?" Dad asked me.

"I'm OK. Just a bit . . . you know . . ."

He looked at me, nodding his head. He was sitting across the room at my desk, and I was still sitting on my bed. He looked tired.

"Mum's really worried about you," he said. "She says you've been feeling a bit down recently, and now she's worried that all this stress and everything might be getting too much for you."

"She worries too much," I said.

Dad smiled at me. "That's what I told her. Mind you, that's what I always tell her, and it's hardly ever true." His smile faded. "Look, I'm not going to pretend that I know how you feel, Pete, because I don't. But I know what something like this can do to you. I know how it can mess up your head. But if there's anything more to it than that — and I'm not asking you to tell me what it is — but if there *is* anything else, any problems, anything that's been troubling you . . . just tell me, OK? We don't have to sort it out now, we don't even have to talk about it if you don't want to, but if Mum's right, and there *is* something else worrying you, I just need to know."

I looked at him, wondering briefly what he would say if I *did* tell him the truth — *well, actually, Dad, I think I might be going a bit mad . . . I mean, I know I'm not going mad, but I keep doing things and seeing things and hearing things that don't make any sense . . .*

"I'm all right, Dad," I said. "Honest . . . I'm OK."

"Really?"

"Well, no . . . I'm not *OK*. I mean, I feel really terrible about Raymond and Stella and everything, you know . . . but apart from that . . ."

"You're OK?"

I shrugged. "Yeah . . ."

He nodded slowly, giving me a long, hard look. It was one of those looks that you just have to sit there and take. So that's what I did. I just sat there, holding his gaze, hoping he couldn't see — or didn't *want* to see — the lies in my eyes.

"Well, all right," he said after a while, "but I think you'd better have a chat with your mum about things . . . try to put her mind at rest."

"Yeah, I will."

He paused for a moment, gazing thoughtfully around my room, but I could tell he wasn't really looking at anything. He was just preparing himself, thinking about what he was going to say next. I guessed it was going to be something to do with Saturday night, something to do with Raymond or Stella, but when he finally got around to focusing on me again, there was something in his eyes that told me I was only partly right.

And I was.

"You don't think much of John Kesey, do you?" he said.

I stared at him, slightly taken aback, not sure what to say.

"It's all right," Dad said. "I'm used to people not liking John. Your mother can't stand the sight of him." He smiled at me. "You don't have to pretend to like him just because he's my friend."

I shrugged. "I don't really know him well enough to like him or not."

"But you probably don't like what you *do* know about him, do you?"

"I don't know," I said, shrugging again. "I mean, I don't really see what difference it makes."

Dad smiled. "John's a good copper, Pete. He's a good man, and he's been a really good friend to me over the years. I'm not saying he's perfect or anything . . . I mean, he's got his problems. Well, one problem, really. He drinks too much." Dad looked at me. "Most of the time it doesn't stop him from doing his job, but sometimes . . . well, sometimes he needs a bit of help. You know, he needs looking after."

"Is that why Mum doesn't like him?"

Dad nodded. "She doesn't think he's worth it. She thinks I'm putting my job at risk."

Neither of us said anything for a while then. Dad just sat there, deep in thought, and I stared blankly at the flickering light of the mute TV. The sun had gone down now, and the sky outside was fading from twilight to dark. The room was dim. The TV was bright. I couldn't take my eyes off it. The faces, the people, the colors, the shapes . . .

It was all meaningless.

"Listen, Pete," Dad said, "the reason I'm telling you all this —"

"You don't have to explain, Dad."

"Yes, I do."

I looked at him. His face glowed eerily in the TV light, and just for a moment — a strange little moment — he was suddenly someone else, someone I'd never seen before. He was still my dad, but I didn't seem to *know* him anymore. It was kind of scary for a second or two, but as I rubbed my eyes and stared at him, the light from the TV shimmered and brightened and the non-Dad instantly morphed back into Dad again.

"What's the matter?" he asked me. "Are you all right?"

I nodded.

He looked carefully at me. "Are you sure?"

"Yeah," I told him. "I'm just tired, that's all."

He carried on looking at me for a while, his eyes full of doubt, but there was nothing for him to see anymore. I wasn't rubbing my eyes, I wasn't seeing things that weren't there. I was just sitting on my bed, looking slightly tired, waiting for him to go on. There was nothing wrong with me.

"All right, listen," he said eventually. "The first thing you need to understand is that John Kesey really *is* just trying to help you. I mean, he might be doing it for me, because he thinks he owes me, and he might be cutting a few corners to do it . . . but that's the way it goes sometimes. You do whatever's necessary. You have to do what you think is right." He smiled at me. "You can trust him, Pete. That's all I'm saying. He wants to help you, he wants to help both of us."

"Yeah," I said, "but I don't see how —"

"Just listen to me a minute," Dad said. "OK? Just listen . . ." He sighed. "Look, I'm a police officer, Pete. It's my job to stop the bad stuff happening. And when it does happen, it's my job to find out who did it and make sure they can't do it again." He leaned forward and looked intently at me. "That's what I *do*, Pete. And I do it because . . . well, I do it because I really *believe* in it. Do you understand?"

"Yeah."

"It's more than just a job, you know . . . it's something special. It's something that *means* something to me." He paused for a moment, looking down at the floor, then he took a deep breath and looked back up at me. "But I'm your dad, too, Pete. You're my son. And that means more to me than anything else in the world."

We looked at each other then, neither of us knowing what to say — both of us feeling stupidly embarrassed. But it was OK — we didn't *have* to say anything else. We just had to look at each other.

It was still kind of hard for us, though, and after a moment or two, Dad sniffed a couple of times and cleared his throat, and I just kind of nodded a bit, as if I was somehow agreeing with him.

"So, anyway," he said, trying to sound casual again, "I suppose all I'm trying to say is . . . well, you know . . . I'm just trying to explain where I *am* in all this, or maybe where I'd like to be." He shook his head and grinned at me. "I'm probably not doing a very good job of it, though, am I?"

"You're doing all right," I told him.

He paused for a moment, a quick smile of gratitude, then he carried on. "I just want to know what happened, Pete. It's as simple as that, really. I want to find out what's happened to Raymond and Stella. And, as a police officer, I know you could help me to do that. Even if you don't *think* you know anything useful, you were *there*. You were with Raymond. You know him. And you know Stella, too. And you also know people who know them both." He looked at me. "If I was part of this investigation, you'd be the first person I'd want to talk to."

"But you're not part of the investigation," I said quietly.

"No, I'm not. But I know what's going to happen. I know how it all works. And I know they're going to be looking really closely at you. And, as your dad, there's no way I'm going to let that happen without giving you as much help as I can."

"Meaning what?" I said.

He shrugged. "We tell each other what we know."

"But I thought you said—?"

"Yeah, I know. I'm not supposed to talk to you about Raymond and Stella. But, like I said before, sometimes you just have to do what's necessary. You have to do what you think is right."

"Right for who?"

"For me, for you, for your mum . . . for Raymond and Stella . . ." He shook his head. "I can't just sit back and not do anything, Pete. It's all too close to me. It means too much."

"Yeah, but what *can* you do?" I said. "I mean, if you can't get involved in the case, and you don't know what's going on—"

"I *do* know what's going on."

"How?"

"John's been keeping me up-to-date. I know *exactly* what's going on, and as soon as anything else happens, I'll know that, too. And so will you."

"Me?"

Dad nodded. "If you want to know . . . I'll tell you."

"But isn't that—?"

"Inappropriate? Yes, it's *totally* inappropriate. And if you want to tell me anything, and I pass that on to John, that's going to be totally inappropriate, too. And if anyone finds out, we're all going to be in big trouble. But I'm willing to take that risk if you are."

"Why?" I said.

"I'm a police officer," he said simply. "I believe in what I do." He looked at me. "And you're my son, and I believe in you, too."

For the next hour or so, Dad told me everything he knew about the investigation so far. Stella's clothes, he explained, the clothes she'd been wearing at the fair, were being forensically examined right now, and the bloodstains had already been matched to her blood type. Further tests for DNA and any other traces would take a while longer. The police were still searching all around the riverbank, he told me, checking out the woods and the bank and all the little pathways, and a team of divers had begun a painstaking search of the river itself, but there was still no sign of a body. Officially, the police were still keeping an open mind, and the case was still being treated as a missing persons inquiry, but it was generally assumed that it was only a matter of time before Stella's body showed up.

"What about Raymond?" I said. "Is he still being treated as just a missing person?"

Dad looked at me. "I know it's hard for you, Pete, but you're going to have to start accepting that Raymond's disappearance can't simply be dismissed as a coincidence. He's missing, Stella's missing, they were both at the fair —"

"Yeah, right," I said sarcastically. "So Raymond *must* have killed her."

"I didn't say that."

"No, but that's what everyone's going to think."

"We have to take everything into consideration, Pete. If Raymond's unbalanced —"

"He's not un*balanced*. He's no more unbalanced than I am."

Dad shook his head. "That's not true."

"Isn't it?"

"His home's a mess, his parents are a mess, he's been bullied and troubled all his life." Dad looked at me. "You might be going through a difficult time at the moment, Pete, but whatever your problems are, they're nothing compared to Raymond's right now. He should have been given some help a long time ago."

"I helped him."

"Yeah, I know you did . . . you helped him because he's got problems."

"Yeah, all right," I admitted, "he's got a few problems. But that doesn't mean he's done anything wrong."

"It doesn't mean he hasn't, either. People with problems can do all kinds of things. Believe me, Pete, I've seen the evidence. I know what a troubled mind can do to a person."

I thought about that for a while, trying to imagine Raymond's state of mind, and what it could do to him, what it could *make* him do . . . and I was surprised to find that I *could* imagine it. I could see him doing dark things, bad things, wrong things . . . but it wasn't *right*. It wasn't Raymond — it was an imaginary Raymond. A nightmare Raymond. And I didn't want him in my head.

I ran my hand over my face, wiping my mind clean, and turned to Dad. "Have the police got anything that actually links Raymond with Stella?"

"Not as far as I know. But they're going to be searching his house, looking into his background, seeing if they can find anything. They've already started examining the dead rabbit and the hutch and everything. It's all a bit of a mess down there after the rain, so they probably won't find much in the way of footprints or anything, but they might get something from the rabbit—"

"I left my backpack there," I said, suddenly remembering.

"What?"

"My backpack . . . I left it in Raymond's shed before we went to the fair."

"Why?"

"Why what?"

Dad sighed. "Why did you leave your backpack in Raymond's shed? What was in it?"

"The bottle of wine," I said, feeling pretty stupid. "You know, the one I stole from you . . . I put it in the backpack so Mum wouldn't see it when I left."

Dad grinned. "Did you think I wouldn't miss it?"

"Yeah, I suppose . . ."

He nodded. "Did you enjoy it?"

"Not really . . ." I looked at him. "I'm sorry, Dad."

He smiled at me. "It doesn't matter."

It doesn't matter.

The whispered echo came from the top of the chest of drawers.

"What?" I muttered, glancing over at the porcelain rabbit.

"What?" said Dad.

I looked at him. "What?"

He stared at the rabbit for a moment, then turned back to me. "What are you doing?"

"Nothing . . . I thought I heard something, that's all. A mouse or something . . . behind the chest of drawers."

Dad's eyes narrowed as he glanced over at the rabbit again, and I could see a germ of suspicion growing in his eyes.

"Where did they find Stella's clothes?" I said, trying to distract him.

"What?"

"Stella's clothes . . . Dad?"

"At the river," he said, still studying the rabbit.

"Yeah, I know . . . but whereabouts at the river?"

He finally tore his eyes away from the rabbit and turned back to me. "They were in some bushes at the foot of the bank, just behind that trailer."

"By the *trailer*?"

He nodded. "There was some blood on the trailer, too. At the back . . . on the same side as the bushes. Forensics are checking it out. The trailer's being searched and they're questioning the owner."

"Raymond knows him," I said, sitting up straight.

"Who?"

"The guy who lives in the trailer . . . we saw him at the top of the street on Saturday night when we were going to the fair. He was coming over the gate. Raymond nodded at him, you know . . . like he knew him. And the guy nodded back. When I asked Raymond who he was, he said he didn't know, he'd just seen him down at the river a few times."

"His name's Tom Noyce," Dad told me. "He was taken in for questioning earlier today. His mother works at the fairground. She's a fortune-teller —"

"She's a *what*?"

"A fortune-teller. You know . . . Tarot cards, crystal balls, all that kind of stuff. She calls herself Madame Baptiste, but her real name's Lottie Noyce. As far as we can tell, her son helps her out sometimes, and he seems to travel around with the rest of the carnival, but for some reason he always parks his trailer away from the other vehicles . . ."

I tried to listen as Dad carried on talking, but my head was filling up with flies again. Disconnected flies, flies of connection, old flies and new flies. The old flies were still there, buzzing away like crazy — Campbell and Pauly, Pauly and Eric, Eric and Campbell, Stella and Raymond, Nicole and me — but now there was a whole bunch of new ones, too. Tom Noyce and Raymond, Tom and his mother, Lottie Noyce, Madame Baptiste, Raymond and Madame Baptiste . . .

It's your fate, Raymond.

Life is not life without death.

The Ace of Spades . . .

Flies.

"Pete?"

I couldn't connect anything.

"Pete?"

There were too many flies.

"Are you *listening* to me, Pete?"

I looked at Dad. "What?"

"I said I'll let John Kesey know about Raymond and Tom Noyce. John's not involved in Noyce's questioning himself, but he'll find a way to pass on the information without letting anyone know that it came from us." He looked at me. "Was that the only time you saw Tom Noyce on Saturday?"

"Yeah."

"You didn't see him at the fair?"

I shook my head. "Do you think he's got something to do with it?"

Dad shrugged. "Who knows?"

His mother, probably, I thought to myself. *His mother probably knows.*

But I didn't say anything.

I didn't really say anything at all after that, I just listened as Dad tried to tell me what to expect over the next few days.

John Kesey hadn't been able to give him any details yet, but they were both pretty sure that at some point soon the police were going to start taking witness statements, and that I was probably going to be one of the first on their list.

"They'll want to talk to everyone who was with Raymond that night," Dad explained, "and everyone who was with Stella, too. It'll be a formal interview this time, so they'll take you down to the station, and they'll want you to give them a written statement. I've talked to your mum about it, and she's going to be with you—"

"Can't I go on my own?" I said.

"No."

"Why not?"

"Because you can't," Dad said firmly. "You have to have someone with you, and I can't do it, so that leaves either a lawyer or your mum. And at this stage I'd rather keep lawyers out of it. So your mum's going with you, whether you like it or not. OK?"

"Yeah, I suppose . . ."

"John's going to try and let me know *when* they decide to take you in, but he might not be in a position to find out."

"Why not?"

"Well, it's complicated . . . I mean, they might give us prior notice, but it's an unusual situation, and although I'm not supposed to be discussing things with you, they probably know that I am, so they might just turn up without any warning. That's why I'm telling you all this now."

He went on to explain what would happen in the interview—how they'd talk to me, what kinds of things they'd ask, what I should do. Apparently, all I had to do was stay calm and tell the truth, and everything would be OK.

Nothing to worry about.

No problems at all.

Simple as that.

Just tell the truth . . .

And everything would be OK.

It was too hot to sleep that night, and as I lay in bed trying to think about things — trying to work out why everything *wasn't* so simple — I kept feeling drawn to the porcelain rabbit on my chest of drawers. Every time I looked over at it, I could see its eyes shimmering in the darkness, and the air seemed to whisper with the coming of a voice . . . and every time I looked away again, the soundless whispering stopped. I didn't know what to do. If I closed my eyes, I saw bad things — dark things, mind things, confusing pictures, flashing lights . . . but if I kept my eyes open, I started seeing other things — carnival lights, carousels, rabbit heads, giants. And all the time, somewhere in the back of my mind, I could hear the sound of flies.

I lay still, soaking up the heat of the night, and I imagined myself burning. I spread out my arms, imagining the heat, and I imagined my pores opening up and the sweat pouring out of me, and I imagined the flies in my head pouring out with it . . . and I knew it was all ridiculous — lying there in the middle of the night, spread out on the bed like a sweat-soaked Jesus — but the longer I lay there, the less ridiculous it seemed, and after a while I began to feel something happening.

My head was emptying.

The flies were leaving me.

I don't know where they went, but within half an hour or so I knew that most of them had gone. And when I looked inside myself, all that was left was a pair of simplified outlines — the outlines of two black flies. But they were on their own now, and they weren't moving, so I could see them for what they really were.

One of them was the memory of a sound, a voice . . . a voice on the telephone earlier that night. It was Eric's voice, asking me if I thought the police would want to talk to us about Stella. And when I'd told him that they probably would, he'd said *Yeah, they'll have to, won't they? We all knew her . . .*

We all knew her.

Not, We all *know* her.

We all *knew* her.

The second thing left in my head was the memory of a scent, a perfume . . . a memory I'd already remembered but tried to forget. It was the perfume I'd smelled on Wes Campbell when he was choking the life out of me down at the gas towers, that darkly sweet scent that had made me wonder where I'd smelled it before . . . and now I knew where I'd smelled it before.

It was the same perfume that Nic had been wearing on Saturday night.

NINETEEN

ad was right about the police turning up without any warning, but he was also right about John Kesey letting us know. So when the unmarked police car pulled up outside our house at ten o'clock the next morning, we'd not only been waiting for it for almost an hour, but we also knew who was in it and who was going to be questioning me at the station.

As the doorbell rang, and Dad went to answer it, I went into the kitchen with Mum and we both sat down at the table.

"Shouldn't one of us be doing something?" I said to her.

"Like what?"

"I don't know . . . anything. Dad told us to act normally, didn't he? Act as if we're not expecting anyone." I looked at her, sitting rigidly opposite me, and I couldn't help smiling. "We couldn't look less normal if we tried."

"Speak for yourself," she said.

I heard the front door closing then. Muttered voices in the hallway. Footsteps coming toward the kitchen . . .

"Go on, then," Mum whispered, "talk to me."

"What about?"

"Anything . . . just pretend we're having a chat."

"A chat?"

She gave me a very false-looking chatty smile. "Yes, a *chat* . . . you know, a talk, a discussion."

I smiled at her. "What do you want to discuss?"

Before she could answer, the kitchen door opened and Dad ushered two men inside. One of them was Detective Barry, the other one was a younger man with a beaky nose and a mop of curly black hair.

"I think you both know George Barry," Dad said to Mum and me.

We both nodded.

Barry nodded back.

Dad gestured toward the younger man. "And this is Officer Gallagher."

More nods.

"They want to talk to Pete about Raymond," Dad explained to Mum. "He'll have to go down to the station with them."

"Why?" said Mum, looking at Barry. "Why can't you talk to him here?"

Barry looked at Dad.

Dad said to Mum, "It's all right, love. It's just routine. They need to take Pete's fingerprints and record the interview. There's nothing to worry about."

Barry said, "You're very welcome to accompany your son if you wish, Mrs. Boland."

Mum looked at him. "Are you asking him to come with you? Or are you telling him?"

Barry smiled wearily, like he'd heard it all before. "At this stage, we're just asking." He looked at me for the first time then. "Is that OK with you, Peter?"

I looked at Dad.

He nodded.

I looked back at Barry. "Have you found Raymond yet?"

"We can talk about that at the station."

The street was pretty quiet when we left the house and followed Barry and Gallagher to their car. The top end of the road was still taped off, and the path to the river was quietly busy with search teams and CSIs calmly going about their business. Two police vans were parked outside Raymond's house, and as I followed Mum into the back of Detective Barry's car, I saw a figure in protective clothing coming out of Raymond's front door carrying a computer terminal in a clear plastic bag.

The interview room at the police station wasn't as stark and intimidating as the interview rooms you see on TV, but apart from that it looked pretty much the same: plain white walls, a dark carpet, a table, four chairs. There was a double tape deck on a shelf in one corner, and a stack of video equipment on a table against the far wall.

I was seated beside Mum, and Barry and Gallagher were sitting opposite us. As Gallagher turned on the tape recorder, and Barry started explaining all kinds of stuff about why I was here, and how I was free to leave at any time, I looked down at my freshly washed hands and rubbed at the traces of fingerprint ink that were still ingrained in my skin. They'd taken my fingerprints shortly after we'd arrived at the station. I could have refused, just as I could have refused to let them take a sample of my DNA, but they'd told me it was purely for purposes of elimination, and that it might help to speed up their inquiries about Raymond . . . so I didn't really have much choice.

I rubbed at the ink on my fingers again, staring at the faint patterns on my fingertips — the whorls and loops, the islands and ridges — and for a moment I saw them as contours on a map, and I felt as if I was way up in the sky, looking down at a landscape of mountains and hills . . .

"Is that OK, Peter?"

I looked up at Detective Barry. "Sorry?"

"Do you understand what I've just been telling you?"

"Yeah."

"Are you sure?"

"Yeah, I understand."

"Good." He smiled tightly. "Well, let's get started then."

For the first ten minutes or so, everything was pretty straightforward. Detective Barry asked me what happened on Saturday night, I started telling him, and Officer Gallagher wrote it all down. Every now and then, Barry would stop me briefly and ask me to clarify something — what time it was, or some little detail about something — but most of the time he didn't say anything at all. He just sat there, staring at me, listening intently to my every word.

But then, just after I'd told him about seeing Tom Noyce, and how Raymond had seemed to know him, Barry suddenly asked me a question I wasn't expecting.

"Tell me about Raymond," he said.

"What do you mean?"

Barry smiled at me. "You've known him a long time?"

"Yeah, since we were kids."

"What's he like?"

"What do you mean?"

"Well, how would you describe him?"

I shrugged. "Shortish, dark hair—"

"No," said Barry. "I don't mean physically, I mean what kind of person is he?"

"What kind of person?"

Barry nodded. "Is he quiet? Noisy? Shy? Sociable? Does he get on well with other people?"

"He's pretty quiet," I said. "I wouldn't say he's all that sociable."

"Why not?"

"I don't know, he's just a bit . . ."

"A bit what?"

I looked at Mum.

She said to Barry, "Raymond's always been a bit of a—"

"I'm sorry, Mrs. Boland," Barry said, holding up his hand. "I'd rather hear it from Peter, if you don't mind." He smiled quickly at her, then looked back at me again. "You were saying?"

I stared at him for a moment, annoyed by his patronizing smile, but then I remembered what Dad had told me—*stay calm*—and I took a deep breath and carried on. "Raymond's just a bit different," I told Barry. "He's had a lot of problems, I suppose—"

"What kind of problems?"

"Bullying, problems at home . . . that kind of stuff."

"Would you say he's an introvert?"

"I suppose so, but not in a—"

"Has he got a temper?"

"No."

"Has he ever shown any odd behavior?"

"Like what?"

"Anything out of the ordinary . . ."

"We all do strange things now and then."

Barry smiled. "That's true. But this isn't about us, is it? This is about Raymond. Has he ever been violent at all?"

"No," I said firmly. "Never."

"He's never retaliated to any bullying or anything?"

"No."

"Does he have a girlfriend?"

"What's that got to do with anything?"

"Just answer the question, please. Does Raymond have a girlfriend?"

"Not that I know of."

"Has he ever had a girlfriend?"

"I don't know . . ."

"Boyfriend?"

"He's not gay—"

"Girlfriend, then."

"I already told you. I don't *know* if he's ever had a girlfriend or not."

Barry frowned. "He's your friend, isn't he?"

"Yeah."

"A close friend?"

"Yeah."

"Well, surely you'd know if he'd ever had a girlfriend or not?"

"He doesn't tell me everything."

"Does he tell you what he thinks about things?"

"What kind of things?"

"Girls, sex . . ." He smiled. "The usual kind of things that boys talk about."

"Excuse me," Mum butted in, "but is all this really *necessary*?"

Barry looked at her. "I wouldn't be asking if it wasn't."

"Yes, but surely—"

"Please, Mrs. Boland," he said, holding up his hand again. "I understand your concerns, but would you please let Peter answer my questions?"

Mum shook her head, showing her displeasure, but she kept any further thoughts to herself.

Barry turned back to me again. "Look, Peter," he said, "I'm just trying to build up a picture of Raymond's character. His personality. Do you understand? If I can get inside his head—"

"I know exactly what you're doing," I told him. "You're trying to find out if Raymond is some kind of twisted pervert or something. You want to know if he's fucked up enough to go crazy and—"

"Pete!" Mum snapped. "There's no need for that!"

"Yeah, but—"

"I know you're upset," she said sternly, "but there's no need for language like that."

"Yeah, well," I said sulkily, staring at Barry. "It's true, isn't it? That's what you're trying to do."

"I'm just trying to do my job, Peter," he said. "That's all. I need to find out if Raymond's disappearance has anything to do with Stella's."

"Yeah, but what if it hasn't?"

"Well, if that's the case—"

"You're not even considering it, are you? You're just assuming that Raymond's got something to do with whatever's happened to Stella."

"We're not *assuming* anything—"

"No?"

Barry just stared at me for a while then, his eyes cold and hard, and it was pretty obvious that he was getting pissed off with me. I was questioning his integrity. I was accusing him of jumping to conclusions. I was being a pain in the arse. And he didn't like it at all.

"All right, Terry," he said quietly to Officer Gallagher. "I think we'd better take a look at the tape."

I watched curiously as Gallagher took a videotape from a bag at his feet and took it over to the VCR. He slotted it in, picked up a remote, and came back over to the table. I looked at Barry. His face showed nothing, but there was something in his eyes that made me think I was about to see something that I'd prefer not to see.

It wasn't hard to guess what it was.

Barry nodded at Gallagher. Gallagher pointed the remote at the VCR and pressed PLAY. As the screen flickered into life, I recognized the images immediately: Stella at the fair, her laughing face, Nicole looking grim in the background. It was the same piece of film that Sky News had been showing over the last few days, only this time it had sound. I could hear Stella's laughter, the crash and boom of the rides in the background, the music, the crowds, excited voices . . .

"I'm sure you've seen all this before," Barry commented. "The footage was shot by an independent filmmaker called Jonathan Lomax. He's been making a documentary about Stella over the last few months, traveling around with her, filming her wherever she goes . . . you know the kind of thing." He paused for a moment, looking at the screen, watching the bit where Stella blew off Nic, then he turned back to me and continued. "Unfortunately for us, Mr. Lomax has been busy selling his film to the TV companies, so it's taken us a while to persuade him to let us see the rest of it." Barry gave me a look. "We've persuaded him now, though. And it's proved very interesting." He nodded at Gallagher. Gallagher hit the FAST-FORWARD button, and I watched in hopeless silence as the blur of images sped inevitably toward my meeting with Stella and Raymond.

Mum looked at me. "Do you know what this is about, Pete?"

I shrugged, unable to speak.

I heard a click as Gallagher stopped the tape, then another as he pressed PLAY again. The film started playing, the soundtrack filled the room, and for the next five minutes or so, no one said anything. We all just sat there, watching and listening as the fairground lights flashed, the music blared, the drums crashed . . . and after a while, I began to feel that I was back there again. I could *feel* it all again, thumping away in my heart—people screaming, sirens wailing, everything spinning . . . whirling wheels, stars and spaceships, thousands of faces, a million booming voices swirling around in the air—*HERE WE GO!! HERE WE GO!! EVERYONE'S A WINNER!! . . . IT'S C-C-C-C-CRAZEEE!!!*—the lights burning my eyes, the crash of the rides rolling and ripping all around me—TERMINATOR! METEOR! TWISTER! FUN HOUSE!—throwing out madness into the night . . .

The film rolled on.

It was hard to distinguish Stella at first. There were so many people—pushing and shoving, laughing and shouting—and the camera was jiggling around all over the place, jerking and zooming, moving in and out of focus . . . but then a close-up of Stella's face suddenly appeared, and the camera panned out, and all at once I could see her quite clearly. Bouncing along, smiling and waving, surrounded by her entourage and crowds of curious onlookers. She had her arm around Raymond's shoulder, and now she was hugging him, talking to him, smiling her bright white smile at him.

He was smiling, too.

And I was close to crying.

I almost told Barry to stop the tape then. I just couldn't stand it. The images of Raymond and Stella, their smiles, their eyes . . . it was like looking at pictures of dead people.

♥ ♠ ♦ ♣

You know that feeling you get when someone's died, and you see their photograph on the TV, or in the newspaper, and even though they were alive when the picture was taken, you somehow just *know* they're not alive anymore? Well, that's how I felt as I sat there watching Raymond and Stella on the screen. There was just something about them — an emptiness, a lack of presence . . . something missing. Something that told me they weren't here anymore.

I felt as if I was watching ghosts.

And I didn't want to watch ghosts.

But I knew Detective Barry wasn't going to stop the tape, and even if I closed my eyes, I'd still be able to hear it. And hearing it in the darkness of my head would probably only make it even worse. So I didn't say anything, and I didn't close my eyes, I just swallowed my tears and kept on watching.

The screen-Stella was kissing Raymond now . . . holding him close, planting her bright red lips on his cheek. But she wasn't looking at him. Her eyes were grinning at the camera. And as she kissed him again, smearing lipstick all over his face, I could see all the people around her smiling at each other, having a good laugh, watching the beauty playing with the beast . . .

Teasing him like a dog.

And Raymond was just going along with it — smiling at Stella, wide-eyed and excited, grinning while everyone laughed at him . . .

I still didn't get it.

Raymond *wasn't* stupid.

He *must* have known what was going on.

I watched, barely breathing now, as the camera panned away from Raymond and focused on a familiar-looking figure shambling through the crowds toward Stella, and as my face appeared for the first time, and the two big security guys cut across the shot to block me off, I heard Mum take a startled breath.

I didn't look at her.

I couldn't.

My eyes were glued to the screen.

I could hear my screen-self calling out — *Raymond! Hey, Raymond!* — and although the camera didn't show Raymond's reaction, I remembered him grinning at me and raising his thumb. My voice sounded weird, like it was someone else's voice, and as the camera zoomed in on me, I realized that I didn't just *sound* pretty weird, I looked pretty weird as well. My eyes were bugged out, like two black marbles, barely blinking at all. I was sweating, pale, my muscles tense. And I understood now why the security guys had been so worried about me. I looked like something from hell.

It's all right, I heard myself telling them, *I'm a friend* — *Get back.*

I just want to —

Get BACK.

One of them put his hand on my shoulder, starting to force me back, and then Stella's voice rang out.

It's all right, Tony! He's a friend. You can let him through.

Big Tony took his hand away and stepped to one side.

Hey, Pete! Stella called out. *It is Pete, isn't it? Pete Boland?*

I watched myself walking up to Stella and Raymond. The camera followed me. As I stopped in front of them, the camera drew back a bit, and now all three of us were in the shot. Stella with her arm around Raymond's shoulder, Raymond smiling at me . . .

Sorry about that, Pete, Stella said, nodding at the security guy. *I didn't know it was you.* She flicked back her perfect blonde hair and smiled at me again. *How are you, anyway? You look* great . . . *God, I haven't see you for —*

Raymond? I said, looking into his eyes. *Are you OK?*

He nodded.

Come on, I told him. *Let's get out of here.*

Hold on, Stella said to me. *What do you think you're doing?*

I just looked at her.

She glanced at Raymond, gave him a squeeze, then looked back at me. *Ray's with me tonight,* she said with a smile. *I'm showing him how to have fun. You're welcome to join us, if you want.*

No, thanks.

Raymond was beginning to look uncomfortable now. I could see the growing fear in his eyes, the anxiety, the confusion. It was almost as if he'd only just realized where he was and what he was doing.

Come on, Raymond, I said quietly. *I'll buy you a hot dog.*

He flicked a quick glance at Stella, then started to move away from her. She tightened her grip on his shoulder and pulled him back.

What's the matter? she said to him. *Don't you* like *me anymore?*

He grinned awkwardly at her.

She smiled at me.

It was at that point that I'd glanced at the guys with the camera and the microphone, and as I sat there watching myself now, it was a really disquieting experience. Just for a moment, as my eyes looked right at the camera, I was watching myself watching myself. The fairground Pete Boland; the interview-room Pete Boland. Something white. Then and now. Something sad. Joined together. In and out of time . . .

And suddenly I was hearing Raymond's voice in my head. *I mean, we don't live in the past, do we? And we don't live in the future. So that only leaves the present. But when's the present? When is now? How long does it last? A second, half a second . . . a millionth of a second? You can't just be alive in a millionth of second, can you? It doesn't make sense.*

None of it made any sense to me.

I turned my attention back to the screen and saw myself walking up to Stella and stopping right in front of her. I looked at her for a moment, then leaned forward and spoke quietly into her ear, so no one else could hear what I was saying.

And no one could.

"Turn it up, Terry," Detective Barry told Gallagher, leaning in toward the screen as Stella whispered back to me.

Gallagher pressed the volume control, but Stella had already stopped whispering to me, and the two of us were just standing there — Stella smiling coldly at me, while I just looked back at her. As I watched us watching each other — in a crackle of full-volume silence — I saw again the mocking emptiness in Stella's joyless eyes. It was the look of a girl who truly believed she was the only worthwhile thing in the world.

After a second or two, the screen-Stella started speaking again, her voice booming out too loudly from the speakers.

YOU'RE GOING TO WISH YOU HADN'T DONE THIS.

AM I? I heard myself roar.

She smiled. *YOU'VE GOT NO IDEA . . .*

Gallagher pressed the volume control again, trying to turn it down, but he must have hit the wrong button or something, because all at once the speakers in the interview room made a horrible crackling noise, and just for a moment the soundtrack became strangely distorted. The background noise of the fairground got louder and more muffled, booming dully like underwater explosions, and the babbling chatter of the crowds seemed to phase in and out of time, like some kind of weird choral nightmare. I watched, entranced, as the screen shimmered, the picture faded, the brightness dulled . . . and then suddenly the speakers crackled loudly again — a big crashing sound — and everything was back to normal. The music, the lights, the crowds, the rides . . .

Stella and Raymond.

I watched as she laughed and took her arm from his shoulder. *I was only looking after him for you*, she said to me. *You can have him back now.* She glanced at Raymond. *All right?*

He nodded at her.

Go on, then, she told him. *Go and get yourself a hot dog.*

As I watched Raymond look at me, I suddenly felt really tired again. I was too hot, too sweaty. My body was aching all over, my head was buzzing with too much of everything. I wanted to reach out to the screen and say something to Raymond, something helpful and reassuring, but I knew it was pointless. He wasn't there anymore. He wasn't there, he wasn't here . . .

I watched myself step over and take Raymond by the arm. The camera stayed on us for a while as I quietly led him away, and then it lost interest in us, sweeping away over the crowds, blurring the lights against the dark sky, before finally refocusing on Stella. She was staring after us, watching us go — her eyes cold, her mouth cruel and ugly, her jaw clenched tight.

Gallagher stopped the tape.

The silence was overwhelming for a few seconds, and all I could do was stare at Stella's face on the screen, frozen in its cruelty, and wonder what was inside her head at that moment. What was she thinking in that millionth of a second? What was I thinking? What was Raymond thinking?

"What did you say to her?" Barry said quietly.

I looked at him. "What?"

"Stella . . . when you were whispering to her. What did you say?"

"I told her to stop fucking about with Raymond."

Barry nodded. "Is that what you thought she was doing — fucking about with him?"

"I *know* that's what she was doing." I looked at him. "It's obvious, isn't it? I mean, you just saw her — she was playing with him, laughing at him . . ."

"How do you think Raymond felt about that?"

"He told me afterward that he didn't care. He said he knew she was taking the piss, but it didn't really bother him."

"And you believed him?"

"Why shouldn't I?"

Barry shrugged. "It seemed to bother *you* quite a lot."

"So?"

He smiled. "I'm not criticizing you, Peter. I think you're probably right — I think she *was* fucking him about. And I think you had every right to be angry about it. I would have been angry, too. And if I was Raymond, I think I would have been *really* angry."

"Yeah," I said, "but you're not Raymond, are you?"

He looked at me for a long time then, staring thoughtfully into my eyes, but I was too tired to do anything about it. I just looked back at him, letting him think whatever he wanted. Eventually he took a breath, looked down at the table, and almost immediately looked back up at me again. "What did Stella say to you when you told her to stop fucking about with Raymond?"

"'Or else what?'"

"Sorry?"

"That's what she said — *Or else what?*"

"What do you think she meant by that?"

"I don't know."

"Did you think she was threatening you?"

"I didn't think anything."

Barry glanced across at the picture of Stella's face still frozen on the screen. "She doesn't look very happy, does she?"

I didn't say anything.

Barry looked back at me. "Why didn't you say anything about this before?"

"I told my dad that I'd spoken to Stella."

"You didn't tell him that you'd seen her with Raymond, though, did you? And you didn't say anything about it when Detective Kesey spoke to you, either."

"Kesey never asked me about it."

Barry shook his head. "Didn't you think it might be important? Raymond's missing, Stella's missing, her clothes have been found, her *bloodstained* clothes . . . and you're trying to tell me that you didn't mention anything about meeting the two of them together at the fair because no one *asked* you?" He stared accusingly at me. "It's a pretty poor excuse, Peter."

He was right, of course. It *was* a poor excuse, and there wasn't much I could say to make it any better. So I didn't say anything.

Barry stared at me for a second, then he did his looking-down-at-the-table-then-looking-up thing again. I wasn't sure what it was supposed to achieve, but I guessed he knew what he was doing.

"Had you been drinking?" he asked me.

"When?"

"Before you met Stella."

"Yeah, a bit."

286

"How much is a bit?"

"I don't know . . . I suppose I was slightly drunk."

Barry smiled. "Slightly drunk?"

"Yeah."

"What about Raymond? Was he *slightly drunk,* too?"

I shook my head. "He didn't have much to drink."

"What about drugs?" Barry said. "Did either of you take any drugs?"

I was acutely aware of Mum sitting beside me now, and I desperately wanted to say no — *no, of course we didn't take any drugs, absolutely not . . .* but there was something about the way Barry was looking at me that made me think he already knew. He *knew* we'd been drinking, and he *knew* we'd been smoking dope, too. And I really didn't want to let him catch me out in any more lies.

So, forcing myself not to look at Mum, I said, "I had a couple of puffs on a joint, that's all. But Raymond didn't touch it."

"A couple of puffs?"

"Yeah."

"That's all?"

"Yes."

"Nothing stronger?"

"No."

"Who had the cannabis? I mean, where did it come from?"

"I don't know . . ."

"Was it yours?"

"No."

"Whose was it, then?"

"I don't know . . . one of the others must have brought it. I can't remember."

"One of the others?"

"Yeah."

"So that'd be either Paul Gilpin, Eric Leigh, or Nicole Leigh? Is that right?"

I shrugged.

He looked at me, nodding his head. "All right . . . well, we'll leave that there for now. But I think—"

"Is this going to take much longer?" Mum said suddenly.

Barry looked at her. "We've only just started, Mrs. Boland."

"In that case, I think Pete needs a break. He's had a tough time over the last few days, and he hasn't been getting much sleep. Is there somewhere we can go for a cup of tea?"

Barry looked at me. "Do you want a break, Peter?"

There was nothing I wanted *more* than a break, but I knew that would mean talking to Mum about things, and I really didn't feel like talking about those kinds of things right now.

"I'm all right, Mum," I told her. "I'd rather just get it all over with, if that's OK with you."

"Are you sure?"

"Yeah."

"Do you want them to get you a drink or something?"

"No, I'm fine. I mean, if *you* want a cup of tea . . ."

She shook her head.

Barry said, "So we're all OK to carry on?"

Mum nodded.

Barry looked at me. "Peter?"

I nodded.

"Good." He turned to Gallagher and nodded. Gallagher reached down to the bag at his feet and pulled out a large plastic evidence bag. He placed the bag on the table in front of me. "For the benefit of the tape," Barry said, "I'm now showing the witness a yellow backpack that was recovered from Raymond Daggett's back garden." He looked at me. "Do you recognize this, Peter?"

"Yeah, it's mine."

"Can you tell me what it was doing in Raymond's yard?"

"I left it there on Saturday night, before we went to the fair."

"Why?"

"The bottle of wine was in it, the one I stole from Dad. I didn't want Mum to see it when I left the house, so I put it in the backpack. When I got to Raymond's, I left the backpack in his shed."

"It wasn't in the shed when we found it."

"I know—"

"What time did you get to Raymond's on Sunday morning?"

"About six-thirty—"

"And what did you see when you got there?"

My voice trembled a little as I told him what I saw—the blood on the ground, Black Rabbit's head impaled on the gate, the smashed-up hutch in the garden, the bits and pieces scattered around the shed doorway, the headless remains of Black Rabbit . . .

"That must have been quite upsetting for you," Barry said.

"Yeah, it was."

"Do you have any idea who might have done it?"

"No."

He nodded. "Did you touch anything while you were there?"

"Yeah, the gate. I opened the gate. But I used my elbow."

"Did you touch anything else?"

"No . . . I was sick before I went through the gate."

"Sick?"

"I threw up."

"Right . . . but once you'd gone through the gate, you didn't touch or move anything?"

"No."

"OK." He turned to Gallagher again and held out his hand. Gallagher reached down to the bag and brought out two more evidence bags, small ones this time. He gave them to Barry and removed the backpack from the table. Barry placed the two clear envelopes on the table in front of me. "For the benefit of the tape," he repeated, "I'm now showing the witness two items found in a recently recovered article of clothing that is believed to belong to Stella Ross." He looked at me. "Have you seen either of these two items before, Peter?"

I was already studying one of the objects in front of me. In fact, I was more than just studying it, I was mesmerized by it. It was a pebble—a shiny black pebble. Round and flat, about the size of a £2 coin, it was the kind of pebble that's perfect for skipping across rivers. It was a beautiful thing — glossy and smooth, shiny and black — but the most astonishing thing about it, and the reason I couldn't take my eyes off it, was the strange little stick-figured picture that had been painstakingly scratched into its surface. It was a picture of a rabbit. The crude simplicity of the etching somehow gave the natural perfection of the stone a weird kind of extra dimension, an *extra* beauty, and although I'd never seen Raymond scratching a picture into the surface of a pebble, I just knew it was the kind of thing he'd do. Find a pebble, clean it up, scratch a little picture on it . . .

Swallowing hard, I turned my attention to the other object.

It wasn't quite so mesmerizing as the pebble — just a shortish length of fine gold chain, the chain of a necklace. A broken necklace. There wasn't anything distinctive about it — no charms, no markings — but it somehow seemed vaguely familiar. I didn't know why. There was just something about it, something that reminded me of something . . .

"Well?" said Barry.

"What?" I said quietly, staring at the pebble again.

"Have you seen them before?" Barry asked.

"No . . ."

"Are you sure?"

I nodded. "What are they?"

"They were found in the coin pocket of Stella's shorts. Are you absolutely certain you've never seen them before?"

"I've never seen them."

"Have you ever been in Raymond's bedroom?"

I looked up at him. "What?"

"His room, Raymond's bedroom. Have you ever been in it?"

"Why?"

"Just answer the question, Peter."

"Well, yeah . . . I've been in his room. Not recently, though . . ."

"When was the last time?"

"I don't know . . . years ago, when we were little kids."

"How little?"

I shrugged. "Six, seven years old . . . something like that. Raymond's parents started getting a bit funny about things around then . . . they didn't like other people being in the house. So whenever I went around to Raymond's after that we spent most of our time in his backyard." I glanced at the pebble again, then looked up at Barry. "What's this got to do with anything?"

"This pebble," he said, tapping the plastic envelope, "it's very similar to a number of other pebbles we found in Raymond's room. Same color, same size, same markings." He looked at me. "It also has Raymond's fingerprints on it."

I found it really hard to concentrate after that. Detective Barry didn't say anything else about the pebble or the necklace, he just started asking me all about Saturday night again, and I started telling him what he wanted to know . . . but I was only semiconscious of what I was saying. Half of me was just opening my mouth and letting the words come out—*I did this, we did that, I don't know, yes, I think so*—while the other half, the inside half, was thinking about Raymond's pebbles. Why didn't I know about them? Why hadn't he told me about them? And why had he given one to Stella? I mean, it wasn't hard to imagine him doing it . . . smiling shyly, mumbling awkwardly . . . *you don't have to keep it if you don't want to . . . I mean, I know it's a bit . . . well, you know . . . I mean, if you don't like it . . .* and it was easy enough to imagine Stella taking the pebble from his hand . . . looking at it, maybe laughing at it, then stuffing it carelessly into her pocket.

But why?

And why hadn't he given one to me?

I would have really liked one of those pebbles . . . I could have kept it next to my porcelain rabbit on top of the chest of drawers. But then maybe, I thought, maybe Raymond only gave the rabbit-pebbles to people he didn't like? Maybe they were some kind of bad-luck charm, something he gave to people who'd pissed him off. Or maybe . . .

No, I didn't want to think about that.

The pebble meant nothing.

Just like everything else.

Stella means star.

The star's going out tonight . . .

Stella's going out . . .

None of it meant anything.

♥ ♠ ♦ ♣

By the time I'd finished telling Barry about Saturday night, and Gallagher had written it all down, and I'd read through what he'd written, and I'd watched Mum read through it all, and I'd signed it at the bottom of each page . . . by the time I'd done all that, I'd just about had it. I was drained, exhausted, sick of talking, sick of sitting in that dull white room, sick of everything. I'd told Barry a lot more than I'd told anyone else — mainly, I think, because I was too busy thinking about Raymond to concentrate on lying — but there was still quite a lot that I hadn't told him. Wes Campbell, for instance. And Nicole's behavior in the den, and afterward at the fair, and almost everything that Raymond had said to me that night. I'd told Barry about the fortune-teller, which he seemed to find pretty interesting, but I didn't go into any detail about what she'd said. I'd even told him about the guy with the mustache. But when Barry had asked me what he looked like, and where I'd seen him, and why I thought he was worth mentioning, my answers were so vague that Barry had stopped listening after a few seconds.

He didn't want feelings, he told me, he just wanted the facts.

What happened next?

Where did you go?

Who did you see?

What time was this?

So that's what I'd given him — the facts. Times, places, people, things . . . I just kept talking. Talking, talking, talking. I thought we'd finished when I got to the bit about

294

waking up Mr. Daggett after I'd found Black Rabbit's head on the gate, but I was wrong. Barry had one more little surprise for me.

As Gallagher wound on the videotape again, Barry said, "I'm sorry we've taken up so much of your time, Peter. And you, too, Mrs. Boland. And I'd like to thank you both for being so helpful." He smiled at Mum. She just scowled at him. He looked back at me and continued. "I just want to show you something before we start going over your statement, if that's all right."

"Oh, come *on*," Mum sighed. "He's had enough—"

"It'll only take a minute," Barry said. "I just need to clarify something."

Gallagher had stopped the tape now. The picture on the screen was a blurred shot of the ground—trampled grass, cigarette ends, litter. Then Gallagher pressed PLAY and the image on the screen lurched upward. The camera swung aimlessly around the fairground for a while, showing us dizzying pictures of the crowds and the lights and the rides, and then suddenly it steadied again—and now I knew where the cameraman was. He was standing near the Portaloos. I could see the rows of blue cubicles, the people going in and out . . . and I could see the ragged square of shadowed ground at the far end of the toilets. There was no sound on the film now, so I guessed the microphone had been switched off, and there was no sign of Stella, either.

"According to the timer on the camera," Barry said, "this was filmed at twenty past midnight. Stella was last seen heading off to the Portaloos about ten minutes earlier."

I stared at the screen, watching the camera as it panned slowly around the fairground. Then Gallagher hit the PAUSE button, and the picture froze, and I was looking at a stuttered image of myself. I was sitting on a bench, a bottle of Vodka Reef in my hand. I was staring across at the patch of ground by the Portaloos. I looked lost — dumb and dazed, overloaded. In the background, another dazed-looking figure was standing on her own, quietly watching me from a distance. Her face was slightly blurred, and she was partly hidden behind the awning of a tent, but there was no mistaking those darkened eyes, those reddened lips . . . the slicked back hair, the low-rise jeans, the flimsy little cropped white vest.

It was Nicole.

She was watching me.

I leaned forward in my seat and squinted at the screen. Behind Nicole, about thirty feet farther back, another blurred figure was standing in the doorway of a tent. I recognized the tent. It was the fortune-teller's tent. And there she was, Madame Baptiste, Lottie Noyce, watching Nicole as Nicole watched me, as I watched Pauly, as Pauly went after Eric and Campbell . . .

And now here I was, sitting in this silent white room, watching it all over again.

"That's you, isn't it?" Detective Barry said. "Sitting on the bench."

"Yeah."

"What are you doing there?"

Feeling bad, I thought to myself. *That's what I'm doing there. Feeling bad. I've forgotten what I'm supposed to be doing. I'm wondering what's the matter with me. Why can't I do anything right? Why can't I do anything?*

"I'm not doing anything," I told Barry. "I'm just sitting there, you know . . . I was tired. I'd been looking for Raymond. I was just taking a rest . . ."

"You just happened to be there?" he said. "Ten minutes after Stella disappeared, and you just *happened* to be there?"

I shrugged. "Everyone's got be somewhere."

Barry looked at me, unable to keep the disbelief from his eyes. But he didn't say anything. He just nodded at Gallagher, and Gallagher pressed PLAY again, and I watched myself stutter into life on the screen — looking at the bottle of Vodka Reef in my hand, knowing that I shouldn't drink it, that it wouldn't do me any good, but not seeming to have any choice. I didn't have any choice. The bottle just lifted itself to my mouth, tipped itself up, and the next thing I knew it was empty.

I carefully put it down.

Burped sweetly.

And closed my eyes.

The screen went blank.

TWENTY

Mum didn't say anything to me as Officer Gallagher escorted us out of the interview room and led us down to reception. She didn't look at me, either. And as we followed Gallagher along the corridors and down the stairs, I wondered what she was thinking. Was she angry with me? Was she concerned? Was she shocked? Disappointed? There was no way of telling from the look on her face, but I didn't think I'd have to wait very long to find out. Before we'd left the interview room, Detective Barry had started arranging for someone to drive us home, but Mum had told him not to bother.

"Thanks all the same," she'd told him, "but we'll make our own way back. We've got a few things to do first, anyway."

And I was pretty sure that those "things to do" consisted mostly of talking to me.

As we passed through the security doors into reception, Gallagher stopped by the open door and nodded toward the exit.

"If you go through those glass doors and turn right," he told us, "that'll take you out onto Westway."

I glanced at him, surprised at the squeakiness of his voice, and I suddenly realized that I hadn't actually heard him speak until now. He'd been with us since ten o'clock that morning, and it was just gone two o'clock now. Four hours, and he'd never said a single word. *Mind you,* I thought to myself, *if I had a voice like that, I wouldn't say very much, either.*

"All right?" he squeaked at me.

"Yeah, thanks," I told him, trying not to smile.

As we started heading toward the glass doors, I could see that Mum was trying to keep a straight face, too, and just for a moment everything felt OK. Mum was Mum again — the Mum I knew. The Mum who made me laugh at things I shouldn't really laugh at — like men in bad wigs, or women in stupid clothes, or tough-looking policemen who talked like Mickey Mouse — and I knew if I'd looked at her then, we would have both started giggling like idiots. And that would have been fine with me. But just as I was about to look at her, something else caught my attention.

The glass doors had opened and four figures were entering the reception area. Two of them were uniformed police officers, the other two were Eric and Nic.

They both looked pale and anxious — their heads bowed down, their eyes fixed worriedly to the floor — and neither of them noticed me at first. They were being led over to the reception desk on our left, while Mum and me were heading in the opposite direction, toward the doors, and for a moment or two it looked as if Eric and Nic weren't going to notice me at all. Which would have been OK with me, because I had no idea what I was going to do if they *did* see me. Should I say something? Was I *allowed* to say anything? What should I say? But even as I was thinking about it, I saw Nic raise her head and look over at us. Her eyes widened as she suddenly recognized me, and almost immediately Eric sensed her reaction and he looked over at me, too. I smiled awkwardly and nodded at them. Nic smiled back — just as awkwardly — but Eric was too tense to smile. All he could do was stare at me, his eyes burning with silent questions — *what have you told them? did you tell them about me? did you tell them I lied to you?* The intensity in his eyes transfixed me for a moment, and as I stared back at him, his face seemed to take over my mind. It was all I could see. Eric's face. It was all there *was* to see. And as I gazed into it, I could see that it was changing again — shimmering, melting . . . the angles shifting, blurring that beautiful ugliness into something else. Only this time, it wasn't Nicole's face that emerged from the shimmer, it was a much more angular vision. A lean and chiseled face. Dark, narrow eyes, a slightly crooked mouth, a high forehead topped with cropped black hair . . .

Wes Campbell.

I saw trails in the air . . .

My throat tightened, I couldn't breathe.

I smelled gas.

A dark sweetness.

I heard his voice: *You don't know anything. You didn't see anything. This never happened.*

I closed my eyes.

"Come on, Pete," I heard someone say.

The voice sounded odd — slow and deep, thick and distorted.

"Pete?"

When I opened my eyes again, Mum was standing there staring at me, Eric and Nic were being led over to the security doors, and Eric's face was pure Eric again.

"Are you all right?" Mum asked me.

"Yeah."

"Come on, then," she said. "Let's get out of here."

I was right about Mum wanting to talk to me about things, and she didn't waste any time getting down to it. As soon as we left the station, she led me along the sidewalk to a little grassy area beside some office buildings and sat me down on a bench. It was one of those places with trees and flower beds where office workers spend their lunchtimes sitting out in the sun, eating ice cream and drinking Coke. It was too late for lunchtime now, though, and apart from a few empty Coke cans and a scattering of ice-cream wrappers, we had the place to ourselves.

It was hot.

I was sweating.

My throat hurt.

As the traffic on Westway streamed up and down in the heat, filling the air with a gray haze of exhaust fumes, Mum started talking to me. She said she was sorry I'd had to go through all that, and she was sorry she hadn't done more to help me. But, she told me, she was also very concerned about some of things she'd found out.

"I know you probably don't want to talk about it right now," she said, "and I want you to know that I'm not angry with you, and that I'm not going to give you a lecture. But nevertheless . . ."

Nevertheless.

"You promised me you *weren't* taking drugs, Pete," she said sadly. "And I believed you."

I looked at her. "I'm *not* taking drugs—"

"Oh, come *on* . . . you just admitted it to Detective Barry. You were in that den of yours, you and the others, drinking yourselves stupid and smoking pot—"

"It was only a *joint*, Mum. And I only had a couple of puffs. And we weren't drinking ourselves stupid—"

"Only a joint?" Mum said. "You think that makes it OK?"

"No, but—"

"Is this something you do regularly?"

I shook my head. "It was just *there*, you know . . . someone lit a joint and started passing it around, and when it came to me I just had a couple of puffs and passed it on." I shrugged. "It happens, Mum. It's no big deal. It happens all the time. I don't even like it, really."

"But you still smoked it, didn't you?"

"Yeah, but it's only cannabis, Mum. I mean, it's not like we were smoking crack or anything. It was just a bit of dope."

"That's not the point."

"Didn't you ever try it?"

She hesitated. "We're not talking about *me* . . ."

I smiled at her.

She frowned at me. "It's not *funny*."

"I know," I said. "But it's not the end of the world, either. Honest, Mum . . . it's nothing to worry about. I mean, I'm not stupid—I know what I'm doing. If I'm at a party or something, and someone's passing a joint around, I might have a couple of quick puffs, but that's it. I'd never take anything else. And I've never *bought* any drugs in my life." I smiled at her. "I've got enough going on in my head as it is. I don't need to *take* anything to make me feel weird."

Mum smiled at me then, and I knew she believed what I was saying, but as her smile quickly faded and the sadness returned to her face, I realized that believing me wasn't enough. "It was just so frightening," she said quietly. "When I saw you on that video . . . the way you looked . . . God, you looked *awful*, Pete. It was as if you weren't *there*." She shook her head at the memory. "Your eyes, your face, everything about you . . . I don't know. It just made me feel really sad."

I didn't know what to say to her.

What could I say?

"I'm sorry, Mum," I said.

She smiled at me.

And this time her smile didn't fade.

We sat there for a while longer, talking about Raymond and Stella and all kinds of other stuff. We didn't really go into any great depth about anything, and I got the impression that Mum was just keeping me talking so she could check out the state of my mind. It felt a bit odd, actually, trying to behave how I thought she *wanted* me to behave, but I think I convinced her that — all things considered — I was coping with things pretty well.

"Right, then," she said eventually, looking at her watch. "I suppose we'd better start getting home." She glanced across Westway. "There's a taxi stand just over there—"

"Would you mind if I walked back?" I asked her.

She looked at me. "On your own?"

"Yeah . . . I mean, if that's all right with you."

"Well, I don't know, Pete. I'm not sure it's a good idea to be on your own right now."

"Please, Mum," I said. "I just want to be by myself for a while. You know, clear my head, sort myself out . . ." I gave her a reassuring look. "I'll be fine, honest."

She frowned at me. "*Honest* honest?"

I smiled. "Yeah."

"And you'll go straight home?"

"Yeah."

"Well, OK," she said. "I suppose it'll be all right. I need to do some shopping, anyway. I'll walk up to the Sainsbury's in town and get a taxi back from there." She reached into her handbag and pulled out her wallet. "Here," she said, digging out a £10 note and passing it to me. "If you change your mind, or if you get too tired or anything, just call a taxi."

"Thanks," I said, pocketing the note.

"Have you got your phone?"

"Yeah."

"All right, then. Well, I'll see you later."

"OK."

I watched her head off into town, and I waved at her when she looked over her shoulder and smiled at me, and then as soon as she was out of sight I started hurrying off to the taxi stand.

It was around three o'clock when the taxi driver dropped me off outside Eric and Nic's place. I paid him, watched him drive away, and then I just stood there for a while, gazing up at the house. There was no sign of any movement inside. Everything felt still and empty. And, of course, I *knew* there was no one at home — Eric and Nic were at the police station, Mr. and Mrs. Leigh were still away — but as I opened the front gate and started walking up the path, I couldn't help feeling that there was something about the emptiness of the house that just didn't feel right. I couldn't quite put my finger on it, but it somehow felt as if the house was expecting someone, waiting for someone . . . and I didn't think that someone was me.

I didn't really think it was Eric and Nic, either, but that's what I made myself believe as I stepped up to the front door and rang the bell. The house was waiting for Eric and Nic to come back, that's all it was.

Nothing to worry about.

The distant *ding-dong* of the doorbell faded to silence inside the house.

There was no one home.

The house was empty.

I stepped back from the door and made my way over to a wrought-iron gate at the side of the house. I took a quick look around—glancing down the street, checking the windows of the house next door—then I opened the gate and followed a pathway around to the back of the house. The garden was as ragged and wild as it had always been—tall trees, overgrown hedges, a lawn that looked like a meadow. A bonfire was smoldering at the bottom of the backyard, filling the air with a pungent smell of burning plastic and cloth.

I stopped by the back door and wondered what I was doing here.

It was hard to think.

Hard to know.

What are you doing here?

I don't know.

What are you looking for?

I don't know.

Are you looking for clues?

I don't know.

How are you going to get in?

I don't know . . . but I seem to remember that Eric and Nic usually leave a spare key somewhere . . . under a plant pot or something.

Why didn't you think of that the other night?

I don't know. I was drunk, screwed up . . . I didn't know what I was doing.

What are you doing?

"Christ, it's hot," I said, wiping the sweat from my head.

I was looking around for a plant pot now — a plant pot, a brick, a garden gnome . . . anything that might have a key hidden under it. But there were dozens of plant pots, hundreds of bricks, thousands of possible hiding places . . . it'd take me hours to check every one. And I didn't have hours. Eric and Nic had already been at the police station for over an hour . . . they could be on their way back any minute.

"Shit," I said, reaching out for the door handle.

It was a futile gesture, the kind of thing you do when you can't think of anything better to do, but as I grabbed the door handle and gave it what I thought was a pointless shove, there wasn't any resistance at all.

The door swung open.

It wasn't locked.

I stood there for a second, staring stupidly at the open door, then I stepped through into the kitchen and closed the door behind me.

I might not have known *what* I was looking for — although, thinking about it now, I think *part* of me probably knew — but whatever it was, and whether I knew about it or not, there was no doubt in my mind *where* to look for it. So I didn't bother checking out any of the downstairs rooms — most of which were piled up with packing crates and cardboard boxes anyway — I just went straight up the stairs, straight along the landing, and straight into Nicole's bedroom.

♥ ♠ ♦ ♣

It hadn't been all that long since I'd last been in Nic's room — two years ago, maybe three at the most — but there was nothing about it now that held any memories for me. In fact, I wondered for a moment if I'd got the right room. It felt kind of strange, standing there looking around, trying to remember the room as it used to be . . . when I was thirteen or fourteen, when I'd sit around in here with Eric and Nic and Pauly and Raymond, or sometimes with just Nic . . . just the two of us, me and Nicole, alone together, in her room . . .

In this room.

But it wasn't the same room anymore.

It *was* Nic's room, I realized now. There were no cardboard boxes in sight, so she obviously hadn't started packing yet, and as I gazed around the room I started recognizing some of her stuff: her makeup things strewn all over the dressing table; bottles of perfume, boxes of jewelry; bracelets and necklaces hanging on hooks on the wall. And the clothes, piled in heaps around the floor, they were definitely Nic's clothes. And the theater posters, the black walls, the arty ornaments, the bookshelves lined with Shakespeare, Chekhov, Brecht. It was Nic's room, all right. There was no doubt about that. But it wasn't the thirteen-year-old Nic's room. That room was gone forever.

What are you looking for?

I carried on looking around the room for a while, trying to ignore the pounding in my heart and the skin-tingling jelliness of my legs, then I took a deep breath and forced myself to go over to the dressing table. Nicole has never been the tidiest person in the world, and I wasn't surprised by the chaotic mess on her table. It looked as if she'd been to a garage sale and bought a box marked "Girls' Stuff," then come back home, lifted the box over her head, and emptied the contents onto the table. I knew what some of the stuff was—tubes of lipstick, mascara, eye shadow—but most of it meant nothing to me. It was just stuff: pots, tubs, bottles, packets, sachets, tins, tiny little boxes . . . all of it dusted with fine sprinklings of powder. White powder (talcum?), pink powder, sparkling metallic powder. I stood there, looking down at it all, trying to find whatever it was that I was trying to find . . . and I suppose I must have known what it was, because after a while I found myself reaching out and picking up a slender glass bottle with a flat black top. It was a small cylindrical bottle, about the size of a cigarette lighter, and it was made from shiny black glass. The word *JOJANA* was written in faint gray script on the front, so I guessed that was the name of the perfume: *JOJANA*.

I unscrewed the top, held the bottle to my nose, and breathed in the scent.

Everything seemed to change then. The atmosphere of the room, the heat, the silence . . . it was all suddenly different. Different time, different place. Different feelings. As the dark sweetness of the perfume filled my head, I was momentarily back in the den again, alone with Nicole . . . alone in the darkness, in a bubble of light . . . inside something alive . . .

What happened to us, Pete?

I could feel the sweat oozing from my skin.

And then, as I sniffed the perfume again, the air got heavier, stiller, more intense, and the dark sweetness became sweet darkness, and I was smelling gas again, the gas of the wasteground, and my head was shoved down between Wes Campbell's legs and he was squeezing my throat so hard that I thought my neck was going to break and all I could see was the white white whiteness of his jeans . . .

I slammed the bottle down on the table.

The visions cracked.

I was nowhere else but here.

In this room.

I was in Nic's room, here and now, and I knew what I knew: that Wes Campbell smelled of Nicole, that they shared the same scent, and that I didn't know what that meant.

As I started poking around through Nic's jewelry — her boxes of trinkets, her bracelets and necklaces hanging on the wall — I tried to imagine what kind of connection there could be between Wes Campbell and Nic. Was it an indirect connection? A connection through Eric or Pauly? Or was it something more than that? A direct connection? The indirect option seemed more likely, given that Eric and Pauly both knew Campbell, but I couldn't see how that fit in with the perfume. As far as I could see, the only rational explanation for the perfume connection was that Campbell and Nic had some kind of direct involvement with each other. But I just couldn't see that, either. Nicole had never liked Wes Campbell. He was everything she hated. He was brutish, artless, thoughtless. He had no grace. He was the last person in the world that Nic would want anything to do with. So the idea that they shared something together, something that hinted at some kind of intimacy . . .

No.

It just didn't make sense.

I stopped thinking about it then, forcing myself to concentrate instead on what I'd been staring at for the last few minutes. Because what I'd been staring at was a string of gold chains hanging on a hook above Nicole's dressing table. There were a lot of them, at least a dozen or so, and they weren't all the same. There were different lengths, different designs, different thicknesses. None of them were broken, and they were all pretty ordinary — much the same as any other plain gold chain — but there was no doubt that some of them were very similar to the piece of necklace that Detective Barry had shown me at the police station . . . the broken necklace they'd found in Stella's pocket. No doubt at all. And now I was remembering something, or at least I *thought* I was remembering something . . . it was hard to tell the difference anymore. I didn't know if the flickering memory that I was seeing now, a memory of Nicole on Saturday night, with a fine gold chain around her neck . . . I didn't know if it was a real memory, something that I'd actually seen, or if I was simply imagining it.

Making connections.

A gold chain glinting on a pale-skinned neck . . .

♥ ♠ ♦ ♣

I couldn't stay in Nic's room anymore. It was too confusing, too maddening. Too much. I had to leave. And as I did, I told myself that it wasn't just time to leave Nic's room now, it was time to leave the house. *Get out of here. Go home. This place is driving you mad. And besides, Nic and Eric are probably going to be back soon. What the hell are you going to tell them if they find you in here?*

But as I left Nic's room and walked along the hallway through sunlit clouds of dust, I knew I wasn't going to leave. It was as if I'd already seen myself stopping at Eric's room, opening the door, and going inside. And because I'd already done it, there was nothing I could do to stop myself. I had to do it. My future was already set. And you can't start messing around with your future, can you?

Eric's room stank of cigarette smoke. It also smelled of something else, something that reminded me of something, but the smell of cigarettes was so overpowering that it was impossible to tell what it was. Even so, I somehow got the impression that it was a human smell, a bodily smell, the smell of someone else, and when I looked over at Eric's bed I realized I was probably right. It was a double bed, and it wasn't made up, so I could see that there were two pillows on either side, and I could also see that there were two distinct impressions in the mattress. Two people had slept there. One of them, the one who'd slept on the right-hand side, had left a half-finished joint and an opened can of beer on the bedside table. On the other bedside table, the one on the left, there was a paperback book (*Les Fleurs du Mal*), a glass of water, and an overflowing ashtray.

I guessed that was Eric's side of the bed.

And I wondered who'd made the impression on the other side. A long-term boyfriend? A one-night stand? A mysterious twenty-five-year-old guy who Eric didn't want anyone to know about?

I looked around the rest of the room. It wasn't as messy as Nic's — and there was no sign that Eric had started packing, either — but it was still pretty untidy. There was a computer desk, lots of books, a TV and DVD player. There were clothes on the floor, more clothes hanging neatly in an open wardrobe. There were framed prints on the wall, some of which I recognized — Matisse, Picasso, Kandinsky — and a lot that I didn't. And there was a dressing table, just like Nic's. Only not quite so chaotic. This time I knew what most of the stuff on the table was — combs and hair brushes, tubes of gel, moisturizer, zit cream, a mobile phone — and this time I didn't have to stand there, looking down at it all, trying to find whatever it was that I was trying to find. I just went over to the table and picked up the phone. It was a good one — sleek and slim, silver and black — and as I flipped it open and turned it on, I could already imagine the connections clicking together.

Numbers and names.

Eric and Pauly.

Eric and Campbell.

Eric and Stella and . . .

"What do you think you're doing?"

The voice came from behind me, slamming into my head like a sudden crash of thunder, and as I spun around to face it, quickly shoving Eric's phone into my pocket, I saw the menacing figure of Wes Campbell in the doorway. He was staring coldly at me, his eyes still and dark, and he had a dull silver box cutter gripped in his hand.

"You don't listen, do you?" he said quietly, stepping into the room and closing the door behind him. "You just don't listen."

TWENTY-ONE

"So," Campbell said, casually tapping the box cutter against his leg, "this is what you call keeping your nose out, is it?"

"I can explain—"

"Yeah? What makes you think I *want* you to explain?" He smiled at me. "I mean, I'm just a concerned passerby, stumbling across a break-in . . . I'm not going to stand here and wait for you to explain anything, am I? For all I know, you might be a gun-toting maniac or something." He held up the blade. "No one's going to blame me for defending myself, are they?"

"I didn't break in. The back door was open."

"Right," he grinned. "So if someone leaves their back door open, that makes it OK to steal all their stuff, does it? You can just walk in and do what you like."

I shook my head. "I'm not *stealing* anything—"

"No?"

"Look," I said, "I came around to see Nic and Eric, that's all. There wasn't any answer when I rang the bell, and the only reason I came around the back was that I smelled something burning. I thought I'd better check it out."

"You smelled something burning?"

"Well, yeah . . . I mean, it turned out it was only a bonfire, but—"

"You checked out the bonfire?"

"No . . ."

"Why did you go into the house?"

"The back door was open—"

"How did you know it was open?"

"It was wide-open—"

"No, it wasn't."

"How do *you* know?"

His eyes narrowed then and he stepped toward me, brandishing the knife at my face. "You ever been *cut*?" he hissed. "You want to know how it feels?"

"I'm telling you the truth," I said, forcing myself not to move. "The back door was open, so I thought someone was in . . . you know . . . I just thought they hadn't heard the doorbell ringing or something."

Campbell touched the blade of the box cutter to my face. "I think you're shitting me, Boland."

"I'm not," I said quietly, trying to sound calm. "Honest . . . the door was open, I went into the kitchen, called out a couple of times, but no one answered."

"So why did you go upstairs? Why did you come in here?"

"I needed to use the bathroom."

He grinned again. "You thought this was the bathroom, did you?"

"No . . . I was in the bathroom when I heard a phone ringing in here. I thought it might be Eric."

"Ringing his own phone?"

I shrugged. "I just thought—"

"Who was it?"

"What?"

"On the phone. Who was it?"

"I don't know. It stopped ringing just as I picked it up."

"Where is it?"

"Where's what?"

"The phone."

I thought I'd been doing OK until then. I was pretty sure that Campbell knew I was lying, but at least my lies had been believable enough to give him something to think about. But now . . . well, what could I say? I couldn't tell him where the phone was, could I? But I couldn't tell him that I didn't know where it was, either. I was stuck for an answer. And from the satisfied look on Campbell's face, and the way he was pressing the box cutter to my face, I could tell that he knew it.

"Get over there," he said, nodding at the bed.

"Why?"

"Just do it."

I didn't move. I couldn't move. Campbell's face was inches away from mine now. I could smell his breath, the sour breath of his lungs. I could feel him thumbing the knife blade into my skin . . .

"You should have listened to me when you had the chance," he whispered.

I opened my mouth to say something, but before I could make a sound he'd clamped his finger to my lips and was shoving me back against the dressing table.

"Uh-uh," he grinned, shaking his head at me. "We're through talking now. The only noise I want to hear from you is—"

He stopped suddenly, freezing at the sound of the front door opening downstairs. Despite the pounding of blood in my head, I could hear the faint mutter of voices, familiar voices . . . and then the door slammed shut and I heard some keys being thrown on a table, and as the voices became clearer, moving along the hallway toward the kitchen, I breathed a silent sigh of relief.

Eric and Nic were back.

I wouldn't say Campbell panicked, exactly, but for a moment or two I could see a burst of indecision racing through his eyes as he tried to work out what to do. He was still holding the knife to my face, and instead of just having a finger to my lips, he'd now clamped his whole hand over my mouth. I wondered briefly if he was thinking of just keeping quiet—keep quiet, stay up here, hope that Eric and Nic go out again, then get back to whatever he had planned for me. But even as I was thinking about it, his eyes fixed hurriedly on mine again and he started whispering instructions at me.

"You tell them what you told me, OK? All that shit about smelling the fire and needing a piss, you tell them that. D'you understand?"

I nodded.

He leaned in closer to me. "You weren't in here. I wasn't in here. I found you on the landing outside the bathroom. I never touched you."

I nodded again.

He moved the knife blade toward my mouth. "You say anything else and I'll cut your fucking tongue out. All right?"

As he stared at me, waiting for an answer, I didn't know whether to shake my head — *no, I won't say anything else* — or nod — *yes, all right, I won't say anything else.* So I didn't do anything. I just looked at him, hoping he'd take it for granted that I wouldn't do anything to risk losing my tongue.

And I suppose he must have, because after a couple of seconds he slowly removed his hand from my mouth and stepped away from me. He stared at me for a moment — his head cocked to one side, his mouth tight, his eyes drilling into mine — then he closed the box cutter, put it in his pocket, and went over to the bedroom door. He quietly opened it and listened for a few moments, then he waved his hand at me, beckoning me over. As I joined him at the door, he reached up calmly and grabbed me by the throat.

"Everything's fine," he hissed at me. "All right?"

"Yeah," I croaked.

"No problems."

"No."

"You tell them you can't stay long, you have to get home. Right?"

"Right."

He let go of my throat, gave me a final glare, then he walked out onto the landing and casually called down the stairs. "Hey! Eric? Is that you?"

♥ ♠ ♦ ♣

It wasn't surprising that Eric and Nic were surprised to see us, but what *was* surprising was that they seemed more surprised to see me than they were to see Campbell. I might have been mistaken, of course. I mean, my state of mind wasn't particularly stable just then, and as we joined Nic and Eric downstairs, and Campbell started explaining what we were doing there, my concentration was pretty much focused on other things. Like trying to behave normally, trying to avoid getting my tongue cut out, trying to work out what the hell was going on. So maybe my brain was just overloaded, and I was totally misreading Eric and Nic's reaction to Campbell . . .

But I didn't think so.

Campbell seemed almost at home here. Unfazed, comfortable, relaxed. Which would have been odd enough in itself, but what made it even odder was that the overall atmosphere was anything *but* relaxed. As we sat together at the kitchen table, I could sense all kinds of tensions between Eric and Nic and Campbell. They were the kinds of tensions that aren't blindingly obvious — the kind that bubble away beneath the surface — but I knew they were there. I could see them, feel them, hear them. The only thing I couldn't do was understand them.

I didn't understand anything.

For example, when Campbell told Eric and Nic that he'd come into the house and heard a noise upstairs, and that when he'd gone upstairs to see what it was, he'd found me coming out of the bathroom . . . why didn't they ask him what he was doing here in the first place? And why, as Campbell went on to explain my story about smelling the fire and finding the back door open and going upstairs to use the bathroom . . . why did Eric suddenly glance at Campbell with a strangely subservient look in his eyes? And why did Campbell ignore him? And why did Nic keep staring at me as if she was stuck in the middle of a secret, a secret she didn't believe in? And why . . . ?

"Why did you come around here?" Eric said to me.

"Sorry?"

"Why did you come around to see us?"

"No reason," I shrugged. "I just thought I'd come around, you know . . . I just wanted to see you . . ."

Eric frowned. "But you'd only just seen us at the police station. You must have known we weren't in."

I shook my head. "I didn't come around straight after I'd seen you. It was about an hour later, maybe an hour and half. I was going this way anyway and I thought you might have been back by then. So I just called in, you know . . . and that's when I smelled the fire."

"Right," said Eric.

"And then I found the back door open . . ."

"And you needed to use the bathroom."

"Yeah . . . I didn't think you'd mind." I looked at him. "I was just leaving when Wes showed up."

Eric looked away.

I glanced at Nic.

"Wes was here when we left," she told me. "That's why we left the back door unlocked."

I waited for her to go on, waiting for her to tell me *why* Campbell had been here when they left, but instead of answering me herself she raised her chin slightly and gazed over at Campbell, as if to say — why don't *you* tell him, Wes? They stared at each other in silence for a while, and I could see there was something going on between them, but I had no idea what it was.

Eventually, Campbell just shrugged and said, "I went out to get some cigarettes. I forgot to lock the back door."

I saw Nic give him a little shake of her head, but Campbell had already looked away from her and was focusing his attention on Eric.

"Are you all right?" he asked him, his voice unexpectedly gentle.

After a moment's hesitation, Eric gave Campbell a disdainful look and said, "Yeah, why *shouldn't* I be all right?"

Campbell blinked. "I was only asking . . ."

Eric stared at him.

I still didn't understand anything.

I looked at Nic.

She shrugged.

Eric lit a cigarette and looked at me. "Did the police ask you about Raymond?"

"Yeah."

He nodded. "I reckon they think he did it."

"Did what?"

"Killed Stella."

I looked at him. "What makes you think she's dead?"

He paused for a moment, taking a long drag on his cigarette. "Well," he said, blowing out a long stream of smoke, "they've found her clothes, haven't they? They've found her blood on them . . ."

"That doesn't mean she's dead."

Campbell laughed then, a short snort of derision.

I looked at him.

"What?" he said, staring at me.

I shook my head, saying nothing.

He grinned at me. "What's the matter — cat got your tongue?"

As he carried on staring at me, I saw him lick his lips, showing me his tongue, and I felt like saying to him — *Yeah, all right, I'm not stupid. I got it the first time: Tongue equals threat. And, no, I haven't forgotten that you want me to leave, either. But thanks for the reminder, anyway, you fucking twat.*

"What are *you* smiling at?" he said to me.

I looked at him for a second — his face, his eyes, his slightly crooked mouth — and then I just gave up and looked away. I didn't want to do this anymore. I didn't want to think about it. I didn't want to be here.

I sighed heavily and started to get up. "Yeah, well," I said to no one in particular. "I suppose I'd better get going . . ."

Eric glanced up at me and opened his mouth, as if he was about to say something, but then he flinched slightly — the kind of flinch that comes from a nudge beneath the table — and he closed his mouth and just nodded at me.

"See you around, Boland," Campbell said.

I didn't look at him.

"I'll see you out, Pete," said Nic, getting to her feet.

"It's all right . . ." I started to say, but before I could finish telling her not to bother, she'd already left the table and was halfway across to the back door. There was something about the way she was walking that said — *just keep your mouth shut and follow me.*

So that's what I did.

Nic didn't say anything to me as I followed her out the back door and along the path to the front of the house. She didn't look at me, either. She just walked on in hurried silence — along the path, through the back gate, across the yard, up to the front gate . . .

The afternoon sun was blazing down now, shimmering white in a dazzled blue sky, and the air was thick with too many smells: the neighboring sweetness of freshly cut grass, the promise of rot and decay, hot metal, dry earth, burning plastic and cloth. And darkness, too. I could smell darkness. A trail of darkness in the sunlight.

Nic had stopped at the front gate and was watching me thoughtfully as I walked up and stopped beside her.

"Are you all right?" she asked me.

I smiled at her. "Not really."

She glanced back at the house, then quickly turned back to me. "Listen, Pete," she said quietly, "I can't really talk right now, but I just wanted to let you know —"

"What the hell's going on, Nic?" I said, cutting her off. "I mean, what's Wes Campbell doing here, for Christ's sake?"

"He's just a friend—"

"Yeah?"

She shook her head. "You don't understand—"

"I don't think I *want* to."

She glared at me for a moment, clearly angry about something, but whatever it was, she wasn't going to share it with me. "Look," she said slowly, trying to calm herself down, "if you don't want to listen to me, that's fine. You're probably going to find out soon enough, anyway—"

"Find out what?"

"It's about Raymond—"

"What about him?"

She glared at me again.

"What?" I said.

"Just shut up for a second and *listen* to me, OK?"

"I *am* listening."

"Yeah, well, stop interrupting then."

"Sorry."

"Right," she sighed. "OK. Well, it's probably nothing . . . I mean, it probably doesn't mean all that much . . . and the thing is, I would have told you earlier, but I didn't remember it until a few hours ago . . ."

"Just tell me, Nic," I said quietly.

She nodded, lowering her eyes, as if she was slightly embarrassed. "OK, well . . . you know that guy I was with at the fair? The one from the tilt-a-whirl?"

"Yeah."

"His name's Luke," she said, shaking her head. "And he's a piece of shit. Not that it really matters, but . . . well, you know." She laughed sadly. "We all make mistakes."

"Right."

"Anyway," she went on, "I was pretty wrecked even before I got to the fair . . . I think it was that shit we were smoking, you know, the stuff that Pauly brought. I think it did something weird to my head . . . I don't know. Christ, I didn't know *what* I was doing. I remember getting to the fair and meeting a couple of girls from school, and *they* were drinking and smoking, too, and I suppose I must have joined in with them and got even more wrecked, because after that . . . I don't know. I can hardly remember anything about Luke. Don't remember meeting him, don't remember what we did, or how we got to his trailer . . ." She paused for a moment then, staring at the ground. "I think I remember something," she muttered distantly. "Something about . . . I don't know. It was like we were fighting . . . or I was shouting at him or something." She was rubbing her bare arm now — rubbing it up and down, as if she was freezing cold.

"Are you all right?" I asked her.

She didn't say anything, she just kept on rubbing her arm, staring at nothing.

"Did he hurt you?" I said gently.

"What?"

"This Luke . . . did he, you know . . . did he hurt you or anything?"

She shook her head. "No . . . no, I don't think so. I think we just . . . we were both really out of it, you know? I don't even know if we did anything or not." She sighed heavily and looked up at me. "I just remember being in his bed, this horrible filthy bed . . . and I didn't really know what was happening, or where I was, and my head was throbbing like hell . . . and then suddenly Luke was jumping out of bed and running to the window, shouting like a madman . . ." Nic looked at me. "That's when I saw Raymond."

"Where?"

"He was at the window. That's what Luke was going mad about. He'd seen Raymond watching us through the window."

"He was *watching* you?"

"Yeah . . ."

"Are you sure it was Raymond?"

She nodded. "I *saw* him, Pete. He was staring at me . . . I looked back at him. We were looking right at each other. It was definitely Raymond."

"Christ," I whispered.

"I don't think he was *doing* anything."

"What do you mean?"

"Well, I'm not sure, but I just got the feeling that he wasn't, you know . . . he wasn't being *pervy* or anything. I mean, he wasn't watching us in a creepy way. He was just watching us. Watching *me*, really."

I looked at her, hearing the fortune-teller's words again: *You care for others without thinking of yourself.*

"Watching out for you," I mumbled to myself. "He was watching out for you . . ."

"What?" said Nic.

"What time was this?" I asked her.

"God knows — one o'clock, two o'clock . . . maybe later."

"What did Raymond do when this Luke guy started shouting at him?"

"Nothing at first. He just stayed where he was. Then Luke ran over and whacked the window with the palm of his hand . . . and Raymond just kind of disappeared. I don't think he actually ran off then, because Luke was still shouting and screaming at him through the window. God knows what Raymond was doing . . ."

"Probably just standing there looking at him," I said.

Nic smiled. "Yeah, probably . . . but then Luke suddenly turned from the window and ran over to the door." Her smile faded. "I was yelling at him now, trying to get him to calm down, but I don't think he even heard me. He just yanked the door open and charged outside."

"What happened then?"

She shook her head. "I don't know . . . I just heard him running and shouting, Luke swearing his head off . . . and then after a while all the noise just kind of faded away into the distance. I don't think he caught Raymond, though."

"Why not?"

"When Luke came back, about ten minutes later, he was still swearing and cursing . . . saying stuff like — *I'll kill the little bastard if I ever find him, dirty little fucker, I'll cut his fucking throat . . .*"

"Nice."

Nic shrugged. "Yeah, well . . . I just thought you'd want to know, that's all. And I'm sorry I didn't remember it until now. But, like I said, I was in a bit of a state, you know . . ."

"Yeah. Well, thanks, anyway." I looked at her. "What did the police say when you told them?"

"Not much . . . I think they're probably going to talk to Luke, if they can find him."

"He'll be with the fair, won't he?"

"Yeah, but most of them have moved on now. And I'm not sure if Luke was going with them or not. He only works at the fair for part of the year." She looked at me. "Listen, Pete, I didn't mean —"

"Did they show you the video?"

"What?"

"When you were at the police station — did they show you the film of Stella at the fair?"

"Yeah, some of it. They wanted to know —"

"Nic!"

She stopped suddenly at the sound of Eric's voice, and we both looked up to see him gazing down at us from an upstairs window.

"Come on, Nic," he called out to her. "We haven't got all day."

"Yeah, all right," she called back. "I'm just coming." She turned back to me. "Sorry, Pete, I'd better go." She smiled at me then, a slightly sad-looking smile, and she reached out and touched me gently on the cheek. "You're bleeding," she said.

"Am I?"

"Just a bit." She showed me a spot of blood on her fingertip.

"Must have cut myself shaving," I muttered, rubbing at a sore spot on my chin where I guessed Campbell's knife must have nicked me.

Nic grinned at me. "Shaving?"

"Yeah . . ."

"You *shave*?"

"I'm not thirteen anymore."

"No," she sighed, looking into my eyes. "I don't suppose any of us are thirteen anymore."

TWENTY-TWO

As I walked back home along Park Road, I couldn't stop thinking about the phone in my pocket. Eric's phone. I could feel it tap-tapping against my leg as I walked, almost as if it was calling out to me —*I'm here, I'm here, I'm here in your pocket*. But I didn't need telling. I knew it was there. I also knew that it *wasn't* calling out to me, because — unlike everything else I'd been experiencing — I knew it was real. It was there. In my pocket. It was simple, solid, undeniable. It wouldn't lie to me. It wouldn't confuse me. It wouldn't threaten me or intoxicate me or fill my head with flies.

It was just a phone.

And it just might have some answers.

So I was desperate to start checking it out, and I could feel my fingers tingling as I walked, itching to answer the nonexistent call of the phone, but I knew it was best to wait. I needed time to concentrate. And, in any case, Mum was probably waiting for me now. Waiting to ask me where I'd been and what I'd been doing and how I was feeling . . .

So I left the phone in my pocket and concentrated on hurrying home.

♥ ♠ ♦ ♣

Mum was surprisingly quiet when I got back. She *did* ask me where I'd been and what I'd been doing and how I was feeling, but after I'd told her that I hadn't really been anywhere, that I'd just been walking, and that I felt a lot better now, thanks very much, she pretty much left it at that.

We ate together in the kitchen.

We watched the news.

She asked me about the little cut on my face. I told her I must have scraped myself on something when I'd ducked under the crime tape at the end of the street.

I asked her where Dad was, she told me he'd gone into work.

"Is he coming back tonight?" I said.

"I think so. They've got him covering all the stuff that everyone else is too busy to deal with, but there's not really all that much he can do on his own. He's just going through the motions, really."

She lit a cigarette.

I frowned at her.

She shrugged and looked out the window. "Did you have any trouble getting past all the reporters out there?"

"Not really. A couple of them called out to me as I ducked under the tape, but the police are still keeping them well back, so I couldn't really hear what they said. I think one of them used my name, though."

"You mean they recognized you?"

"I suppose so."

Mum shook her head. "This is all getting ridiculous."

♥ ♠ ♦ ♣

Eric's phone was still calling out to me from my pocket as I went upstairs to my room after we'd eaten, and I was still desperate to turn it on. But I didn't. I don't know if I was just trying to savor the sensation of knowing it was there for a little while longer—in the same way that you leave the tastiest thing on your plate until last—or if it was simply that I didn't *want* to know the truth.

I didn't know.

And I didn't want to think about it.

And besides, I told myself, *you really need to take a shower. You stink of sweat. Your skin feels grubby. Your hair's all matted and dirty, your head's too hot . . .*

I took a shower.

Changed into some clean clothes.

I went back into my room, shut the door, sat on the bed, and stared at Eric's phone . . .

Then I put it back in my pocket and switched on Sky News.

The first thing I saw was a really bad photograph of Raymond. It was taken from a school photograph, one of those panoramic photos they take of the whole class. You know the ones—where you all line up in rows, smallest at the front, tallest at the back, and you have to keep as still as possible, and there's always some joker making a face or waggling their fingers behind someone's head . . .

Rabbit ears . . .

Anyway, the newspeople had obviously got hold of one of these photos, and all they'd done was cut out Raymond's face and enlarge it. So, for a start, it looked all blurry and grainy, which made him look like some kind of fugitive. And, secondly, he was wearing his secondhand school uniform, with his shirt buttoned up to his neck, but without a tie, which made him look kind of poor and desperate. But, worst of all, the camera had caught him just as he was looking to one side, smiling nervously at something, and that made him look like a deranged serial killer.

Which I guessed was probably the point.

Because although the news anchors were being careful not to explicitly link Raymond's disappearance with Stella's, there was something about the tone of their reporting, the way they kept *emphasizing* things, that made it pretty clear what they *really* thought. Raymond Daggett had been at the same *fairground* as Miss Ross. Raymond Daggett had once been a pupil at the same *school* as Miss Ross. And although the two teenagers weren't *known* to be closely acquainted, and the police weren't ruling *out* the possibility of a double abduction, reporters close to the investigation believed that such a likelihood was *extremely* unlikely . . .

And then they'd show a picture of Stella's house — security gates, high walls, acres of rolling lawns — followed by a picture of some dingy little terraced houses (which weren't even in St. Leonard's, let alone Hythe Street) just to show us the kind of hovel that Raymond came from . . . and then more pictures of Stella looking well groomed and beautiful, and the same picture of Raymond looking deranged and desperate . . .

I watched it all for a while, my initial anger quickly fading to a sense of numbed resignation, and then I just gave up and turned the TV off. It was pointless watching it. Pointless and sickening. It didn't tell me anything, it didn't say anything, it didn't do anything.

It was just TV.

It wasn't real.

Nothing felt real anymore.

Even this, I realized, taking Eric's phone out of my pocket, *even this doesn't feel quite so real as I thought. It's just a lump of plastic, a handful of stuff that goes* beep beep beep . . .

But it was all I had.

And I knew I had to see what it could tell me.

I flipped it open and turned it on . . . and then I quickly turned it off again as Dad knocked on my door and walked in.

Mum must have already told him how the police interview had gone, because the first thing Dad did was try to explain why Detective Barry had been so hard on me.

"I'm not apologizing for him," he said, "and I'm not trying to say that, underneath it all, he's a really nice guy. Because he's not. He's a coldhearted bastard, always has been, and personally I can't stand the man. But he's good at his job. He knows what he's doing. And he gets results. So whatever you think of him, Pete, however he made you feel today, try not to take it to heart, OK? It's just how it has to be done."

"Yeah, I know."

"I mean, if it had been me on the other side of the table, I would have been just as hard on you as Barry was."

I grinned at him. "Mum wouldn't have let you."

"True," he agreed, nodding thoughtfully. "I probably could have outwitted her, though."

"You think so?"

He smiled at me, which made me feel pretty good, and I think I realized then that there was something about these recent little chats of ours that I was beginning to enjoy. I mean, I'm not saying that we hadn't talked like this before, because we had, but Dad was usually so busy most of the time, or so tired, that he couldn't always spend as much time with me as he'd like. Now, though . . . well, now it was different. Now we had time. And it felt kind of nice — just me and my dad, sitting in my room, talking quietly in the fading light of the evening sun . . .

It was good.

Like it should be.

It was just such a shame that it'd taken something so bad to bring us together.

"They brought in quite a few people for questioning today," Dad told me. "Some of Stella's friends, her security men, the guys who made the film . . ." He looked at me. "Do you know where Paul Gilpin is, by the way?"

"Why?"

"He wasn't at home when they went around to bring him in. Apparently, no one's been home all day, and no one knows where Paul is. Any ideas?"

I shook my head. "He could be anywhere . . . I mean, you know what Pauly's like — he's always out and about somewhere . . ."

Dad nodded. "Well, I'm sure it doesn't mean anything. But if he doesn't show up soon, it's only going to make things worse for him. So if you hear anything . . ."

"I don't really know him that well anymore, Dad. I mean, we don't hang around together like we used to."

"What about Eric and Nicole? Are they still friends with him?"

"Not really."

Dad nodded again. "They were interviewed today — Eric and Nicole."

"Yeah, I know. We saw them on the way out of the station. Did they have anything interesting to say?"

"I'm not sure about Eric . . . John Kesey wasn't involved in his interview, and he hasn't heard the tape yet, but he was in on the interview with Nicole." Dad looked at me. "John hasn't had time to tell me everything yet, and it seems as if Nicole was fairly vague about a lot of things, anyway, but she remembers being with you in the den."

"Yeah," I mumbled, slightly embarrassed. "I think she'd had a few drinks before I got there . . . I mean, she seemed all right at the time, but I suppose she was fairly . . ."

"Vague?"

"Yeah," I grinned.

"And what about you?" he said. "How 'vague' were you?"

I sighed. "Come on, Dad . . . I've already been through all this with Mum."

"I know." He gave me a stern look then, and I guessed Mum had told him about the dope and everything, and from the look on his face I thought he was going to start lecturing me about it. But, surprisingly, he didn't.

"Did you drink any of the tequila?" he asked me.

I looked at him. "How do you know—?"

"Your den in Back Lane was searched yesterday morning," he told me. "Forensics have been analyzing all the stuff you left behind."

"What stuff?"

"Bottles, cigarette butts, spliffs, condoms . . ." Dad shook his head at me. "Christ, Pete, what the hell was going on in there?"

"It's not as bad as it sounds, Dad. It was just . . ."

"Just what?"

"I don't know . . . it was just *stuff*, you know?"

He stared at me. "What about the tequila? Did you drink any of it?"

"Why?"

"Just answer the question, Pete."

"I had a bit, yeah."

"Whose was it?"

"Does it matter?"

"Yes, it matters."

"Why?"

He leaned forward in his chair and looked me in the eye. "Forensics have identified traces of a drug called TCI in the tequila. Do you know what that is?"

"No," I said quietly.

"It's a synthetic hallucinogen, a phenethylamine, the same group of drugs as Ecstasy. It's not all that common yet, but it's starting to become popular at raves and nightclubs.

It's sometimes known as 'glitter' or 'ice.' Other people call it 'juice.'"

"Juice?" I said.

As Dad nodded his head, Pauly's grinning face suddenly flashed into my mind. I could see him laughing, lighting a cigarette . . . I could hear the echo of his voice calling out to me in the den . . . *Jooooseeee!*

I looked at Dad. "This TCI stuff was in the tequila?"

He nodded again. "Didn't you know?"

"No . . . Christ, I wouldn't have touched it if I'd known. I just thought it was tequila."

"Well, it wasn't. Forensics think the TCI was probably mixed into the tequila as a powder. You can get it as a tablet, apparently, but it's usually sold as a sparkling white powder."

"What does it do to you?" I said, remembering the powder I'd seen in Pauly's drawer.

"It's a powerful psychedelic. The effects usually come on within about an hour of taking it, and they can last for anything up to ten hours."

"What kind of effects?"

"Heightened stimulation, hallucinations, increased sensitivity to visual images, smells, tastes . . . and, depending on the dose, and how you react to the drug, you might experience all kinds of other things. Nausea, anxiety, stomach pains, headaches, depression . . ." Dad paused, taking a deep breath, keeping his eyes fixed worriedly on mine. "Did *you* feel anything like that?"

It was hard to concentrate now. My mind was racing with all kinds of mixed-up emotions — shock, anger, realization, relief . . . and I *was* strangely relieved. If Pauly had drugged the tequila, and I didn't doubt that he had, then that would explain everything—all the weirdness, the visions, the voices, the madness inside my head . . .

It wasn't madness; it was drugs.

But I didn't really want to share that relief with Dad, because I didn't think he'd find it very relieving. So I lied.

"I don't think I felt anything particularly strange," I told him. "I mean, I was pretty drunk, I suppose, and I felt a bit sick and dizzy a couple of times, but that's about it."

"Are you sure?" Dad said.

I nodded. "It was the first time I've ever tasted tequila, and I didn't really like it that much. I only had a tiny little sip."

"What about the others? Did they drink a lot of it?"

I pictured Nicole in the den, taking constant little sips from the bottle, and Pauly, glugging it down like a maniac . . .

"Pete?" Dad said.

"Yeah, sorry . . . I can't really remember if the others were drinking it or not. I'm pretty sure Raymond didn't have any."

"Well, someone must have drunk it," Dad said. "The bottle was almost empty. Are you sure you can't remember who brought it?"

I shook my head. "It was just there . . . I didn't see where it came from. And it was almost empty the first time I saw it, anyway, so maybe there wasn't much in it to start with."

"Maybe not . . . but it was still a ridiculously stupid thing to do. Whoever did it — and it has to be *one* of you . . . you *do* realize that, don't you?"

"Yeah."

"One of your so-called friends tried to *poison* you, Pete. It's as serious as that. So if you're trying to cover up for them —"

"I'm not."

"You'd better not be. And I want you to tell me immediately if you start feeling anything strange, anything at all. This TCI stuff can continue affecting you for weeks after you take it. It can make you feel ill, depressed, it can give you flashbacks . . ." He looked at me. "Do you know what a flashback is?"

"Like a memory of something?"

"It's more than a memory. It's when you experience the full effects of a psychedelic drug again without actually taking it. You might suddenly start hallucinating, seeing things, hearing things, imagining things . . . so, if anything like that happens, if you start feeling weird or sick or anything, I want you to tell me straightaway. Do you understand?"

"Yeah."

"Good."

I looked at him. "Have Eric and Nic been told about this?"

"Not yet."

"Why not? Shouldn't they be warned?"

Dad looked at me. "What makes you think that one of them didn't spike the tequila? Or both of them."

"Nicole wouldn't do anything like that."

"No? What about Eric? Or Pauly? And Raymond can't be ruled out, either—"

"Raymond doesn't know anything about drugs."

"Are you sure about that?"

"I know him, Dad. I've known him for years. I probably know him better than anyone."

"Did you know he was spying on Nicole that night?"

I had to feign surprise for a while then as Dad told me about Nic's encounter with Raymond at Luke's trailer. He didn't go into as much detail as Nic had, and I guessed he was trying to spare me from whatever embarrassment I might have felt. I'm not sure if he understood *why* I might be embarrassed, but I suppose it was pretty obvious that there was a good chance I would be. My childhood "girlfriend" had got hopelessly drunk and spent the night with a casual fairground worker who she'd only just met, and that was after she'd tried to seduce *me* just a few hours earlier . . .

There had to be *something* there to embarrass me.

And I suppose, in a way, there was.

But it was an oddly distant kind of embarrassment, and I don't think there was any bitterness attached to it. I didn't think Nic had done anything wrong. I didn't blame her for anything. I just felt a little bit sorry for her.

When Dad had finished telling me what happened, I asked him what he thought it all meant.

"Well, they need to corroborate Nic's story first, which means bringing in Luke Kemp for questioning, and at the moment they don't know where he is. And then there's the question of Nic's reliability as a witness, given the state she was in. Particularly if it turns out that she'd been drinking the spiked tequila. But even if she *is* telling the truth, and her story checks out, I'm not sure it's going to help Raymond that much."

"Why not?"

"He was *watching* them, Pete. He was peeping through the window in the middle of the night, watching them doing . . . well, whatever they were doing."

"I think he was just watching out for Nic," I said. "You know, like keeping an eye out for her, making sure she was OK."

"Well, maybe," Dad said, shaking his head. "But I don't think anyone else is going to see it like that. They're just going to see a mixed-up kid who gets his kicks by watching people have sex. They're going to think he was sick and frustrated, and then he got chased away, and maybe that made him even him more frustrated, so maybe he turned his attention to someone else."

"Or maybe Luke didn't *just* chase him away," I suggested. "Maybe he caught him."

"Possibly," Dad said. "And if that's the case, he'll have left some trace in his trailer, which forensics will match up with Raymond. But Nicole said he wasn't gone for very long, and she didn't see any signs of a struggle when he came back."

"But if Raymond was at the trailer, doesn't that mean he couldn't have done anything to Stella?"

Dad shrugged. "It all depends on the timing. Nicole isn't sure what time she saw Raymond, and the pathologist is still working on the exact time of . . . I mean, until all the reports are in . . ." Dad hesitated for a moment then. His eyes flicked away from mine, and he seemed to think about something for a second before quickly looking back at me. "They think the car had something to do with it."

"What car?"

"The burned-out car at the river. It's possible that Stella was driven down to the river that night, and then the car was torched to get rid of any evidence. It's being checked, but there's not much chance of finding anything. They're still checking Tom Noyce's trailer, too—"

"She's dead, isn't she?" I said.

Dad stared at me.

I looked back at him. "That's what you were talking about just now—the pathologist's report, the exact time of death. They've found her body, haven't they?"

Dad didn't say anything, he just kept on staring at me, but I knew I was right. I could tell by the sound of his silence.

"When did they find her?" I asked him.

He sighed. "Early this morning . . . in the river. About a quarter mile downstream."

"Shit . . ."

"I'm sorry, Pete. I didn't want you to find out like this, but the investigation team is trying to keep it quiet for as long as possible, and I promised John Kesey I wouldn't tell anyone." He took a deep breath and let it out slowly. "Stella's parents have been informed, and they've agreed not to go public yet, so it's imperative that you don't tell anyone, either. All right? Not a word to anyone. Because as soon as this gets out, there's going to be absolute chaos, and that's going to make it almost impossible for the police to do their job."

"How did she die?" I asked quietly.

Dad looked at me. "Do you promise to keep quiet about this?"

"Yeah."

He nodded. "Well, at the moment, the cause of death seems to be a head injury. The autopsy isn't conclusive yet — they're still waiting for the outcome of some more tests — but the only apparent injury she suffered was the wound to her head."

"What about her clothes? I mean, was she . . . you know . . . ?"

"No, she wasn't sexually assaulted. Her body was naked, but there were no signs of assault."

The full horror of what we were talking about suddenly sank in then, and I don't think I've ever felt so empty and dark. I think it was the words "naked" and "body" that did it. Those two simple words had somehow managed to strip away the frail illusion that Stella was still alive. Even when I'd seen her on the videotape, and I'd got the feeling that I was looking at a ghost, there'd still been something inside me that wasn't willing to accept the reality of her death. But now . . . well, now she was nothing but a naked body. A dead naked body. Pale and white, cold and lifeless.

I could smell dark water.

I shuddered.

I could feel myself shrinking, my senses fading, and I just wanted to sit there and do nothing. I didn't want to talk, I didn't want to listen, I didn't want to do anything . . . but I could already hear Dad talking to me, asking me if I was feeling OK, and I knew that I was listening, because I could hear myself telling him not to worry, that it was just a bit of a shock, that I was fine . . .

"Are you sure?"

"Yeah."

My voice sounded a long way away, and it didn't seem to have anything to do with me.

"What about Tom Noyce?" it said. "Is he still a suspect?"

"Well, he's been questioned, and they're still taking his trailer apart, but apart from Stella's blood on the outside, they haven't found anything of interest yet. His mother has given him an alibi for most of the night, anyway. He's been released for now, but they might want to talk to him again."

"I suppose they still think that Raymond did it, don't they?"

"You can't blame them, Pete. Everything's pointing that way. They've even found pictures of her on his computer. Photographs, film clips—"

"That doesn't *mean* anything," I heard the distant-Pete say. "Everyone I know has seen those pictures on the Internet. I've seen them, everyone at school has seen them, including most of the teachers. You've probably seen them, too."

"I haven't seen them," Dad said prudishly.

"Yeah, but you didn't go to school with her, did you? I mean, come *on*, Dad . . . if you went to school with a good-looking girl and you found out there were naked pictures of her on the Internet, wouldn't you be just a little bit curious?"

"That's not the point—"

"Yes, it is."

My voice was becoming more and more distant now. I could still hear it, and it wasn't actually getting any quieter, it just seemed to be moving further away from me. And for a while then, as Dad and I continued talking, I was totally unaware of what we were talking about. I was deep down inside myself, thinking—without thinking—of other things. My thoughts were raw and black.

Pauly.

Powder.

Why?

Phone.

When?

Who?

Stella.

Naked.

Body.

Dead.

Stella.

Naked.

Body.

Dead.

Rabbit.

Pebble.

Raymond.

Dead.

♥　♠　♦　♣

I don't know what made me come back to myself, but when I did — emerging quite suddenly, my head thick and dull — Dad was still talking to me, but I had no idea what he was talking about.

". . . and when I put that into the CCA system," he was saying, "I found at least three incidents that shared some similarities, and quite a few more that might be worth looking into."

"Sorry?" I said.

He looked at me. "What?"

"You lost me there for a minute. What's CCA?"

"I've just *told* you. Weren't you listening?"

"Sorry," I smiled. "I must have drifted off or something . . ."

"Maybe you'd better get some sleep," he said, giving me a concerned look. "I can tell you all about this in the morning."

"No, it's all right. I'm not tired. I just wasn't concentrating, that's all." I smiled at him again. "I'm listening now."

"All right," he said. "Well, do you remember what I told you about the PNC?"

"The what?"

"PNC. Police National Computer." Dad looked at my blank face and sighed. "I'll start again from the beginning, shall I?"

"Please."

I listened then as he told me how he'd gone into work that afternoon and his boss had sent him up to an isolated room on another floor to keep him away from the investigation, and he'd spent the morning reading through case files and transferring data to computer records, and after a while he'd got so bored that he'd logged on to the Police National Computer and just started browsing around.

"I wasn't really *looking* for anything to do with all this," he told me. "But I suppose it was on my mind, and I didn't think it'd do any harm to try a few things. So I started seeing if I could find any links to this case on the CCA system." He looked at me. "CCA stands for Comparative Case Analysis. It's basically a national database application that can be used to compare and analyze crimes of a similar nature."

"You mean like serial killers?"

He nodded. "Serial killers, serial crimes . . . it's especially useful if you're trying to find patterns between crimes committed in different parts of the country."

"But this isn't—"

"No, I know this case doesn't *sound* anything like that, but as I said, I was just having a look, seeing if I could find anything."

"And did you?"

He frowned. "I don't know . . . I might have found *something*, but I'm not sure if it means anything or not. You see, the system works by analyzing certain aspects of a crime and seeing if they match the identifying aspects of other crimes. But the trouble with this case is that most of the identifying elements are too wide-ranging to be of any use."

"What do you mean?"

"Well, I knew that if I put in quite general keywords— things like *missing teenager, abduction, murder*—I'd get literally thousands of matches, so I realized that I had to work out a way to narrow it down. I tried everything I could think of—time of day, time of year . . . I searched by age group, by town, by county . . . I even started putting in things like *river, rabbit, celebrity*—but none of it really got me anywhere. It wasn't until I tried narrowing down the location even more that I finally started to see something." Dad looked at me. "In the last four years, fourteen teenagers have been reported missing after visiting a carnival."

"Fourteen?"

He nodded. "Five of them either returned home later or were subsequently found to have simply run away, but of the remaining nine, six are still missing and three are dead. Two girls, one boy."

"How did they die?"

"Two from strangulation, one from a knife wound. All three murders are still unsolved."

"Shit, Dad—" I whispered. "That could mean—"

"It *could* mean anything, Pete. That's the trouble. There's no pattern to any of it yet. None of the missing kids knew each other, none of them had anything in common, and there's no obvious parallels between the three murders. The only thing that links all three cases is the carnival connection, and even that's pretty shaky."

"Yeah, but if it was the same fair every time—"

"It wasn't. Two of the kids went missing from a Bretton's Funfair, and another two disappeared after visiting a Funderstorm Fair, but on both occasions the fairs were in different towns, and all four cases occurred at different times. The rest of the kids all went missing from different fairs. Different fairs, different times, different parts of the country. So if there *is* someone out there taking all these kids, it's probably not a fairground worker."

"Unless they move around a lot and work for different fairs," I suggested.

Dad shrugged. "They'd have to work for a *lot* of different fairs."

"Yeah, but it's not impossible, is it?"

"I suppose not . . ."

"And if—"

"Listen, Pete," he said calmly. "Don't get too carried away with this, OK? It's all just conjecture at the moment, and there's a pretty good chance that it won't come to anything in the end. I've passed it on to John Kesey, and he's going to try and get someone to look into it in more detail, but I don't want you to start getting your hopes up too much." He looked at me. "Yeah, I *know* I'm contradicting myself—giving you the possibility of hope and then telling you not to get carried away with it . . . and I know that sounds really stupid. And maybe it is. But I just wanted you to know—"

"The man with the mustache," I said suddenly.

"What?"

"It could be *him.*"

"What are you talking about? What man?"

I looked eagerly at Dad. "When I was leaving the fair, I saw this creepy-looking guy hanging around the exit, and then later on I saw him going into Back Lane."

Dad frowned. "What do you mean *creepy-looking*? What was he doing that made him look creepy?"

He was standing in the shadows, I thought, *watching a vision of Raymond on a nonexistent merry-go-round. An old-fashioned fairground organ was playing and I could hear the sound of children's laughter and I could see Raymond sitting on a jet-black horse that wasn't a horse but a horse-size rabbit with shining black eyes and I wanted to join him on the carousel . . . I wanted us to ride those horse-rabbits together like two lost cowboys riding in circles . . .*

It was too late.

"He had a mustache," I muttered.

"That's all?" Dad said. "He was creepy because he had a mustache?"

"No . . . he was creepy because . . . I don't know. I mean, he wasn't actually *doing* anything, he was just kind of hanging around, you know . . . lurking in the shadows, watching people as they left."

"Did you see him talking to anyone?"

"No."

"Have you mentioned this man to anyone else?"

"I told Detective Barry."

"Did he take a description?"

I shook my head. "He didn't seem that interested."

"All right," Dad said, taking a pen and a notebook from his pocket. "What did this man look like?"

All I could really remember about the man with the mustache — apart from his mustache, obviously — was that he was slightly odd-looking, slightly hunched, and that he'd reminded me of an overconcerned father keeping an eye out for his child . . . only there hadn't been any children around. It wasn't much to go on, and I wasn't totally convinced that Dad was taking me seriously, anyway, but I did my best to describe the man I thought I'd seen.

By the time I'd finished, it was dark outside, and as I got up and went over to the window to close the curtains — yawning and stretching my arms — Dad got wearily to his feet and suggested that we both get some sleep.

I nodded and smiled at him, stifling another yawn.

He smiled back at me. "Are you going to be OK?"

"Yeah, I think so."

"Well, try not to think about things too much. Just get your head down and get some sleep. You'll probably feel a bit better in the morning."

"Yeah . . ."

He nodded. "Good night, then."

"Yeah, night, Dad."

"See you in the morning."

I waited for him to shut the door, listened to his footsteps going down the stairs, then I took Eric's phone out of my pocket and sat back down on the bed. I flipped it open, turned it on, and muted the ring tone.

I'd never felt more awake in my life.

TWENTY-THREE

t didn't take me long to get the hang of Eric's phone, and the first thing I found out was that he'd deleted all his text messages. Of course, it was possible that his out-box was empty simply because he hadn't sent any texts recently, but, knowing Eric, I somehow doubted that. He'd always been a text maniac. He couldn't let a day go by without sending a text to someone.

His in-box was empty, too.

I exited the MESSAGE menu, opened up his phone book, and started scrolling down through all the entries. Some of them were just abbreviated first names — Jo, Mart, Mich, Nic — while others were abbreviated first names with the initial letter of the surname — Ali F, Pet B, Rob S. The names that interested me the most, though, were the names that didn't really look like names. There were three of them: Pyg, Amo, and Bit.

Pyg I guessed was probably Pauly — Pauly Gilpin — but the other two, Amo and Bit, they didn't mean anything to me.

I selected the details of all three entries. They were all mobile numbers and they were all on speed dial.

Amo and Bit . . . ?

I hit more buttons and checked out the CALLS RECEIVED menu. The last ten calls were listed as follows:

10) Voice mail

9) Pyg

8) Pyg

7) Amo

6) Amo

5) Amo

4) Pyg

3) Voice mail

2) Amo

1) Bit

Calls 2–10 were received between Sunday and today. The call from Bit was received on Friday. The day before the fair. The last ten dialed calls were:

10) Amo

9) Amo

8) Amo

7) Pyg

6) Amo

5) Pet B

4) Amo

3) Pyg

2) Amo

1) Amo

All these calls were made in the last two days.

♥ ♠ ♦ ♣

I sat there for a long time, staring at the phone, staring at the ceiling, staring at the phone, staring at nothing . . . trying to think, trying to work out if anything meant anything . . . trying to work out how to find out if anything meant anything, and what that might mean . . .

If anything.

Maybe *none* of it meant anything? I mean, so what if Eric had been in regular contact with Ƥყɠ, Ꮟ𝗆ᴏ, and Ᏼɪt? The calls to and from Pauly didn't necessarily mean anything—apart from the fact that Eric had been lying to me when he'd told me he didn't have Pauly's number—and Ꮟ𝗆ᴏ and Ᏼɪt . . . ? Well, they *could* be anybody. They could be just friends of Eric's, perfectly innocent friends who didn't have anything to do with Pauly or Stella or Raymond . . .

But I didn't think so.

Eric had been up to something with Campbell on Saturday night.

They'd both been around when Stella had last been seen.

Eric had lied to me.

Campbell had twice warned me off.

Pauly had been in touch with Campbell.

Pauly had drugged the tequila . . .

Black flies buzzing . . .

Connecting disconnecting connecting disconnecting . . .

I knew that it all meant something, and I knew that the key to it all—if there *was* a key to it all—was finding out who Amo and Bit were, and it was incredibly tempting to just dial their numbers and see what happened. But it was also kind of scary, too. What should I say to them? What would they say to me? Would they know it was me? Would I know who they were? And what if one of the numbers was Stella's and someone found out that I'd called it? How was I going to explain that?

On the other hand, though, if I *didn't* ring the numbers . . .

I stared at the phone, emptied my head, and hit the speed dial for Bit.

The line hummed for a few moments, then hissed, and then it went dead. Nothing at all. No tone, no message, no nothing. Completely dead.

I tried Amo next, and this time I got an automated message: *This person's phone is switched off. Please try later or send a text.*

I closed the connection and hit the speed dial for Pyg. The line clicked in, the dial tone rang, and after a couple of seconds I heard Pauly's voice in my ear. "Eric? Is that you?"

I didn't say anything.

"Eric?" Pauly said.

I ended the call and switched off the phone.

Pauly sounded worried.

He sounded small.

He sounded a bit like Raymond.

And I hated him for that. How *dare* he remind me of Raymond? He was Pauly Gilpin, a conniving piece of shit, a sly little bastard who didn't care about anyone but himself. He used people, abused people . . . he put drugs in people's drinks. He was Pauly *Gilpin*, for Christ's sake. How could he *possibly* remind me of Raymond?

It was obscene.

But it was true.

And that hurt. Because it made me realize how much I missed Raymond, and how much I wanted him to be here right now. If only he was here, sitting with me in this room . . . I could talk to him. I could trust him. I could tell him things that I couldn't tell anyone else . . .

But he wasn't here.

I knew that.

And as I closed my eyes to the whispered darkness, I knew that his ghost wasn't here, either. Ghosts don't exist. The ghosts haunting me were chemical ghosts — hallucinations, flashbacks . . . I *knew* that. But I also knew that I'd heard Black Rabbit's voice on Friday. In Raymond's garden. When I'd sensed a soundless movement, and I'd looked down at my feet and seen Black Rabbit flopping past me and hopping back into his hutch . . .

Be careful. Don't go.

I'd tried to convince myself that I hadn't heard it, but I had. And that was on *Friday*. Before the fair, before the den, before I'd drunk any psycho-tequila.

And that didn't make sense.

How could I be hallucinating *before* I'd taken the drug?

Unless . . . ?

No, there were no *unless*es.

I'd heard Black Rabbit's voice on Friday.

Be careful. Don't go.

And again on Sunday.

Take me home . . . bring me home . . .

And Monday . . .

Or was it Tuesday?

It doesn't matter.

And now . . .

In the silence of my head, I was hearing it again.

You know who knows . . .

My skin tingled.

You know.

I didn't have to open my eyes to know that the porcelain rabbit was looking at me. I could feel its black eyes in the darkness, shining like moments of light, like saddened stars . . .

The mother knows.

"Whose mother?" I breathed.

See her dark eyes, her white skin . . . she knows.

"Who knows?"

You like animals, they make you feel good. She draws me on the black table to show him she knows him. You know who knows . . .

"The fortune-teller?"

She knows.

It must have been some time around midnight when I tiptoed downstairs, opened the front door, and crept out into the darkness. Mum and Dad's bedroom light was turned off, so I guessed they were sleeping, but I didn't want to take any chances. So I'd turned off my mobile — and Eric's, too — and I didn't stop walking on tiptoe until I'd opened the front gate and stepped out into the street.

I didn't look back to see if there were any police at the top of the road, I just turned left and walked briskly in the opposite direction, hoping that I looked perfectly normal. I wasn't sneaking out of the house. I wasn't following the advice of a black porcelain rabbit. I wasn't going to see a fortune-telling woman whose dreadlocked son's trailer was stained with the blood of a dead girl.

Not me.

I was just going for a walk, getting some fresh air . . .

That's all I was doing.

The park was dark and silent when I got there. There were no flashing lights tonight. No crashing music, no screams of laughter, no whirling wheels or booming voices swirling around in the air. It was just a park at night, a blurred black emptiness stretching out beyond the padlocked gates.

But it wasn't completely empty.

In the distant dimness I could just make out a faint gathering of lights, and around the lights I could see the grayed outlines of several vehicles. I couldn't tell what kind of vehicles they were, but I was fairly sure that one of them would be Lottie Noyce's trailer. Her son had only been released from questioning today, and the police were still checking his trailer, *and* they might want to talk to him again . . . so he had to be staying somewhere.

As I clambered over the locked gates and began heading across the park toward the lights, I could see that the vehicles were parked in a rough semicircle in the shade of some tall park trees. A generator was chugging away quietly somewhere out of sight. The ground was packed hard, rutted with wheel tracks, and I guessed this was the place where all the fairground vehicles had been parked on Saturday night. It was hard to imagine now, but this must have been the far edge of the fairground, the place where I'd seen Nicole and Luke staggering off into the darkness . . .

It was *all* hard to imagine. The lights, the chaos, the whirling confusion . . . Nicole's dead eyes as Luke led her off into the shadowed maze of trucks and vans and trailers . . .

There'd been dozens of vehicles then, but most of them had gone now. All that was left — standing quietly in the green-gray darkness — were two trailer vans, an RV, and a Toyota pickup with a deflated bouncy castle in the back. Both of the trailers had lights in the windows, and neither of them had any markings.

I suppose I was half-hoping that one of them might say *Madame Baptiste* on the side, or maybe *Noyce & Son* or something. But they didn't. So I just stood there for a while, about thirty feet away from the trailers, watching and listening, trying to work out which one of them belonged to Lottie Noyce. It was a pretty pointless thing to do. The curtains were closed, so I couldn't see anything, and the only sounds I could hear were the soft *chug-chugging* of the generator and the whisper of a night breeze in the trees. But I didn't seem to mind. I was quite content just standing there, soaking up the dark tranquillity of the park, breathing in the scent of the sleeping grass, listening to the silence . . .

The sky was clear and starry black, and for the first time in days there was a slight chill to the air. I turned and gazed out over the darkness. Where was Saturday night now? I wondered. Where had it gone? Where were all the laughing faces, the streaming crowds, the bumper cars and the teddy bears and the whirling wheels? Where was Raymond? Where was the past? Where was —?

I sensed something then — a soundless movement.

Right behind me.

A quiet breath, the whisper of a presence . . .

"Raymond?" I muttered, turning around.

Despite the hope in my voice, I don't think I really believed it was Raymond, but there was still something inside me that died a small death when instead of seeing Raymond I saw the tall figure of Tom Noyce in front of me. He was standing very close, still and pale in his grubby white coveralls, his eyebrow studs and his lip ring glinting dully in the night. His icy blue eyes looked down at me through a tangle of dirty blond dreadlocks.

"Who are you?" he said.

His voice was a gentle growl.

"I'm Pete Boland," I told him. "I'm a friend of —"

"What do you want?"

I looked up at him, wondering briefly how a man so tall and with so much hair could creep up behind me without making a sound.

"What do you want?" he repeated.

"Tell your mother I'm here," I said.

"Why?"

"She'll know why."

He stared at me for a long time then, and as I gazed back at him, looking into those cold blue eyes, I tried to imagine if he was capable of having blood on his hands. I thought I could sense *something* about him, a vague impression that had something to do with life and death . . . but there wasn't anything malicious about it. It was more of a down-to-earth kind of feeling, a practical acceptance that life *depends* upon death. Animals eat animals. Life has to be taken. Blood has to be spilled.

I could imagine Tom Noyce catching a fish or killing a chicken, but that was as far as it went.

"Come on," he said simply, turning around and heading off toward one of the trailers. "She's waiting for you."

TWENTY-FOUR

I suppose I was expecting Lottie Noyce to look exactly the same as Madame Baptiste—the same thick braid of dark brown hair, coiled into a bun on her head, the same old-fashioned brown woolen dress, buttoned up tightly to her neck. But, of course, that was Madame Baptiste, the fortune-teller. And Lottie Noyce wasn't Madame Baptiste. She was just Lottie Noyce: a middle-aged woman with long brown hair, wearing a plain black T-shirt and jeans, sitting at a table at the back of the trailer, drinking tea and smoking a hand-rolled cigarette.

That's all she was.

Just a middle-aged woman smoking a cigarette.

But as Tom Noyce showed me into the trailer, and Lottie just sat there, gazing calmly at me through a cloud of bluish-gray smoke, I still found it hard to take my eyes off her.

"Come in, please," she said, beckoning me over.

The trailer rocked slightly as I crossed over to the table. Pale light glowed from a tall pewter lamp stand in the corner, and the air seemed to shimmer in the light. Lottie was sitting with her back to a curtained window, and as I settled myself down at the small and flimsy table, I could feel her watching me, just like she'd watched me before — studying me, reading me, searching me for secrets.

"Would you like some tea?" she asked, smiling at me.

"No, thanks," I told her.

I glanced over at Tom. He was standing at the other end of the trailer in a cramped little kitchen area. He wasn't doing anything — just standing there, leaning casually against a fridge, quietly keeping an eye on me. The fridge looked ancient. In fact, as I gazed briefly around the trailer, I realized that almost everything around me looked ancient. The pots and pans hanging on the walls, the sparse and simple furniture, the china ornaments, the varnished shells, the primitive paintings in crude wooden frames . . . it all looked like something from another age.

"There's juice if you'd prefer," Lottie said.

"Sorry?"

"Orange juice, pineapple . . ."

I shook my head. "I'm fine, thanks."

She nodded, puffing on her cigarette, and I saw her glance down at a pack of playing cards on the table. They looked the same as the cards she'd used on Saturday night — plain, dark red, no pictures or patterns. Lottie breathed out a long stream of smoke.

"So, Peter," she said, smiling at me again, "what can I do for you?"

I looked at her, not sure what to say. I mean, what could I say? *A porcelain rabbit told me to come and see you. He thinks you know what happened to Raymond. He thinks you know his fate. And he thinks you know why Stella's blood was found on your son's trailer.*

I didn't say anything.

"It's all right," Lottie said gently. "I know how hard this is for you. I know how you feel about your friend."

"Do you?"

She nodded. "You know I do. That's why you're here."

"I don't *know* why I'm here," I said. "All I'm trying to do is find out what happened to Raymond. I just want to know if you know anything, that's all. I mean, if you *really* know anything."

"What do you mean by *really*?"

I looked at her. "I think you know what I mean."

She stared back at me for a while without saying anything, then she smiled quietly to herself and stubbed out her cigarette in a small metal ashtray. "It's not *all* deceit, Peter," she said quietly. "The cards mean nothing, of course — they're just part of the show. Some people like to believe in them, just as some people like to believe in gods and devils and miraculous stories." She paused for a moment, staring thoughtfully into space, then she shook her head, dismissing whatever it was she was thinking about, and went on. "But I do *know* things, Peter. No matter what you believe or disbelieve, I *can* see things that other people can't see. It's how I make my living. It's how I make people believe in me."

"What kinds of things can you see?" I asked.

She looked at me. "Simple things . . . like the sleeplessness in your eyes, the fresh cut on your chin, the very faint bruising around your neck —"

"What about Raymond?" I said. "What did you see in him?"

She smiled. "I saw traces of black rabbit fur on the shoulder of his jacket."

"And what did that tell you?"

"That he had a black rabbit . . . and that he was in the habit of holding it close to him." She shrugged. "And that told me how much his rabbit meant to him, which for a boy of his age . . . well, it suggests a certain way of life, a certain set of emotions." She tapped the side of her head. "It's all about perception, Peter — and perception can be trained just like anything else. You can teach yourself how to observe, how to ask the right questions, how to deduce . . . and after a while, these things become second nature. You're not even aware of what you're doing most of the time. You see things, hear things, smell things . . . and without even thinking about it, you just add them all up and something inside you tells you what they probably mean." She smiled. "All you have to do then is tell people what they want to hear."

"Is that what you did with Raymond?" I said. "I mean, is that all you were doing — telling him what he wanted to hear?"

"What do *you* think?"

"I don't know," I muttered, suddenly realizing the stupidity of my question. "I just thought . . ."

"Yes?"

"Well, all that stuff you told Raymond about his kindness, his selflessness —"

"Simple observations and deductions, nothing more."

"And the stuff about life and death —"

"Life and death comes to us all."

"But you were talking about somebody dying—"

"Raymond was talking about somebody dying. Not me."

"All right," I said. "But what about at the end, when Raymond was leaving and you came up to me and told me to look after him. You told me to take care. You told me to take him home. Why did you do that?"

She hesitated then, and there was something in her eyes—a look, a feeling—that made me wonder if all she was doing was telling me what *I* wanted to hear. She knew I didn't believe in magical powers or mysterious insights, and she was simply trying to convince me that I was right. That it *was* all a scam, that it *was* just a show . . . that I was right not to believe in things that aren't real.

And I knew that I *was* right.

But I wanted to be wrong.

"Do you ever get feelings you don't understand?" Lottie asked me.

"Like what?"

She looked at me. "Like when you're going to see someone, and you don't know whether they're at home or not, but when you get to their house and knock on their door . . . you somehow just *know* if they're there or not. And you *know* that your feeling is right."

"You can trust it," I said quietly.

She nodded. "I felt something like that about Raymond, something I trusted but didn't understand, something that went beyond what my perceptions were telling me.

I didn't know exactly what it was, but it didn't feel good. Something was going to happen to him. Or he was going to do something . . ."

"Do you *know* what happened to him?" I asked bluntly.

She shook her head. "I don't think he hurt anyone."

"What about Stella Ross? Do you know what happened to her?"

Lottie glanced over at her son. He hadn't moved, he was still just standing there, leaning casually against the fridge. "Tom doesn't know anything about Stella Ross," Lottie said, turning back to me. "He didn't even know who she was until the police started questioning him."

"I wasn't suggesting—"

"I know you weren't."

"I just thought you might have seen something, you know . . ."

"I've already answered all the policemen's questions."

"Me, too," I said. "But that doesn't mean I've told them everything."

She smiled. "You think I know more than I'm telling?"

"I don't know . . . you told me just now that you can see things that other people can't see." I looked at her. "I don't suppose you told the police that, did you?"

She shook her head. "They wouldn't have listened." She looked at me. "Why haven't *you* told them everything."

"I don't know . . . I just . . ."

"Are you frightened?"

"Of what?"

"Anything . . . fear is often a motivation for lying."

"Fear of what?"

"Whatever it is you're frightened of."

I thought about that for a moment, wondering about all my fears — physical, mental, emotional, invisible — trying to work out if any of them *could* be the motivation behind all my lies . . . but it was too much to think about. Too *scary* to think about.

I looked at Lottie. "Why didn't *you* tell the police everything?"

She shrugged. "Like I said, they wouldn't have listened. Why would they listen to someone like me?"

"I'm listening," I told her.

She smiled at me again, idly shuffling the cards in her hand. "I thought you didn't believe in the power of the cards?"

"I don't."

"But you believe in me?"

"I don't know. You haven't told me anything yet."

"I can only tell you what I think."

I didn't say anything for a moment, I just looked at her, trying to read her eyes, trying to work out what she was all about . . . but I couldn't do it. Her eyes were like mirrors. All I could see in them was a study of myself.

"Go on, then," I said to her. "Tell me what you think."

"I think this is all about love," she said.

"Love?"

She nodded. "It's a heartless business."

♥ ♠ ♦ ♣

As Lottie began telling me what she'd seen that night, and what she thought it might mean, I noticed that the pack of playing cards never left her hands. She didn't do anything with them at first — she didn't even seem to be aware that she was holding them. They were just there, in her hands, almost as if they were part of her. Which I suppose, in a way, they were.

"As soon as Raymond came into the tent that night," she told me, "I knew there was something different about him. And I could tell by the way he was looking at things that he thought he knew something about fortune-telling. I wasn't sure if he believed in it or not, but I sensed that he knew what to expect." She looked at me. "Am I right?"

"I don't know," I admitted. "Raymond's always liked reading, and he reads about all kinds of weird stuff. So I wouldn't be surprised if he knew a bit about fortune-telling."

She nodded. "He knew what the cards are meant to symbolize. That's why I didn't manipulate them for his reading." She smiled at me. "I usually just pick out the cards that fit in with what I'm getting from the person in front of me, but with Raymond . . . well, I just thought it'd be interesting to see what happened without any help from me."

"Is that why you were so surprised when you saw his cards?"

"Yes . . . they were *very* dark cards. Darker than I'd ever choose to select. And even though I know they're just cards, and I *know* there's nothing in them . . ." She glanced at the cards in her hand. "They're just bits of patterned card, numbers and shapes and colors . . . they're just tools. They can be whatever you want them to be." She slowly turned over the top card of the pack and placed it faceup on the table. "The Queen of Spades," she said. "The woman with come-to-bed eyes." She turned over another card. "The Queen of Hearts. A woman with purpose." She looked at me. "I saw Stella Ross after you and Raymond had left that night. She walked past my tent, parading herself like a queen, surrounded by all her servants and worshippers. I never saw her again."

"What did you think of her?"

Lottie closed her eyes. "She wants to be adored, but she despises those who adore her. She's insecure, self-obsessed, vengeful, bitter. She likes to play cruel games. She likes to manipulate people."

"You got all that from one brief look at her?"

Lottie smiled. "We're all sorcerers, Peter. We all live in a wonderland of marvel and beauty if we did but know it."

"What?" I frowned.

"Sorry," she said, opening her eyes and grinning at me. "I spend most of my life talking crap—it's hard to break the habit."

"Right. So you didn't see Stella again that night?"

"No. But, as I told you before, I *am* very good at reading people, and I did get the impression from her that her overriding desire was to have what she couldn't have." She looked at me. "Just like the boy you were sitting with on the bench later on."

"Pauly?"

She turned over a card: the Four of Diamonds. "Intoxication," she said simply. "His face is dulled with drink and drugs." Another card. "The Two of Spades. He loves an illusion." Another card. "The Seven of Spades, the fascination of the moth to the flame." She looked at me. "He, too, wanted what he couldn't have."

"Who — Pauly?"

"Yes."

"What couldn't he have?"

She narrowed her eyes, thinking about it. "Well, at first I thought that the object of his desire was one of the two lovers he was watching, that he wanted one of them, and that it angered him to see them together. But after a while I realized there was more to it than that. I think there was something *else* he wanted —"

"Hold on," I said, getting confused. "Are we still talking about Pauly here?"

She nodded. "The boy on the bench. You watched him for a while, and then you went over and sat down next to him."

"Right . . . so who were these two lovers he was watching?"

"The same ones that you were watching."

I looked at her in disbelief. "You mean Eric and Campbell?"

"I don't know their names—one of them was the brother of the girl you know, the other one was an older boy with a slightly crooked mouth."

"Yeah," I muttered. "Eric Leigh and Wes Campbell. But they're not . . ."

Lovers, I was going to say. They're not *lovers*. But all at once a whole load of stuff started popping and crackling inside my head—the sound of everything coming together—and suddenly it all seemed so obvious. Eric and Wes Campbell: together at the fairground, together at Eric's house, together in his bedroom . . .

Eric and Campbell were *together*.

That's why Campbell had warned me off.

That's why Eric had lied to me about where he'd been all night . . . he'd been with Wes Campbell.

They were *together*.

"Didn't you know?" Lottie asked me.

"No . . . well, I know that Eric's gay—"

"He's the brother?"

"Yeah, I mean everyone knows about Eric. He came out years ago. But Wes Campbell . . . ?" I looked at her. "Are you sure about him?"

She nodded. "The way they were looking at each other, the way they were standing together, their closeness, their intimacy . . . of course, they were both doing their best to disguise it." She paused, looking at me. "The older boy . . . Wes Campbell, is it?"

"Yeah."

"There's no doubt that he loves the brother, but he loves himself too much to show it." She turned over a card. "The Two of Diamonds . . . he fears that his love will meet with disapproval and suspicion."

"Christ," I said, shaking my head. "Wes Campbell . . . shit. I can't believe it." I looked at Lottie. "I mean, I'm not saying . . . you know, I'm not saying that guys like Wes Campbell *can't* be gay or anything, it's just . . . well, it's just a bit of a shock, that's all."

Lottie lit a cigarette. "It was clear to me that they were both very troubled about concealing their love, but I think the brother was the more concerned of the two." She turned over a card: the Seven of Clubs. "Guilt," she said. "Embarrassment. Shame. The brother's fears of revelation are based on shallowness, but I think he dreads the consequences much more than his friend."

I thought about that for a moment, wondering why Eric should be more concerned than Campbell. I mean, as far as I was aware, no one knew that Campbell was gay — and I guessed he didn't *want* anyone to know — so I could understand why he'd want to keep things quiet. But Eric had been openly gay for ages, and I'd always got the impression that he genuinely didn't care what other people thought of him . . .

But maybe I was wrong about that.

Maybe I'd always been wrong.

I looked at Lottie. "Is this what you meant when you said that it's all about love?"

"Partly . . ." She turned over two cards: the Two of Hearts, the Three of Hearts. "The sister," she said, looking up at me. "The one who was watching you . . ."

"Nicole," I said.

Lottie gazed down at the two cards. "The last love is always the best . . ." She looked into my eyes. "She's loved you for a long time."

"Who?"

"Nicole."

"She's *loved* me?"

"For a long time."

I shook my head. "No . . ."

"Yes."

"No," I said firmly. "She *used* to like me . . . and maybe she still does a bit. But she doesn't *love* me. Absolutely not."

Lottie shrugged, smiling. "Perhaps I was mistaken."

"Yeah."

"I just thought, from the way she was watching you—"

"You made a mistake."

Lottie nodded. "If you say so."

"I do."

Lottie tapped ash into the ashtray. "She's very much like her brother, isn't she?"

"They're twins."

"They're close, then."

"Yeah, I suppose so. I mean, they've always spent a lot of time with each other, you know—hanging around together, doing stuff together, always sharing everything . . .

clothes, makeup, jewelry, even boyfriends sometimes . . ."
I paused for a moment, looking down at the table, struck
by a sudden thought.

"What is it?" Lottie asked me.

Sharing, I thought to myself. *They're always sharing
everything . . .*

"Peter?"

I looked up at Lottie. "Did you see Nicole later that
night?"

"She was with Luke Kemp," she said solemnly. "Luke
was working the tilt-a-whirl."

"I know."

"He took her back to his trailer."

"I know that, too."

"She didn't want to be with him. She was . . . well,
I think at first she was just doing it to spite you, and I don't
think she meant it to go so far . . . but Luke always takes
things too far."

"What do you mean?"

Lottie shook her head. "He always makes sure he gets
what he wants, and he doesn't care how he does it."

"What are you trying to say?"

"There's no proof . . . it's all just rumors. But it's been
suggested that some of the girls he takes back to his trailer
don't have a clue what they're doing."

"You mean he *drugs* them or something?"

"It's possible, yes."

"Shit."

"Sometimes, of course, they're just very drunk . . ."

"Nicole *was* pretty out of it."

"Yes . . ." Lottie stubbed out her cigarette. "I think that's why your friend Raymond followed her to the trailer. I think he was worried about her. He cared for her."

"Without thinking of himself."

"Yes. He had great kindness."

I looked at her, wondering if she remembered saying that about Raymond before . . . and I could tell by the way she avoided my eyes that she did. "Did you see Kemp chasing him away from the trailer?" I asked her.

"Yes."

"Did he catch him?"

She shook her head. "Raymond was too quick. Luke never even got near him."

"Where did Raymond go?"

"The fair was closed by then. The lights were out. I saw Raymond running through the fairground, down toward the exit, and then he just carried on running off into the darkness."

"Which way?"

She pointed over my shoulder. "Toward the far end of the park, where the main gates are."

"Did you see him go through the gates?"

"Yes."

"Which way did he go?"

"He turned right."

"And then?"

"I don't know. That was the last I saw of him."

I looked down at the cards on the table again. They were all arranged in a circle around the first card she'd turned over, the Queen of Spades. Stella's card. I studied them, gazing at the shapes, the colors, the faces . . . trying to remember who they were supposed to represent . . . trying to work out the connections . . . the nonconnections . . . the black flies, the pops, the crackles in my head . . . the colors, the shapes, the faces . . .

The cards meant nothing.

I was trying to see the patterns *beyond* the cards.

"Where am I in all this?" I asked Lottie.

"You're here," she said, tapping the card on top of the pack.

I looked at her.

She said, "You know it doesn't mean anything."

"Yeah . . ."

"You can be whatever you want to be."

"Can I?"

She smiled. "What do you *want* to be?"

"I don't know . . ."

"What's your card?"

"What?"

She tapped the pack of cards with her finger. "Your card — what do you think it is?"

"I don't know . . ."

"Yes, you do. Tell me what you think it is." She smiled again. "What harm can it do?"

I looked at the card under her finger, and I knew it meant nothing. I knew I couldn't know what it was, or what

I wanted it to be. And I knew I didn't know what I wanted it to be. So I just said the first thing that came into my head. "The Five of Spades."

She turned the card over, and of course it was the Five of Spades. It was never going to be anything else.

"What does it mean?" I heard myself say.

"Whatever you want it to mean — it could mean that you're growing up, you're beginning to think about yourself and the nature of the universe and your place within it. It could be a lucky omen. It could mean a lover's quarrel. It could foretell a summer of madness."

"But it's just a card."

"That's right."

She placed my card on the table, outside the circle of other cards, and then she just sat there looking at them in thoughtful silence.

It was late now. Early morning. The air was cold and still, the world outside was asleep.

I was here.

Now.

I was here.

I gazed at the cards on the table. I was there, I was here. Everyone else was there. Everyone else except . . .

"Where's Raymond?" I said quietly to Lottie.

She turned over the top card of the pack and placed it faceup on the table.

It was blank.

TWENTY-FIVE

The predawn sky was silent and black as I walked the empty streets back home. The world was asleep. The houses, the parked cars, the walls, the gates, the hedges, the sidewalks, the air . . . everything was frozen in the eternal dawn of streetlights.

Nothing moved.

Nothing made a sound.

Apart from me.

Tap tap tap tap . . . my steady footsteps echoing dully in the night.

Tap tap tap tap . . . my unsteady mind trying to think.

One thought, another thought.

One step, another step . . .

One step at a time.

One thought at a time.

Eric and Wes Campbell are lovers.

Stella liked to play cruel games.

Pauly wants what he can't have.

What can't he have?

Eric? Wes Campbell?

Stella?

One step, another step . . .

Nicole doesn't love me.

Stella despised those who adored her.

It's all about love.

One thought at a time.

It's all about love.

It's not all deceit.

The cards mean nothing.

Gods and devils.

Pauly adored Stella.

One thought.

Sharing . . . Nic and Eric . . . they're always sharing everything.

Clothes.

Perfume.

Jewelry.

I paused then, my mind suddenly fixed on the image of a broken necklace. A shortish length of fine gold chain in a clear plastic envelope . . . *it was found in the coin pocket of Stella's shorts.* A string of gold chains hanging on a hook above Nicole's dressing table. Chains, connections . . .

Stella, Nicole.

Nicole, Eric.

They're always sharing everything.

The images skimmed through my mind like weightless pebbles skipping over a slurred black pond. The connections ticked — *tick tick tick* — barely touching the surface, like summer birds drinking on the wing. I saw arrows, darts, stars, hooks, flat black stones, too fast to see. I saw the rippled trace of movement in the still black waters of the night. Circles, trails, patterns . . . coming together, moving apart.

I knew it all meant something, but I didn't know what. I squeezed my eyes shut and opened them again. I was standing by the old factory gates in Park Road. I could see the lights of the town in the distance. I could smell the iron and the dust of the factory. Iron and dust, concrete and flesh. I could smell . . .

Darkness.

And heat.

I could feel a presence.

I heard a click then, a very faint click from across the road, and as I turned toward it, peering into the darkness, a pair of headlights suddenly snapped on, blinding me with their brightness. As I shielded my eyes against the glare, I heard a car starting up. The engine revved loudly a couple of times, tires squealed, and before I knew what was happening, the car was roaring toward me in a blaze of dazzling lights.

My body froze.

My head emptied.

All I could do was stand there, glued to the spot, watching dumbly as the car screamed toward me in nightmarish slow motion, and just for an instant I wondered stupidly why I wasn't feeling anything, why I wasn't doing anything, why I wasn't trying to get out of the way, why my life wasn't flashing before my eyes . . .

At the very last moment, just as the car was about to hit me, it swung to the left, missing me by inches, and skidded to a sudden screeching halt. And all at once the rest of the world came back to life again. I could hear my heart beating. I could smell the burning rubber of the tires. I could feel my hands shaking. And I could see Wes Campbell staring at me through the open window of a small black hatchback.

"Get in," he said.

I just looked at him.

He leaned across the passenger seat and opened the door. "Get in."

I shook my head.

He smiled at me. "I just want to talk, that's all."

"What about?"

"Get in," he said, "and I'll tell you."

"I don't think so."

I stepped away from the window then and started edging my way around the back of the car. But before I'd gotten very far, Campbell slammed the car into reverse and lurched back across the pavement to block me off. I stared at him for a moment, then I started moving back the other way, back around the front of the car. Campbell hit the gears again and screeched forward, this time swinging the car toward me, and I had to jump back to get out of the way.

"You're not *going* anywhere," he said to me through the window. "You might as well get in."

"What do you want?" I asked him, breathing hard.

"I want you to get in the fucking *car.*"

I stepped back a little more and glanced over my shoulder. The road was as empty as ever. There was no one around, no one to call out to. The world was still asleep. The houses, the parked cars, the walls, the gates, the hedges, the sidewalks, the air . . .

"All right," Campbell said calmly. "Listen, just give me the phone, OK? Give me the phone and I'll let you go home."

I turned to him. "What phone?"

"Don't fuck with me, Boland. I'm giving you a chance here. Just throw the phone through the window—"

"I don't know what you're talking about."

He stared coldly at me. "What do you think's going to happen?"

"What?"

"If you make me get out of this car . . . what do you think's going to happen?"

I said nothing.

He grinned at me. "You're going to start running, *that's* what's going to happen. You're going to start running, and I'm going to come after you, and I'm going to catch you. And I'm going to be really pissed off with you for making me get out of this car and chase you around these shitty little streets, and I'm already pretty pissed off with you anyway, so when I catch up with you, the very *least* I'm going to do is kick the living shit out of you, and then, one way or another, I'm going to get Eric's phone off you." He smiled at me. "So it'd save us both a lot of bother if you just gave it to me right now."

"You're Amɒ, aren't you?" I said to him.

"What?"

"Amɒ . . . amour. It's French for love."

"What the fuck are you talking about?"

"Eric's mother is French." I stared at Campbell. "You're Eric's lover. You're Ⱥⱬⱷ."

The color had drained from Campbell's face now, and just for a moment he was a different person—frail, human, almost pitiable—but then, almost immediately, his rage kicked in, a cold and intense physical fury, and suddenly he was anything *but* human. He was a stone-cold killer, calmly opening the glove compartment and taking out his box cutter. He was opening the car door, getting out, moving toward me with the measured steps of a man who knows exactly what he's doing and doesn't care what it means . . .

And I was already stepping back, starting to turn around, getting ready to run . . .

When someone grabbed me from behind.

I couldn't see who it was at first, all I could feel were two strong hands on my shoulders, holding me firmly in place, and the imposing presence of someone behind me. I squirmed and struggled for a moment, trying to break free, trying to see who it was, and then I heard Tom Noyce's deep voice.

"It's all right," he said quietly. "Just stay where you are."

I twisted around and gazed up at him.

"OK?" he asked me.

"Yeah . . ."

He took his hands off my shoulders and looked slowly at Campbell. I looked at him, too. He'd stopped about ten feet away from us and was staring over my shoulder at Tom.

"Who the fuck are you?" he said.

"Tom Noyce."

"Yeah? Well, listen to me, Tom fucking Noyce—"

"Get back in the car," Tom said calmly.

"*What?*"

"Get in the car and go home."

Campbell glared at him. "And what are *you* going to do if I don't?"

Tom didn't say anything, he just sighed quietly and started moving toward Campbell. Campbell hesitated for a moment, nervously blinking his eyes, then he held up his box cutter and waved it at Tom.

"I'll cut you," he warned him, backing away. "You come any closer, I'll fucking cut you . . . don't think I won't . . ."

Tom just kept on walking, his eyes fixed silently on Campbell, and I could see that Campbell was beginning to realize that Tom Noyce wasn't just big—far too big for the suddenly very small knife in Campbell's hand—but he was fearless, too. Tom Noyce didn't care what happened to him. And Campbell wasn't prepared to face that.

"Yeah, all right," he said to Tom, backing away to the car. "Look, I'm going, for Christ's sake . . . OK? I'm going."

Tom stopped, watching him as he opened the car door.

Campbell looked at me. "I'll see *you* later, Boland." He glanced at Tom, then turned back to me and grinned. "And you won't have your pet yeti to look after you next time. I'll make sure of that."

As Tom took another step toward him, Campbell laughed and quickly got in the car. The engine was still running, the exhaust fumes misting in the still night air, and even before the door slammed shut, Campbell had put the car into gear and hit the accelerator. The tires spun for a moment, squealing loudly, and then the hatchback screeched away from the curb, swung around to the right, and sped off down Park Road.

I watched it until it was out of sight, then I turned to Tom Noyce. He was still just standing there, staring down the road.

"Thanks," I said to him.

He turned to me and nodded. "No problem."

"That was Wes Campbell," I explained. "He's one of the guys your mother was telling me about."

"I know—I saw him earlier, in the park. He was following you."

"Following me?"

Tom nodded. "He was parked across the road when you were in the trailer. He drove off after you left."

"So you followed me?"

He shrugged. "I thought you might need some help."

I didn't know what to say. I mean, I *wanted* to ask him why—why had he bothered to help me when he hardly even knew me?—but it seemed such a shitty thing to say. So I just smiled at him and thanked him again. And he just nodded his dreadlocked head at me and told me it was no problem again.

And it felt OK.

"Well, anyway," I said, "I'd better be getting home now."

"Do your parents know you're out?" Tom asked.

"No."

"Have you got far to go?"

"Hythe Street."

He nodded. "I'll come with you."

"It's all right," I told him. "I'll be OK."

"Fair enough," Tom shrugged. "If that's what you want. But I wouldn't be surprised if Campbell's waiting for you somewhere."

I thought about that for a moment, imagining Campbell sitting in his car in a side street somewhere, waiting for me to walk past, waiting for his chance to get me on my own . . .

And then I thought about Tom, and I couldn't help wondering about his motives again. Why was he helping me? Why was he looking out for me? Why should I trust him? I mean, Stella's blood was found on his trailer, wasn't it? And his trailer had been parked down by the river. And now here he was, offering to walk me back home, back to my house in Hythe Street . . . just a few hundred feet from the river. And just because he'd *told* me that he'd followed me from the trailer because he'd seen Campbell following me and he'd thought I might need some help . . . well, I only had his word for that, didn't I? Maybe he'd followed me for his own reasons, and maybe he'd saved me from Campbell for his own reasons, too?

I looked at him, smiling nervously, and as he looked back at me with those cold blue eyes, I found myself reimagining his capabilities . . .

I didn't know who Tom Noyce was.

I had no *idea* who he was.

"Are you all right?" he asked me. "You don't look so good. Do you want me to—?"

"Has your mother ever worked with Bretton's Funfairs?" I heard myself ask him.

"What?"

"Or Funderstorm?"

He shook his head. "I don't know what—"

He stopped abruptly as the piercing wail of a police siren suddenly blipped on and off behind him, and as he spun around to see where it was coming from, I saw the flashing blue lights of a police patrol car accelerating up the street toward us. The headlights flashed, the siren blipped again . . . and then the patrol car was pulling up at the side of the road, the doors were opening, and two uniformed officers were getting out and moving purposefully toward us.

"Shit," sighed Tom. "Here we go again."

Mum and Dad were waiting for me at the police station. They were both in the reception area when one of the officers took me in, sitting with Detective Barry on a red metal bench, and they both looked pale and exhausted. As soon as Mum saw me, she jumped up from the bench and hurried over to me.

"Pete!" she cried, pushing the officer out of the way and flinging her arms around me. "Christ . . . I was so *worried*. We didn't know where you'd gone. We've been looking *everywhere* for you." She stopped hugging me for a moment and held me at arm's length, looking intently into my eyes. "Are you all right? Has anything happened to you? You're not—?"

"I'm all right, Mum," I told her. "I'm fine—"

"Where the hell have you *been*?" she said, letting herself get slightly angry now. It was the kind of relieved anger that parents allow themselves when everything has turned out OK in the end, but they know that it might *not* have turned out OK.

I could see Dad and Detective Barry coming over to us now. Dad looked surprisingly calm, but I knew that didn't mean anything. He always looked pretty calm when things were really bad.

"I'm sorry, Mum," I said. "I didn't *know* you were looking for me, I thought you were asleep—"

"Have you been with *him*?" she asked me, shooting a look at Tom Noyce as the other officer led him past us toward the security doors.

"I'm sorry, Mrs. Boland," Detective Barry said as he came up and stopped beside us. "We need to ask your son a few questions."

Mum ignored him, keeping her eyes fixed on me. "What's going on, Pete?" she said. "What have you been doing all night?"

"Nothing. I was just—"

"Please, Mrs. Boland," Barry said. "I know you've been through a lot tonight, and I know you want to be with Peter right now, but we really need to ask him some questions first."

"You're not questioning him without me," Mum said firmly.

"Of course not." Barry looked at Dad. "I need to talk to him, Jeff. The sooner the better."

Dad nodded and turned to me. "Are you all right, Pete?" he said quietly.

"Yeah . . ."

"Are you up to answering questions?"

I shrugged. "I suppose . . ."

"You don't have to if you don't want to, but you're going to have to do it at some point. You might as well get it over with now."

I looked at him. "Can you come with me?"

Dad glanced at Detective Barry.

Barry shook his head. "Sorry, Jeff."

Dad turned back to me. "Mum'll be with you. Is that OK?"

I looked at Mum.

She smiled at me. "You'll have to make do with second best again."

"I didn't mean that—"

"I know. I was only joking."

"I just meant—"

"It's all right, Pete," she said reassuringly. "I know what you meant."

"Sorry . . ."

Dad put his hand on my shoulder. "Let's just get this done, OK? The sooner it's over, the sooner we can all go home."

I looked at him. "I didn't mean to cause any trouble, Dad. I was just trying to—"

"Later, Pete," he said, giving me a look. "We'll talk about it later."

It was the same interview room as before, and I was sitting there, just like before, with Mum sitting next to me and Barry sitting opposite, and the red light of a tape recorder blinking away in the corner, and a stack of video equipment piled on a table against the wall. The only difference this time was that Officer Gallagher's place at the table had been taken by John Kesey, which Mum didn't like one bit. And she didn't try to hide it, either.

Kesey had stood up and smiled at her when we'd first come in. "Hello, Anne," he'd said, offering his hand. "It's good to know that Pete's safe and sound—"

"Yeah," she said, ignoring his hand and sitting down. "Can we just get on with it, please? It's late. Everyone's tired." She glared at Detective Barry. "You've got twenty minutes and then we're leaving. So you'd better start asking your questions."

Detective Barry did as he was told.

"Where did you go tonight, Peter?"
    "I went to see Lottie Noyce."
    "Why?"
    "I wanted to talk to her."
    "About what?"
    "Raymond, Stella . . . anything she might know."
    "Did she tell you anything?"
    "Not really."

"Not really?"

"She didn't tell me anything that I didn't already know."

"Like what?"

I told him some of the stuff we'd talked about — how she'd guessed things about Raymond, how she'd thought he was troubled, how she'd understood why I was worried about him.

"She told me she'd seen him following Nicole back to Luke Kemp's trailer," I said. "She thought he was worried about her."

"Raymond was worried about Nicole?"

"Yeah."

"Why?"

"Because he cared about her. Because she was drunk, and she didn't know what she was doing . . . and Raymond probably didn't like the look of Luke Kemp." I looked at Barry. "Did you know he's suspected of drugging girls?"

Barry nodded. "We're looking into it. Was Tom Noyce at Lottie's trailer tonight?"

I looked at John Kesey. He was taking notes. "Have you *looked into* all these fairground disappearances yet?" I asked him.

Kesey smiled, showing tobacco-stained teeth. "We're looking into everything, Pete."

Detective Barry said, "Please answer my question, Peter. Was Tom Noyce at the trailer tonight?"

"Yeah."

"Have you ever met him before?"

"I saw him once, that's all. I told you before, I saw him on Saturday night—"

"So you've never met him before?"

"No."

"Did you talk to him tonight?"

"What about?"

"Anything."

"Not at the trailer . . . well, he saw me outside and asked me what I was doing there, but after that, when I was talking with Lottie, he never said anything."

"So how did you end up on Park Road together?"

"He said he was worried about me . . . he'd seen some kids from Greenwell Rise hanging around when I left, and he thought they might be following me or something. They were in a car."

"Why would they be following you?"

I shrugged. "I was on my own, it was late . . ."

"And why would Tom Noyce be worried about you?"

"I don't know. You'd have to ask him."

"We will." Barry smiled briefly. "So he followed you home, is that right?"

"I didn't know he was there until some guy pulled up in a car and started hassling me."

"Where was this?"

"On Park Road, by the old factory. This guy just pulled up and asked me if he could use my phone, and when I asked him why, he started getting all nasty about it."

"What do you mean?"

"He was threatening me, telling me to give him my phone . . . and then he started getting out of the car and waving a knife at me. And that's when Tom Noyce showed up."

"What did he do?"

"He told the guy to get back in his car and go home."

"Just like that?"

"Yeah."

"And what happened then?"

"The guy got back in his car and drove off."

"Lucky for you."

"Yeah."

"Did you know him — the guy in the car?"

"No."

"Could you describe him?"

I described someone who could have been anyone — mid-twenties, dark eyes, short brown hair — and as John Kesey wrote it all down, I kept my eyes fixed firmly on the table. I was pretty sure that Barry knew I was lying, but if I'd told him the truth then — if I'd told him that the guy in the car was Wes Campbell — Barry would have wanted to know who Campbell was, and how I knew him, and how he knew me, and why I hadn't said anything about knowing him before . . . and I really didn't think I could cope with all that.

"So," Barry said, "after Tom Noyce had scared this guy off, what did you do then?"

"Not much . . . I thanked him, asked him what he was doing there, and that was about it. I was just about to get going when the police car showed up."

"Where were you going?"

"Home."

"What about Noyce? Did he say where he was going?"

"No."

"Didn't you ask him?"

"No."

"Where do you think he was going?"

"I don't know. Back to his mum's trailer, I expect."

Barry stared at the table in silence for a moment, then he let out a long sigh and looked up at me. "All right, Peter . . . let me ask you something else." He paused, staring at me. "What would you say if I were to tell you that we'd found your fingerprints on Tom Noyce's trailer?"

The question surprised me, as I suppose it was meant to, and I found myself glancing instinctively at Mum. She looked back at me for a moment, equally surprised, then she turned to Barry.

"If you're going to ask questions," she said to him, "just ask them. Don't give us all that *what would you say if I were to tell you* rubbish. Were Pete's fingerprints found on the trailer or not?"

"Yes, on the door handle."

"And you'd like to know how they got there?"

"I would."

"Right, so ask him."

Barry looked at me, trying to hide a hint of embarrassment. "All right, Peter. Your fingerprints were found on the door handle of Tom Noyce's trailer. Would you like to tell me how they got there?"

It didn't take long to explain everything: how I'd gone looking for Raymond on Sunday morning, how I'd seen the trailer down at the river and wondered if Raymond might be inside, how I'd knocked on the door and called out, and how, when there'd been no answer, I'd tried the door. It was simple. The truth. The simple, straightforward truth.

But I was pretty sure that Barry didn't believe it.

"Did anyone see you at the trailer?" he said.

"I don't think so."

"Why didn't you mention it before?"

"I didn't think it was important."

"Didn't you see the blood on the trailer?"

"No."

"Did you see Stella's clothes?"

"No."

"How long have you known Tom Noyce?"

"I don't know him."

"What were you were doing at the fairground on Saturday when Stella Ross disappeared?"

"Nothing."

"Why were you sitting on that bench near the toilets? Were you waiting for someone?"

"I've already *told* you —"

"All right," Mum said. "That's enough."

"What are you hiding, Peter?" Barry said quietly.

"He's not answering any more questions," Mum said firmly, starting to get up. She looked at me. "Come on, Pete. We're leaving."

"Sit down, please, Mrs. Boland," Barry said.

She glared at him. "Is Pete under arrest?"

"No, but—"

"Are you going to arrest him?"

"We're just trying to find out—"

"Are you going to *arrest* him?"

"No," Barry sighed.

"So he's free to go?"

"Yes."

"Right," Mum said, turning to me and almost dragging me to my feet. "Come on, we're going home."

TWENTY-SIX

As I sat in the back of Dad's car on the way home from the police station, all I could feel was a brain-deadening tiredness and a hopeless desire to go back in time and start all over again. I wanted to be lying on my bed again on that hot Thursday night, just as the sun was beginning to go down. I wanted to be busy doing nothing again, not caring about anything . . . I wanted to be happy enough doing nothing. And when the telephone rang, and I heard Mum calling out to me from downstairs—*Pete! Phone!*—I wanted to stay where I was, just lying on my bed, staring at the ceiling, minding my own mindless business . . .

I wanted to make myself stay there.

Happy enough doing nothing.

I looked out the car window. We were heading out of town now, heading home, and I realized that Dad was taking the long way around, so I guessed all the press reporters and TV crews were still camped out in the old factory parking lot. The sun was coming up, rising over the blued horizon in a blaze of burning orange, and as its tireless light streamed in through the car windows, I could already feel the first faint promise of another scorching day.

The back of my neck was sweating.

I couldn't be bothered to wipe it.

"Is there any news about Raymond?" I asked Dad.

He looked at me in the rearview mirror. "You might not realize it, Pete, but I've had more important things to think about than Raymond tonight." He shook his head, and his voice hardened. "I mean, what do you think we've both been doing all night? Do you think we've been sitting around thinking about *Raymond*?"

"No, of course not —"

"I'll tell you what we've been doing," he said. "We've been trying not to panic, we've been trying not to imagine the worst . . . we've been ringing your mobile, ringing the police, ringing your school friends . . . Christ, Pete, we've been up all night worrying ourselves to death. *That's* what we've been doing."

"I'm sorry . . ."

"Don't *ever* do that again. Do you understand?"

"Yeah . . ."

"And wherever you go," Mum added, "whatever you're doing, always keep your mobile turned on."

"Yeah, sorry."

"Christ," Dad sighed. "Why can't you just do what you're *told* for once in your life?"

I looked at him in the rearview mirror. "You told me that sometimes you have to do whatever's necessary. You have to do what you think is right."

"Yes, I know —"

"I'm only doing what I think is right."

Dad sighed again. "Well, that's as may be . . ."

"That's what you *told* me."

"Yes, I know, but I didn't tell you—"

"Not now," Mum said, touching his arm. "Let's just get home first, OK? We're all tired. We need a rest. There'll be plenty of time for talking later."

Dad went quiet.

Mum looked at him for a moment, then she turned in her seat and smiled at me. "You must be hungry."

"Not really."

"How does bacon and eggs sound?"

"Sizzly," I said.

She smiled.

I sat back in my seat and looked out the window.

I had no conscious intention of doing what I did next, and considering what Dad had just been telling me about how much pain and worry I'd caused, I'd like to think that it was beyond my conscience, too. Or maybe I'm just making excuses. Maybe I'm just trying to kid myself that I had no control over my actions.

I don't know.

But as the car pulled up outside our house, and Dad turned off the engine, I heard myself saying, "I have to go somewhere. I'm really sorry, but I'll be all right. I just *have* to go somewhere."

And as Mum and Dad turned around, their faces blank with disbelief, I opened the car door, stepped out, and started running.

♥ ♠ ♦ ♣

I was perfectly aware of myself as I ran down Hythe Street and ducked into the alleyway — I could feel my tired feet slapping on the ground, I could feel the rush of air on my face, I could hear Mum and Dad shouting out after me, their voices strained with shock and desperation . . . and as I jumped up onto a trash can and clambered over the wall into the old churchyard, I knew exactly what I was doing. I could hear Dad now, running down the street and following me into the alleyway, yelling at me to come back . . .

But I was gone now.

My awareness didn't belong to me anymore.

I couldn't go back.

I had to keep running — out of the churchyard, down St. Leonard's Road, down toward the docks — I had to get where I had to go. I had to go back to the beginning and find the key to the end.

I don't know how long it took me to get to Back Lane, but I'm pretty sure I ran all the way, and by the time I finally got there I was panting so hard and sweating so much that I could feel my body oozing out of my shoes. My legs were on fire, my arms were burning . . . I was sucking in so much air that it was making me feel drunk. I could feel the oxygen buzzing around in my head, making me dizzy, and for a while I thought I was going to be sick. But, strangely enough, I didn't really mind the nauseous feeling. It felt OK . . . like some kind of weird, floaty sensation, as if something soft was hovering in my stomach. Like a small cloud of friendly gas.

So when I reached the point along the lane where the pathway led up to the den, I didn't bother stopping to get my breath back, I just kept going — clambering up the bank, past the tree stump, through the brambles, up the overgrown path . . . until eventually I was back at the den again. Back to where it had all begun. Back to the same old brambles, the same old wooden boards, the same old faded blue roof . . .

Back to when? I asked myself. When *had* it all begun?

Four days ago?

Four years ago?

Four *friends* ago?

As I stepped over to the den and crept in through the door, I wondered if that's what it was all about. Friends. People you know. People you used to know. People you *think* you once knew, but you probably never did. You probably just knew a part of them, the part of them that was your friend. And the rest, the parts of them that you didn't know — the twisted parts, the untrue parts, the parts you're seeing now — well, back then you just ignored them. But now you can't. Because now you *can* see it all, and now you know that "back then" wasn't all wonderful and innocent. It was just a time and a place, just like every other time and place. The only difference now is that the things — the people — that belonged to the old time and place aren't here anymore, and things that aren't here anymore don't hurt anymore. The only things that hurt are the things that hurt right now.

I stooped over to the far wall of the den and sat down.

The air was cool.

I could feel the sweat drying on my skin.

I looked around the den. There were no bottles left, no cigarette butts, no traces of Saturday night. It'd all be in a police laboratory now, I realized — chopped up in test tubes, sliced up under microscopes, liquidized in smart machines that whizzed round and round and analyzed crap.

The right-hand wall of the den was buckled and broken, and I guessed that someone — a burly policeman, probably — had either fallen against it or given it a hefty kick. A fresh bramble stem was already beginning to creep in through the gap in the boards. It wouldn't be long before more stems squeezed through, and then the hole would get bigger, and then more stems would squeeze through . . . until eventually the board would break and the brambles would take over and the whole den would start to collapse.

It wouldn't be long.

It doesn't matter.

A whispered voice.

It came from a placeless place somewhere in front of me, a place that somehow didn't exist. In the middle of the den, but not in the middle of the den. Floating, but not floating, about a foot and a half above the ground.

But the ground wasn't there. And neither was Black Rabbit, or the fine gold necklace around his neck, or the single red flower that hung from the necklace like a pearl drop of honey-sweet blood. And Black Rabbit didn't have Raymond's face, either. I watched in silence as Raymond blinked his shining black eyes, and a perfect red teardrop fell slowly from the flower on his necklace to the ground.

It's all about Pauly, isn't it? he whispered.

"It's all about everyone."

But Pauly's the key.

"Maybe . . ."

The key to the end.

I pulled Eric's mobile from my pocket and flipped it open.

My hands were shaking as I turned on the phone, and my fingers and thumbs seemed to have doubled in size, so it took me a while to find the MESSAGES menu, and it took me even longer to key in the text, but after a lot of deleting and backspacing and swearing, I got there in the end.

This is what I wrote:

```
Pauly—they kno what hapnd satdy nite.
need tlk urgnt! meet me @ bld asap.
dont tel others. come alone—Eric
```

Because Eric had deleted all his texts from the phone, I had no way of knowing how he usually texted, so I had no way of knowing if my message was sufficiently Eric-like to fool Pauly or not. I spent a few minutes trying to imagine what kind of texter Eric might be — did he abbreviate? did he use capitals? did he sign himself Eric, or E, or EL? — but I knew I was wasting my time. There was no way of guessing that kind of thing. All I could do was hope that Eric's texts were pretty much the same as everyone else's. Or, if they weren't, that Pauly wouldn't be in the right frame of mind to notice.

If the message behind my message was correct, I was pretty sure that Pauly's frame of mind would be so messed up that he wouldn't notice *anything*.

I read through the message again, just to make sure that it couldn't be misunderstood . . . then I pressed OK, scrolled down to Pyg, and hit SEND.

Pauly's reply came almost immediately — b thr 15mins.

And that was it.

All I had to do now was wait.

It was a timeless fifteen minutes, and as I sat there in the cooling shade of the den, my mind drifting sleeplessly in the wooded silence, I tried to imagine how Raymond must have felt when he used to come up here on his own — sitting quietly among the brambles, breathing the warm earthy air, his eyes half closed, his head full of nothing . . .

Hidden away in a secret place.

No one knowing where he was . . .

"Were you happy then?" I heard myself wondering. "I mean, when you came up here on your own . . . did it make you happy?"

I don't know about happy . . .

"But you liked it?"

It made me feel calm. I didn't have to worry about anything.

"What did you do in here?"

Nothing.

"Did you think about stuff?"

No.

"You must have thought about something."

Why?

"Because . . ."

Because what?

"I don't know . . . just because."

You're getting confused, Pete. You're beginning to think you're me.

"I know," I grinned.

At least, that's what you think *you're thinking. But you know what you're really thinking about, don't you?*

"What?"

You're thinking about Pauly.

"Am I?"

Yeah, you're remembering those times when you saw him on his own and you hated him for reminding you of me, and now you're beginning to realize that that's why he hated me, too, because I reminded him of himself. He could see himself in me. And that scared him to death.

"I don't understand . . ."

Yeah, you do. You just don't want to admit it.

"Admit what?"

How close everything is. Me and you, me and Nicole, Campbell and Eric, Pauly and me . . . we all could have been each other. I mean, if things had been just a little bit different, you could have been me, I could have been Nic, Campbell could have been Eric, Pauly could have been me—"

"No."

It's pointless arguing with yourself.

"I'm not *arguing*, I'm just saying—"

He's coming.

"What?"

Listen . . .

I could hear it now, the sound of Pauly coming up the bank—struggling through the undergrowth, slipping and stumbling, cursing under his breath.

"Do you think this is going to work?" I whispered to Raymond.

He didn't answer me.

"Raymond?" I said.

But I knew he'd already gone. And now the door to the den was opening and Pauly was stepping in . . . and just for a moment he *was* Raymond—the shocked face, the mixed-up eyes, the sudden look of fear and confusion.

"Hello, Pauly," I said.

"Pete?" he muttered, quickly scanning the den. "Where's Eric?"

"Eric's not here."

He stared at me then, beginning to realize that he might have been tricked, and as his eyes narrowed slowly in anger, his resemblance to Raymond just floated away into nothing. "What's going on?" he said. "I got a text—"

"I sent it."

"What?"

I took Eric's phone from my pocket and held it up for him to see. "I sent you the text."

He stared at the phone, blinking slowly. "Where did you get—?"

"Sit down, Pauly," I said.

"Where's Eric?"

"Sit down."

Pauly shook his head and started edging back through the door. "No, no way. I'm going to get Wes—"

"I know what happened to Stella."

Pauly froze. "What?"

"Eric told me all about it."

"No . . . no, he wouldn't do that."

"How else would I know?"

"No," he said, shaking his head. "You're lying. You don't know anything—"

"I know about the car," I told him. "I know you drove down to the river and dumped Stella's body. I know you smeared blood on Tom Noyce's trailer. I know about Eric and Wes." I looked at him. "Do you want me to go on?"

He didn't say anything, he just stood there, staring hopelessly at me, and just for a moment all I could do was stare back at him. I'd taken a huge risk, pretending to know about the car and the river and everything, and if I'd got any of it wrong . . . well, that would have been the end of it. But it was obvious from Pauly's reaction that I hadn't got it wrong, and that was a big relief. Which made me feel pretty good . . . for about a millionth of a second. And then suddenly the reality hit me, and I realized that I wasn't just guessing anymore, I was finally facing the truth. And it was sickening. Pauly Gilpin, the boy standing in front of me now, the boy I'd known for years and years . . . Pauly had been there. When Stella had died . . . Pauly had *been* there.

"Sit down," I told him.

He looked at me. "What are you going to do?"

"I just want to talk to you, that's all."

"Have you told anyone?"

"Sit *down*, for Christ's sake."

He didn't seem too steady as he stepped away from the door and lowered himself to the ground in the middle of the den, and as he sat there — cross-legged, swaying slightly, his eyes staring blankly at me — I realized that he wasn't just shocked and confused, he was drugged to the eyeballs, too. His face was pale, his skin was tense, his hands were shaking. He was drenched in sweat and his eyes were black and hollow. He looked as if he hadn't slept for a week.

"Are you all right?" I asked him. "You don't look so good."

"What do you care?"

"How long have you been taking it?"

"What?"

"Juice, TCI . . . the stuff you put in the tequila."

"You know about that?"

I nodded.

He grinned. "What d'you think? D'you like it? I got some more if —"

"Why did you do it?"

"Do what?"

"Spike the tequila. I mean, why didn't you just *ask* us if we wanted to try TCI?"

Pauly laughed. "You're all too chicken to try stuff like that. You're all too fucking *clean*." He grinned again. "And, anyway, my way was more fun."

"Fun?"

"Yeah . . . fun." He stared at me. "You know what that is?"

"Are you having fun now?" I asked him.

He shrugged and looked away.

I said, "You know the police are looking for you, don't you?"

"So?"

"You can't hide forever."

He looked at me, smiling strangely. "You reckon?"

"They're going to find you —"

"They don't know anything. They can't *prove* anything . . ."

I didn't say anything, I just sat there watching him as he tried to maintain his Paulyness — Pauly the tough guy, Pauly the joker, Pauly the kid without a care in the world. But he couldn't do it anymore. His face was twitching, his lips were trembling, his eyes were out of control — he was falling apart.

"What did Eric tell you?" he said suddenly, staring wide-eyed at me. "Did he say it was me? Is that what he said?" He shook his head. "It wasn't *just* me . . . did he say it was me?"

"Why don't you just tell me what happened?" I said quietly, trying to calm him down.

"Are you going to tell? *Are* you?" He was jabbering now. "What did Eric say? Has he told the police — ?"

"Listen," I said. "All I want to do is find out if Raymond had anything to do with it. I'm not trying to rat you out or anything. I just want to know about Raymond."

Pauly frowned. "What's Raymond got to do with it?"

"That's what I'm trying to find out."

"Did Eric say Raymond was there?"

"No, but I don't think Eric was telling the truth about everything." I looked at Pauly. "I think he's trying to blame it all on you."

"No," Pauly said desperately, shaking his head again. "It wasn't *just* me . . . it was Eric and Wes. I mean, it was *their* thing. Not mine. It was them and Stella. I didn't even know what they were doing." He looked pleadingly at me. "It was an accident, anyway . . . it wasn't my fault. If Stella hadn't . . . if she hadn't . . ."

He was crying now.

"Pauly?" I said quietly.

He sniffed hard and looked at me. "It was *her* fault . . . all of it. It was Stella who started everything."

"What do you mean? How did she start everything?"

He wiped his nose with the back of his hand and looked at me with a snot-covered grin. "You really want to know the truth?"

"Yeah."

"Everything?"

"Yeah."

"You promise not to tell anyone?"

"I promise."

"Cross your heart?"

I crossed my heart. "Hope to die."

Pauly stared at me for a moment, his sunken eyes moist with tears, then he wiped his nose again, looked down at the ground, and started talking.

TWENTY-SEVEN

aturday night. It's late, around midnight, but the fairground is still busy. The walkways are crowded, the lights are flashing, the lunatic music is still blaring out. Two boys are sitting on a wooden bench set back in a little gap between a burger stand and a row of litter-filled oil drums. While one of them just sits there looking lost and confused, the other one gets up from the bench and starts hurrying across the fairground walkway, his spaced-out eyes searching frantically for two other boys. Where are they? Where did they go? What are they doing together?

Pauly *has* to know.

He *needs* to know.

Why?

Because Wes Campbell shouldn't be with Eric, that's why. Wes Campbell should be with Pauly. Wes and Eric don't *belong* together. It's just not right. It's wrong. It's unfair.

Pauly doesn't know why he feels like this, and he doesn't want to know, either. All he knows is that he has to do something about it.

So he pushes his way through the crowds, and he marches into the square of shadowed ground by the Portaloos, and then he pauses for a moment, looking around. He sees the fairground trucks and the chugging generators, he sees the thick black cables snaking across the littered ground, he sees the hard and empty hooded faces slouching around in the darkness . . . but he doesn't see Eric or Wes. He starts walking again, heading toward the park railings and the dimly lit street beyond. Pauly knows there's a gate there, a gate that leads out to the street. And his pace quickens. He's running now — around the back of a high-sided truck, down to the railings, through the gate, into the street . . . and he pauses again, looking left, looking right, up the road, down the road, across the road . . . and then he sees them. They're on the other side of the road, away to his right, about fifty feet away. They're getting into a car. A Ford Focus. The doors are open, the interior light glowing faintly. Pauly can see Wes Campbell getting into the driver's seat. He can see Eric standing by the open passenger door. And at the back of the car, leaning casually against the open door and saying something to Eric, he can see Stella Ross.

She's smiling, laughing, ruffling Eric's hair.

Eric shrugs her hand away.

She laughs again.

Pauly stares at her for a moment, thinking of all the secret times he's stared at her on the Internet . . . then he blanks those images out of his head and starts running again.

"Hey, Eric!" he shouts. "Eric! It's me . . ."

The three figures at the car all turn and look at him. They see him running toward them, crossing the road, yelling and waving — "Hold on, Eric . . . wait a minute, wait for me!"

Wes Campbell says, "Shit . . . what's that little fucker doing here? Quick, get in the car."

Eric and Stella start clambering into the car, slamming the doors shut, yelling at Wes to get going, but Pauly's almost there now, and Wes has just realized what that means.

"Come *on*, Wes!" urges Eric. "Start the car!"

Wes shakes his head. "There's no point. He's seen us now. If we leave him behind he's going to talk."

"We can't take him *with* us."

"What else are we going to do?"

"Shit," says Eric, glaring at Pauly as he runs up and stops at the car. "You stupid bastard," he mouths through the window at him.

"What?" says Pauly, grinning at Stella.

Stella looks back at him, her face screwed up in disgust. "What's *that*?" she says, as if Pauly's some kind of walking disease.

"It's Pauly," says Eric. "Pauly Gilpin. He went to school with us, remember?"

Stella shakes her head, grimacing.

Pauly raps on the window. "Where're you going, Wes? What's going on?"

"Let him in," sighs Wes.

"No," says Stella. "He'll fuck it all up."

"He'll fuck it all up if we *don't* let him in."

"Christ," snaps Stella. "I told you, didn't I? No one else. I *told* you that. Why can't you just run him over or something?"

"Yeah, right," says Wes, "run him over. *That* won't draw any attention to us, will it?" He turns in his seat and looks at Stella. "Just open your door and let him in. The longer we stay here, the more likely it is we'll get noticed."

"Why can't he sit in the front?"

"For Christ's *sake*, Stella — open the fucking door!"

Stella sighs and reluctantly opens the door. As Pauly stoops into the car, she shuffles along the seat, keeping as far away from him as possible.

"Hi," Pauly says to her, grinning like a starstruck kid.

She says nothing.

Eric turns to face him. "What are you doing, Pauly?"

"Nothing. I was just, you know . . ." He wipes sweat from his face and looks excitedly at Campbell. "Where're we going, Wes? We going to a party or something?"

"Yeah," mutters Wes, starting the car. "We're going to a party. "

They drive away from the fairground, heading out of town for five minutes or so, and then Wes starts circling back toward St. Leonard's Road. Pauly knows they're going in circles, and part of him wonders why. But he doesn't really care. He's *with* them, that's all that matters. He's with Eric and Wes in a car — which he's guessing is stolen — and he's going wherever they're going. *And* he's sitting right next to Stella Ross.

That'll do for him.

He looks at her. "I saw you in that rap video," he says.

She scowls at him. "What?"

"You know, the one with the black guy . . . what's his name? He's in that big white car with all those girls, and they're all drinking champagne and stuff—"

"Limousine," she says.

"Yeah, that's him."

"No," she sneers, "that's not his *name*. It's the car, the big white car . . . it's a limousine."

"Right, yeah . . . that's what I meant." He smiles at her. "You're the one he picks up off the street, aren't you? Like he's got all these other girls in the limousine with him, and they're all wiggling around all over the place, but then he sees you, standing on the street corner, looking really cool, and he stops the car and kicks all the rest of them out—"

"Really?" she says sarcastically.

"Yeah, and then you get in the car with him—"

"I know what *happens*, for fuck's sake."

"I know . . . I was just saying, that's all." He runs his hand through his hair. "You look really good in it."

"Yeah?" She smiles coldly at him. "You liked it, did you?"

"Yeah, it's great."

"What did you like best about it? My tits, my ass, my legs? What's your favorite bit?"

Pauly blushes. "I didn't mean I like it like that."

"Yeah, you did. Everyone likes it like that." She smiles again, nodding at Eric and Wes. "Everyone except them, of course."

Pauly glances at Eric and Wes, then looks back at Stella. "What do you mean?"

Stella laughs. "Can't you guess?"

Pauly looks up and sees Wes watching him in the rearview mirror. His eyes are angry, threatening, staring, cold . . . but there's something else there, too, something Pauly hasn't seen in Wes before. Something that looks like fear.

"Are you going to tell him?" Stella says to Eric. "Or do you want me to do it?"

"It's nothing to do with him," says Eric. "He doesn't have to know—"

"Yeah, but he's going to find out anyway, isn't he? I mean, once we get there, once we start doing it . . . he's going to start asking questions."

"So? We don't have to answer them."

"If he doesn't know what's going on, he's going to keep wondering. And if he keeps wondering, he's going to end up talking. And I can't have that. So either we tell him what's going on, or we kill him." She glances at Pauly, smiling pleasantly, then she turns back to Eric. "It's up to you, *darling*. What do you want to do?"

"Bitch," Eric mutters. "You're loving this, aren't you?"

Stella winks at Pauly. "He thinks I'm bitter. He thinks I'm only doing this because he humiliated me."

"I didn't mean to *humiliate* you, for Christ's sake," Eric snaps. "I was just a kid then . . . I was confused. I didn't know what I was—"

"Yeah," hisses Stella, "but as soon as I started getting hot with you, you suddenly knew what you were then, didn't you?"

"It wasn't anything to do with you . . . how many more times do I have to tell you? I just happened to realize—"

"Yeah, I know. I was there, remember? I was the nice little girl with her hand down your pants when you just *happened* to realize you were gay. You think I'm going to forget that? You think I'm going to forget how it felt when you stood up on that fucking stage and announced to everyone that Stella Ross had just turned you gay?"

"I didn't say that—"

"That's what everyone thought."

"No, they didn't."

Stella turns to Pauly, her eyes burning with some kind of madness. "How would you feel if someone did that to you?"

Pauly shrugs. "I don't know . . ."

"All right," she says, "how about this? Say you used to really like someone, OK? You really liked this guy, and you were happy to do stuff with him, you know, the kind of stuff you'd never done with anyone else before, but then this guy goes and does something really shitty, he makes you feel ugly and stupid and embarrassed. You with me?"

"Yeah . . ." Pauly says hesitantly.

"All right. So then, one day, about a year after this guy has *ruined* your life, you see him doing something that he doesn't want anyone else to know about."

"Like what?"

"Oh, I don't know," says Stella, glancing nastily at Wes, "let's say you catch him in a storage room in the basement of the school theater, him and this other guy. And they're doing stuff you wouldn't *believe*, and you just happen to have your mobile with you, and you just *have* to take a picture—"

"All right, Stella," Eric says quietly. "He doesn't need to know any more."

"And the thing is," Stella continues, "it's not what he's *doing* that this guy wants to keep secret . . . it's who he's doing it *with*." She stares at Wes now. "I mean, this other guy's no *drama queen*, is he? He's hard, he's *street*. He's inarticulate, thick as shit. He likes to hurt people—"

"You got that right," says Wes.

"He's embarrassing." She looks at Eric. "You're ashamed of him."

"I'm not *ashamed* of anything," says Eric. "It's just—"

"So, anyway," Stella says to Pauly, "how would you feel if you're this guy, and you've been hiding this secret shame for years . . . and, by the way, this other guy doesn't want anyone to know about it, either, because he's got his reputation to think of. So they're both living this secret life, creeping around like a couple of dirty old men, and then suddenly one of them gets a phone call from that nice little girl from all those years ago, only she's not so nice anymore. And she's not so little, either. And she's rich, and she's famous, and she can do whatever she fucking wants. And she tells this guy that she wants him to do something for her. And he says — what? And she says — I want you to kidnap me."

"We're here," says Eric.

Pauly looks out the car window and sees that they're driving along Park Road, and now Wes is slowing the car, cutting the headlights, and they're turning left down a potholed track that runs alongside the main entrance to the old factory.

"Where're we going?" asks Pauly.

No one answers him.

He gazes through the window at the gloomy shapes of towers and chimneys and crumbling warehouses. Security lights are glowing in the main entrance parking lot, but that's behind them now, and as they continue on down the narrow track, everything around them gradually merges into a dim and derelict darkness. The abandoned buildings, the pathways, the rusted hulks of ancient machinery . . . it all just lies there, silent and dead, like a vast black carcass of stone and metal.

"Over there," Eric says to Wes, pointing through the window.

Wes bumps the car over a strip of grassy wasteground, and then they're rolling across a concrete square toward a huddle of pale stone buildings with corrugated iron roofs. Beyond the buildings, the vague shapes of towering tree-tops are dimly visible against the black sky. Pauly has lost his bearings now, but he wonders if the trees are the trees that line the bank along Back Lane.

Wes steers the car around a heap of old tires and slows to a stop. He turns off the engine.

The silence is complete.

Eric opens the door and steps outside.

Wes follows him.

Stella looks at Pauly. "I bet you wish you were somewhere else now, don't you?"

Pauly grins at her.

There's nowhere else he'd rather be.

As they head through the darkness toward the buildings, Stella and Eric start arguing about something, their voices instinctively whispering, and Wes shakes his head and leaves them to it. Pauly moves up alongside him and offers him a drink from a bottle he takes from his pocket.

"What is it?" says Wes.

"Vodka Kick."

"What kind of kick?"

Pauly grins. "It might have a bit of juice in it."

Wes shakes his head. "Fucking idiot."

Pauly says, "I got some blow if you want."

Wes says nothing.

Pauly shrugs and takes a drink from the bottle. Up ahead, he can see Eric and Stella entering one of the buildings.

"What's going on?" he asks Wes.

"She's out of her mind, that's what's going on."

"Is it true . . . all that stuff she was saying about you and Eric?"

Wes stops and stares at Pauly. "What if it is? What's it to you?"

"Nothing," says Pauly. "I mean, you know . . . it's up to you what you do. It's nothing to do with me—"

"Fucking right. And it's nothing to do with anyone else, either. All right?"

"Yeah . . . yeah, of course."

Wes grabs Pauly by the hair and jerks his head to one side. "You know what I'll do to you if you don't keep your mouth shut, don't you?"

"Yeah," Pauly winces, "I won't say anything . . . I promise."

Wes yanks Pauly's head toward him, stares hard into his eyes, then suddenly lets go and slaps him across the face. Pauly takes the slap without a sound. He just stands there for a moment, rubbing his face, then he quietly follows Wes into the building.

Inside, Wes takes a small flashlight from his pocket and turns it on. The building is empty, the windows boarded up. There's a rusted filing cabinet in the corner, its drawers buckled open and half-filled with rainwater. The floor is littered with empty beer cans, bottles, used condoms, needles, unidentifiable items of soiled clothing screwed up into wet rags. One wall is pocked with hammer marks, the others are smeared with graffiti.

At the far end of the building, Eric is pulling a metal shelf unit away from the wall. Stella is standing next to him. Behind the shelf unit, there's a door-size gap in the wall. Eric takes a flashlight from his pocket and shines it into the gap. Pauly sees stone steps leading down into a basement.

Stella looks over at Wes. "Stay there a minute," she tells him. "I want to talk to Eric about something."

Wes stares at her for a moment, looks at Eric, then nods.

Eric and Stella squeeze past the shelf unit and go down the steps into the basement.

Pauly looks questioningly at Wes.

Wes shakes his head again. "You don't want to know."

"What did she mean about kidnapping?"

Wes says nothing for a moment, just stares into the darkness, then he breathes in deeply and lets out a sigh. "She called Eric a couple of weeks ago," he reluctantly tells Pauly. "She had this mad idea about faking her own kidnap and getting her parents to pay the ransom. She wanted Eric to arrange it."

"Why?"

"Because she hates his guts."

"No, I mean why did she want to fake her own kidnap? She must have loads of money."

Wes shakes his head. "I don't know . . . I think it's got something to do with her parents. She's got this thing about them . . . you know, they were always stinking rich but they never gave her any money. They didn't help her when she was trying to make it, they made her go to an ordinary school . . . all that kind of shit. I think she's trying to pay them back." He shrugs. "Or maybe she just wants to get her name in the papers again . . . I don't know."

"So why are you helping her?"

"Why do you think?"

"I don't know . . ."

Wes turns and stares at Pauly. "She's got a picture of me and Eric, OK? She's going to put it on the Internet if we don't do what she wants. So we don't have any *choice*, do we?" He spits on the floor. "You got any *more* questions?"

"No," says Pauly.

Wes glares over at the gap in the wall. "Hey!" he shouts out. "What the fuck are you *doing* down there?"

Eric calls out from the basement, telling Wes to come down, and as Pauly follows him through the gap and down the stone steps, he can feel the juice-spiked vodka racing through his blood.

As far as Pauly can tell, the way it's supposed to go down is that Eric will call Stella's parents and make the kidnap demand. He'll tell them to drive down to the factory before first light and leave the ransom money in the trunk of the car outside, and that if they don't do exactly as they're told, their daughter will be sent back to them in shrink-wrapped chunks. Pauly doesn't know how much the ransom is, but according to Stella, it won't be a problem. Her father, she says, keeps a stash of ready money in a cast-iron safe in the attic.

So that's how it's supposed to happen.

But not just yet.

Pauly doesn't know *why* they're waiting, and he doesn't care, either. He's happy enough down here in the basement, down in the flashlighted dirt, sitting on a wooden crate, sipping his psycho-vodka, looking around at the industrial debris—the dilapidated machines, the rotten boards, the piles of garbage, the heaps of rusting girders . . . he's happy enough with all that. The air is cool, his head is buzzing, his skin is tingling . . . he's in a basement with Stella Ross. What more could anyone want? I mean, look at her, standing over there by the wall, talking to Eric . . . pouting, posing, showing it all off. It's even better than the picture Pauly knows so well, the one on the Internet, the one on his wall. That wonderful thing over there isn't trapped inside a computer monitor or pinned to his wall — it's right there. Moving, breathing, pulsing . . . every single bit of it. The flat belly, the skin, the lips, the legs, the eyes, the neck, the breasts, the flirty peep of her underwear . . .

Jesus, thinks Pauly.

Christ.

The TCI is burning him up, pumping him up . . . he can feel every cell in his body bursting with blood.

"What are you looking at?" Stella says to him.

"What?"

"You got nothing better to do than stare at my tits?"

Pauly blinks, raising his eyes to her face. She's staring at him, her hand on her hip, her body half-turned toward him.

"I wasn't . . ." he mutters, standing up. "I wasn't staring . . ."

"Yeah, right," she says, turning to face him now. "I know what you're thinking about."

Pauly hopes it's too dark for his blushes to show. "I'm not thinking about anything."

"No?" Her eyes flick down at his crotch. "You could have fooled me."

Pauly's starting to hallucinate now, and as he looks at Stella he sees her flesh-and-blood head on a naked paper body, then his vision suddenly flips and he sees her pouting paper head on the barely clothed figure of her flesh-and-blood body.

He grins to himself.

"Is dreaming about it all you can do?" Stella says, moving toward him.

"What?"

She licks her lips, puts her hands on her hips, posing, pouting, leading him on. "You want to try it for real?" she says huskily.

"Try what?"

"Everything you've ever dreamed about . . ." She winks at him. "You can try it if you want."

Pauly's breathing hard now, trying to control himself. But he knows he doesn't want to control himself.

"Come here," Stella says.

"Me?" Pauly says dumbly.

"Yeah, you. Come here."

He moves cautiously toward her, half-expecting her to start laughing at him. But she doesn't. She just stands there, a pulsing vision in the underground darkness, gazing innocently into his eyes. Pauly moves closer, his mouth bone-dry, his heart pounding, his belly burning.

"It's all right," Stella says babyishly. "I'm not going to bite you." Her face is a picture of virginal innocence now. She's posing like a shy little child—her head held slightly to one side, her hands clasped demurely in front of her—and she knows that Pauly can't resist it.

And he can't.

He stops in front of her, his body trembling.

"Closer," she whispers.

He edges forward until their faces are almost touching. He can feel the heat of her breath on his lips. He can feel her arms against his chest, the feathered touch of her passive hands . . . down there. He's embarrassed, but he doesn't care. This is it. He leans toward her, his lips trembling . . . and his heart stops beating as he feels her hands move. He freezes for a moment, waiting breathlessly for that impossible touch . . .

And then Stella puts her mouth to his ear and whispers, "Never in a million years."

And an instant later a sickening pain explodes in his groin and he's doubling over in agony, sinking to his knees, moaning and groaning, his eyes watering, his hands clutching desperately at his groin. Christ, it's the worst pain in the *world* . . . it's unbearable, it's *unbelievable*. It hurts so *much* . . .

He's down on his knees, his head in the dirt, and he's howling and crying and moaning . . . and he can hear them laughing. Eric and Wes, Stella . . . she's laughing at him, and he knows now that she always was.

"Serves him right, dirty little bastard," he hears her say.

"Yeah, nice one," Wes says admiringly. "What d'you do — grab his balls?"

"No, just a little flick," Stella says. "Like this . . ."

Pauly looks up through his tears and sees her flicking her thumb, and it seems such a trivial thing, just a stupid little thumb flick . . . as if that's all he's worth. And as he watches her walking away from him—like he's nothing at all, just something to laugh at, something to flick in the balls—he realizes that she's not even laughing at him anymore. She's already forgotten about him. He's not even worth laughing at for more than a few seconds. And it's that that tips Pauly over the edge.

His head goes black, blanking the pain.

He sits up.

His blood is hot, bursting in his veins.

No thoughts.

He gets to his feet, swaying a little, and looks over at Stella. She's walking in slow motion, her body haloed in a shimmer of light. Her long legs are skinless, like raw meat hanging in a butcher's window. Her hair is a nest of snapping yellow snakes.

Pauly runs at her.

Someone shouts, "No!"

Stella turns, sees Pauly coming at her, his teeth bared in a monstrous grin. She steps back, her eyes shocked. She loses her footing, stumbles slightly, and now Pauly is almost on top of her. A weird kind of howling noise erupts from his throat, and he raises his hands . . . and then Eric is there, barging into him, wrapping his arms around him, pulling him away from Stella. But Pauly is out of control now, his strength pumped up with madness and drugs, and with a violent twist of his body, he rips himself free from Eric's grip, grabs him by the shoulders, and shoves him violently away. Eric staggers backward, his arms flailing wildly as he tries to stay on his feet, but he can't see where he's going. He can't see where his feet are taking him. He doesn't know that Stella is right behind him, struggling to get out of his way. He hears her crying out, but even as he looks over his shoulder to see where she is, he's already losing his balance. And as he starts falling, his right arm whips up and catches Stella full in the face. She lurches back, clutching her face, and then it happens — she trips on something, or maybe she puts her foot in a hole, or steps on a brick . . . nobody really knows. Her feet just suddenly fly out from under her, and as she crashes heavily to the ground, her head cracks dully into the rusted hulk of a girder.

Silence.

No one moves.

Pauly, Eric, Wes. They all just stare at her, waiting for her to sit up. Waiting for her to groan, or to start crying. Or to roll over and start swearing . . .

Anything.

But nothing happens.

She just lies there, dead in the dirt.

TWENTY-EIGHT

s Pauly sat there telling me all this, everything about him seemed to shrink and wither away: His voice got weaker, his eyes dulled, his shoulders sagged . . . even his breathing got shallower. By the time he'd got to the end of the story, there was hardly anything left of him. He was just sitting there, staring emptily at the ground, drained of all emotion. It was like watching somebody die.

"Whose idea was it to dump Stella's body in the river?" I asked him.

"Uh?"

"Her body . . . how did it end up in the river?"

He slowly looked up at me. "The river?"

"Yeah . . . you put the body in the car and drove it down to the river, didn't you?"

Pauly nodded. "Is that what Eric told you?"

"Never mind what Eric told me—"

"Did he say it was me?"

"What?"

"Did he say it was me that pushed Stella? I know he did. He's a liar, it wasn't me—"

"What happened when you got to the river?"

Pauly stared angrily at me for a moment, then all at once his face went blank again. "It was Wes's idea," he said dully. "He said if we took her clothes off, it'd look like a sex killer had done it. Eric undressed her. He took her clothes off." Pauly blinked. "I don't suppose it mattered to him, you know . . . it's not like he wanted to *see* her or anything. He just took off her clothes and then . . . I don't know. I was pretty out of it by then. I didn't know . . . I was just . . . I don't know." He shrugged. "I didn't do much. Eric and Wes put her in the river. Wes torched the car . . . there was a can of gas in the trunk. And that was about it, really."

"Who put the blood on the trailer?"

"Wes. There was some blood on Stella's shirt. He wiped it on the trailer, chucked the clothes in the bushes."

"Why?"

"Wes is smart. He knows what he's doing."

"You reckon?"

Pauly shook his head. "It wasn't anything to do with Wes. The whole thing . . . it was all about Eric and Stella. Wes was just trying to help."

"How did Eric's necklace get in Stella's pocket?"

"What?"

"The police found a bit of broken necklace in Stella's pocket. They showed it to me. I think it was one of Nic's that Eric had borrowed."

Pauly frowned. "It was in Stella's pocket?"

"Yeah."

He hesitated. "She must have snatched it off his neck when they were struggling—"

"You never said anything about a struggle."

"Didn't I?"

I shook my head. "Eric staggered backward into Stella, whacked her in the face, and then she fell over and hit her head on the girder." I looked at Pauly. "That's what you said, wasn't it?"

"Yeah . . ."

"So when did she snatch his necklace?"

"I don't know . . . maybe she grabbed it when she was falling."

"And when did she put it in her pocket?"

He shrugged. "After she fell, I suppose."

"You said she didn't move after she'd fallen."

"Maybe I got that bit wrong . . ."

"Right. So now you're trying to tell me that she *didn't* die straightaway?"

Pauly stared angrily at me. "I was drunk, all right? I was fucked up . . . my fucking head, you know? I can't remember *every*thing."

"Yeah, OK," I said, trying to calm him down. "I'm just trying to get everything clear in my mind, that's all."

He was staring at the ground again now.

"What about Raymond?" I asked him.

"What about him?"

"Did he have anything to do with it?"

"No."

"Nothing at all?"

"No."

"He wasn't even there?"

"No."

"Did you see him after you'd got to the fair?"

Pauly rubbed his eyes.

"Did you *see* him, Pauly?"

"See who?"

"Raymond."

Pauly shook his head. "You're not going to tell anyone about Stella, are you?"

"I don't know . . ."

His eyes widened. "What do you mean? You said you *wouldn't* . . . you said . . . you fucking *promised*—"

"I was lying."

His head started shaking from side to side. "No . . . no, no, you can't do that . . . you *can't*—"

"All right, calm down. I'm not saying that I *will*—"

"You crossed your fucking *heart*."

"Look," I said patiently, "if I don't tell the police what happened, and they don't find out, they're going to think that Raymond did it."

"So?"

I stared at him, momentarily speechless.

He stared back, his eyes bright with a frenzied hope. "I mean, it's only *Raymond*, for Christ's sake . . . who *gives* a shit? He's probably dead anyway." Pauly grinned. "And even if he's not . . . well, it's not going to make any difference to him if he gets locked up for it, is it?"

"Why not?" I said.

"Come on, Pete, we're talking about Mental Ray here . . ." Pauly grinned again, tapping the side of his head. "Once they find out how fucked up he is, they won't even bother putting him on trial. They'll just stick him in one of those psycho places and stuff his head full of drugs. He'll be all right. I mean, shit, he's not going to have much of a life anyway, is he? What's he got going for him? No one's ever going to give *him* a job, are they? He'll spend the rest of his life living at home with his pissed-up parents, talking to his fucking rabbit all day . . . so, you know, he'll probably end up in the funny farm anyway . . ."

I was trying very hard to contain myself now—breathing slowly, keeping still, telling myself to stay calm, don't get riled, don't let him get to you. And I knew I was right, I knew it was pointless getting angry. Pauly was an idiot. He was sick, he was stupid, he was selfish and weak. He couldn't help what he was.

I *knew* all that.

But I still wanted to rip his head off.

I didn't, though.

I just sat there in silence, staring at him as he jabbered away, letting my hatred sweat itself out. And as the dark feelings seeped out of my skin, I began to realize that not all of my hate was for Pauly—some of it was for myself. Because I'd always known what Pauly was like . . . I'd *always* known. But I'd never done anything about it, had I? And why not? Because he was Pauly . . . he was one of us. And we were all *friends*, weren't we? Eric, Nic, Pauly, me . . . we'd grown up together. We'd done things together. We'd spent our summers together. We'd built dens together.

We were friends.

But had we ever really *liked* each other?

Maybe some of us had . . .

Now and then.

But that's not enough, is it?

I mean, that's not friendship — it's just being together. Being one of us. And the only one of us who'd never been one of us was the only one who'd ever meant anything to me. And now that Raymond was gone, it was too late to do anything about it. All I could do was hate myself, and even that was a waste of time.

"So?" Pauly said.

"What?"

"Are you going to tell anyone what happened or not?"

"I don't know yet. I'll have to think about it."

"Come on, Pete," he pleaded. "I *told* you it was an accident . . . I mean, it's not like we did it on purpose or anything —"

"I said I'd think about it."

"I'd do the same for you."

"No, you wouldn't."

"Yeah, I would . . . I mean, we're friends, aren't we? We've always been —"

"Shut up."

"All you've got to do is —"

"Do you want me to call the police right now?" I said, pulling my phone from my pocket.

He didn't say anything, he just sat there staring at me like a hurt little boy. For a moment I thought he was going to start crying, and I almost felt sorry for him again. But I was all out of sympathy now.

"Go home," I told him.

"Yeah, but—"

"Just go home, OK? I'll think about what I'm going to do, and when I've made up my mind I'll come around to your place and let you know. I won't say anything to anyone else till then."

"What if the police come around for me?"

"Are your parents home?"

"No."

"Don't open the door then. Just stay in your room and wait for me."

"You'll definitely come around?"

"Yeah."

"When?"

"When I'm ready."

"This afternoon?"

I stared at him.

"What?" he said.

I sighed and turned on my phone.

Pauly looked confused for a moment, but then he realized what I was doing, and he quickly started getting to his feet. He lost his balance for a moment, almost falling over, but he managed to steady himself, and then—with a strangely prescient look—he turned around, lowered his head, and stumbled out through the door.

I was so tired now—my body so heavy and numb—that I didn't want to do anything at all. I didn't want to think about Pauly. I didn't want to walk back home. I didn't even want to stand up. I just wanted to close my eyes and forget about everything and fall into a dreamless sleep. And as the sound of Pauly's unsteady footsteps faded away down the bank, I stared blearily at the phone in my hand and imagined myself calling Dad. I could tell him everything right now. I could tell him what Pauly had told me. I could tell him that Pauly was on his way home. I could tell him where I was, that I was sorry I ran away, that I was too tired to move and would he please come and get me . . .

There was no signal on my phone.

I put it in my pocket and forced myself to stand up.

My legs felt like stone.

My head was throbbing.

I breathed in a lungful of warm earthy air and shuffled wearily outside.

The sun was high in an electric-blue sky as I started walking along Back Lane, and for a second or two I seriously wondered if I had enough energy to keep going. The sweat was already pouring out of me from the effort of clambering down the bank, and now I was beginning to feel that foggy kind of sickness you get when you haven't slept for a really long time. I felt like I was going to throw up, but not from my belly. I felt like I was going to throw up from inside my head.

But then, as I paused for a second and took a few deep breaths, trying to steady the nausea, I suddenly saw something up ahead that stopped me worrying about being sick.

At first I thought I was just seeing things — another juice-induced flashback — and for a timeless moment it was Saturday night again, and I was standing in the lane with Raymond, and he was staring straight ahead, his eyes glazed with fear . . .

Raymond?

You said he wouldn't be here . . .

Who?

You said . . .

But I knew it wasn't Saturday night now, it was Wednesday morning, and the bunch of Greenwell kids I could see standing in the lane up ahead . . . they weren't a flashback. They were right there, right now, less than fifty feet away. A dozen or so skanky white eyes, staring the shit out of me.

I turned around and started walking back the other way . . .

And suddenly stopped again.

Staring at Eric.

And Wes Campbell.

And Pauly.

Eric was closest to me, about thirty feet away, and Campbell and Pauly were just behind him. Eric looked haggard and drawn. He was just standing there, gazing wearily at me, his hands in his pockets, his shoulders slouched. He didn't seem aware of what was going on behind him, or maybe he just didn't want to admit to himself that anything *was* going on. But it was. I couldn't hear what Wes Campbell was saying to Pauly, but I could see the box cutter in his hand, and I could see the way he was leaning into Pauly's face, baring his teeth, hissing and spitting into Pauly's petrified eyes.

I saw Eric glance over his shoulder and say something to Campbell then. Campbell looked at him, glanced at me, and then — without so much as a final quick look at Pauly — he grinned and started walking toward me. As he passed Eric, Eric touched his arm and said something. Campbell paused for a moment, looking at Eric, and although there were no smiles, no obvious signs of affection, the intimacy between them was unmistakable. And now that I was aware of it, it was hard to believe I'd never noticed it before.

Not that it made much difference to me.

Campbell was walking toward me again now. Eric was right behind him, and Pauly was tentatively following along a few feet farther back.

"Piss off, Gilpin," Campbell called back, his eyes still fixed on me.

Pauly paused.

"Go on," Campbell said dismissively. "Fuck off home."

Pauly just stood there for a moment — his eyes blinking rapidly, his face pale and confused — then he turned around and walked off dejectedly in the opposite direction. I couldn't see his face, but it wasn't hard to imagine the look in his eyes . . . the loneliness, the darkness, the sadness . . .

But I didn't have time to think about Pauly.

I looked over my shoulder. The Greenwell kids were still there, still blocking the lane up ahead. I had nowhere to run. Nowhere to go. I looked back at Eric and Campbell again. Campbell was about fifteen feet away, smiling crookedly at me.

"You're on your own this time, Boland," he said. "Your luck's just run out."

I stared at him for a moment, looked over his shoulder at Eric, then I turned and started running toward the Greenwell kids.

I could see them grinning at me as I ran toward them — smiling at my stupidity, getting ready to have some fun. I could see their feet fidgeting, their shoulders twitching, their fists clenching. They knew they wouldn't have much time with me before Campbell and Eric called them off, and I could see them moving toward me now, jostling for position, each of them trying to get to the front so they could get a few good kicks in while they had the chance.

But they weren't going to get the chance.

I kept on running straight at them, running as hard as I could — my arms pumping, my legs pounding — and I didn't make my move until the very last moment. Just as I reached the first of the Greenwell kids, just as he was slowing down and spreading out his arms to stop me, I leapt up onto the bank and started scrambling up through the undergrowth. There wasn't a path here, just a thick spread of brambles and weeds and moss-covered roots, and the bank was a lot steeper in this part of the lane. It was almost impossible to stay on my feet, and I didn't even try. I just crawled and slithered, scrabbled and groped, heaving myself up the bank. The brambles were ripping me to shreds, tearing at my clothes and gouging my skin, but I didn't care. The Greenwell kids weren't going to come up here and get *their* clothes messed up. I could hear them down below, laughing at me as the brambles got thicker and thicker, and my crawling got slower and slower. They knew I wasn't going anywhere.

And I knew it, too.

I wasn't even trying to go anywhere now. All I was doing was rolling around in the undergrowth, looking for somewhere to hide for a moment — a dip in the ground, a hollow, a broad-trunked tree. Anywhere. As long as it kept me out of sight for a second or two.

"Boland!" I heard Campbell shout out. "You might as well come down . . . there's nowhere to go."

A dead oak tree loomed up in front of me. It was lightning-struck, blackened and burnt, with bare branches and a hollowed-out trunk. The ground around the base of the tree had been dug out by a badger or something. I looked around, memorizing the surroundings — halfway up the bank, directly below a group of old factory buildings, just to the right of a drooping holly tree, about thirty feet to the left of an overgrown path . . .

"Boland!"

I rolled into the ditch at the base of the oak tree, lay on my back, and pulled my mobile out of my pocket. Still no signal. I dug Eric's phone out of my pocket.

Campbell yelled out again. "If you're not down here in thirty seconds, I'm coming up. D'you hear me?"

I didn't bother checking Eric's mobile for a signal, I just reached inside the hollow trunk and placed the phone out of sight. It was safe now. I didn't know what good it would do, hiding it away, but Eric's phone was the only piece of solid evidence I had. Names, places, times, texts. It was all in there somewhere. Eric might have deleted his texts, but that didn't mean they weren't there anymore. And his calls could be traced. Calls to Amo and Bit . . . Campbell and Stella. Amour. Bitch. Amour. Bitch. Amour . . .

It's all about love.

"All right, Boland, that's it. You've had your—"

"I'm coming down!" I shouted, getting to my feet.

I climbed out of the ditch and looked down the bank. They were all there—Campbell, Eric, the Greenwell kids. They were all looking up at me, squinting into the sun, waiting for me to come down.

They looked pretty small from up here.

But as I started edging my way down the bank, I knew it wouldn't be long before they looked pretty big again.

TWENTY-NINE

B y the time I got to the foot of the bank, I was sweating all over and covered in dirt, and every inch of my skin was either bloodied-up with bramble scratches or itching like hell from a million gnat bites.

"Give me the phone," Campbell said, holding out his hand.

I looked beyond Campbell at Eric. He was standing on his own, a little way down the lane. Away to his right I could see the bunch of Greenwell kids sloping off down the path toward the wasteground. They'd done their job, they weren't needed anymore.

"Phone!" Campbell snapped.

I pulled out my mobile and flipped it open. "I've just called my dad," I told him. "He knows where I am, he's called the police, they'll be here in a few minutes —"

"Yeah?" Campbell said, grabbing the phone and glancing at the display. He hit a couple of buttons, stared at the screen for a moment, then looked back at me and grinned. "No signal," he said. "No calls to Daddy." He snapped the phone in half and threw the pieces over the fence into the wasteground. "Now give me Eric's phone."

"I haven't got it with me. I left it at home . . ."

Campbell stepped up to me, grabbed me by the shoulders, and hooked his foot around the back of my leg. A quick shove in the chest and I was flat on my back on the ground. Campbell planted his foot on my chest, pinning me down.

"Eric," he said, "come here."

Eric came over.

"Search his pockets," Campbell told him.

As Eric crouched down beside me and started going through my pockets, I stared silently at him, trying to make eye contact, but he wouldn't look back at me.

"I know what happened, Eric," I said quietly. "I know it was an accident—"

"Shut up," Campbell told me, stomping on my chest.

I shut up and lay still, trying to get some air back into my lungs. Eric continued rummaging through my pockets.

"Nothing," he said after a while.

"You sure?" Campbell asked him.

Eric nodded. "He hasn't got it."

"Maybe he ditched it somewhere?"

Eric glanced up the bank. "We don't have time to look for it up there. It could be anywhere . . ."

"All right," Campbell said. "We'll have to leave it for now." He looked at Eric. "Shit, if you'd done what I told you—"

"Yeah, well, I didn't, did I?"

"All you had to do was—"

"I know what I *should* have done, Wes. You don't have to keep going *on* about it." He stood up. "Anyway, it's not going to make any difference now, is it?"

"I suppose not." Campbell took his foot off my chest and looked down at me. "Get up."

I got to my feet. He took out his box cutter, grabbed me by the arm, and dragged me down off the bank.

"Wait there," he said to me. He turned to Eric. "You go first."

Eric stepped down off the bank and began walking along the lane, heading in the direction of St. Leonard's Road. Campbell gave me a shove in the back, and I stumbled forward and started following Eric.

"I'm right behind you," Campbell whispered, breathing down my neck. "You want to make a run for it, that's fine. See how far you get with a box cutter stuck in the back of your head."

I didn't say anything, I just kept on walking, as carefully as possible, following Eric along the lane. I tried not to imagine how it'd feel to have a box cutter stuck in the back of my head, but the more I tried not to think about it, the more it made my skull shiver. And the more my skull shivered, the harder it was to concentrate on not doing anything that could possibly be mistaken for trying to make a run for it.

Which wasn't easy . . .

Especially as another part of me was trying to think about where we were going and what was going to happen when we got there, and when and where I *should* try making a run for it. But then, just as I was starting to seriously consider the options, I realized that Eric had stopped in front of me and was peering up the bank.

I stopped, too, my skull instinctively flinching.

"Is this it?" Eric asked Campbell, still gazing up the bank.

"Yeah, I think so."

I could see the outline of a path now, a barely visible track winding up the bank.

Eric looked back along the lane. "There's another one over there . . ."

"No," Campbell said, "this is it. We tried the other one, remember? It's blocked off at the top."

I glanced over my shoulder, recognizing the overgrown path that I'd seen near the dead oak tree.

Campbell slapped the back of my head. "What are *you* looking at?"

I quickly turned back.

Eric was stepping up onto the bank now, beginning to climb the narrow path. Campbell gave me another push in the back, and I got moving again. Up onto the bank, up the path, back up through the brambles . . . with Campbell close behind me all the way, breathing heavily.

I followed Eric.

Into the undergrowth.

Through the trees.

Sweating and stumbling . . .

Slipping and sliding . . .

There was something distantly familiar about the path and the surrounding woodland, something that reminded me of something . . . a feeling, a childlike anxiety, an expectation. Or maybe it was just the feeling itself that was familiar? It was hard to tell, but I kept getting the sense that this was the path I'd taken as a thirteen-year-old boy when I'd nervously followed Nicole up to the old factory that day, the day that Dad had caught us together and gone ballistic . . .

Or maybe not.

Maybe I was just imagining things.

We'd reached the top of the bank now and I could see the old factory spread out in front of us. A narrow strip of level ground ran alongside the high metal fencing that separated the bank from the factory, and as the three of us stopped for a moment to get our breath back, I noticed a gap in the fence. Someone had cut through the mesh. The opening wasn't big enough to see from a distance, but it was easily big enough to squeeze through. As I stood there — sweating and panting — gazing through the fence at the old factory, I found myself trying to remember which one of the buildings I'd been in with Nicole all those years ago . . . but there was nothing there that brought back any memories. I suppose I'd been too busy thinking about other things at the time to take any notice of *where* we were going. It was a building, that's all I'd cared about back then. It was a place for us to be on our own. It could have been a bright red tower block for all I'd cared . . .

But I couldn't see any bright red tower blocks now. All I could see were derelict workshops and offices, abandoned machinery, chimneys and towers, ramshackle warehouses . . . a concrete square, a pile of old car tires . . .

and, over to my left, a huddle of pale stone buildings with corrugated iron roofs . . .

I didn't have to wonder where we were going anymore.

"After you," Campbell said, ushering me toward the door of the abandoned building.

I looked at him for a moment, then opened the door and went inside. It was pretty much as Pauly had described it — boarded-up windows, rusted office furniture, crap all over the floor. Campbell grabbed me by the arm and led me across to the far end of the building. We stopped in front of the metal shelf unit that Pauly had told me about.

"Pull it back," Campbell told me.

I gripped the shelf unit and pulled it away from the wall. Campbell took a flashlight from his pocket and shone it down into the basement.

"Everything all right?" Eric asked him.

He nodded, turning to me. "Down you go."

As I went down into the basement, I could see that Pauly hadn't been lying about that, either. It was just as he'd said — dirt floor, stale air, stone walls, bits of machinery, a pile of rusting girders. Behind me, at the top of the steps, I heard Eric pulling the shelf unit back. As it clanged dully against the wall, the basement suddenly darkened.

"Get over there," Campbell said roughly, pushing me toward the girders.

Although Campbell was shining his flashlight away from me now, the basement wasn't completely dark. A faint chink of sunlight was showing through a small ventilation grid at the top of one wall, and as I shuffled wearily across the dirt floor, I could see well enough to see where I was going. I stopped beside the pile of girders.

"Sit down," Campbell told me.

I sat down on the nearest girder and looked down at the ground. There was a dull red stain in the dirt at my feet. It was crescent-shaped, like a jagged half-moon, and just for a moment I could see Stella lying there, her skull cracked open, her dead eyes staring, her perfect blonde hair matted with blood . . .

I raised my head and looked over at Eric and Campbell. They were standing against the far wall, talking quietly to each other. Eric was smoking a cigarette while Campbell whispered urgently into his ear. I saw Eric shake his head.

Campbell put his hand on his arm.

Eric looked up at him.

Campbell smiled.

Eric sighed.

They looked into each other's eyes for a while — staring at one another as if they were the only living things in the world — and then eventually Eric just nodded. Campbell patted his arm, then turned to face me.

"All right, Boland?" he said. "Comfortable enough?"

I looked at him.

He grinned at me. "It's all right, don't look so worried. No one's going to hurt you. We just want to ask you a few questions, that's all."

"You didn't have to bring me all the way down here just to ask me a few questions."

He didn't say anything to that, he just stared at me for a few seconds, his face pale and blank, then he reached into his pocket and brought out his box cutter again. "What did Gilpin tell you?" he said quietly.

"Didn't you ask him?"

"Yeah, I *asked* him. Now I'm asking you. What did he tell you?"

I glanced at the knife in his hand. "I thought you said you weren't going to hurt me?"

He shrugged. "I was lying."

As he started moving toward me, I looked over his shoulder at Eric, my eyes imploring him to do something. It felt so false, so hypocritical — appealing to a friendship that didn't exist — but what did I care? I'd rather be ashamed of myself than dead.

"Hold on a minute, Wes," Eric said grudgingly.

Campbell shook his head. "This little bastard's been winding me up for days. It's about time he got —"

"We need him," Eric said firmly. "Remember? We *need* him."

Campbell hesitated, staring coldly at me, and I could see the conflict in his eyes: Should he go with his gut feeling and rip me apart, or should he listen to Eric? I stared back at him, holding my breath, willing him to listen to Eric.

Eventually, after staring at me for what seemed like a year, he shook his head, spat on the ground, and took a few paces back.

I started breathing again.

Eric sighed and looked at me. "Listen, Pete, there's no need for things to be like this. All we want to know is what Pauly told you, OK? Just tell us what he told you, and then we can sort everything out."

I nearly said — *sort everything out? what do you mean we can sort everything out?* — but there didn't seem much point. Whatever they had planned for me, there wasn't anything I could do about it just now. And there was nothing to gain by *not* telling them what they wanted to know . . .

I looked down at the dirt for a moment, thinking things over . . . and then I told them everything that Pauly had told me.

"That's it?" Campbell said when I'd finished. "That's what he told you?"

"Yeah." I looked at Eric. "Is that really how it happened?"

"Not exactly," he said, glancing at Campbell.

"Fucking Gilpin," Campbell said, shaking his head. "Lying little shit . . . I told you we couldn't trust him, didn't I? I *told* you."

Eric looked at me. "I never touched Stella, Pete. It was Pauly . . . he just went crazy and attacked her. All that stuff about me trying to stop him and knocking

Stella over . . . it's all bollocks. I never *touched* her."

"You didn't try to stop him?"

"I didn't have time. One minute he was on the floor, moaning and groaning . . . the next thing I knew he was charging at Stella and shoving her in the back. It was all over before I could do anything."

"What about the rest of it?" I said. "The fake kidnap, Stella threatening you, what she did to Pauly . . . is any of that true?"

"Yeah," Eric shrugged. "Pretty much all of it, really." He let out a sigh. "Stella got in touch with me a couple of weeks ago. She said if I didn't help her with this kidnap idea, she'd put the picture of Wes and me on the Internet."

"So you helped her?"

"I didn't think she was going to go through with it, did I? I just thought it was one of her sick little games, you know . . . getting her own back on me, having a laugh, *controlling* me. That's how she got her kicks, Pete. Playing games. Messing with your head. Fucking with your emotions." He shrugged again. "I just went along with it. I didn't think anything was going to happen . . ."

"But then Pauly showed up."

"Yeah . . ." Eric shook his head. "Christ, you should have seen him, Pete. I mean, he's always been mad about Stella, hasn't he? Even before she was famous, he was always watching out for her, talking about her, drooling every time he saw her. So you can imagine how he felt when he thought she was coming on to him, especially with all the booze and shit he'd been taking. He must have thought he was in dreamland. But then she goes and flicks him in the balls . . . right in front of me and Wes. And he's crawling around on the ground, bawling his eyes out, and we're all laughing at him . . . shit, it's not surprising he lost it."

"Are you saying he killed her?"

Eric blew out his cheeks. "I don't think he *meant* to . . . he just went berserk, you know? He just lost it. Ran up behind her, screaming like a madman, and shoved her really hard in the back." Eric shrugged. "She never knew what hit her. She just kind of flew off her feet and went headfirst into the girders and then—"

"*Whack*," said Campbell, smacking his fist into the palm of his hand.

I looked at him.

He smiled at me.

I glanced down at the bloodstain in the dirt, imagining Stella's dead eyes again, then I looked back at Campbell. "You dumped her body in the river?"

"So?"

"You didn't have to do that."

"What were we supposed to do—take her body back to her mummy and daddy and say sorry?"

"You could have just left her here."

"Yeah, but someone would have found her eventually, wouldn't they? And then the cops would have started digging around, and they would have found out that we'd been here—"

"But it was an accident—"

"So fucking *what*?" Campbell said. "I mean, what the fuck's it got to do with you, anyway?"

It was a good question, and as I sat there in the dusty gloom, I realized that Campbell was right. I *didn't* care what they'd done. It *didn't* have anything to do with me. Now that I knew that Raymond hadn't killed Stella . . . well, the rest of it was irrelevant. It didn't matter to me who *had* killed her, or whether it was an accident or not, or why they'd try to cover it up. I just didn't care. And I know that probably sounds pretty callous, but the simple truth is — I didn't *like* Stella Ross. I'd never liked her. And I didn't care much about Eric or Pauly, either. I mean, I'm not saying that I didn't feel *anything* for them, and if I could have clicked my fingers and brought Stella Ross back to life, I would have done it.

But I couldn't.

She was dead.

And Raymond might still be alive.

I looked up at Eric and Campbell. They were both standing in front of me now, the light from the ventilation grid outlining their figures with haloes of shimmering dust.

"What are you going to do?" I said to Eric.

"What are *you* going to do?" Campbell answered.

"Nothing," I said, looking at him.

He laughed. "You got that fucking right."

"Look," I started to say, "I really don't care what happened down here —"

"Get up," Campbell said.

I looked at him.

"Stand up," he told me.

I glanced at Eric.

"Just do what he says, Pete."

As I looked up at Campbell again, he grabbed me by the hair and yanked me to my feet. I reached up instinctively, trying to get hold of his hand, but he just tightened his grip, pulled even harder, and then — with a sudden sharp yank — he ripped out a handful of hair. I yelped, a pathetic little sound, and stared wide-eyed at him.

He was studying the clump of hair in his hand, feeling it carefully with his thumb. "Nice," he said distantly. "A bit sweaty, maybe . . ."

He smiled at me.

I didn't know what to say. I rubbed at the sore patch on my scalp, watching curiously as Campbell stepped to one side, walked around me, and sprinkled the handful of hair over the ground. As he rubbed his hands together, getting rid of every last hair, I turned and looked at Eric.

"What the hell's he doing?" I asked.

"Sorry, Pete," Eric said, stepping toward me. "But this is the only way."

I saw him glance over my shoulder then, and as I turned to see what he was looking at, Campbell stepped up and flat-handed me hard in the nose. My head roared, screaming with pain, and as I staggered back into Eric, I could already feel the blood streaming out of my nose. Eric grabbed hold of me, clamping his arms around my chest and pinning my arms to my sides.

"All right?" I heard him say to Campbell.

"Yeah," Campbell said. "Get him down on the ground."

I felt a sharp kick in the back of my knee then, and as my leg buckled, Eric pushed me down to the ground and threw himself on top of me. I was facedown in the dirt now. Eric was straddling my back, holding me down . . . and I was too shocked and breathless to do anything. For a second or two, all I could do was lie there, spitting out strings of blood and snot, trying to get some air into my lungs . . . but then I felt Campbell crouching down beside me, and as he reached out and gripped my head in his hands, I suddenly started struggling like a maniac — twisting and squirming, kicking and screaming, shaking my head from side to side, trying to break free, trying to get up . . .

"Fuck *off*," I spat. "Fuck*ughh* —"

Dirt filled my mouth as Campbell shoved my face into the ground. It didn't really hurt that much, but it kind of knocked all the fight out of me, and as I jerked my head to one side, coughing and spitting out blood, I was just about ready to give up struggling and let Campbell do whatever he wanted.

But then, to my surprise, I heard him say, "That'll do," and I felt him let go of my head, and a moment later I felt Eric clambering off me . . . and all of a sudden everything was silent and still, and I was just lying there, trying not to cry.

I didn't move for a while, I just lay there in the dirt, my eyes closed, my heart thumping, my head spinning dully, numbed with shock. My nose was throbbing like hell, but it was a strangely distant kind of pain. I mean, it *hurt* . . . but not as much as the feelings that went with it. They were small and childish feelings — self-pity, shame, humiliation — the kind of feelings that make you want to curl up into a ball and cry. But I wasn't going to cry. I was sixteen years old, for Christ's sake. I wasn't a child anymore. And even if I was, even if I *did* feel like the smallest thing in the world, I still wasn't going to let myself cry.

Not yet, anyway.

I sat up slowly and wiped my face. My nose seemed to have stopped bleeding now, but there was plenty of blood on the ground. Dull red stains, already soaking into the dirt. Blood and spit. And hairs . . . my hairs, scattered among the blood and dust.

"Are you all right, Pete?" I heard Eric say.

I looked up at him. He was standing beside Campbell, smoking a cigarette. His eyes were so mixed up that I couldn't tell what he was feeling. I don't even think that *he* knew what he was feeling. I struggled wearily to my feet, steadied myself for a moment, and looked at him again. He was half-smiling at me now, half-shrugging . . . half-wanting to help me, half-knowing he couldn't.

"I'm sorry, Pete," he said unconvincingly. "I didn't want it to be like this, neither of us did . . . but we didn't have any choice. We had to do it. It was the only way." When I didn't say anything, Eric glanced at Campbell for support. "Tell him, Wes."

"Tell him what?"

"It's over now, isn't it? We're finished. He can go."

Campbell stared at me. "Your old man's a cop, right?"

"So?" I said.

"So you know how it works." He nodded at the ground. "That's your blood down there. Your hair. Your fingerprints are on the door handle and the shelf unit. There's probably all kinds of other crap around, too — sweat, spit, bits of skin, whatever." He grinned at me. "You see where we're going with this?"

"DNA," I said.

"Right. Your DNA's all over the place." He shrugged. "Of course, there's nothing to stop you coming back here and trying to get rid of it, but you're never going to get rid of *all* of it, are you? There's always going to be a bit of you down here. So, you know, if you start shooting your mouth off about Stella, and the cops come down here with all their forensic shit . . . well, they're going to *know* that you were down here, aren't they? Your blood, Stella's blood. Your fingerprints, Stella's fingerprints. Your DNA, Stella's DNA."

"And yours," I said, "and Eric's —"

"That won't change anything for you, though, will it? You'll still be part of it. And we're not going to say you weren't. Me and Eric don't have anything to lose, neither does Pauly. It'll be our word against yours. Three against one. Who do you think the cops are going to believe if we all say that it was you that killed Stella?"

"They already know who killed her," I said.

Campbell barely blinked. "Yeah, right . . ."

"They found a bit of Eric's necklace in Stella's pocket."

Campbell's eyes darkened. "They what?"

I looked at Eric. "The gold chain you were wearing on Saturday night, the one you borrowed from Nic—"

"What's he talking about?" Campbell said, turning to Eric.

"I thought I'd got rid of it," Eric muttered.

"Got rid of what?"

Eric sighed. "She broke it . . . Stella. When she brought me down here on my own—remember? She said she wanted to talk to me about something—"

"Yeah, I remember. What did she break?"

"Nic's necklace . . . you know, the one you really like? The gold one. Stella broke it."

"How?"

Eric put his hand on Campbell's arm. "Look, I didn't want to tell you about it at the time because I didn't want to upset you . . . and it was just so pathetic, anyway. She was just trying to . . ."

"Trying to what?"

"She was, you know . . . she was coming *on* to me, trying to kiss me . . ." He shook his head in disgust. "She said she was trying to *convert* me, the stupid bitch."

"*What*?"

"It's all right—"

"No, it's not *fucking* all right. Why didn't you *tell* me?"

"Because nothing *happened*, Wes. She was just messing about, you know . . . grabbing me around the neck, trying to stick her tongue down my throat. I just pushed her away, told her to piss off . . . and that's how the necklace got broken. When I pushed her away, she just kind of lashed out at me, and somehow the necklace came off in her hand. I snatched it back off her, but I just thought the clasp had broken, you know. She must have had some of the chain left in her hand."

Campbell took a breath, calming himself. "What did you do with the bit of necklace you had?"

"I got rid of it."

"Where?"

"In the fire."

"You *burned* it?"

"Yeah . . . well, you told me to burn all my clothes and stuff, didn't you?"

"Christ," Campbell said, shaking his head. "I told you to burn your *clothes* . . . I didn't tell you to burn your fucking jewelry." He stared angrily at Eric. "Metal doesn't burn in a bonfire, does it? Shit. If the cops find it, they can match it with the bit they found in Stella's pocket . . ." He paused for a moment, thinking about something. "I thought you checked all her pockets, anyway."

"I *did*," Eric said.

"So how come you didn't find it?"

"It was in the little coin pocket," I said.

Campbell stared at me, his face as tight as a drum. "How do you know?"

"The police told me. They showed me the chain—"

"Did you tell them it was Eric's?"

"No, but—"

"So they don't know anything, do they?" A crooked grin cracked his face. "As long as you keep your mouth shut, and as long as Eric finds his burnt fucking *necklace* before the cops come snooping around, we're all still cool, aren't we?"

"You don't look too cool," I said.

"You what?"

I gazed steadily at him. "What are you scared of, Wes?"

"*What*?"

"I mean, if everything happened like you say it did, what have you got to worry about? Stella was blackmailing Eric. The kidnap was all her idea. And you didn't kill her, anyway. It was Pauly."

"Nothing to *worry* about?" Campbell said. "We were there when she died, remember? We didn't report it. We dumped her naked body in the river, we tried to frame the guy in the trailer—"

"Why?"

"Why what?"

"Why go to all that trouble? Why didn't you just blame it all on Pauly?" I looked at Eric. "Were you scared of what he'd tell people about you?"

Eric glanced nervously at Campbell.

"Don't listen to him," Campbell said. "He's just trying to fuck with you."

"I just don't get it," I said, shaking my head.

Eric turned back to me. "Get what?"

"You and Wes . . . I mean, are you *really* that ashamed of him?"

Eric just stared at me, his eyes cold and white in the gloom.

I stared back at him, my heart pounding. "What do you think's going to happen if people find out you're in love with him? Do you think it's going to make the newspapers or something? 'Middle-Class Gay Kid In Love With Backstreet Thug'? I mean, come *on*, Eric — do you really think anyone *cares*?"

"You don't understand," Eric said quietly.

"No?"

"It's nothing to do with being *ashamed* of anything —"

"You used to be so proud of yourself," I said, cutting him off. "Remember when you first came out and you used to wear that Gay Pride T-shirt all the time . . ." I looked at him. "Where's your pride now?"

"You don't know what you're talking about —"

"And you," I said, turning to Campbell. "You're just scared that no one's going to be scared of you anymore if they find out you're gay." I smiled nastily, taunting him. "Tough guys aren't supposed to be gay, are they? Tough guys aren't supposed to fall in love with poofs like Eric — they're supposed to beat the shit out of them. They're supposed to *hate* them. I mean, they're disgusting, aren't they? Fucking queers, they're unnatural —"

Campbell hit me then, a vicious crack in the mouth that sent me lurching back into the wall. I wiped blood from my lips and looked at him . . . and I saw what I was hoping to see. Pure hate. Despite the jagged pain in my mouth, and the jagged fear in my heart, I smiled to myself. I'd got to him. He was losing it. I spat blood on the floor and grinned at him.

"Tough guy," I said.

His eyes went blank as he pulled the box cutter from his pocket and started moving toward me, and I knew he was without a conscience now. There was nothing to him — no feelings, no emotion, no fear. He didn't even hate me anymore. I was just a thing he had to shut up. A thing he had to cut up. Simple as that. There was nothing I could do to stop him.

I was banking on Eric to do that.

But as Campbell got closer and closer to me, and Eric just stood there doing nothing, it suddenly dawned on me that I was making a big mistake. A *really* big mistake. Eric wasn't going to do anything to stop Campbell. Why should he? He loved him.

Simple as that.

Campbell was bearing down on me now, his right hand gripping the box cutter, his left hand still holding the flashlight . . . and I knew it was too late to do anything. I couldn't move. There was nowhere to go. He was too close, too big, too determined. *He's going to cut me*, I realized. *It's really going to happen. I'm going to get cut.* And all I could do was stare at him, watching in dumb disbelief as he raised the blade in his hand . . .

And then all at once Eric was there, barging into him, wrapping his arms around him, pulling him away from me . . . and Campbell was fighting back like a madman — twisting and writhing, grunting and cursing, dropping his flashlight as he tried to break free from Eric's grip — and the beam from the fallen flashlight was glowing weirdly through the dust-scattered half-light, casting strange shadows across the walls . . . and as I was standing there watching it all, I felt a sudden black crack inside my head, like the sound of shattering glass, and just for a moment I could see and feel everything all at once. Everything and everyone. I was Stella Ross, the Stella of Pauly's story. I was a lie. I was Campbell, fighting like crazy. Raymond was Pauly. Pauly was Campbell, out of control, pumped up with madness and drugs. Eric was Nicole, Eric was Campbell, Eric was Eric. Wednesday morning was Saturday night. It was dark outside. A storm was coming. It was bright outside, the sun was shining. I was dead. I was alive . . .

The inside of my head flashed white.

I was alive.

I was here.

I was Pete Boland.

Eric was Eric, and Campbell was Campbell, and they were dancing together in the middle of the floor . . . no, they weren't dancing. They were holding each other in anger. Red-faced, tempers lost, embraced in the passion of a lovers' fight. They were screaming at each other.

"You can't just —"

"I was only going to *hurt* him, for Christ's sake."

"There's no *need*—"

"Fuck your *need*," Campbell yelled, pushing Eric away. "Shit," he spat, "we wouldn't even *be* here if you'd listened to me—"

"About what?"

"*Everything*. I *told* you to get rid of your phone—"

"I was going to—"

"Yeah, but you didn't, did you? Now this fucker's got it hidden away somewhere." He shook his head. "*And* you fucked up with the necklace."

"I didn't do it on purpose, did I? It was a mistake—"

"The whole fucking thing was a mistake. You should have told Stella to fuck off in the first place."

"I couldn't, could I?"

"Why not?"

"You know why not."

"Yeah," Campbell sneered. "We can't let anyone *know* about us, can we?"

Eric shook his head and turned away. "I'm not getting into all this again. It's ridiculous—"

"Don't turn your back on me," Campbell said angrily, grabbing him by the shoulder and spinning him around. "I asked you a question."

Eric glared at him. "What are you going to do, Wes? Beat me up?"

It only took a moment for Campbell to whip the box cutter from his pocket and grab hold of Eric by the neck, but then—just as suddenly—he froze, as if he'd only just realized what he was doing. I saw him look at Eric, his eyes shocked, and I'm sure that if Eric had just waited a second, everything would have been all right. Campbell would have said sorry. Eric would have forgiven him. They both would have calmed down and stopped fighting.

But instead of waiting, Eric started laughing. It was a nasty laugh, cold and mocking, and when he spoke his voice was equally nasty.

"You're going to *cut* me now, are you?" he sneered. "You're going to cut me up?"

Campbell tried to control himself, and I could see him staring intensely at Eric, silently telling him to shut up, that's enough, no more. But Eric wasn't in control of himself, either. Campbell had pulled a knife on him . . . he'd pulled a *knife* on him.

"Fuck you, Wes," he hissed, twisting away from Campbell and chopping his arm away. "Why don't you just piss off back to where you belong?" He turned angrily and started marching toward the steps.

Campbell went after him, his eyes burning black. "Hey! *Hey* . . . who the fuck d'you think you're talking to?"

Eric ignored him and kept walking.

Campbell hurried after him, not bothering to say anything now, intent only on stopping him. Eric was just starting to climb the steps when Campbell came up behind him. Eric heard him coming and increased his pace, but Campbell was already reaching out for him now. He made a grab for him, almost caught hold of his belt, but Eric dodged out of his way. Campbell scrambled up the steps and tried to get hold of him again, and this time Eric stood his ground. He was a couple of steps above Campbell, his feet about level with his head, and the only real option he had was to kick out at him. And that's what he tried to do — spinning around, launching a kick at Campbell's head . . . but Campbell was ready for it. As Eric kicked out at him, he lurched forward and grabbed hold of his leg, pushing Eric back . . . and then all of a sudden Eric let out a sharp scream of pain and fell to one side, grasping his thigh.

I didn't think it was anything to worry about at first. I just thought he'd pulled a muscle or twisted his leg or something . . .

But then I saw all the blood.

THIRTY

don't think Campbell meant to stab Eric. I think he was just trying to get hold of him and he forgot that he still had the box cutter in his hand, or maybe Eric was trying to kick the box cutter out of his hand or something . . . I really don't know. One second I was watching them struggling—and all I was thinking about was making a run for it—and the next thing I knew, Eric was sitting on the steps with blood squirting out of his leg, moaning in agony, and Campbell was crouching down beside him, desperately trying to comfort him.

"Shit, Eric . . . I'm sorry . . . I'm so *sorry* . . ."

"It's all right," Eric grimaced. "It just won't stop bleeding. Christ . . ."

"Here, let me see . . ."

As I crossed the basement toward them, Campbell gently eased Eric's jeans to his knees, and I could see that the knife had caught him on the inside of his thigh, about halfway between his knee and his groin. It was only a small cut, and it didn't look that bad, but the blood was really pouring out.

"You need to put pressure on it," I said.

Campbell looked up at me. "What?"

"Have you got a hanky or something?"

He just stared at me, too shocked to react. I pulled off my shirt, ripped off one of the sleeves, and moved around to the side of the steps. I was level with Eric now, and I could see that he was really scared. His hands were shaking. His eyes were white. His skin was very pale.

"We need to stop the bleeding," I told him. "OK?"

He nodded.

I folded the sleeve in half and placed it carefully over the wound in his thigh.

"Give me your hand," I said to Campbell.

He looked at me.

I took hold of his hand and placed it on top of the folded sleeve. "Keep it pressed down," I told him, pushing his hand down. "Like this. Not too tight . . . just keep your hand there and hold it down."

"Why's he bleeding so much?" Campbell said.

"It could be a severed vein or an artery . . ." I moved to one side and put my hands under Eric's arms. "Help me get him down off the steps."

"We need to get him out of here . . ."

"No," I said firmly. "If we start moving him around too much it's only going to make things worse. Just help me stop the bleeding first and then I'll call an ambulance. All right? Wes?"

"Yeah . . ."

"Come *on*, are you going to help me or not?"

We got Eric off the steps and laid him down on the floor. While I carefully raised his leg and rested it on the steps,

I told Campbell to keep pressing down on the wound. "And keep his leg up there," I told him. "It'll help to slow down the bleeding." I turned to Eric. "Try to stay calm, OK?"

Eric nodded. His face was deathly pale now.

I stood up and looked down at Campbell. "Give me your phone."

He shook his head. "I got rid of it."

"Shit. What about . . . ?"

Eric's phone, I was going to say. *What about Eric's phone?*

"Shit," I said again.

"He's still *bleeding,*" Campbell said desperately. "We've got to *do* something . . ."

He was still crouched down beside Eric, still pressing down on the wound. His hands were red with blood, his face almost as pale as Eric's. He didn't look so tough anymore. He looked like a scared little kid. And I wondered for a moment why I wasn't getting any enjoyment out of this. Campbell was suffering, wasn't he? And I hated him. I'd *always* hated him. And I'd always wanted to see him suffer. But now that he was . . . well, it didn't seem to matter anymore.

I looked at Eric.

His eyes were half-closed.

"Give me his lighter," I said to Campbell.

"What?"

"His cigarette lighter. Give it to me."

Campbell dug into Eric's pocket and passed me his lighter.

"Stay there," I told him, heading up the steps. "Keep his leg up and keep the pressure on the wound."

"Where are you going?" Campbell said.

"Just stay there and wait for the ambulance. When you hear it coming, go outside so they can see where you are. I'll be as quick as I can." I shoved back the metal shelf unit at the top of the steps and hurried out into the daylight.

After the cool underground air of the basement, the sudden heat of the afternoon sun almost knocked me off my feet. I was tired, I suppose. Beaten up and exhausted. And as I scurried around the concrete square, picking up handfuls of twigs and bits of old newspaper, I could feel the sweat pouring down my bare-skinned back, sucking me dry.

I went over to the pile of old car tires, stuffed all the newspapers and dried twigs into a gap at the bottom of the heap, then took Eric's lighter out of my pocket and set light to it. There was more litter inside the pile — bits of paper, plastic bags, ancient candy wrappers — and it was all so dry that within a few seconds the pile of tires was burning away like mad. I waited a few moments, watching as the flames took hold, and the smoke turned thick and black, then I turned around and started running.

Back through the gap in the fence, back down the bank, back down the overgrown path . . . there was nothing familiar about it anymore. It didn't remind me of anything, it didn't bring back any feelings, it didn't take me back to a time when everything was wonderful and exciting . . .

It was just a path.

The same as it had always been.

About halfway down, I stopped running for a moment to get my bearings. After a quick look around, I realized that it'd be easier to cut through the undergrowth here than to go all the way down to the bottom of the bank and then clamber back up through the brambles to the oak tree. I could see the oak tree from here. I fixed it in my mind, stepped off the path, and started cutting across through the undergrowth.

It was pretty thick, and most of it was pretty thorny, but there was no way of avoiding it, so I just gritted my teeth and plowed on through. I could smell the smoke from the burning tires now, and when I glanced over my shoulder I could see plumes of thick black smoke billowing up into the sky. Hopefully, somebody else would see it, too. And even if they didn't, at least it would show the ambulance where to go.

I came out of the undergrowth just below the oak tree, and for a second or two, as I stood there wheezing and panting, I couldn't remember what I was doing. Where was my shirt? Why was my mouth hurting? Why the hell was I staring at an oak tree?

"Oh, yeah . . ." I heard myself say.

And then I was scrambling over to the tree, crawling down into the ditch, reaching inside the hollow trunk, trying to remember where I'd put Eric's phone. Where was it? All I could feel was dirt, dead leaves, twigs, more dirt . . .

Plastic.

I grabbed the phone, pulled it out, and sat back against the tree. Still breathing hard, I flipped open the phone and turned it on. And then I just waited. Staring at the display, dripping sweat . . . waiting . . . staring . . . hoping for a signal. The phone beeped. MAIN MENU. I wiped a drop of sweat off the screen and stared at the reception indicator. Three bars. I punched in the number and put the phone to my ear.

Dad answered almost immediately. "Hello?"

"Dad, it's me—"

"Pete! Christ, where *are* you! Are you all right? What the hell—?"

"Listen, Dad," I said quickly. "I'm all right—"

"Where *are* you?"

"Dad, *please*," I said sharply. "Just listen to me, OK? I might lose the signal any second. Are you listening?"

I heard him take a breath. "Yes . . . yeah, I'm listening."

"I know what happened to Stella, Dad. I know who did it. It was Pauly and Eric and a kid called Wes Campbell—"

"Say that again. You're breaking up. Eric and who?"

"Never mind, I'll explain everything later. Eric needs an ambulance, Dad. He's been stabbed in the thigh and he's bleeding really badly. He's in the basement of one of the old factory buildings. Tell the ambulance crew to look for the fire. There'll be someone waiting outside the building."

"Are you with Eric now?"

"No. Wes Campbell's with him, but I'm not far away. I'll go back now and wait for the ambulance."

"I'll be there in five minutes. Do you need anything?"

"Just get here as quick as you can, Dad."

"I'm leaving right now."

He put the phone down.

I breathed out heavily, closed my eyes, and slumped back against the tree. I could rest for a minute or two now. I didn't have to think about Eric and Campbell anymore, I didn't have to think about Stella. All that was over. Finished. It was out of my hands. I just needed to rest for a minute. Then I could get back to the old factory, let Dad take me home, try to explain everything to him . . . take a bath, get some sleep . . . and then I'd be ready to start thinking about Raymond again.

Raymond . . .

I opened my eyes and looked up at a blue sky darkened with smoke.

I couldn't see anything in it. No rabbits, no faces, no visions.

I closed my eyes again.

Eric's mobile beeped twice.

Ignore it, I told myself. *You're not thinking about Eric anymore. All that's over. Finished. It's out of your hands . . .*

I opened my eyes and looked down at the phone.

The display read: 1 New Message From Pyg.

I wasn't really thinking as I instinctively pressed READ, I just assumed it was a message from Pauly to Eric. But then, as the message came up, I suddenly remembered that Pauly had seen me with Eric's phone. He knew that I had it. He knew that I'd answer it.

His message wasn't for Eric, it was for me.

```
petepete — it said — imbad im 2bad im2fukD
HA! cntdoit gottadoit nw kil me itKIL me
KILME nw imded
```

I didn't get it at first. I just thought it was Pauly being Pauly again. He'd probably been drinking his juiced-up booze again, I imagined, and now he was just lying around somewhere, his brains in a mess, sending me meaningless text messages.

But then I started feeling something, something wrong . . .

And as I tried to work out what it was, a half-forgotten image suddenly flashed into my mind, an image of Pauly in the den that morning: his face twitching, his lips trembling, his eyes out of control.

You can't hide forever, I'd told him.

And he'd looked at me, smiling strangely. *You reckon?*

With the sound of his words echoing ominously in my head, I started reading through his message again . . .

I'm bad.

Gotta do it now.

. . . and suddenly it didn't feel so stupid anymore.

Kill me.

Now.

I could see Pauly's house now, I could feel it inside me — the emptiness, the coldness, the lightlessness. I could feel the grubbiness of his room — the smell of sweat and stale air, the flies buzzing around unwashed plates . . . the dirty floor, the dirty furniture, the dirty pictures tacked to the walls . . .

I'm bad.

. . . and Pauly himself, closing his eyes and putting his hands to his face.

Kill me.

Now I'm dead.

"Shit."

It was a long, hard run to Pauly's place, and even before I'd got halfway I didn't think I was going to make it. My legs were like lead, my chest was exploding. My lungs were on fire, my heart was bursting . . . I didn't think I could walk any farther, let alone run. But I couldn't let myself stop. If I stopped, I'd stop hurting. And if I stopped hurting, I'd start thinking. And I didn't want to start thinking, because I knew it would hurt too much.

So I just kept running.

Across the wasteground, through the fence, along the dock road and up into Greenwell Rise . . .

I don't remember any of it.

I was nowhere now.

Everywhere and nowhere.

The world was melting.

Pauly's house felt dead when I got there. The windows were shut, the curtains were closed. The house was silent and still. I walked up to the front door and rang the bell.

No answer.

I hammered on the door.

No reply.

I crouched down and called out through the mail slot. "Pauly? Hey, *Pauly*! *PAULY*!!"

Nothing.

I stepped back and started shouting at the upstairs windows. *"PAULY!! Are you there? PAULY!!"*

The door of the house next door swung open and an angry-looking woman leaned out. "What d'you think you're *doing*?" she yelled at me. "Jesus! I'm trying to watch TV in here—"

"Is he in?" I snapped at her. "Have you seen him?"

"Seen who?"

"Pauly. Pauly Gilpin. Have you seen him?"

"No, I haven't *seen* him. And I can't say that I want to, either . . . hold on, what are you doing?"

I'd turned away from her and picked up a lump of concrete from the side of the path. I could hear her saying something else to me as I stepped over to the front window, hefting the lump of concrete in my hand, but I wasn't listening anymore. I wasn't anything anymore. I was just desperate to get into the house.

I heaved the concrete slab at the window. The glass exploded, shattering all over the place. I scrambled up onto a broken skid that was leaning against the wall, reached in through the broken glass, unlatched the window, and clambered through into the sitting room.

It was dark and dingy inside. A small TV flickered silently in one corner, and the air was lifeless and dull.

I thought about calling out again, but somehow it didn't seem right. It was too quiet for shouting . . . too hushed. It just didn't feel right.

I crossed the sitting room, opened the door, and went out into the hallway. The stairs were on my left. I paused for a moment, gazing up into the dimness, trying to convince myself that I didn't *have* to go up there, that it probably wasn't going to make any difference now, anyway . . . but I knew there was no going back.

As I climbed the narrow stairs, the silence of the house seemed to close in all around me. I could feel it in the air, drifting over my skin like a film of oily gray water.

I stopped at the top of the stairs.

The sheet of stained newspaper was still on the landing. I stepped around it and went over to Pauly's door. It was closed. I stood there for a moment, listening hard, and I thought for a moment I heard something. A faint creaking . . . once, twice . . . then it stopped. I breathed out, breathed in. The air smelled bad. Sour and stale, sweaty and dirty . . . and worse. There was something else, another smell, something awful.

I closed my eyes.

Took a deep breath.

And opened the door.

The smell hit me first, the rank odor of human shit, and I was already starting to retch as I looked up and saw Pauly hanging from the ceiling. A belt was looped around his neck, the other end tied to the light fixture, and as I stood there — choking and gulping — the flex of the light fixture creaked and twisted, and Pauly's bloated face turned slowly toward me. He was grinning — a final agonized grin — and his thickened tongue was sticking out between his teeth. His eyes were bulging, the whites flecked with blood. His neck was swollen. His bowels had emptied, staining his jeans, and there was a small pool of piss on the floor.

I closed my eyes.

Held my breath.

Please don't let it be true.

But when I opened my eyes again, it was all still there: the body, the flies, the empty burger boxes, the dirt, the grief, the stink of guilt, the upended chair on the floor . . . and lying on the unmade bed, a computer printout of Stella Ross, her face scribbled out, a ballpoint pen stuck through her heart.

"Christ, Pauly," I muttered.

I was drenched in sweat now. My legs were shaking, my blood was cold, and as I lowered myself unsteadily to the floor and sat down in the doorway, a flood of wretchedness welled up inside me, filling my eyes with tears.

I buried my head in my hands and started sobbing.

THIRTY-ONI

don't know how long a moment lasts—a second, half a second . . . a millionth of a second—and I don't know how the timelessness of a moment can invade your mind and turn itself into an everlasting memory . . . but I know I'll never forget what I saw in that room. I *want* to forget it. I want to stop seeing it every night, every time I close my eyes, every time I think I've forgotten it. But I know it's impossible to forget. It's seared into my memory, burned into my mind—as sickeningly vivid now as it was all those months ago.

Pauly Gilpin.

Dead.

I still don't know why he did it.

And I don't think I'll ever know.

Because I don't think I ever knew him at all.

Not that it really matters.

Why he killed himself, and whoever he was—he's still dead.

And so is Stella.

They're both gone now.

And the rest of us . . . ?

Well, we're all still here.

We're all still living our moments.

Eric Leigh and Wes Campbell were both arrested that day at the old factory. Campbell was taken in for questioning straightaway, but Eric was still bleeding pretty badly, so he was rushed to the hospital for emergency treatment. He'd lost a lot of blood, and he had to stay in the hospital for a while, but it turned out that the knife hadn't severed his artery after all, it'd just cut through a couple of veins, so there wasn't any serious damage. He was interviewed by the police while he was still in the hospital, and questioned again at the police station as soon as he was well enough to walk.

I don't know what he told them about Stella, and I don't know what Campbell told them, either, but they were both eventually released on bail, pending further inquiries. I'm not sure what's going to happen to them. I'm pretty sure they'll end up facing some kind of charges, but whether or not they'll ever stand trial for anything . . .

I really don't know.

I really don't care, either.

I haven't seen either of them since it all happened, and I'm hoping it stays that way. It's not that I feel particularly bitter about what they did to me, and I'm certainly not frightened of them anymore . . . in fact, I don't really feel anything about them anymore. I just don't want to see them again.

Ever.

Which probably isn't going to be all that easy, especially where Eric's concerned, because I've kind of started seeing Nicole again.

After her parents postponed the move to Paris because of everything that was happening with Eric, Nic decided that she might as well go on to college and start taking some prep courses. She told me all this when we bumped into each other in the college cafeteria on the first day of the fall semester.

"I'm trying to enroll in the Drama and Theater Studies program," she told me, "but I've left it a bit late, you know . . ."

"Yeah," I said awkwardly, not knowing what else to say.

At the time, neither of us had the courage to talk about what we really wanted to talk about, and we were both quite happy to pretend that we were in a hurry to be somewhere else. And it was pretty much the same a couple of weeks later when I saw her again at the bus stop: a few mumbled words, lots of awkward glances, strained smiles, fidgeting feet . . .

But then, the next night, she called me.

And we talked.

And we both cried a little.

And since then we've been meeting up quite regularly, and we've talked a lot more, and we've gradually gotten over the awkwardness and gotten back to being good friends again . . . or maybe even more than just good friends.

But it's hard.

I mean, it's good when we're together. It feels really good. And I think it's probably going to work out for us in the end.

But it's still really hard sometimes.

For lots of reasons.

There's Eric, for one thing. I mean, whatever I think of him, and whatever Nic thinks of him, he's still her twin brother. He's still part of her life. And that's bound to make things difficult for us. And then there's Raymond . . .

There's always Raymond.

Raymond and me . . .

I don't know.

It's just so hard.

Because a lot of the time I simply don't care about the rest of it — Pauly, Eric, Campbell, Stella, the police, Nicole, Mum and Dad, the rest of the world . . . it's all out there somewhere — the horizons, the skies, the days and the nights — I just don't want anything to do with it.

All I want to do is talk to Raymond.

But he's gone.

Disappeared.

Vanished.

No one knows where he is, no one knows what's happened to him, no one knows whether he's dead or alive.

He's just gone.

It took the police a long time to start treating Raymond as a victim rather than a suspect, but after questioning

Eric and Campbell, Detective Barry finally got around to launching a full-scale investigation. Raymond's parents made an emotional appeal on TV, too, with lots of tears and lots of anguish, which I'm sure was all very genuine . . . but I can't help feeling that it was all far too late. If the police had started looking for him earlier . . . if Mr. and Mrs. Daggett had shown him some emotion when he needed it . . . I mean, it's all very well going on TV and telling the world how much you love your missing son, but how about telling *him* once or twice? You know, *before* he goes missing.

Anyway, they made an appeal, and the police kept looking for him — searching the river, searching the factory, searching the wasteground and the woods around Back Lane — but so far they haven't found anything. The only useful thing to come out of all the publicity has been a spate of reports about mutilated animals — a couple of slaughtered cats, a stray dog found hacked up in a park, chickens with their heads off. All of these incidents have occurred in the last year or so, and all of them happened in and around St. Leonard's. Which could mean something. It could mean that there's a madman out there, a bloodthirsty lunatic who might have something to do with Raymond's disappearance. Or it could just mean that there's a madman out there who killed Black Rabbit and cut off his head and hung it on the gate but who *didn't* have anything to do with Raymond's disappearance. It could be just a coincidence — a pointless and barbaric coincidence.

The police are still looking into it.

They're also still looking into the possibility of a link between Raymond's disappearance and the other kids who went missing from fairgrounds, and apparently there are one or two promising leads, but as yet there's nothing definite.

It's all just possibilities.

Theories.

Suspicions.

Maybes.

Maybe Raymond was abducted.

Maybe he just ran away.

Maybe he's still out there somewhere.

Maybe he's still alive.

I don't know . . .

All I know is that he'll always be with me—in my head, in my heart . . .

He'll always be here.

No matter what.

♥ ♠ ♦ ♣

ABOUT THE AUTHOR

Kevin Brooks was born in 1959 in Exeter, Devon, England. He studied in London and Birmingham and spent much of his adult life writing and recording music before becoming a full-time writer in 2000.

His debut novel, *Martyn Pig,* was critically acclaimed by British and American reviewers for its edgy wit and intelligence. Described as a cross between J.D. Salinger and Raymond Chandler, the novel was shortlisted for the Carnegie Medal and won the Branford Boase Award. His award-winning second novel, *Lucas,* has been compared to such classics as *To Kill a Mockingbird* and *The Ox-Bow Incident.* An ALA Best Book for Young Adults in 2003, *Lucas* was the recipient of the North East Book Award and the Kingston Youth Book Award in the United Kingdom and winner of the coveted Buxtehuder Bulle in Germany.

His other novels include *Kissing the Rain*; *Candy,* recipient of the Angus Book Award and the Stockport

Children's Book Award; *The Road of the Dead,* shortlisted for the Carnegie Medal and nominated for an Edgar Allan Poe Award by the Mystery Writers of America; and *Being,* which *Publishers Weekly* called an "adrenaline-laced adventure" and a "thought-provoking exploration of the very nature of . . . existence" in a starred review.

Kevin Brooks lives in North Yorkshire, England, with his wife, Susan, and their two dogs, Shaky and Jess.